FROM THIS MOMENT ON

Titles by Lynn Kurland

STARDUST OF YESTERDAY
A DANCE THROUGH TIME
THIS IS ALL I ASK
THE VERY THOUGHT OF YOU
ANOTHER CHANCE TO DREAM
THE MORE I SEE YOU
IF I HAD YOU
MY HEART STOOD STILL
FROM THIS MOMENT ON

A KNIGHT'S VOW
(an anthology with Patricia Potter, Deborah Simmons,
and Glynnis Campbell)

LOVE CAME JUST IN TIME
(an anthology)

THE CHRISTMAS CAT
(an anthology with Julie Beard, Barbara Bretton, and Jo Beverley)

CHRISTMAS SPIRITS
(an anthology with Casey Claybourne, Elizabeth Bevarly,
and Jenny Lykins)

VEILS OF TIME
(an anthology with Maggie Shayne, Angie Ray, and Ingrid Weaver)

OPPOSITES ATTRACT
(an anthology with Elizabeth Bevarly, Emily Carmichael,
and Elda Minger)

TAPESTRY
(an anthology with Madeline Hunter,
Sherrilyn Kenyon, and Marie Moning)

FROM THIS MOMENT ON

LYNN KURLAND

BERKLEY BOOKS, NEW YORK

FROM THIS MOMENT ON

A Berkley Book / published by arrangement with
the author

PRINTING HISTORY
Berkley edition / October 2002

ISBN: 0-7394-2928-0

BERKLEY®
Berkley Books are published by The Berkley Publishing Group,
a division of Penguin Putnam Inc.,
375 Hudson Street, New York, New York 10014.
BERKLEY and the "B" design
are trademarks belonging to Penguin Putnam Inc.

PRINTED IN THE UNITED STATES OF AMERICA

FROM THIS MOMENT ON

Prologue

A hearty brew shimmered and danced in the firelight as it tumbled into waiting cups. It was swirled about, admired, sniffed by noses well accustomed to that sort of work. Experienced hands brought cups to lips where the contents were confidently consumed with the full expectation of a hearty belch to follow and a bit of hand-slapping on the table to show appreciation.

Only the hand-slapping that followed this imbibing had less to do with appreciation than it might have another time.

"By the fires of Hell, Magda," bellowed one of the guzzlers, spewing her drink onto the floor and gasping for air, " 'tis the *foulest* thing you've foisted off upon us yet!"

Magda, a white-haired, sweet-faced woman of advanced years, held her own well-herbed ale in her mouth, her eyes wide, her brew unswallowed.

"Tell her," the first said, glaring at the third occupant of the chamber. "Tell her, Berengaria, that at no time will she *ever* succeed in brewing a proper potion!"

Berengaria reached for a bit of wine to wash down the unappetizing swill, but refrained from criticizing. "It wants but a bit of sweetener, Nemain."

"No honey ever fashioned by any bee this side of Hell could turn this into anything drinkable," Nemain grumbled. She turned her attentions to the hapless potion maker. "Drink yours down, you silly nun."

Magda's eyes widened even further.

Nemain, never one to let words attempt where actions would succeed, reached over and pinched Magda's nose closed.

It was done, Berengaria noted, with more vigor than was truly necessary, but it certainly accomplished what it was meant to. Magda swallowed in desperation, then coughed out her own concoction—all over the front of Nemain's gown.

Ah, well, there would be hell to pay now. Berengaria rose and left the luxurious chamber she shared with her fellows before the curses and cursings began flying about. No sense finding herself in Nemain's sights unnecessarily.

She made her way down the stairs and through the great hall, nodding and smiling to those who greeted her. It was a strange thing, she supposed, to find herself so generally welcome in a lord's hall. Her chosen occupations—midwife, healer, or witch, depending on who was offering an opinion—gave some reason enough to shun her. Then again, she made her home currently at Blackmour where there were souls about in abundance with reputations black enough that hers seemed rather pale by comparison.

She left the hall, stumbling a bit as the pull of future events drew her sight from that which surrounded her. She gained the garden before she was no longer seeing what was before her, but rather something beyond the castle walls.

The vision of a young woman came to her, an amply rounded girl with a cloud of pale hair and eyes so light they were almost painful to look at. Straining further to see what was yet unrevealed, Berengaria took note of the girl's companions: a trio of giggling maids and a young knight charged with the guarding of them all. Berengaria peered more intently at the little company, but no further illumination came to her. Was she beginning to lose her gift? Perhaps the white hairs in her crown spelled not only the ending of her youth, but the wilting of her powers as well.

She came to herself to find that she was staring down at the frail beginnings of the spring garden. The vision had to do with events yet to come to pass in the keep; of that she was certain. But who was the girl? Her companions? When would they arrive and what troubles would they bring with them?

Well, this was a puzzle, to be sure, but one she was obviously not going to solve at present. Further intuition would no doubt come to her in time. For the moment, perhaps plucking a few errant weeds would be a work worthy enough for her.

Her labors were abruptly interrupted by the arrival of a rather loud and energetic soul who had the most unwholesome knack of knowing just what plant she had in her sights. He smiled a gap-toothed grin at her, then with a screech made straightway for the only thing growing with any vigor.

"A dwink," he announced, holding up crushed stems of tender rue. "For me."

Who was she to resist such a command? "Aye, Robin, my lord," she agreed, "I'll make you a drink, but not of that. 'Twould work a foul work upon your sweet self. Let us be about finding something more toothsome for you, shall we?"

Robin nodded enthusiastically, then turned and began to pluck up all of the green shoots that fell within his reach. Berengaria hastily refocused his efforts. The choices were few, but there were enough goodly herbs about for her to fashion him a drink that wouldn't finish him before his time.

But even as she carefully guided the hands of Blackmour's curious heir, she found herself distracted by what she'd seen. It troubled her greatly that she could not divine who the girl in her vision was, or what ailed her. With a gaggle of handmaids and a young knight to attend her, what could she possibly run afoul of?

Unless it was not the girl who needed aid.

Berengaria considered again the wenches from her vision, then dismissed them. They were silly girls with the usual cares and malice in their souls that came from petty jealousies. Nay, there was nothing noteworthy there.

The knight received her scrutiny next and 'twas only after a pair of moments that she realized with a start that this one was definitely not what he seemed.

"Bewengawia, *now!*"

Berengaria came back to herself and nodded to her charge. "Off to the kitchens with us, aye?"

Robin took her hand and began to pull her back toward the hall. Berengaria followed willingly, now fully satisfied that she had an idea of who the players involved in the near future might be. She could readily divine what their roles were and was happy to see events moving along as they should have. She suspected, though, that there might be others at Blackmour who would be less than cheerful over the arrival of this little company.

Ah, well, such was the course of true love.

But with her there to aid faltering feet along that road, how could it be anything but a pleasant and fairly uneventful journey?

"Bewengawia," Robin said, with an imperiousness that would have pleased his father greatly, *"now."* Then he paused and sighed. "Pwease," he added reluctantly, in a manner that would have pleased his father just as well.

Berengaria reached out to ruffle his hair. "Forgive me, little one. I have been distracted by other things, but I am yours for the rest of the morn."

His long-suffering sigh was truly impressive, but he ruined it by grinning up at her and darting across the hall, leaving her to follow.

She suppressed the urge to have a final peek at her vision. Her efforts were best spent now on keeping young Robin from poisoning himself. The future would proceed as it cared to; there was nothing she could do about that.

But she could offer aid where needed, and that she would do.

She suspected the young knight she'd seen would have need of all the aid she could give.

Chapter 1

A delicate brew shimmered as it was poured forth from a newly opened bottle into a gracefully made cup. It was subsequently swirled about, admired, sniffed appreciatively by a nose that was consummately accustomed to sniffing those kinds of things to judge their quality and ingestability. The mixture was sampled, hesitantly, on the off chance that it wouldn't taste as good as it smelled. That sampling was followed by a quick imbibing, then a refilling of the cup by a loyal handmaid who stood nearby. It was a scene that no doubt could have been repeated at any number of keeps in France on a night such as this, a simple scene, a scene that no soul would have considered out of the ordinary.

Only the imbiber, Sybil of Maignelay-sur-mer, was not a drunkard, despite how frequently and fully her cup was refilled. Her ladies were not exactly ladies, but serving wenches elevated in station to care for the last of Maignelay's eight daughters on the night before she was to leave her home and ride off into the gloom to meet her betrothed. And the soul leaning against the wall watching the proceedings was not a brave knight prepared to defend the lady Sybil against all enemies, but rather a girl hiding behind mail and hose for the express purpose of avoiding the matrimonial fate Sybil had neither the courage nor the wit to avoid herself.

Aliénore of Solonge leaned against that wall, fair to dropping with fatigue and worry, and wondered how it was she found herself trapped with creatures who seemed bent on stretching out the torture of the day as long as possible and thereby, wittingly or not, inflicting as much suffering upon her own sorry self as possible. Why couldn't these girls become fully and happily inebriated so she could escape and at least forget her own desperate straits by plunging herself into a few hours of peaceful sleep?

Her day already seemed endless, what with all the fetching of foodstuffs, the carrying of sewing, the delivery of sundry messages, and more fetching of foodstuffs that she'd been required to do. But those were tasks that allowed her to keep herself mostly far from others in the castle, and for that she was grateful. After all, keeping herself hidden was the way to keep herself alive, and she shunned no opportunity to continue to enjoy that condition. For now, she supposed she should be content to lean against something sturdy, watch her charges consume what she'd just fetched for them, and hope that they wouldn't require anything else from her that night.

Unfortunately, such leisurely loitering gave her ample time to consider not only Sybil's future, but her own. And given the fact that her own limited bit of freedom would vanish with Sybil's when they both became the property of Sybil's new husband, was it any wonder that she found herself suddenly tempted to flee screaming down the passageway and through the gates? Her life, which for the past several years had been just a smidgen above unbearable, seemed destined to become perfectly intolerable.

And if that weren't enough torment, a ferocious itch had just sprung up between her shoulder blades. She angled her offending back so it pressed against the doorframe of the solar and rubbed vigorously. Her mail set up a horrendous squeak, causing her to cease all movement abruptly lest she draw Sybil's attention and find herself sent on some other ridiculous errand. How was it men managed to attend to these sorts of itches? She supposed a stick might have served her well enough, if she'd had one to hand. Unfortunately, all she had at present was her sword, and she doubted she could pull it from its scabbard with any success, much less slide it down her back and scratch without cutting herself to ribbons.

She leaned back against the wood with a sigh and tried to ignore her discomfort. There was certainly no use in complaining. Her situation was of her own making and she was not ungrateful for it. It was surely preferable to the alternative, which was marriage to the most abhorrent, terrifying man England had ever produced.

Aye, she could itch far into her old age to escape that.

"Sir Henri," Sybil croaked, holding up her cup and staring blearily at Ali, "the bottle is empty."

Ali blinked, then realized she was being spoken to. By now her alias should have come more naturally to her, even though her choice hadn't been a particularly thought-out one. After her flight from her home, she'd been comforting herself by thinking on the bravery and cleverness of her namesake, Aliénore of Aquitaine. To give the name of Aliénore's rather ruthless English husband, Henry Plantagenet, to the first person who'd asked had seemed logical.

"Sir Henri?" Sybil prompted. "The bottle? And the cup is empty as well." She held out her cup, her arm waving about unsteadily.

"Aye, my lady. I can see that."

One of the serving wenches stomped her foot and gave Ali a glare. "Go fetch her more," she demanded. "Can you not see that she is desperate?"

Ali could see many things, and one was that Sybil's most vocal of attendants could have used a lesson in manners. A pity she could scarce wave her sword about with any success, else she might have taken on that task herself with pleasure.

"More wine," Sybil whispered weakly. "And some of Cook's tender pasties, if possible. I daresay I'm feeling rather faint."

Ali nodded and escaped the solar before Sybil's list could lengthen. At the very least, being sent on an errand meant she would not have to listen to any more speculation about whom Sybil stood to wed, the horrors of marriage, or the possibility that Sybil's new husband might not have a properly stocked larder.

The last, of course, being Sybil's worst fear.

She walked down the passageway quickly, casting aside her usual caution, eager to have her errand over with so she might see Sybil put to bed and then perhaps have a bit of rest herself. There was no telling where Sybil might come to roost, given the fact that Sybil's sire had been completely silent about his choice of husbands for her. It would be wise to have as much rest as she could, whilst she could. The saints only knew how her life might change on the morrow.

She should have had a plan. It wasn't as if she hadn't tried to fashion one—for she'd certainly had ample time to do so during her two years at Maignelay-sur-mer. Unfortunately, concocting plans was not something she did well, nor gladly.

In her youth, she'd never had a need to. Her circumstances had been those of dozens of other lords' daughters, where her most pressing decisions had been limited to what color thread to embroider with, or whether to wear the gown with the longish sleeves or the one with the pointed, beruffled ones. Her mother had died when she'd barely reached her tenth summer, causing her choices to suddenly become limited to merely one: to elude the woman her father had subsequently wed.

Then had followed nine hellish years of doing all in her power to avoid Marie of Solonge's vicious tongue and even more vicious birch rod—all whilst her father buried himself inside himself and noticed not a thing that went on around him. Ali had assumed her life could not worsen.

She'd been quite wrong.

Marie had announced one eve two years earlier that Ali was about to enter into the pleasant state of matrimony with an Englishman.

The Butcher of Berkhamshire, to be exact.

Ali's memories of what had transpired after that were still a bit unclear. She was fairly certain she'd burst into tears. She was almost sure her father had escaped the chamber and left Marie to the unpleasant task of convincing Ali that such a choice was the best one that could be made. Ali was almost positive that Marie had gone about her convincing in her usual manner.

She'd had the welts across her back for a fortnight to show for it.

What she did remember with perfect clarity was the terror of the next several days. Marie had lost no opportunity to remind her of every rumor that had ever been spewed forth regarding Colin of Berkhamshire, every tale of horror, every whisper of his limitless cruelty. And after having heard them all, and having no reason to doubt anything she'd heard, Ali had taken the only path left to her.

She had fled.

She'd done it at night, when Marie had been well into her cups. Her first happy bit of fortune had been finding one of her brothers senseless and naked in the stables, where he'd no doubt been about his usual occupation of tumbling a serving wench. Ali had helped herself to his mail, his sword, and his horse. That pleasure had been followed directly by the agony of having to bribe the gate guards with a necklace her mother had given her—the only thing of value she possessed.

The rest of that journey was likely better forgotten, for it had seemed endless. She'd had no choice but to set her brother's horse loose after a pair of days, lest his mount be recognized—

She shook her head sharply to clear it of the memories of those very perilous few days. They were better left in the past, where they belonged. What was worthy of memory was how she'd been rescued by Sybil's mother, who had been out on a hunt. Ali had been invited to come back to Maignelay-sur-mer, where the lady Isabeau had given her the less-than-taxing assignment of being Sybil's keeper. Aye, there was aught to be grateful for in that.

But now that she wouldn't be under Isabeau's watchful eye, who knew what her future would hold? It hardly bore thinking on.

She thumped down the stairs and was halfway across the great hall before she realized that the hall was not as empty as she would have expected it to be at this time of night.

Worse yet was the identity of the occupants.

Humbert of Maignelay-sur-mer sat at his high table, a cup in his hand. Nearby sat Ralph of Beaumont, Humbert's staunch ally, with his own cup. And next to him, completing the trio of powerful lords, was none other than Denis of Solonge.

Her lord father.

Ali skidded to a halt, then looked about her frantically for somewhere to hide. She found nothing but inadequate shadows. Well, better that than loitering in the midst of the chamber. She began to ease toward her right.

The lord of Beaumont cleared his throat and pointed at her. "You, there," he said imperiously. "Come pour me more wine."

Ali found quite suddenly that not only could she not move, she couldn't breathe. All she could do was stare at Beaumont in terror. If he should recognize her . . .

"Damnation, man, come here," Beaumont said impatiently. "I'll not stick you, though the urge is powerfully strong at present."

Ali realized she had no choice but to do as he asked. She approached the table with the same amount of enthusiasm she might have for a field full of angry knights bent on attacking her. She came around to stand behind Lord Ralph, then reached for his bottle of wine. She managed to get it close to his cup without incident. Just a moment or two more, then she could escape—before her father looked up and noticed who was serving his comrade, of course.

"So, Solonge," Beaumont said, with a hearty belch, "since Maignelay won't tell us whom he's betrothed Sybil to, let's discuss your gel Aliénore. How long is it since she fled? Two years?"

Ali flinched sharply. Wine sloshed over the sides of Beaumont's cup and began to liberally cover the table.

Beaumont cursed as he brushed aside the spilled wine. "Clumsy fool," he complained, throwing her a glare. Then he looked at her more closely and frowned. "Why, this one looks hardly old enough to be a squire, Maignelay. Are you knighting boys scarce weaned these days?"

Sybil's sire shrugged. "My lady found him with spurs in hand. He didn't balk at guarding my gel. That was reason enough to keep him."

"Girl-faced, pampered puss," Beaumont began.

Ali made Lord Maignelay a low bow, then fled before Beaumont could comment further on her very cherubic and unmanly features—liberally smudged with dirt and soot though they might have been—and before her father could look up and decide if Beaumont had it aright or not. She hastened to the kitchens as quickly as she could, obtained the required items, then paused at the entrance to the great hall. How was she to avoid these three again? The saints be praised that her sire never traveled with Marie. Ali suspected an encounter with that one would result in more being spilt than just wine.

And then a miracle occurred.

The men rose and stretched. Apparently their wine was finished and so were their conversings. She watched as they slapped each other several times on the back, then quit the great hall. She, however, found that her poor form was unequal to carrying her quite so easily across that expanse. Her only choice seemed to be to lean back against the wall and wait for her knees to stop quivering underneath her.

By the saints, she'd been a fool to think all danger had passed and that mail would keep her safe.

Well, at least she would be escaping with Sybil on the morrow. She would find a way, somehow, to make a life for herself far away from both her stepmother and her erstwhile betrothed.

Though how she was to do that with no skills and no coin, she couldn't have said.

She watched the great hall until she was certain no one would come back to enjoy its minimal comforts, then took what courage remained her in hand and walked through it. She made her way up the stairs and down the passageway toward the solar, wondering if her night could worsen before she managed to seek her bed.

She paused before the solar door, lifted her hand to knock, then found the door pulled back before she could do so.

"Sybil, my love, I can only wish you the best for your nuptials." Marie of Solonge began to come out of the chamber.

Ali flung herself into an alcove as her stepmother left the solar and stepped out into the passageway. She wondered quite seriously if she just might be heartily sick. How had Marie come to be here? And why now, when she herself was so close to having escaped the woman for good?

"Marie, a good night to you," Sybil's mother said. "We're so pleased you came with your husband."

"How kind you are, Lady Isabeau," Marie said, in the voice that Ali easily recognized as the one she used when trying to pass herself off as the grand lady she wasn't. "I'm so pleased to be here to see Sybil off on her journey. Wherever that might be."

"None of us knows," Isabeau said with a small laugh. "Humbert is very closed-mouthed about this."

"No doubt Sybil's husband will be a fine one. After all, what parent wouldn't want the best of all men for his girl?"

Ali suppressed a snort. The only thing more astonishing about Marie than her cruelty was her ability to hide it. Then she found herself ceasing thought abruptly as Marie came down the passageway toward her.

Her mouth went dry.

"Marie! Do wait, my lady!"

Ali watched as Isabeau rushed down the passageway to take Marie by the arm.

"I'll see you settled," Isabeau said pleasantly, blocking Marie's view of Ali. "Such a chill in the hall still, aye?"

Ali held her breath until the pair passed by, waited until she could hear them no longer, then bolted for the solar.

"Here," she said, shoving her burdens at one of Sybil's handmaids. "The lady Sybil should be abed now, don't you think?"

Sybil moaned weakly from the chair. "I must eat a bit more, I think. To keep up my strength."

Ali suppressed the urge to curse. Would these silly wenches never tire? Then again, when they went to bed, she would have to go to bed and that meant a pallet in the alcove she'd just hidden in.

Too accessible by far to Marie's investigations.

Ali sighed, turned to close the door, then jumped at the sight of a body there. Relief flooded through her as she realized it was just the lady Isabeau.

"My lady," Ali said.

"Ah, Sir Henri," Isabeau said, inclining her head. "Heavy labors today?"

Ali shook her head. The day, nay, her very life at Maig-nelay could have been so much worse, and that it hadn't been was due completely to the intervention of the woman stand-ing before her. Isabeau had sheltered her, fed her, and kept her far from the lists and the great hall as often as possible.

A boon indeed when visitors came to call.

Well, at least she could look back over the list of guests and not count Colin of Berkhamshire amongst them. He'd never come looking for her in France, and she'd heard no rumor that he intended to in the future. She fervently hoped that he'd given up waiting for her to be found and concen-trated on getting himself another wife. Surely after so long, he would have resigned himself to the idea that said wife would not be she.

"Heavy?" Ali repeated, dragging herself back to the pres-ent. "Nay, my lady. Easy tasks, for which I am most grate-ful."

Isabeau smiled. "You never complain, do you? For that, I think you should be rewarded tonight. I'll see Sybil put to bed. Why don't you seek yours now? You'll no doubt be awake for days on your travels."

Ali wondered how Isabeau could be so calm, not knowing where her daughter was going to be sent—or if she would ever see her again intact. Perhaps she had more faith in her husband than Ali had had in her own father. Or perhaps it was that Sybil would likely not notice if she had a good husband or bad. It wasn't as if she were endowed with an overabundance of wit. And she was also the last of eight daughters. Perhaps Maignelay was merely glad to be rid of her, and as cheaply as possible, and Sybil expected no more of him than that.

"I daresay you will not be traveling in France," Isabeau said quietly, too quietly to be heard over the feasting going on inside the solar.

"My lady?" Ali asked politely.

"Humbert intends to wed her elsewhere. In England, no doubt."

Ali considered that. Well, at least it would mean she would be out of the wet, unless by some unhappy bit of fortune

Sybil's new keep would be on the shore as well. Nay, with luck it would be inland, on some sunny bit of soil where Ali might finally lose the mold that seemed to be growing between her toes. That would be pleasing enough, to be where other things might grow, perhaps a place with a garden . . .

Then she realized the truth of it. She might be near those things, but she could never enjoy them. Suddenly, the whole of her life stretched before her, her life as Sybil's guardsman, forever hiding who she was.

It was enough to make her want to seek out her bed and never rise again from it.

She blinked, startled, to find that Isabeau had pressed something into her hand. Ali could feel without fingering it overmuch that it was a bag of coins.

"Go to England," Isabeau said softly, "and buy yourself a new life, far from France, far from where Sybil will come to rest. I wish I had more to give you, but Humbert would notice otherwise."

Ali felt her jaw slide down of its own accord. "My lady?"

"Go," Isabeau said, motioning toward the door. "Seek your bed in the stables, where 'tis safe."

"But—"

"The lady Marie might rise from her bed during the night, as we all do from time to time, and I daresay you wouldn't want to encounter her," Isabeau continued. "Such an unpleasant woman, don't you agree?"

Ali could only shut her mouth and endeavor to swallow in something akin to a normal fashion. But before she could comment further, she had been turned around and pushed out of the solar. The door was shut firmly behind her, leaving her no choice but to do as the lady Isabeau had bid her.

She fetched a small bundle of belongings from her spot outside the girls' chamber, then made her way to the stables. The lads there were used enough to seeing her, given that 'twas in the stables she loitered if Sybil had no need of her. The stable master only grinned at her.

"Out of favor with the gel, eh?"

"You could say that," Ali agreed.

"Up there you go, then," the man said, pointing to the hayloft. "You could wish for a poorer bed, no doubt."

Ali could have wished for much poorer indeed, but she didn't say the like. She crawled up into the hay and made a place inside her clothes for the little pouch of coins she'd been given. As she put it away, she realized there was more than coins inside.

The note was difficult to read in the gloom, but she managed. For that gift of knowing how she could thank her sire, for, despite Marie's protests, he'd insisted she be educated along with her brothers. Of course, she'd paid for the privilege with Marie's displeasure, but those were memories better left unexamined at present.

My dearest Aliénore,

Take this gold and find yourself a place far from those who would see you harmed. Would that I could have aided you more, for your mother was my dear friend and it has been my joy to have the keeping of her daughter for this too short time.

I have told no one of your secret. Be well, my girl, and may God grant you peace and safety.

Isabeau

Ali found the last words hard to read, mostly because the tears had blurred everything before her. By the saints, how had Isabeau known? Then again, Isabeau had been the one to find her after she'd fled Solonge, half-dead from exhaustion and hunger, sporting her brother's gear and pretending to be a knight. Perhaps being surprised by the woman's clarity of vision was foolish, given the circumstances.

But if Isabeau had recognized her, who else had?

She forced herself to breathe normally. If anyone else had known, they would have exposed her long before now. She knew she could trust Isabeau. Indeed, hadn't she unknowingly done so for the past two years?

Ali tucked everything back into the pouch. On the morrow, she would hide herself in the crowd as well as she could, pray she could avoid Marie's assessing gaze, then ride off calmly in Sybil's company. She would travel to England and see Sybil safely delivered to her new husband. Then, her duty done, she would make a new life for herself, just as Isabeau had said. Aye, a new life, one where she could move about freely, without fear of discovery, without fear of a knife between her ribs, far from France. A life of peace and safety.

Any kind of life, actually, would be far better a life than the one she would have had as the bride of the most feared man in England.

Chapter 2

Colin of Berkhamshire, surely the most feared man in England *and* France alike, moved stealthily across the bridge that spanned from the mainland to the island that was Blackmour's foundations. Stealth was never a problem for him. Despite his height and his strength, he was lithe and graceful.

Even he was driven to admit the like, though the only pride he took in it was that such grace gave him the advantage of sneaking up on an enemy and clouting him into insensibility before the man was the wiser—though he did that very seldom indeed. He was more inclined to announce his presence and demand a fair fight where he could see the terror in his foes' eyes before he sent them on their way out of this world. Few even heard his name but they didn't find their legs unsteady beneath them and their lips inclined to babble out the most heartfelt and sincere prayers of their life.

Unfortunately, at present even his own hard-won reputation did nothing for him. His current dilemma demanded nothing but stealth.

He was, and it galled him to admit it, being stalked.

For the first time in his life he had a small bit of sympathy for foxes, deer, and the like who found themselves being chased down and slain for the amusement of others. It was not a pleasant feeling and he suspected he might be hard-pressed to ever hunt again for the sheer sport of it.

Having gained an appreciation for the perils of being the prey, as it were.

He looked up at the barbican before attempting to creep through its gate. The parapet sported only the reassuring glint of steel and men wearing surcoats adorned with the blood-red dragons of Blackmour.

Colin moved through the barbican gate with care, looking before him into any nook that could have hidden an assailant. He would have drawn his sword as well to test the shadows, but that might have made him look weak. Better that he use his bare hands to torment his adversaries until other measures were called for.

He paused at the other end of the tunnel and eased his head out, his sharp eyes missing no detail. Nothing seemed out of place. Men worked in the lists. Peasants went about their labors. Servants did what they were supposed to be doing. Indeed, it looked like a score of other keeps in England might have looked at any given moment.

But Colin knew better.

Herein lurked his attackers.

Their number was three, that much he knew, and their work was foul. Their fate for him was fouler still, and 'twas a fate he was just as certain he could avoid—with enough stealth.

He had taken but one step into the inner bailey when he saw a page come racing across the lists toward him.

"Sir Colin! Sir Colin!" said the lad, waving what looked to be a rolled missive over his head.

Colin folded his arms over his chest and waited with an impatient frown. This distraction would do him no good. He had need of keeping his wits about him, not deciphering a message that would no doubt do nothing to improve his mood. No missive ever contained anything worthwhile, to his mind. Either they were calls to arms or messages from his sire telling Colin another of his intended brides had begged off.

It was tempting to run a hand over his face and examine it yet again for fatal flaws, but he was nothing if not disciplined when it came to that sort of thing. His visage was what it was, flaws and all, and no amount of examination would alter it.

Oddly enough, only a handful of his intended brides had ever seen that face, so he couldn't help but wonder if the others had fled for other reasons.

Of course, he knew what their *given* reasons had been. Brush with death, pox, plague, unstaunchable wounds. Aye, they'd all come up with something plausible for why they could not, in the end, attend their own marriage ceremonies with him as bridegroom.

Well, all except that wench from Solonge who hadn't even possessed the imagination to invent a decently clever reason to avoid him. Nay, she'd merely fled, leaving him humiliated.

Not that as pitiful a thing as an errant bride would humiliate such a one as he.

Or so he told himself.

Of course, he'd vowed to slay her should she ever dare show her face to him, but that had been, to his mind, the least he could have said under the circumstances. It had been a far sight more palatable than admitting she'd bruised his tender feelings.

He sighed, wondering not for the first time just what might be the *true* reasons a woman would find him a less than pleasing marital prospect. His fiercesome reputation, perhaps? That was nothing he could change. He was what he was and his reputation served him well on the battlefield.

Perhaps 'twas rumors of his unyielding sense of justice or tales of his skills in the hunt. He couldn't understand what was amiss there. What wench could fail to be moved by such fine, manly qualities? Unless, of course, the wench in question wanted a man who was soft, foolish, and willing to be controlled.

Which Colin most definitely was not.

Nay, there was no point in trying to divine the reasons a woman would avoid the pleasant state of matrimony—unless she had the same good sense Colin had, a good sense that had kept him his own man for nigh onto a score and twelve years. And, the saints willing, he would manage to hold on to that precious freedom a bit longer.

Unless, of course, the missive was from his sire. Then who knew what tortures might await him?

He waited until the page had come to a skidding halt before him and proffered the missive. With a sigh, he took it, broke the seal, and unrolled it.

To Colin of Berkhamshire from his loving sire, Reginald of Berkhamshire.

Colin snorted. Loving? Nay, his sire's self-stated mission was to make Colin's life as miserable as possible. *Loving* had merely been inserted to impress anyone who might have intercepted the missive and passed judgment on Colin's sire. Colin pursed his lips and read on.

After such troubles in finding you a wife to thereby assure myself of heirs to carry on my illustrious name, I have finally found a solution even you cannot befoul. A bride will be arriving at Blackmour shortly. You will bring her to Harrowden where I will give you further instructions regarding her fate. Do not fail to see to this, else you will leave me no choice but to take drastic measures.

I remain your patient and loving father, Reginald.

Colin cursed fluently and at great length, dismissing the page with the frown he normally used for that purpose. He rolled the missive up and wondered if it might be possible to escape Blackmour before his bride arrived. He could imagine quite well just what kind of wench his father had found for him this time and could only speculate how far afield his father had had to go in order to procure her. She was likely cross-eyed, palsied, and of so little wit that she wouldn't know him from a post shoved into the earth.

His father's preference in brides for him had become markedly less particular as time had marched doggedly on.

One could hardly lay the blame for that at his own feet, though. He'd done nothing but be what he was—arguably the fiercest warrior in the realm and certainly the warrior with the fiercest reputation. Not even Artane on his best day could inspire an immediate drop to the knees and a spewing forth of pleas for mercy that Colin could just by making his presence known. Was it any wonder no woman ever found herself equal to him, either in wit or in courage?

Nay, he didn't want to think about what poor child his father had found for him this time. That she stood to arrive at Blackmour soon was proof enough that she was either from a far distant land where his reputation did not extend—

and was there really such a place? he couldn't help but wonder—or she was, as he'd first suspected, completely witless.

That he was required to bring her to the monastery at Harrowden was no less a foul portent of things to come. No doubt his father wished both Colin and his bride to come to his brother's monkish home where they could be wed as quickly and as easily as possible.

He sighed and marched across the bailey toward the great hall. Had he been a lesser man, such desperation on the part of his sire to find him a bride might have wounded his feelings. Of course, he was not a lesser man, and his father's search for a bride was merely an annoyance to be endured every so often and then forgotten when the wench begged off.

Of course, none of his irritation over his father's fruitless searches meant that he was completely opposed to marriage. Even a man such as he couldn't help but have a foolish wish for home and hearth cross his mind now and again.

Occasionally.

During the odd, maudlin moment.

He gave himself a good mental shake to rid himself of his foolish thoughts, then continued on his way. He stepped inside the great hall, but hadn't taken two paces forward before he found himself meeting the fate he had so carefully tried to avoid.

One vile practitioner of even viler arts stood before him with a smile on her face that fooled him not at all.

"My lord Berkhamshire," she said pleasantly.

He hadn't opened his mouth to speak before he was flanked by her accomplices. The attack came without hesitation and he found himself facing the calamity he had so strenuously tried to avoid.

Dust floated up in the air and descended upon him with a heavy weight of doom.

"That ought to do it," said the old woman on his right with a grumble. "If he won't drink it down, sprinkling will have to do."

Colin scowled at her, then turned to look at the woman on his left only to find her rearing back for another fling of foul matter his way. Before he could command her to stop, she'd finished her business and he found himself with a face full of some foul substance. He sneezed heartily.

"Forgive me, my lord," the woman said contritely. "My aim needs improvement."

"Ha," said the one on his left. "What needs improving is more than your aim."

"I did my best, Nemain."

"Magda, your best would be dangerous in an empty field!"

Fierce bickering began. Colin felt the overwhelming urge to step out of the fray so he could cease being argued around, but that might have suggested to any of the three women surrounding him that he conceded them any kind of power at all.

Which, of course, he did not.

He frowned at the woman before him. "Might I ask what I am covered with now, Mistress Berengaria?"

Berengaria only smiled pleasantly. "Husband dust, my lord."

Colin felt one eyebrow go up of its own accord. "Husband dust?" he mouthed, finding quite suddenly that he had no voice.

"I put a pinch of handsomeness in it," Magda added brightly.

"Like as not, 'twas a bit of pox you added," Nemain countered.

Colin felt alarm sweep through him. His poor visage was hard enough to look at without marks from the pox adorning it.

"With any luck, my additions will outweigh any foul effects from her mistakes," Nemain said heavily. "Never worry, my lord Berkhamshire. I am your ally in this."

The saints pity him if she ever chose to be his enemy. Colin dragged his scattered thoughts back to the forefront of his mind and stared down at the harmless-looking old woman before him.

"Tell me again what that was, Mistress Berengaria," he commanded. "And pray make it something other than the foolishness you just spewed forth."

" 'Twas husband dust," Berengaria said, sounding neither afeared of him, nor remorseful over what she'd just commanded be flung in his face. "We thought it needful."

"I don't need a wife!" he exclaimed.

She looked unconvinced.

"I don't *want* a wife," Colin amended. "They're naught but a burden and a worry. I've enough of both without the affliction of a woman in the bargain."

Berengaria looked at him skeptically. "You need a son, my lord, and I know only one way to get yourself a proper one. Isn't that what your father just told you?"

He felt his jaw slide down of its own accord. "Did you read that missive?" But nay, that was impossible. The seal had been intact. He looked at her with narrowed eyes. "I vow, lady, that you've some powerful unwholesome skills that I've no desire to acquaint myself with further."

"Your father's desires are no secret," she said mildly. "I'm merely trying to make the fulfilling of them less fraught with anguish than they might be otherwise."

"Humoring my sire is hardly my fondest wish."

"But a son, my lord," Berengaria said. "Surely that is a thing to be wished for."

Colin spared a brief thought for Blackmour's two sons, one almost three years and one not even a year, and the simple pleasure of holding them both in his arms from time to time. Young Robin was more inclined to pat Colin's person for potentially hidden sweets than he was to agree to a bit of mild swordplay, but perhaps a young lad of three summers couldn't be blamed for that.

The wee babe, William, however, indulged in no such pleasantries. His main purpose seemed to be inserting his fingers into whatever opening he could find on Colin's head as often as possible. Nose, ears, mouth—the lad was not choosy. Colin found himself unable to deny the lad his curiosity, though he was the first to admit that it was difficult to intimidate any of Blackmour's men whilst he had a babe's finger delving into the depths of his ear or trying to scratch the back of his head by means of a passage up one of his nostrils.

A son?

By the saints, the thought was almost enough to bring him to his knees, faint with the responsibility and the joy of it.

But a son would entail a wife, and that was a thought he could not bear. Nay, rather he should find himself rotting in an enemy's dungeon and die a manly death full of courage. Far better that than a slow death of matrimonially induced boredom.

"Could I sire myself a legitimate babe without a wife," Colin answered finally, "then a son I would be happy to have. Find an answer to that riddle, mistress, then I will subject myself to whatever substance you wish to fling upon me."

Berengaria inclined her head. "As you will, my lord. And I wish you luck of your desire to avoid wedded bliss."

Colin assessed her sincerity with a single piercing glance, and found it to be sadly lacking. He scowled at her, glared at her companions, then politely parted the gaggle of witches and strode to the back of the great hall before they could scatter anything else on him.

It seemed that the beginnings of supper were arriving at the table, so he took his place on the left hand of his former brother-in-law and his dearest friend, Christopher of Blackmour.

"By the saints, Colin," Christopher said with a grimace, "when was the last time you bathed?"

Colin grunted as he reached for a platter of meat and served himself a hearty portion. "I don't remember. 'Tis an unhealthy practice I can't understand your fondness for. Besides, if I bathed, how would you know 'twas me next to you?" he asked, shoving the platter toward Christopher. "There's meat there before you."

Christopher nodded his thanks before reaching for his goblet of wine.

"Here you are, my lord," said his wife, putting it into his hand. "I poured it for you, of course, because I know you like that sort of thing."

"And you do your best to humor me at all times," Christopher agreed with a small smile.

"I daren't do anything else," Gillian said pleasantly.

Colin snorted over that. It wasn't just one of them humored, it was Christopher and Gillian both, and so often that it fair turned his stomach to watch them at it. He applied himself industriously to his supper, but found that he was drawn continually to the spectacle of watching Christopher with his wife. They seemed to find themselves in an endless contest to love and care for the other. 'Twas exhausting and Colin often wondered how they kept it up.

He had to admit, though, that they were well suited to that task, and to each other. Christopher was happier than Colin had ever known him to be, and Gillian likewise. And Gillian was certainly a far better woman for Blackmour's lord than his first wife had been—never mind that that first wife had been Colin's younger sister, Magdalina.

Apparently, there was no accounting for lack of character in one's siblings.

Nay, Gillian loved Christopher, and he her, and the arrangement suited them well enough to have produced two sons. Colin scratched his chin thoughtfully with the edge of his knife as he contemplated the potential for such a thing in his own life. A pity Gillian had no sister, for Colin supposed he could have wed that sister and been happy enough.

But would she have been happy with such a one as he? He gave that some thought and decided that she wouldn't have been. He had no chivalry where women were concerned, and surely no woman would be willing to settle for a lack of it. Perhaps 'twas best that he discourage whoever had come to wed him. It was the least he could do for her.

"So," Christopher said around a mouthful of supper, "you've a bride arriving soon."

"Do the walls have ears?" Colin asked in astonishment. "I vow I just received the missive but a handful of moments ago!"

"It was but a matter of time," Christopher said sagely. "How long has it been since the last wench your sire tried to foist off upon you—a year?"

"Two years," Colin said absently. "She was of Solonge. Ali-something. I scarce remember what it was."

Actually, that wasn't exactly true, for he'd thought the

name Aliénore to be quite lovely—or as lovely as a warrior would allow himself to think a name. That she'd disappeared without a trace had led him to wonder what had truly befallen her. Perhaps she'd taken the veil, though how any priory would have accepted her without her dowry, he didn't know.

Her sire, the lord Denis, had offered Colin the dowry just the same, plus a goodly bit more, if Colin would but go and search for the girl. Colin had declined. 'Twas pitiful enough that he couldn't get a bride to come to him freely. That he should have to track one down like a hapless rabbit was more than he'd been able to stomach. There were some things his pride simply would not allow.

And, of course, after his vow to slay her had been made, it had seemed a pity to find her only to have to do her in.

"Aliénore is a fair name," offered Gillian. "And I heard she was quite beautiful."

"And clever," Christopher said. "Managed to avoid facing the altar with you."

"Like as not, she met an unwholesome end," Colin said, ready to not think on her any longer. "Why else would my sire be sending me a replacement?" He downed a goblet of wine and looked about him for more. Perhaps if he ingested enough drink, he might forget about his upcoming nuptials. "The saints only know whence my sire dredged this wench up. At least she won't arrive for some time."

He had just settled down to truly making deep inroads into the dishes before him when the hall door burst open and a weary messenger stumbled across the rushes and up to the high table.

"Colin of Berkhamshire?" He panted.

Christopher pointed to his left. "In all his glory."

Colin scowled at the man before him, a nicely cooked thigh of fowl grasped in his hand and halfway to his mouth. "Aye?"

"Tidings from your sire," the messenger gasped out. "Your bride has left France and will arrive within the se'nnight. Perhaps even as soon as three days' hence."

Christopher smothered a laugh in his cup. Colin didn't spare Christopher a glare that he wouldn't have seen anyway.

Instead, he turned the full force of his displeasure on the hapless fool before him.

"So soon?" he demanded.

"Apparently the company is, um, *eager* to be here," the messenger said faintly. "In truth."

Christopher's laugh wouldn't have been smothered by half a dozen goosefeather pillows held over his face. Colin cursed and waved the man away to seek his meal at the lower table. And he cursed some more as he looked at the leg he'd been contemplating with such relish not a handful of moments before and now found completely unappetizing.

"Poor Colin," Christopher said, between snorts of laughter. "You'll not escape your fate so easily this time."

Gillian looked around her husband. "Perhaps," she said kindly, "the lass will be a good one."

Colin pursed his lips in answer.

"One never knows," she said.

"What?" Colin asked. "That my sire picked a decent, woman for me despite his best intentions? Nay, lady, that he should find me a wife to make me happy would only be the worst of misfortunes in his eyes."

"Well, mayhap the worst will come about," she said firmly.

"Not without help from us," Christopher said, slapping his hands on the table. "The lad needs a bath, clean clothes, and a bit of tidying. Surely Berengaria would have something to freshen up his aspect—"

"I've already been assaulted by those three practitioners of shady arts," Colin said grimly. "I'll not be tortured by them again."

"Perfumes," Christopher continued, as if he hadn't heard Colin. "Aye, sweet oils for his smell, herbs to improve his visage, and a comb to his locks. And the sooner the better, don't you think, Gillian?"

Colin thought many things, but chose not to give voice to any of them. He might submit to a bath, aye, for 'twas only a fool who didn't take advantage of whatever positive impression he might leave—and if there was one thing he certainly had experience with, it was preparing to meet future brides—but that would be all. He had his own labors to see to and they weren't going to be interrupted by something as foolish as the arrival of a wench. Let her seek him out in the lists when she came. He certainly didn't intend to be languishing about the hall, waiting for her to arrive and bestow her no doubt very witless and likely very insincere smile on him.

And whilst he was out in the lists, perhaps he could think of a fitting revenge to wreak on his sire for all the anguish of soul the man had caused him over the years.

Marriage? Ha! 'Twas a waste of a man's strength, a dagger plunged into the tenderest place of his heart, a burden heavy enough to crush him to the ground with the bearing of it. He would avoid it at all costs for as long as he could, despite whatever plans his father might have for him.

"We should be about this fine, matrimonial alchemy," Christopher began. "And as soon as possible—"

Colin shoved back from the table and leaped to his feet.

Christopher didn't spare him a look. "Run if you like. We'll find you and have you washed just the same."

Colin favored his former brother-in-law with a snort, then fled from the hall with as much dignity as possible.

A bride?

Not if he could help it. There was a good reason he was the fiercest warrior in England *and* France and 'twas far past the time when his father became familiar with it.

Chapter 3

Ali put her hand over her belly, fingered her coins through her tunic, and contemplated the possibilities for her future. It was the first chance she'd had for any such thought. She'd spent the whole of the shipboard journey leaning over the railing, heaving into the heaving sea. She hadn't even had the strength to wonder how it was that seamen bore such a life. Rolling, heaving, bucking—just the thought of the ocean was enough to bring back very foul memories she sincerely hoped she would never have to make any more of. And she wouldn't, if she could help it. She was now on England's pleasant soil and had no intentions of ever leaving it again.

England being, of course, so comfortably far from France, Solonge, and Marie.

And England would be even a more pleasant place when Sybil's little company had been deposited at their destination and their escort, Sir Etienne of Maignelay-sur-mer, had been sent back to France.

He was, to put it mildly, a complete arse.

She watched as he sauntered over to where Sybil and her maids sat huddled near their gear in a little glade, then backed away from them as inconspicuously as possible. No sense in being too close. Sir Etienne was as free with his slaps as he was with his orders and she had no desire to elicit any more of either than necessary. Now that she was under his command, she realized how completely she had been shielded from him and those like him at Maignelay-sur-mer. Apparently Isabeau had tried to keep her safe in England as well, for Isabeau had commanded that Ali was to answer only to Sybil. Those were instructions that Sir Etienne had, of course, ignored immediately and fully. As far as he was concerned, she was his to torment.

He cleared his throat imperiously. "We will arrive at our destination on the morrow," he announced in the booming tones of one who relished the power of having kept them ignorant of that destination for well over a se'nnight. "Ready yourselves. And you, Henri," he said, with an unfriendly look thrown her way, "stop hiding in the shadows and see to their gear."

Ali nodded quickly, so that she might not draw his ire.

"Your husband awaits, my lady Sybil," he continued crisply. "Pray, manage to brush the crumbs from your gown and tidy your hair on the day we arrive. Those at Blackmour will expect a more worthy emissary from Maignelay-sur-mer than a gaping half-wit wearing the remains of her last score of meals on her front."

Ali felt her jaw slide down at the insult and she continued to watch, open-mouthed, as the offensive oaf swept them all with a final glance of disgust, then stomped away.

She looked to see how Sybil was reacting, only to find her charge staring after Sir Etienne with the same slack-jawed expression.

And then it occurred to her just what Sir Etienne had said.

Blackmour?

Sybil's husband was to be found at Blackmour?

Sybil's maids had ceased to gape after Sir Etienne and were now blathering on in their usual witless fashion. Ali listened to them only because the shock she'd just had was so great, she could do nothing else. And why was it, she wondered absently, that serving wenches seemed to congregate in threes? It boded ill, every time.

"Blackmour," one of the girls whispered, crossing herself. "We're going to Blackmour!"

"He's a warlock," another whispered, her knuckles white as she clutched her hands together.

"But there is no one of marriageable age there," said the third, looking suddenly rather relieved. "Blackmour's eldest son is not yet four."

Sybil sighed in relief and plopped a hefty chunk of cheese in her mouth. Ali felt a wave of relief as well. Whatever Sybil's faults might have been, she surely didn't deserve a warlock for a husband. Ali wondered briefly how these wenches knew so much about Blackmour's lord, then dismissed the thought. Everyone knew of him, for his foul reputation stretched over the whole of England and much of France. The only person she knew of with a more widespread reputation than the Dragon of Blackmour was his closest friend, Colin of Berkhamshire. Well, at least Blackmour was safely wed and his sons far too young to be taken as serious matrimonial prospects.

But if not Blackmour and his spawn, then who?

"But wait," insisted the first, "he said we *were* going to Blackmour. Why there?"

There was silence in the little clearing. Well, silence except for Sybil chewing.

The second wench snapped her fingers. "I know! It isn't to Blackmour's lord, but someone else there!"

Well, surely no one could fault her wit.

As if they'd planned it, all three girls clapped hands over mouths, then crossed themselves as if against the Devil himself.

"Not Blackmour."

"Nay, not him."

"That leaves only his blood-brother."

Sybil gulped a bit of wine. "And who's that?" she asked, sucking her teeth, apparently searching for an overlooked tidbit.

The three girls looked at her, their eyes wide, their visages pale.

"The Butcher of Berkhamshire," they said as one.

Ali watched as Sybil stopped the investigation of her mouth. Her lips twitched. Her fingers fluttered up and pressed against her mouth, as if they sought to stifle a large, endless scream. Then her eyes rolled back in her head and she slumped back against the provision sacks she'd been guarding with her very self. She lay sprawled bonelessly over grain and other foodstuffs.

Ali watched all this happen, then felt her knees grow just as unsteady as they always did when faced with that name. Indeed, her legs grew so unstable, she soon found herself on the ground with her legs folded beneath her. She could scarce believe what she'd heard, and she frantically tried to find some other explanation for Sir Etienne's destination.

Unfortunately, she could find nothing.

In truth, there was likely only one man at Blackmour who was looking for a bride and that man was Colin of Berkhamshire.

Well, at least his bride was apparently no longer to be her own poor self.

A wave of relief washed over her so strongly that she shook. And then she began to laugh. She was free, truly free. Colin of Berkhamshire no longer searched for her, no longer planned to make her his wife, no longer had any hold over her.

Or did he?

Her relief was gone as quickly as it had come. What if she were discovered? If he knew she was alive, would her betrothal to him still stand? If her mail were stripped away and she were revealed to be what and who she was, would that leave her as the pitiable girl standing next to him at the altar instead of Sybil?

She couldn't go to Blackmour. How could she when Christopher of Blackmour would see through her disguise and know who she was the moment she rode into his courtyard? She had no doubts he could, and would. He was, after all, a warlock. The saints only knew what kinds of powers he had that she couldn't even imagine.

What would happen to her once he'd discovered her? Would they send her immediately back to her home, back to the keep at Solonge where Marie would be waiting to murder her? Or would Blackmour deliver her into Berkhamshire's hands for him to dispose of as he would? And based on very reliable rumor, she already knew what *he* would do the moment he had his hands around her throat.

The panic that swept over her felt altogether too much like what she'd experienced at Solonge. Her instinct, and it was so strong an instinct that she found herself quite suddenly on her feet, was to flee. But even as her feet began to move of their own accord, she remembered the vow she'd made herself after her flight from Solonge, her vow to never again act so impetuously.

But that was before she knew she was heading directly into a Dragon's nest, especially when within that nest loitered one Colin of Berkhamshire, butcher extraordinaire.

Before she could decide in which direction to bolt, a heavy hand grasped her by the back of the tunic.

"Lazy whelp," Sir Etienne barked. "Be about your business. The Butcher contracted for a wife, three handmaids and a pitiful excuse for a knight to attend them and I intend to see all of you delivered in goodly time." He gave Ali a shove toward Sybil. "See to her gear and pray I find nothing more taxing than that for you to do."

Ali stumbled toward a partially rousing Sybil, then straightened. A look over her shoulder revealed Sir Etienne watching her with his hand on his sword.

No chance of escape there, then.

With a deep sigh, she started to gather up the things Sybil and her maids had scattered about. At least seeing to that simple task gave her something to do besides concentrate on the irony of her life. The two years she'd spent hiding, looking over her shoulder, praying she could succeed with her ruse, all in an effort to avoid being anywhere near the Butcher of Berkhamshire, wasted.

All wasted.

She had escaped the Butcher by becoming Sybil's keeper—and as her keeper she would now travel with Sybil to meet none other but the very man she'd given up her freedom to avoid.

Who could have possibly imagined such a chain of fiendish events?

"Henri, make haste!" Sir Etienne bellowed. "We've a long way to ride this afternoon."

Ali bent her mind and her shaking hands to her task. She would simply have to think on a plan as she rode. Escape was unlikely, what with Sir Etienne watching as he seemingly was. And where would she escape to, even if she did manage it? She had no idea where she was, nor what was nearby.

Nay, she would just have to remain close to Sybil, make herself as inconspicuous as possible, and hope that a solution to her problems would present itself before the Butcher's hands presented themselves around her neck.

Or mayhap a miracle would occur and the morning would never come.

*U*nfortunately, the morn did arrive in its normal, relentless fashion and Ali found herself with no choice but to continue in the direction Sir Etienne dictated. He ordered her about as often as possible, and when he wasn't shouting at her, he was smirking at her. No doubt he had his own secret enjoyment over the thought of her spending the rest of her life as Berkhamshire's man. Perhaps in his mind that was punishment enough for someone he considered completely useless with a blade.

Which she was, of course, despite her brother François's spurs. She couldn't feel anything but satisfaction each time she heard the comforting *clink* of metal at her heels. Then again, she owed him for several instances of torture—not only to her own poor person, but to her childish playthings. A pity that bit of metal couldn't have endowed her with skill enough to have wielded her blade as well as François could.

But perhaps wishing for things she would never have could be put aside for a while. Blackmour was rising up before her, coming closer with every hoofbeat. Her hands were so slippery with sweat that she could scarce hold her reins. Her horse seemed to sense her fear, for he danced continually beneath her until she was firmly convinced she would humiliate herself by losing her seat—and likely before the Dragon and the Butcher themselves.

Ali looked at Sybil and found a girl riding next to her whose hands were empty of all foodstuffs. Too nervous to eat? It spoke fully of the poor wench's terror.

Ali put her face forward and prayed for death.

It didn't come, of course. What did come was a castle that seemed ever larger and more gloomy as they approached it.

The walls were dark, cast in shadows from stormy clouds above that seemed to gather more densely as they approached. Ali half wondered if the Dragon was conjuring up a bit of thunder simply because he could. After all, what else had the man to do to occupy his time?

Or perhaps Lord Colin was preparing to send a few sniveling souls along to the afterlife by his frowns alone and Blackmour was simply providing an appropriate accompaniment. The screams of terror and the litany of pleas for mercy would be drowned out quite nicely by a ripe thunderstorm. Perhaps Lord Colin preferred it that way—having spent the greater portion of his life listening to men babbling piteously to be spared. That likely grew tiresome after a few years. And by her count he was a year or two past a score and ten. How was it one man could fill so few years with so many tales of terror?

Perhaps 'twas better not to think overmuch on that.

It seemed far too soon that they were riding into the courtyard after a harrowing journey across a bridge that surely was too thin to hold the combined weight of their entire company. Ali was thankful to be once again on solid ground, never mind that the Dragon's nest was naught but an island thrust away from the whole of England. Perhaps the land itself couldn't bear the thought of sheltering him and thus continually tried to rid itself of his presence.

They stopped in the courtyard. Ali looked about her reluctantly and had to admit that as far as castle courtyards went, it looked much like every other one she'd ever seen. There was a great hall that gave no outward sign of the evil that lurked within. A pleasant-looking garden sat to one side, full of the first blushes of herbs, tender flowers, and a handful of blossoms and fruit trees. Stables, a smithy, peasant huts: These were all things she would have expected to see, and nothing about them seemed untoward. Indeed, the garden looked like something she might have enjoyed passing her time in, if she'd had the chance.

The door to the great hall opened suddenly, interrupting her scrutiny and sending her heart racing. People came down the steps and gathered together before their small company.

And then the Dragon came to the door.

Ali felt her mouth go dry, and she wasn't sure if it was from the horror of seeing him in the flesh or from the surprise at finding he was powerfully handsome. What sort of devilry was that, that a fiend so foul should possess such commanding features as well?

He was accompanied by a woman of comely appearance who held his arm so easily that she could have been none other than his wife. Ali couldn't even begin to give thought to how she had found herself in the Dragon's talons. That was a story she suspected she wouldn't be equal to hearing even on her best day.

The Dragon stopped before the company and spoke briefly with Sir Etienne. Ali realized belatedly that only the women were still mounted and she slid off her horse, trying to be as unobtrusive as possible. Of course, her sword chose that moment as the appropriate time to twist around, trip her, and make her look the fool. Her horse followed suit by putting up a struggle that sent the entire company into a panic.

Sir Etienne appeared before her. Whatever else her failings, her ears seemingly worked well enough, for she had no trouble hearing him shout at her. And then she found herself quite suddenly sprawled in the dirt with her ears ringing. She realized only then that she'd been struck, and forcefully enough that sparks of light danced in the world around her.

"Have you no skill at all?" Sir Etienne snarled. "Get yourself over and hold your lady's horse." He spat on her, then turned and walked back to the front of the company.

Ali struggled to her feet, wishing she were anywhere but where she was. She staggered over to hold on to the reins of Sybil's horse, keeping her eyes down to the ground. Then she heard the collective gasp of those around her and suspected that gasp was not for her sorry self. She looked up and saw that another body had come to the doorway of the great hall.

And knew that she was gazing upon none other than the Butcher himself.

The tales did not exaggerate. He was enormous. He filled the doorway not only with his foul self, but with his reputation as well. She could almost see it wrapping itself around him like a sorcerer's cloak.

Ali wished she'd had a place to sit down as Lord Colin walked down the stairs. She suspected that one of the reasons Lord Colin was so successful in battle was that all he needed to do was walk onto the field and half his opponents would throw down their weapons in an effort to save themselves from his wrath.

Ali didn't dare look at him as he approached. It was all she could do to continue to suck in air and keep Sybil's horse under control.

The footsteps ceased.

The Butcher spoke.

The heavens wept in fear.

"And you are?" he demanded.

Ali stole a look to determine that he hadn't been speaking to her before she ducked her head again and did her best to fade to insignificance.

Unfortunately, Sybil seemed not to be suffering from the same desire. She whimpered loudly enough that Ali looked up in surprise. She swayed in the saddle, swallowed that last little bite of whatever last meal she'd decided to ingest before meeting her doom, then her eyes rolled back in her head and she slumped sideways toward Ali. Ali managed to catch her, but the girl was substantial and her dead weight bore both of them to the ground. Ali lay comfortably covered by the voluminous folds of Sybil's wimple and veil—made excessively ample for the hiding of various sweets, no doubt—while Lord Colin's displeasure washed over them in a rush.

"Can someone tell me what this child's name is?" he demanded.

Ali would have stayed happily where she was for eternity, but it was not to be so. The cloth was suddenly ripped back from her face. And if that weren't unpleasant enough, she found herself facing not an annoying drizzle, but the furious-looking visage of none other than the Butcher of Berkhamshire himself. She squeaked in surprise—belatedly remembering that manly knights never squeaked. She tried for a more knightly exclamation of surprise.

"I take it you are her keeper?" he demanded.

Ali stared at him, his face so close to hers, and for the briefest of moments she felt surprised that she faced a man and not a foul demon. Indeed, he looked like a very undemonlike man. Two eyes of a color that reminded her of a mossy pool near her home. A nose that had definitely encountered some kind of fist or sword hilt, given the crook in it, but not a bad nose as far as they went. Sun-darkened skin over a face that had a pleasing enough shape. Little crinkles around his eyes, as if there were times he might have smiled—

Over the foul, painful deaths of his opponents, no doubt. Ali came to herself with a start and realized that Lord Colin was scowling at her with enough fierceness that any of the kind thoughts she'd had of him before were immediately shown to be what they were—the idle daydreams of a girl who was being crushed to death by the not-so-lithe Sybil of Maignelay.

"You are her keeper?" Lord Berkhamshire demanded again.

"Aye, my lord," she gasped, wishing intensely that perhaps she had been more diligent in keeping Sybil away from the cellars.

"And your mistress's name? If you can stop squeaking long enough to give it to me?"

"Sybil of Maignelay-sur-mer," Ali said promptly, wishing she could decide what was the worse of the tortures: having Lord Berkhamshire breathing down on her, or Sybil crushing the life from her. She spared effort for a wish that she weren't quaking so hard that she was coming close to flinging Sybil off her without aid.

Lord Colin grunted, straightened, and walked off, leaving a waft of odd-smelling air behind him. Ali sniffed, unable to decide if the man had doused himself in ale or rolled in the herb garden. 'Twas rumored he had a most foul smell. Mayhap he tried to cover that with something less foul.

"The lists," he called to any who would listen. Ali watched him point at Sir Etienne. "You're of that company. Let us see what you're made of, eh?"

Ali didn't even have the brief satisfaction of seeing Sir Etienne hesitate. He merely shrugged negligently and followed Lord Colin to the lists. Perhaps he was too stupid to realize whom he stood to face. Either that, or he thought far too much of his own skill. Ali suspected it was a great deal of both.

For herself, she was left with a picture of complete menace as her first impression of her one-time betrothed. Never mind those crinkles around his eyes; there was no mercy in him. She imagined that he only laughed when he was putting someone to the sword. She closed her eyes and let fly heavenward a heartfelt prayer that she'd never been forced to wed with him.

Ali soon found Sybil removed from her own flattened self. Sybil and her ladies were led inside the hall, leaving Ali to struggle to her feet herself. She had scarce managed to gain them before she found herself confronted by a sight far worse than the Butcher of Berkhamshire.

The Dragon himself stood there, with a young knight at his side. But all he said was, "Best be about your duties, lad."

Ali waited for him to spew out the truth of her identity, but apparently he either hadn't troubled himself with discovering it, or he planned to announce it at another time, for he said nothing else to her. She gaped at him for a moment or two in surprise, then managed to shut her mouth. "Aye, my lord," she whispered. "Thank you, my lord."

Blackmour nodded curtly before he turned to the young man at his side and turned him away to speak in low tones to him.

"Keep an eye on that Sir Etienne," Blackmour said. "I've no liking for what I saw today."

"Of course, my lord," said the young man, who waited until his master had walked away, then turned to Ali with a friendly smile. "And you are?"

Aliénore of Solonge was so far forward on her tongue, she had to bite the words back. She swallowed, then tried again.

"Sir Henri," she said.

The man facing her lifted one eyebrow in surprise. "A knight, are you?"

"Knighted young," she said. "For valor," she added, choking over the words.

The other man seemed to be trying not to smile. "Jason of Artane," he said, "at your service. Knighted early enough as well, though merely for many hours spent sweating in the lists, not for any great deed of valor."

She swallowed with difficulty. Artane? Jason of Artane? By the saints, the de Piagets of Artane were patrons of the priory near her home! She ducked her head, on the off chance he might somehow, beyond reason or logic, recognize her. This was, after all, Blackmour. The saints only knew if the entire keep was bewitched or not.

"Sir Henri?"

She looked at Jason and nodded in her most manly fashion. "My thanks," she said gruffly.

"The stables are that way," he said, pointing over her head. "You'll likely want to see to your lady's horseflesh."

"Of course."

He paused, looked at her closely, then shook his head. "I am," he muttered to himself, "beginning to imagine things. Aye, that's it."

Ali turned away before he could decide that he *wasn't* imagining things. He had looked at her far too closely for her taste. His master might have the benefit of unwholesome magic to aid him, but she suspected that Jason of Artane needed nothing but his own two eyes to divine any and all secrets.

All the more reason to flee.

As quickly as possible.

She gathered up the reins to a pair of horses and headed toward the stables. She deposited the beasts with the grumbling stable master, then stepped back out into the courtyard and headed without hesitation toward the gates. Perhaps the best thing for her to do was simply walk out whilst there was a goodly bit of confusion in the courtyard. Sybil was being fussed over inside, the Dragon had disappeared, and she knew that Lord Colin was no doubt grinding Sir Etienne into the dust in the lists. Aye, this was the perfect time to make good her escape.

She came to a teetering halt and watched in dismay as the portcullis slammed home with a ring that rivaled any death knell she'd ever heard.

Her chest felt as if a large hand were squeezing it so tightly that there was no room for breath, no room for her heart, no room for any life inside her body.

"Sir knight," the stable master bellowed. "Bring me your other horses!"

Ali turned and numbly went to fetch more horseflesh.

Trapped, again.

By the saints, how was she to survive *this* prison?

Chapter 4

C olin parried with Sir Etienne and, finding nothing that required his immediate attention, turned his mind to other things.

Namely the fact that his own smell was driving him mad, and his bride apparently agreed. Surely only a hefty waft of perfumed oil could have been what had knocked her straight from her horse in such a manner. The saints only knew where she was now. Likely weeping buckets in some corner of Gillian's solar, comforted by masses of women whose task it was to comfort those who wept in such volume.

The saints be praised he hadn't been called upon to join that unhappy group.

He fended off Sir Etienne's aggressive attack with something akin to boredom. Would there ever come a man who could truly make him sit up and take notice? Artane himself, perhaps. Lord Robin had white enough in his crown, but he was still a joyously wily warrior who delighted in nothing more than a good skirmish in the lists.

His get were sport enough, to be sure, though of Artane's three sons, Kendrick was surely the most skilled. Jason would be just as skilled, though, in time. Colin took every opportunity to polish up that lad's swordplay so he might someday have a worthy opponent. Jason was improving, to be sure, but still Colin found himself left vaguely unsatisfied. One thing was certain: It would not be this Sir Etienne of Maignelay to make him break a sweat. So, with a sigh of resignation, he continued his play but turned his mind to other matters.

His bride was, unfortunately, the first thing that came to mind. He could recall little of her save masses of pale hair escaping a wimple that could have covered the heads and throats of a half a dozen women with ease. Her eyes he'd had but a brief glimpse of before they'd rolled straight back in her head and she'd pitched off her horse onto that pitiful guardsman who'd been completely overcome by his mistress's substantial self.

"I see fear in your eyes," Sir Etienne said triumphantly. "Do you yield?"

Colin blinked in surprise. "Yield?" he echoed, fair dumbfounded by the very idea.

"I can be merciful," Sir Etienne said magnanimously.

Colin honestly wasn't sure if he should laugh or run the fool through for his idiocy. Surely the latter would have been a mercy to all involved. The very idea of him, Colin of Berkhamshire, *needing* any mercy was just so ridiculous, he had no idea how to respond.

Obviously Sir Etienne thought he was speechless with fear.

"To save your pride, then," Sir Etienne said, "we'll continue."

Colin scowled and dismissed the imbecile before him, though he did, of course, continue parrying with him. Fool or not, the man was hoisting a sword and had a faint idea of what to do with it once it was up in the air. Colin was in need enough of distraction that he would take it from wherever it might come.

Unfortunately, Sir Etienne was a poor enough distraction that Colin found he couldn't keep his thoughts away from his pitiful future—a future he was just certain would be full of torments any man with sense would have avoided like the pox itself.

Marriage. A bride who fainted at the sight of him. His father gloating over finally having saddled him with a wife.

It was enough to make him wish for a hasty retreat to his bed for the afternoon.

He sighed deeply. He would have to consider his journey soon, he supposed, before his bride threw herself off the parapet, or before Colin threw Sir Etienne off the like—and given how much he hated being that far off the ground, the latter was saying something indeed. It was growing more tempting by the heartbeat, though, for the longer they parried, the more vocal Sir Etienne became about his skill and Colin's supposed apparent awe of the same. Colin could finally bear the braggart no longer. He resheathed his sword in disgust, leaving the other man fighting against air.

"You babble overmuch," Colin said briskly, then walked off the field. Mayhap he could get himself back to the house and down to the cellar before anyone caught him. Then he would douse himself in ale and rid himself of the stench that bathing and perfuming had given him. Then, he supposed with a heavy sigh, he would have to seek out his bride and make her acquaintance.

If she could cease fainting long enough for him to do so, of course.

Colin strode back to the hall. His nose recognized the pleasing odors of a yet-to-arrive afternoon repast the moment he entered. He immediately put aside all foolish thoughts of parleying with his bride and made his way without interruption to the high table, took his seat, and looked about him hopefully. When sustenance did not immediately appear before him, he pulled out his knife and began to bang on the wood.

"That really isn't polite."

Colin scowled as his primary tormentor, Gillian of Blackmour, sat down next to him. True that she was his dearest friend's wife. True, too, that he was rather fond of her himself, so he couldn't just up and bellow at her to be silent. But could he bear a meal with her judging his every move and measuring it against some ideal of perfection no man had ever attained?

"I was," he said loftily, "testing the balance of my blade."

"You were," she said archly, "banging for your supper. Patience is a virtue."

"Patience is a virtue that leaves the patient weak-kneed from hunger," Colin countered. "I have manly business. I need to be fed. I smell, but I do not see. Cook apparently needs to be prodded to action."

Gillian raised a single finger and suddenly food appeared before them.

Colin was quite frankly amazed at her powers of persuasion, but he wasn't going to let that admiration of the like get in the way of getting something to his mouth as quickly as possible. He looked to Gillian's far side to find that Christopher had joined them and was making quick work of piling pleasing things upon his trencher. Well, if he was doing it, Colin could as well, without fear of a scolding. He reached for a platter only to hear the dreaded *tsk-tsk* from Christopher's lady.

Colin glared at her. "What now?"

"You should serve me first."

"What the bloody hell for?" Colin asked, astonished. "Have you been out in the lists all morning, working like a fiend?"

Food spewed well across the table as Christopher guffawed out what he'd managed to ingest without having been forced to serve his bride. And a damned goodly bit of food it looked to have been.

"I am your trencher partner," Gillian said.

Don't want you was on the tip of his tongue, but this was the lady Gillian, after all. Colin found himself looking down into her sweet green eyes. When she gave him that smile that seemed to bring all men with any sense straight to their knees, he knew there was no point in protesting. She would have her way with him despite his best intentions.

"Chris?" he said conversationally.

"Aye?" his friend answered around a substantial hunk of bread halfway into his mouth.

"I hate you."

Christopher only continued to chew contentedly. Colin glared at Gillian, just to let her know he wasn't going soft, then with a grumble set to topping her side of the trencher with things that looked fairly edible to him. The saints only knew what Gillian would think of them.

He waited until she had begun to delicately pick through the offerings before he applied himself earnestly to the task of filling his belly. Meat, the occasional vegetable, bread, cheese—in truth he couldn't have cared what he ate as long as there was a goodly amount of it and it was unimpeded in its progress from the table to his mouth.

Once his initial appetite was appeased, he looked about for things to fill in the cracks, as it were. He considered a bowl of eggs. The saints only knew how Cook had decided to ruin these today. Colin reached out and poked one clear through with his finger.

"Colin!" Gillian exclaimed. "Do not poke the eggs."

"I want to know what's in 'em."

"Then take a bite."

"And what if I don't like it?"

"Swallow it anyway."

"Daft notion," he grunted under his breath, and reached for some odd bit of stuff smothered in some odd bit of sauce. Trying to be polite—the saints pity him—he took a bite.

And spewed it immediately forth where it deserved to be, namely on the floor where the dogs could have at it.

"Don't spit!" Gillian exclaimed.

He pulled up a corner of the cloth covering the table and wiped his mouth liberally.

"And don't use the cloth to wipe your mouth!"

He reached in desperation for the goblet of wine before him with every intention of downing the entire cupful. Or he would have, had it not been pulled away from him before he could get it all down.

"What?" he demanded.

"Share," she warned.

He tried to tug it from her, but she was stronger than she looked. He pulled, but she frowned at him, as if she thought that would persuade him to let go. With narrowed eyes, he released the cup, but she'd been pulling so hard that the half-full cup flew from her fingers and landed with a *splat* and a *ding* on the side of Christopher's head.

He, predictably, bellowed with rage.

"Not my fault," Colin said, shoving back his chair. "I'm going elsewhere to eat in peace!"

He lifted a loaf of bread and an enormous chunk of cheese from off the table and escaped the great hall whilst he still could. The thought of facing his bride was sounding more appealing by the moment, especially if it meant his table manners would no longer be scrutinized. He walked down the passageway toward Gillian's solar, wherein was bolted his bride. It wasn't his ideal destination, but perhaps there would at least be an empty seat therein where he might ingest a bit more sustenance without comments on how he was doing it.

He slowed as he approached the solar. The young knight who'd been flattened in the courtyard stood before the solar door, apparently standing guard. Colin snorted to himself. As if that one would ever be able to defend the lady Sybil from any but the smallest and least ferocious of rats.

But at least he was making an effort, despite how feeble an effort it was. Colin came to a halt before the lad, peered at him, and was left again with surprise that such a one as this had ever been knighted. Why, he looked no older than ten-and-five! Not a shadow of beard adorned his face, and there were no lines of living adorning that smooth skin either. A babe, that's what he was, saddled with the task of playing nursemaid to a wench who couldn't even face a true man without fainting.

Colin pitied the boy his task.

Well, the least he could do was do something to strengthen the boy during his unpleasant labors. Colin untucked the loaf of bread from under his arm and held it out.

"Here," he said. "Eat something."

The lad gaped at him.

"All right," Colin grumbled, holding out the bottle. "Take this as well. You may as well not die of thirst whilst you're about your useless vigil."

The boy shut his mouth with a snap and looked as surprised as if Colin had been some kind of bloody angel of mercy, come to give him reprieve from a hangman's noose.

"Thank you, my lord," he whispered.

Colin was hardly accustomed to those kinds of looks of wonder and surprise. Generally, those who thought him to be ruthless were in a position to be recipients of that ruthlessness. He was used to looks of pleading; he wasn't used to such open looks of surprise—as if the lad had fully expected him to remove his head from his shoulders and now that Colin hadn't, he hardly knew what to think.

Colin pursed his lips. If the lady Sybil's keeper was this daft, what did that betide for the lady herself?

Better not to know, likely.

Colin turned his attentions back to the boy before him. "What's your name?" he demanded.

The boy gulped. "Sir Henri."

"Hmmm," Colin said, regarding him skeptically. "A knight?" He shook his head. "Impossible to believe," he muttered. "But then again, this is France spewing forth girls in mail without a decent idea of how to wield their blades. Mayhap I am overdue for a visit there."

Sir Henri began to breathe in a most unsteady fashion. Colin looked at the boy from under his eyebrows and wondered if it would be better to slap some proper breath back into him, or leave him to sorting it out himself. When Sir Henri began to wheeze, Colin decided on the latter. A healthy slap on the back might just do the lad in.

"Don't choke on the bread," he said heavily. "And there's more below, if you can get your delicate self downstairs to ingest any of it. I wouldn't share with your mistress, however. Perhaps she'll find her way out the door if she's hungry enough."

Sir Henri only nodded, his breath still coming in unwholesome-sounding gasps.

Colin walked away before he had to watch the boy humiliate himself further. He had no doubts Sir Henri would break down soon and sob with fear. Apparently the lad was not unacquainted with his own intimidating reputation. No doubt having to see Colin in the flesh had been too much for him.

But France, now that was something he could certainly give more thought to. He'd assumed that he'd left an indelible impression upon the country the last time he'd been there. Apparently, their memories were short and their training methods dwindling to nothing.

Obviously, it was time he returned for a visit.

That thought cheered him considerably. He would finish up the foul work of getting himself wed, then turn his attentions to the more pleasurable work of setting foot on yonder shore and instructing the men there on the proper comportment of a knight. How could they fail to be impressed by his own modest example? Perhaps this time he would stay a bit longer, instruct more men than he'd been able to the last time, and finish his work properly.

It was the least he could do for the noble cause of chivalry.

He found himself eventually out in the stables. Ah, now here was a place he could understand, with occupants he could be at ease with. How often was it he longed for the companionable noise of wickers and the pleasant smells of dung and hay? Too often, likely. Perhaps it *was* time he wed before he found his mount's company preferable to a wench's.

He leaned over the stall and rubbed his stallion's nose. At least here was a being who found him not offensive. And why not? A horse cared nothing but that its master was brave and courageous and Colin was surely those things and more. A pity none of his potential brides had possessed the same good sense. He sighed. It did him no good to wonder why horses loved him and women did not.

Women were, obviously, of less wit than his mount.

He was satisfied with that realization, but it did little to aid him any in his current undertaking. He sighed and bowed his head. Mayhap he could just put Sybil on her horse, drag her to Harrowden and let his sire see to the rest of it. After all, his sire was controlling the rest of their lives. Perhaps he could talk a bit of sense into the wench whilst he was at his scheming. It was a certainty Colin would never manage the like.

He sighed and turned his mind away from unpleasant thoughts of matrimony and travel. Mayhap he could lure the more ferocious part of Blackmour's garrison out into the lists and spend the afternoon grinding them into the dust one by one.

Aye, that was the task for him. Brides and sires could wait. He gave his stallion a pat and left the stables, whistling a happy tune.

Chapter 5

A li fled, terror clutching at her heart, knowing that the sword that swung behind her was coming closer with each swing. She forced herself to go faster and was faintly surprised to find that she was managing it. Perhaps that had aught to do with the fact that she was running on four feet—and she was running on four feet because she had been transformed by some foul spell into a rabbit.

She found it in her to curse her now quite large ears. Smaller ones perhaps wouldn't have been capable of so clearly hearing the ring of the sword coming closer and closer to her. She risked a glance over her furry shoulder to find herself being pursued by none other than Colin of Berkhamshire, his wicked blade in his hand, a ferocious frown on his face. He stooped suddenly, reached out and grasped her by the scruff of her neck.

"Aack!" she cried out in terror.

She was jerked backward.

It was then that she woke fully and found that whilst she was most certainly not a rabbit, she was definitely being hauled backward—into the solar, fortunately. That meant, though, that she'd fallen asleep sitting straight up against the solar door.

She wanted to weep with relief. Her first night had passed safely at Blackmour with only foul dreams to show for it. It could have been much worse. Any number of souls could have happened by and done the saints only knew what to her whilst she slept.

She was deposited without care onto the solar floor and Sybil's maids leaped for the door to heave it to and bolt it. Ali rubbed the sleep from her eyes, then slowly crawled to her feet and turned to find Sybil sitting in a chair. She was looking, unsurprisingly, pale and terrified.

"Henri," Sybil whispered, as if she thought the walls might be eavesdropping, "you are well?"

"Well enough," Ali said, shaking off her unsettling dream. She stood quite happily on two feet and forced herself not to reach up and assure herself of the proper shape of her ears. "And you, my lady?"

Sybil looked to be on the verge of fainting again. One of her maids appeared instantly at her elbow with some strengthening bread and a large goblet. "I will survive it," she said, chewing industriously, then taking a large swallow of wine. "But barely."

In all honesty, Ali couldn't blame her for her terror. Just the thought of being chained to Colin of Berkhamshire for the rest of her life was enough to bring any sensible woman to take drastic measures.

As Ali would certainly know.

"Have you seen him?" one of the maids asked.

"Is he as horrible as the tales say?" asked another.

"Has he killed anyone yet?" asked the third.

Ali pointedly ignored the fact that she'd just spent half the night dreaming of Colin pursuing her, his sword at the ready, no doubt planning on having her for his supper. She could hardly blurt that out without sending Sybil burrowing deeper into her sack of sustenance.

But, aye, she had seen Colin. Not only had she seen him, he'd given her food the night before when it would have been just as easy to have run her through, burst into Sybil's solar, and drag the girl out by her feet to converse with him. He hadn't seemed cruel beyond measure then.

But that was one occasion and perhaps he'd been overcome by unwholesome feelings of pity. She'd certainly given the strong impression of someone about to expire from terror. Would he be moved by such pity again? She had no idea; there was no sense in raising Sybil's hopes unnecessarily.

But neither could she frighten the girl further without good cause.

"I have seen him and, aye, he is fierce," Ali conceded

slowly. "And he does have quite a peculiar smell about him, as the rumors have said. But I haven't seen him kill anyone yet."

"A pity he hasn't done in Sir Etienne," one of the wenches offered.

Ali agreed heartily, but didn't say as much.

"He is so large." Sybil moaned. "So intimidating. So fully without any mercy at all."

How Sybil could tell that when she'd fainted at the mere sight of him Ali surely didn't know, but she didn't bother to point that out to her charge. Sybil was eating and Ali couldn't bring herself to ruin the girl's one pleasure.

"Enormous," one of her maids repeated.

"Merciless," another added.

"And we'll likely see him kill someone before we leave," the third added in a hopeful tone. "Wouldn't you think?"

Ali frowned at the serving maids. By the saints, these three were no help at all. 'Twas little wonder Sybil was so terrified if this was what she listened to for the whole of the day.

Then she clapped her hand to her forehead. She had seen Colin of Berkhamshire, she had thought him as awful as the tales had said, and she was just certain, given the right amount of time, that she would see him kill someone as well. Who was she to think to defend him?

She rubbed her hand over her face and wondered if there was something in the air at Blackmour that rendered all within its reach bewitched. The place certainly reeked of secrets and works wrought in the cover of darkness.

Mayhap someone would take pity on Sybil and render her just as enspelled. It might be a mercy, given the fact that Sybil had no choice but to wed Colin.

Ali steadfastly refused to think on the fact that if she did but reveal herself, Sybil would be freed of her obligation— and Ali would find herself in the wench's unenviable position as the Butcher's bride.

She rubbed her hands together the way her sire had always done when he'd been finished talking of unsettling matters and was ready to be off and doing, then looked about her purposefully. She had business to attend to—somewhere far from Sybil and her foodstuffs, far from Sybil's maids and their foolish babblings.

And very far from her own troubling thoughts.

"Have you adequate sustenance here in the solar, my lady?" Ali asked Sybil politely.

How Sybil managed to look famished with a platter of sweets at her elbow Ali couldn't imagine, but the girl looked fair to perishing.

"Bread," Sybil said weakly. "Meats under sauce, if possible. Anything to keep up my strength."

Which she would need, Ali had to agree. And if food was the girl's comfort, then well was she entitled to it. Ali bowed and left the chamber, charged with her accustomed task of venturing to the kitchens for Sybil's extra rations. This she could do—assuming she didn't meet anyone untoward in the process. There were, after all, so many souls to avoid.

Christopher of Blackmour with his piercing sight.

Jason of Artane with his inquisitive nose.

Colin of Berkhamshire with his ready sword and vast stores of irritation toward any and all past or future brides.

She peered down the passageway and saw no one. Well, that was an auspicious start, at least. She put her shoulders back and did her best to swagger down the way as if she belonged there and was charged with an important errand from an important lord.

There were men milling about in the great hall, but Ali paid them no heed aside from making certain no one loitered therein whom she needed to avoid. She didn't feel Colin's immense reputation filling the chamber, nor Lord Blackmour's dark, bewitching wickedness, so she supposed no one else would mark one lone knight skulking along the back wall.

The kitchens were a marvel of smells. Indeed, Ali couldn't remember a time where she'd smelled things so fine, except perhaps memories of when her mother had been alive. To be sure, things at Solonge had declined greatly when Marie had become chatelaine. Well, unless a meal was destined for her plate alone. Not even Ali's sire was allotted fineries, though Ali suspected he never noticed.

Ali saw a small skirmish going on near the cooking pot. A robust, elderly man, who Ali assumed was the cook by the lordly manner in which he waved his spoon, was scowling down at an equally elderly woman with hair the color of steel, who was glaring up at him and pointing her own spoon at him as if it had been a sword.

"Not enough sage," the old woman accused.

"And you, Mistress Nemain, know nothing of how to make a good stew!"

"I've forgotten more about herbs than you ever knew, you puffed-up pretender!"

The cook puffed himself up—and quite impressively, Ali had to agree—his outrage clearly showing on every feature. *"My* herbs," he said haughtily, *"do not cause warts!"*

There was silence for the space of a heartbeat or two, and then the kitchen folk scattered in all directions.

Ali knew that now was the time to be about her business and then make her escape before an all-out war erupted. She sneaked along the wall to the worktable, took the sack she had brought from Sybil's chamber, and then very quietly and very carefully began to fill it with things that could be carried easily.

She had just begun to creep back toward the passageway when she felt the finger of doom tap her on the shoulder.

'Twas in truth just the cook's spoon, but that was enough to startle her thoroughly. She whirled around in surprise.

"You," Cook said, pointing at her imperiously, "come taste this."

Ali gulped. "Me?"

"Nay, the pot hanging on the wall," Cook snapped. "Aye, you. If you've any wits about you and a tongue that works!"

"Aye," said Mistress Nemain, taking Ali by the sleeve with very bony fingers and pulling her closer. "Have a taste and be the judge. I say it wants for a bit of sage."

"And I say 'tis perfect just as it sits," Cook responded hotly.

"And I say you're a fool who wouldn't know sage from saffron—even if the pots were labeled in a manner that you could tell them apart!"

Ali could see already that there would be no winning this battle here today. Unfortunately, she could also see that there was no escaping her fate. Both Cook and Mistress Nemain were giving her meaningful looks—looks she interpreted to mean that if she ever intended to have anything edible at the table again, she'd best side with them. Her. Him. Ali knew that it wouldn't matter whom she sided with, she was doomed to crack her teeth on rocks in her bread. She sighed, eased Sybil's sack of sustenance to the floor, then accepted the spoons.

Mistress Nemain was looking at her with so piercing a gaze, and Cook so compelling a one, she began to truly believe she had stumbled into some dreadful dream where potions were brewed in the kitchen and men changed themselves into foul creatures at night to harass unwary travelers.

She took a deep breath, tasted each offering in turn, then shoved the spoons back at the squabblers.

"Needs thyme," she blurted out, grabbed her sack, and bolted for the passageway.

"Thyme?" Cook echoed.

"Thyme!" exclaimed Mistress Nemain.

Ali looked over her shoulder to see them shaking their heads.

"Daft lad," they said together.

And, as if Ali hadn't just taken her life in her hands to humor them, they began their argument again.

"Sage!"

"Nothing!"

That proceeded rapidly to assaults on the other's character and ability to taste.

Ali left the kitchens whilst no blood had yet been spilt.

Without any hesitation, she ran through the great hall, fled up the steps, down the passageway and came to a skidding halt before the solar door.

"Open up," she commanded.

The door was flung open, the foodstuffs snatched, and then the door was slammed shut in her face.

Ali stared at the wood in astonishment. Then equal parts of anger and fear swept through her.

"Ungrateful harlots!" she exclaimed, pounding on the door. "Let me in! How dare you leave me out in this accursed place after all I've done for you?"

There was no response, not even any words of censure from within the solar. Ali continued to shout and pound until she realized there was no use. She took a deep breath, leaned her forehead against the wood, and wondered what she was supposed to do now that her only place of safety had been denied her.

And then she realized, quite suddenly, that she was not alone in the passageway.

She wondered if it might be best to just turn and flee without ascertaining who watched her, but 'twould be her luck to have that soul be Christopher of Blackmour, who could no doubt spell her into some foul malady just as easily to her back as to her face. So she took a deep breath, then turned to face her doom.

The lady of Blackmour stood there, a smile tugging at her mouth. "My," she said, "what a tremendous ruckus. And such language from a knight to his lady."

"Um," Ali said, then remembered to deepen her voice. "Um," she tried again, much lower, wondering how she'd sounded whilst she was screaming out her frustration at the door. "It has been, my lady, a very trying morning."

"So I heard," Gillian said. She leaned back against the wall and looked at Ali thoughtfully. "What an interesting face you have," she said finally. "Most delicate, for a man."

"My bane," Ali said with a gulp. "I have pretty brothers, as well."

And then she wondered why she wasn't struck down immediately for lying. Her brothers might have been many things, all bloody five of them, but pretty was definitely not on that list. 'Twas a fortunate thing she'd inherited her mother's face and not her father's, else the same thing might have been said of her.

Though at the moment, she could have wished for much uglier features.

"Well," Gillian said with a smile, "whilst I do feel sorry for your siblings, that doesn't solve the mystery of your features."

Why couldn't these souls here be as blind as those at Maignelay-sur-mer? She'd been in Sybil's company for over two years and the wench had never looked at her twice. In less than two days at Blackmour, all manner of people had peered at her visage, trying to discover all her secrets.

And now she faced the Dragon's wife, who likely had sight as clear as his own.

The saints preserve her, she was doomed.

She looked about her for a means of escape, but before she could decide on a direction, she was caught.

"I think it would be most interesting to hear more of your tale," Gillian said, taking her by the arm. "Perhaps you might enjoy the freedom of the roof after your morning of frustration here at the solar door."

"But—"

"Have you seen the view from the battlements?"

"Nay—"

"Then you should. I'm Gillian, by the way."

"Aye," Ali managed. "I know. I saw you yesterday."

Gillian drew Ali up the stairs, and Ali found herself with little choice but to allow it. Besides, perhaps the view might provide her with some idea of where she was and a direction in which she might flee.

Should she ever get outside the gates, of course.

"Ah, here we are," Gillian said, stopping along one wall. "This is where I come when I have things that trouble me."

Ali supposed there must be an endless list of those kinds of things, beginning and ending with the torments of being wed to the lord of Blackmour. How was it a woman bore living with a dragon? And such a dragon as Blackmour! Why, his reputation stretched to Solonge and farther, surely. The tales of his evil, his cruelty, his very gaze that was rumored to render his foes powerless and enspelled—

Things that troubled the lady Gillian, indeed. Ali could have made the poor woman's list for her!

"What do you think of the view?" Gillian asked.

Ali suspected that this might be one of the lady's few pleasures, so who was she not to admire it? She clutched the rock before her and looked about her carefully. It wasn't that she was afeared of heights; she had escaped to her own battlements at Solonge often to avoid the madness below. But her keep didn't overlook an ocean that churned with a fierceness to rival the fury of Hell.

She closed her eyes briefly, took a deep breath, then decided that looking down was not something she would do again any time soon. Aye, the countryside, what she could see of it from the Dragon's nest, was view enough for her.

"Perhaps you too have things that trouble you," Gillian said quietly.

"Nay, nothing," Ali responded promptly. "Nothing at all."

"Not even the girls below? Your lady Sybil? That poor child. She seems powerfully terrified of something."

Ali looked at Gillian in surprise. "Something? Surely 'tis obvious what."

"I suppose," Gillian said with half a smile. "But is it Blackmour that terrifies her, do you think, or just Colin?"

"Both, I'd warrant," Ali said, realizing only then that she certainly should not be speaking so freely to a woman who, as a lord's lady, was far above a mere knight in station. She ducked her head and tried to look penitent.

"You would think that if anyone at Blackmour here had reason to be afraid, it would be me, wouldn't you?" Gillian continued. "After all, I am wed to Blackmour's lord."

Ali could only snatch a glance at the lady Gillian and bite her tongue. How was she to agree without offending the woman and her husband both?

"Do I look terrified?"

Ali shook her head. Gillian looked anything but that. Then again, the woman had been here for the saints only knew how long and perhaps had come fully under Blackmour's spell. How was her opinion in these matters possibly to be trusted?

"Would you care for the tale of how I came here ... um ... I fear I've forgotten your name, Sir ..."

"Henri," Ali supplied. "Sir Henri."

Gillian looked at her so long and so searchingly, Ali found herself with the intense desire to flee. Unfortunately, Gillian had retaken her grip on Ali's arm.

"Stay," she coaxed. "I think you'll find it much more peaceful here than below."

And Ali thought just the opposite. "I have duties," Ali said, attempting to pull her arm free of Gillian's fingers.

"Those duties can wait, don't you think? Far better that we have speech together."

Ali suspected that a year or two in an oubliette would be better for her than a conversation with Gillian of Blackmour. She just *knew* that if she continued to talk to the woman, she would have no secrets left.

But Gillian had now released her sleeve to hook her arm with Ali's and there was surely no escaping that unless Ali shook the woman right off the battlements. She girded up her loins, as it were, and vowed to remain silent, no matter what sorts of nefarious tactics the lady Gillian might use to pry secrets from her.

"Would you believe," Gillian went on, standing far too close to Ali for her comfort, "that I once thought to escape marriage by disguising myself as a lad?"

Ali choked. She didn't mean to, but she couldn't help herself. She continued to gasp for breath until Gillian had pounded some of it back into her. And once she could breathe again, Gillian took her arm again, as if she sought to stop Ali from escaping.

"Aye," she said, "I know. 'Tis difficult to imagine that a man would be so terrifying as to drive a girl to such a pass, but when I heard to whom my father had betrothed me, I could see no other choice. Christopher of Blackmour?" She shook her head with a dry smile. "I was convinced that being bound to him would only lead to a life of misery."

Ali swallowed with difficulty. Aye, she could understand that feeling well enough.

"But that is the way of things, is it not?" Gillian continued. "A girl has no choice in where she goes or with whom she weds. All she can do is either make of her life what she can, or run."

Was that the sun beating down so strongly as to make sweat begin to trickle down the middle of her back? Ali looked up but saw nothing but clouds. Perhaps 'twas the tension of being up on the roof to cause her such distress. Aye, that was it. Surely.

"I thought my lot worse than most, though," Gillian continued, as mercilessly as any castle torturer, "for after I learned that I was to be wed to the Dragon of Blackmour, I then found that my escort to Blackmour would be none other than the fierce and ruthless Colin of Berkhamshire."

Ali choked again. By the saints, could she control none of her body's traitorous actions? She held up her hand to stop Gillian from pounding further on her back. "I am well," she gasped.

"Are you?"

"Aye," Ali wheezed. By the saints, from one peril straight to another—and that was just the pattern of her own morning so far! Gillian's life's path had been much worse. How had she borne such a thing? Ali would have fled, in her place.

She tried to ignore the irony of that.

"I arrived here," Gillian went on, "certain that I would find myself wed to a warlock of the foulest ilk who would likely offer me up as a sacrifice in the most painful of ways at his earliest opportunity. But," she said, looking Ali full in the face, "I found him to be nothing more than a man. One with a very intimidating reputation, to be sure, but just a man nonetheless."

Ali wondered how the Dragon might feel, did he but know his wife thought so little of his fierceness.

"And you wed him willingly?" Ali found herself asking.

"Willingly?" Gillian asked, then laughed. "Nay, I wed Christopher in sheer terror. 'Twas afterward that I grew to love him. And I daresay he loves me well enough himself."

Ali simply couldn't fathom that. That the Dragon of Blackmour should tenderly care for a woman this gentle was simply beyond belief.

"Not all men," Gillian said, "are what they seem to be."

"But Colin of Berkhamshire—" Ali protested.

"Has as tender an underbelly as my dragon," Gillian said,

"though it flatters his enormous ego to think everyone drops to their knees in terror when he approaches."

"But, my lady, most *do* drop to their knees in terror when he approaches."

"Do you truly think he would require that of his wife?" Gillian asked.

"I've no doubt of it," Ali responded without hesitation.

Gillian only shook her head with a small smile. "Did you but know him as I do, you would think differently. His manners at table are atrocious, and those manners would likely extend to courtesies shown a wife, but I daresay the right woman would inspire in him great love and devotion." She looked at Ali searchingly. "Your lady Sybil will find that for herself, in time. If she is the right woman for him."

Ali forced herself not to snort in disbelief.

"Do you know of another woman who might suit him better?"

Ali could only shake her head, mute.

"Why is it, my girl, that you find yourself hiding in mail?" Gillian asked quietly. "Were you faced with an unsavory wedding?"

"I am no girl. . . ." Ali said desperately.

"Your betrothed must have been powerfully unpalatable," Gillian continued thoughtfully, as if she hadn't heard Ali's protest, "for you to have fled him thusly. How long have you been hiding?"

Ali had wondered, when she'd first seen Gillian coming down the steps holding on to the lord of Blackmour's arm, if the woman might be bewitched. Now she was quite convinced that she wasn't bewitched, she was a witch herself. Either that, or she possessed a kind of sight that only the strongest of souls could counter.

And Ali was certainly not the strongest of souls.

Obviously, there was no use in further denials. All that was left was to speculate on how long it would take for Gillian to give Ali back her own name.

Ali sighed deeply. "Two years have passed since I fled my home."

"Two years?" Gillian asked in surprise. "A very long time to be hiding from a man."

"I had no choice."

Gillian stared out over the water for several minutes. "Maignelay-sur-mer is on the coast, is it not?" She looked at Ali briefly. "I haven't the head for maps. Christopher and Colin both have told me quite a bit about how things find themselves in France, though, so I often try to imagine how things must lie there. Let me see. Maignelay is not far from . . ."

Ali waited grimly for Gillian to solve the rest of the puzzle. It took less time than she'd suspected it might.

"Not far from Solonge, is it?" she asked suddenly.

"Not far enough," Ali muttered.

Gillian paused, then smiled faintly. "Two years ago Colin was set to wed with the daughter of Solonge," she said. "That daughter fled. We were fairly certain she'd met her end in some unpleasant way. But that isn't so, is it?"

"It depends," Ali said, not daring to look at Gillian, "upon how unpleasant one might find the life of a knight."

"Ah, Aliénore," Gillian said, giving Ali's arm a squeeze, "you poor girl."

Ali could only sigh in answer.

"And now to find yourself in the very place you sought to avoid! However did you manage that?"

"It wasn't by choice," Ali mumbled. "I found myself dragged along with circumstances I couldn't control."

Gillian laughed softly. "Such is the course of life, or didn't you know?"

"If I'd had any idea that allowing Isabeau of Maignelay-sur-mer to rescue me from my own ineptness would have resulted in finding myself guarding the Butcher's bride, I would have continued on to Constantinople—which had been my goal from the moment I fled through my father's gates."

"The Butcher," Gillian mused, with a smile. "Aye, that is a title that would certainly please him to hear often. You know, Aliénore, he is not truly the demon he is rumored to be."

"Aye, I know," Ali said darkly. "He's likely worse." She looked at Gillian. "My lady, I crave your silence. I know I have no right to ask anything of you, but—"

Gillian held up her hand. "No one will learn of this from me."

"Not that it would matter," Ali said with a sigh. "Your husband will likely look at me and know anyway, given his foul powers of sight."

Gillian turned to lean on the wall and look at Ali. "And did he manage to see you truly, he would offer you his aid, not his censure, I can assure you of that. But I will not tell him, for your sake. But what is it you'll do now? You cannot hide forever behind your mail."

Ali looked at her miserably. "I've no idea," she said. "I have no skills, no calling, no useful purpose. I have a bit of coin, but I'm not even sure what that will buy me. Worse yet, if my stepmother knew I was alive, she would hunt me down and slay me. And we haven't even spoken of what Lord Colin would do to me, *has* promised to do to me did he but clap eyes on me."

Gillian looked off over the sea for several moments in silence. Ali stared at her, and whilst she did, she couldn't help but marvel at the woman's comeliness and serenity. Indeed, the fairness of her face seemed to have much to do with the peace that seemed to flow from her.

Ali envied her that peace.

Then Gillian turned back to her and gave her arm a squeeze. "We'll think of something. I'll aid you as I can and we'll see your troubles solved. But I must tell you," she added suddenly, "that whilst I understand your two years of hiding, I think they were unnecessary. Colin of Berkhamshire has the most foul of reputations, but he is, like my dragon, only a man in the end."

"A man who vowed to kill a certain woman did he but find her," Ali said pointedly. "What kind of man does that?"

"Men blather on," Gillian said, waving a dismissive hand. "And Colin is more boastful than most."

"I find myself quite unwilling to test that, my lady."

Gillian laughed. "No doubt you do. For now, what you

need is a goodly nap and a fine meal to restore you. Come, I will see you installed inside my overrun solar and keep your lady occupied that you might have your rest on a proper mattress. You must be very tired." She turned Ali toward the door leading down into the castle. "I think that did Colin but know what you'd managed all on your own, he would fall to his knees at your feet and beg you to be his."

"Aye, so he could more easily impale my head on a pike outside his gates," Ali muttered.

Gillian only laughed again. Ali found herself far too weary both in body and spirit to do aught but allow herself to be led—and be profoundly grateful for the aid. At least she might have an afternoon's sleep in peace. For that, she would have paid quite a high price.

She followed Gillian to the solar, then watched in amazement and not a little satisfaction as the solar door was opened, Sybil and her wenches were herded into a corner, and Ali was given a fine couch with a comfortable goose-feather mattress to sleep on. Protests were silenced with naught but a look and Sybil was distracted with such skill that Ali lay down with a smile on her face.

And with her last thoughts, she promised herself she would decide on her life's work at her earliest opportunity. And once that was decided upon, perhaps she would enlist Gillian's aid in having the portcullis raised so she might escape and be about that work. She patted the coins tucked into her belt and was comforted by the weight of them. Aye, there was enough there to buy her some kind of goodly life.

But first, blissful sleep, with the Dragon's lady watching over her.

Chapter 6

C olin stood still, silent and waiting, bursting with the skills he had acquired over a score and twelve years of warring, fighting, and hunting. Hunting it was that now occupied his attentions, and he had no intentions of failing at it. Though he was growing stiff with the lack of movement, he didn't allow himself to shift even the slightest bit. To alert his prey to his presence would have spelled certain failure. So, he forced himself to wait, silently, until such time when his quarry would take flight and he would be able to pounce without mercy.

He wished, absently, that he might have a fine dinner of boar as a result of his efforts instead of merely a bride who apparently had as little enthusiasm for wedding him as he did her.

Damn her anyway.

Unfortunately, that bride had neither shown her face to be pounced upon, nor made her presence inside the solar known so he might remain silent and avoid startling her into flight.

He had, of course, considered scratching at the door in the most womanly fashion he could muster, just to see if Sybil or one of her maids would open up, but that was beneath him. Besides, Sybil likely would have taken one glance at his less-than-pleasing visage and promptly taken flight into senselessness.

Of course, getting her to quit the chamber was proving to be even more difficult. There was nary a sound from inside, and certainly no movement out the door. He wondered if they were tossing the contents of their pots out the window into the garden, for no one had left the chamber since he'd been there and he'd arrived well before dawn. No doubt they had stocked so much foodstuffs that even venturing forth for sustenance was unnecessary. Colin couldn't see how that was possible—unless that young Henri had been filching things from the kitchen.

Colin leaned back against the wall and sighed. Despite his determination to wait out his bride, he was beginning to wonder if it would be worth the effort. Even if Sybil gathered enough courage to poke her nose out the door, what would he say to her? *Come, let us sup together and I'll display for you my fine manners?* Gillian would have aught to say about that, to be sure.

Even if he managed to get Sybil to the table, keep her from fainting, and not offend her with his bad manners, what would they talk on? Horseflesh? The balance of the perfect blade? Battle tactics? The saints pity him should he be reduced to listening to a woman babble about stitches and sleeve lengths and feathers and baubles for her gowns.

Now, could he have found a woman who perhaps didn't care so much for those things, he might have been persuaded to believe that marriage could be something other than a misery. Even Gillian, despite her insistence on those ridiculous manners at table, had more on her mind than sleeves and feathers. The woman had been known to poke her nose in the lists now and then, just to see how the men were being trained, and to assure herself that her firstborn was proceeding with his lessons in the arts of war as he should.

Either that or she was just coming to make certain a particular three-year-old hadn't cut off anything important with his wooden sword, but perhaps that was something better left unspeculated upon.

Nay, Gillian was a fine wench with a fine head for thinking. Colin suspected that if Sybil used her head for anything, it wasn't for the examination of deep thoughts.

He leaned back against the wall, suppressed a very loud sigh, and prayed for a distraction. It came soon enough in the person of none other than Christopher of Blackmour. Christopher paused a pace or two away, then sniffed.

"Colin?"

Colin pursed his lips. "The very same."

"Waiting out your bride?"

Colin scowled. "Nay, contemplating the craftsmanship of your walls and how to best hold them upright with my own fine form."

Christopher whistled. "You've a foul humor today."

"Can you fault me for it?"

"I had no such trouble with my bride."

Colin snorted mightily. "I was there through all your pitiful attempts to woo her and I remember very well the troubles you had."

Christopher clapped a hand on Colin's shoulder. "I have a suggestion."

"I don't want it."

"Don't sing to her."

"Shut up."

Christopher laughed. "Good fortune to you, my friend. You'll need it."

Colin cursed him, even though he agreed that Christopher had it aright. Getting the wench to leave the chamber would take a lifetime's worth of luck. Dragging her to the altar would take nothing short of ropes and a gag. He wondered, absently, what she would blurt out when he untied her. Nothing pleasant, he suspected. A pity they couldn't have settled their differences on the field.

Men, he decided, were much easier to have dealings with than women.

He hadn't passed a quarter hour in peace before Jason of Artane appeared at his elbow, looking serene and lethal, just like his sire, damn the man. Jason leaned against the wall next to Colin and folded his arms over his chest.

"Won't come out?"

Colin scowled. "Little escapes your notice, does it?"

Jason smiled. "Her reticence would be preying even upon my sunny disposition by now. Your self-control is admirable, my lord, to seem so cheerful after so long."

"It *hasn't* been that long," Colin grumbled. "The wench is recovering from her journey."

"And how long do you suppose that will take?"

It was tempting to say *years*, but he controlled himself

before he spewed out his disgust with his life and the cowardice of his future bride.

"Until she's hungry enough, I suppose," Colin said with a sigh.

"That could take a bit."

Colin looked down at him archly. "Are you saying my betrothed is overplump?"

"I'm not saying anything."

"Indeed, I think you're saying too much."

Jason shrugged. "I could play my lute for you, if you like. Lure the poor girl from her hiding place with songs she couldn't possibly resist."

Colin had heard Jason's lute playing. While it was a fair sight better than his elder brother's, it was still not something a body would listen to unless forced. Colin shook his head quickly.

"I want her to come out, not hide beneath whatever she can drag over her ears."

Jason pursed his lips, pushed off the wall, and walked away. "My ballads are not so foul."

Colin had the brief satisfaction of realizing he'd won at least one battle of wits and words that day. That satisfaction was short-lived, however, for who should be coming his way but Gillian of Blackmour, and she looked to be itching to cure some or other of his flaws.

By the saints, were these souls banded together in planning their assaults on him, or was he merely in the midst of a powerfully large piece of poor fortune?

He scowled at Gillian before she'd even opened her mouth, but that didn't seem to deter her.

"You're waiting patiently," she said with a smile.

Colin scrutinized her smile, but found that it contained no teasing or other unwholesome elements. So, he grudgingly allowed her another chance to comport herself well.

"I am an extraordinarily patient man," he agreed.

She paused. "You know," she said slowly, "perhaps this one isn't the one for you."

He could scarce contain his mighty snort. "You speak as if I had a choice."

"What of Aliénore of Solonge?" she asked. "Does not your betrothal to her still stand?"

"The saints pity me if it does," he said grimly, "for then I would find myself saddled with two wenches."

"But if that betrothal still stands, how are you to wed with Lady Sybil?"

"Aliénore is dead," Colin said flatly, "and at this moment I envy her that peace."

"I have the oddest feeling that she isn't dead at all," Gillian said. "Perhaps you should search. Take a month and see where her trail led."

Colin shifted irritably, and that he had allowed such a display of his irritation irritated him further. He gave Gillian a look that he hoped spoke fully of his displeasure with her choice of subject.

"I want a wench courageous enough to come face me, and of more wit than to get herself killed fleeing across the continent by herself," he said curtly. "And that wench from Solonge obviously possesses neither of those qualities."

"And Sybil does?"

"At least she is here," Colin said, then clamped his lips shut. Aye, the wench was there, surely, but she certainly hadn't had the courage to face him. And he suspected that her wit wouldn't keep her safe inside even an inner bailey, if the mere sight of a manly man was enough to fell her from her horse.

But he needed to say none of that to Gillian. He glared at her and was mildly satisfied to see her lower her eyes.

"I still think you should search," Gillian said clearly.

And then she was trotting down the passageway before Colin could gather his wits to bellow at her. He was momentarily tempted to do it just the same, but that would have alerted Sybil to his presence and that he couldn't have. So he clamped his lips shut and cursed Christopher's wife silently. Damn her. Meddling with his manners, meddling with his matrimonial plans, meddling with whatever suited her fancy. How did Christopher bear it in his own life?

Bravely and apparently quite happily, Colin conceded with a grumble. Either that or matrimony had ruined what few wits Christopher possessed. A wife? Ha! Unpleasant creatures just itching to put their hands in a man's life and stir it all about until he scarce recognized it as his own.

He contemplated that grim possibility for far too long. Indeed, he plunged himself into enough of a foul humor that he began to consider giving up the siege. Aye, perhaps that was the only solution. The wench could stay inside the solar forever. It would save him having to wed her.

He had just pushed away from the wall when whom should he see but those three practitioners of the dark and unwholesome-tasting arts who seemed hell-bent on turning him into a husband.

Colin briefly considered tying them up and sending them to his sire. Since the four of them—the witches and his sire—had the most nefarious designs on his happiness, perhaps they deserved to plot and scheme together. At least that way Colin wouldn't have these old women underfoot and overhead, flinging all manner of suspicious herbs upon him.

He steeled himself for another vicious assault.

Nothing, though, came flying at him in the form of herbs. Nemain did give him a poke with an extremely long and bony finger, but at least it was hers, and not someone else's. With Nemain, a body never knew.

"Move," she said without preamble or any such nicety. "We're here to spell the girl into compliance."

Colin blinked. "What?"

"Compliance," she repeated. "Willingness. A burning desire to become your bride."

"Can you *do* that?" he asked.

Nemain looked him up and down, then pursed her lips. "An extremely difficult case," she said bluntly. "But I've brought a variety of very strong herbs. If it can be done, I'll see to it."

Colin wasn't sure if he should be flattered that they were taking up his cause, or insulted that Nemain apparently considered success nigh onto impossible.

"And I've brought my own special brew," Magda said brightly, waving her spoon about and coming very close to taking off the end of Colin's nose with it.

Colin suppressed a shudder. He'd tasted several brews made by that one and found them all to be, without fail, burnt and undrinkable. He looked at Berengaria, wondering if it would be foolish to hope for aid from that quarter. She held in her hands a very comforting-looking sack of something. He leaned forward and sniffed. It smelled passable.

"Courage herbs," Berengaria said with a smile. "To make her equal to her task."

"Are you going to sprinkle them on her?" Colin asked. He'd had the same thing done to him, of course, and it certainly hadn't made him any more likely a prospect as a husband.

"Nay, my lord," Berengaria said. "They'll be put into her wine."

"It will take more than wine with a crust of courage on top to give this girl what she needs to face her doom," Nemain said heavily. "Brews steeped for long periods of time to infuse them with their maximum strength are needful. Nothing less." She looked at Colin. "You'd best be off. We don't want you frightening the girl into insensibility when she opens the door."

"She won't open the door," Colin said.

"Aye, she will," Nemain said. "Perhaps you forget our vast powers."

"I'll let her sniff *my* brew under the door, and the pleasant smell of it will draw her forth," Magda said, holding forth a jug and popping off the cloth on top. "Here, my lord. You smell and see if it wouldn't lure you from the most secure hiding place."

Colin had no choice but to sniff, given that the jug was shoved as closely under his nose as a woman half his size could manage.

The smell of it fair knocked him to his knees.

Nemain pulled Magda away. "Lord Colin can use yours in battle when he wishes to fell his enemies without his blade. Now, move yourself, you silly nun, and let me be about my business."

Colin's nose was so polluted by the stench that he couldn't even smell himself. And if that wasn't enough to give a man pause, he didn't know what was. He was just considering the location of the next foulest stench in the keep so he might repair there and hopefully recover some sense of smell, when he found his hands full of herb sack.

"Try that, my lord," Berengaria said. "And see what you think."

Grateful for something else to smell, Colin sniffed deeply.

And then he sneezed so thoroughly as to knock Magda over with the force of it.

Her foul brew flowed around the broken shards of her jug. Colin watched, his hand over his nose, as the brew began to flow beneath the solar door.

Nemain looked at Berengaria. "Hrumph."

"Knocking may be unnecessary now," Berengaria said. She looked at Colin. "If you will, my lord . . ."

Colin didn't have to hear that again. He handed her back her herbs, then turned and quickly made his way down the passageway. If nothing else, perhaps Sybil would have to quit the chamber to save her nose. Who knew where that would lead?

He strode down the passageway with as much haste as was seemly and made his way through the great hall and out into the lists where there were men doing things he could understand. There were far too many nefarious schemes and vociferous opinions floating about inside the keep for his taste. What he wanted was a bit of swordplay, then perhaps a hearty meal to soothe him. And no more bloody talk of marriage for the day.

He walked out onto the field only to be greeted by Sir Etienne's booming laugh. He scowled. This was another one who would have to go as soon as possible. Colin couldn't abide men who boasted of skill they didn't have. He could only hope Lord Humbert of Maignelay-sur-mer would take the buffoon back. Colin most certainly did not want him as a wedding gift.

"Your lord must trust you," said a man near to Sir Etienne, "to escort his daughter so far."

Sir Etienne snorted. "She's no temptation. And her maids are silly twits."

Colin looked at the man's back with narrowed eyes. Perhaps Sir Etienne wouldn't be offering his opinion so freely if he'd but known who was listening to him.

"Your lord of Maignelay didn't fear attack from ruffians?" another asked. "Odd, that he should send you so far with no men to guard her."

"He has another man," another said. "The young knight. He seems useful enough."

Sir Etienne laughed, but it was an ugly sound. "That girl? Nay, he was sent along to play nursemaid. 'Tis only I with skill—and 'tis mighty skill indeed, as you might imagine. Just me to guard Maignelay's precious treasure."

"My sympathies," a knight said. "Saddled with such wenches and a useless lad as well. Have you not tried to train the boy?"

"Train him?" Sir Etienne snorted. "Train him to do what? Not to scamper away every time someone looks crossly at him?"

Another knight laughed. "Rather you should beat the fear out of him. Unless that task is too heavy for you."

"I'll see to training the lad when it suits me," Sir Etienne said sharply. "Now, who's for the lists? To be sure, none of you has seen my equal."

Colin had heard far too much. Sybil's little keeper was inept and terrified, true, but the saints pity the lad if he had the misfortune of a master such as Sir Etienne. Perhaps if Sir Etienne had a better idea of his own failings as a swordsman, he might not be so eager to take on the instructing of another.

And Colin himself was never one to shy away from giving instruction when it was warranted, and to be certain this oaf was in sore need of a lesson or two.

He cleared his throat. "I'm for a bit of swordplay."

Sir Etienne turned around in a most leisurely fashion. "Ah, Sir Colin," he said, "you have returned for more?"

Colin pursed his lips, not sure if he were more irritated by Sir Etienne disdaining his proper title as lord or his complete lack of respect for Colin's skill.

Perhaps the afternoon stood to be far more interesting and

fulfilling than the morning had been. Colin smiled pleasantly, flexed his fingers, and drew his sword. After all, whilst wooing brides was certainly not his strength, swordplay was.

Best be about something he could do well before he had to return to his unpleasant duties of luring, capturing, and, the saints preserve him, wedding of that cowardly wench locked in Gillian's solar.

Chapter 7

A*li* would have spared a thought for those blissful days when all she'd had to do was rise, go to Mass, then spend the rest of her time doing menial tasks—never mind that it was under Marie's critical eye and ready slap—but she couldn't. She was far too busy trying to keep her head atop her shoulders.

The day was definitely not proceeding as she would have liked. She'd left the solar early in the day, certain she could avoid Lord Christopher, Lord Colin, Jason, and Sir Etienne—and that had been after a miserable night spent smelling whatever foul brew had been dropped in the passageway and subsequently seeped into the solar. It had rendered the place almost unfit for habitation.

She'd intended to sneak to the kitchen, find herself something to eat, and then retreat to the safety of the battlements where she could inhale fresh air and give thinking on her future the attention it deserved. She hadn't managed to shove but a bite or two of bread into her mouth before Sir Etienne had appeared, scowling fiercely. He'd taken her by the scruff of the neck and dragged her from the great hall.

She hadn't had time to even contemplate flight. Sir Etienne had pulled her across the courtyard to the lists, cursing her the entire while and promising her a good lesson that morn on how a *man* comported himself. She'd known that nothing pleasant could come of that. All she'd been able to do was pat her middle quickly to make certain her coins were securely nestled against her belly, then pray for a swift journey into senselessness before the true torture of his instruction began.

Once they'd reached the lists, he had shoved her away and bid her show him what feeble things she was capable of. She had been no match for him from the start, of course. She'd held up her sword as bravely as she'd known how and waved it about in the same manner. As he'd sneered at her, she'd begun to wish that perhaps Isabeau had let her out in the lists more often where she might have learned a bit of sword-play.

Now, she found herself with her sword in both hands, fighting to keep it upright and wondering how the morning could possibly finish any way but in complete misery. And if her own black thoughts weren't bad enough, a crowd had begun to gather—no doubt to be witness to her humiliation.

She could only hope Lord Colin wouldn't be there as well, for then he would see her feebleness and likely know immediately she was not what she purported to be.

Sir Etienne took an enormous swipe at her. Her blade left her hands abruptly; her hands stung as if Marie had been at them with a birch rod for some bad bit of embroidery. Ali watched as Sir Etienne flipped her blade up and into the air with his own. He caught it and tossed it aside with a negligent flick of his wrist. Then he looked at her, his utter contempt for her written plainly on his face.

"You don't deserve your spurs," he said coldly. "And I intend to see you sully them no longer."

"Ah," she began, but got no further.

He slapped her on various parts of her body with his sword until it felt as if she wore nothing, not a mail shirt, not a leather padded jerkin beneath her mail. She was nothing but bare flesh against unforgiving steel. The only mercy was that he used the flat of his blade instead of the fatally sharp edge. Yet still her ears rang from blows, her legs stung from being whipped.

And then he jabbed his sword into the dirt next to him and came at her with his fists.

The fist blow connected with her belly. She immediately lost her wind. When she managed to suck back in air, he did it again.

And this time, despite herself, she heaved up her meager breakfast onto his feet.

The next thing she knew, he had her by the scruff of her

tunic, had forced her to her knees, and had buried her face in her own bile. She struggled to turn her head aside to breathe, but Sir Etienne was far too strong for her. She clawed at the hand that held her head down until she felt the world begin to fade. Perhaps her death approached. Not a dignified way to go, but who was she to find fault with it?

She suddenly found that she could breathe again and the first great gulp into her lungs was full of things she didn't want to identify. She coughed and spit and gasped for more sweet air that smelled of things most foul. She didn't care. She lived still.

"You ruined my sport," Sir Etienne bellowed from above her.

"We don't take kindly here to bullying children half our size," came the reply.

Ali managed to pry her eyes open long enough to see that none other than Jason of Artane stood over her like an avenging angel. Jason gave Sir Etienne a mighty shove backward. She huddled there miserably and watched as swords were brandished and the true business of the morning began. She had no means, nor desire, to protest the rescue. She was simply grateful to be alive and breathing.

It took her half a lifetime to drag herself upright. She made it as far as her knees, and could go no farther. Her body was on fire and she wondered if Sir Etienne had done her a grave injury. Then again, perhaps this was how every man felt after being bested in battle.

She wished, and not for the first time recently, that she could have just been a woman. Surely even childbirth was less trouble than this.

Then the next thing she knew, arms were sliding under hers and she was hauled to her feet—rather gently, all things considered. Heavy hands remained on her shoulders as her surroundings spun violently. She wondered how she could possibly stand—never mind avoiding the temptation to break down and sob.

"It makes you want to kill the whoreson," a deep voice said curtly from behind her, "doesn't it?"

She could only nod jerkily.

One of the hands patted her shoulder with almost enough force to send her back down to her knees.

"Up on your own now," the man said, then moved in front of her. "I believe I'll be enjoying some of this fine play now."

Ali watched in complete amazement as the very man she had risked her life to avoid strode out onto the field.

Apparently to avenge her.

Colin unceremoniously pushed Jason of Artane out of the way and took his place facing Sir Etienne.

"How pleasant to find you here again," Colin said, folding his arms over his chest.

Sir Etienne shrugged negligently. "I've seen you a pair of times. And you've shown me nothing I haven't seen before—and bested."

Ali gasped at his cheek. Jason only laughed and resheathed his sword.

"You'll pay for that," he said, still chuckling.

"Jason, see to the lad," Colin threw over his shoulder.

"Already done," Jason said. He walked over to where Ali was weaving unsteadily and took her arm. "You look fair to falling down. Did he break anything, do you think?"

Ali could only shake her head. "He merely . . . wanted to . . . teach me a lesson," she managed.

"Hardly the way to go about it, was it?" Jason asked. He inclined his head toward the hall. "Let us seek out a healer for you and leave Sir Colin to his play."

Ali hesitated. There would be something quite satisfying about witnessing Sir Etienne's defeat. After all, how many souls had the luxury of watching a warrior of Colin's mettle when that skill was directed at someone else?

"I believe that lad is mine now," Colin was saying conversationally.

"He isn't yet. I've things I intend to teach him before you have him and you'll not interfere with that. Not," he added contemptuously, "that you'd be able to with your paltry skills."

"Well, perhaps we can come to an agreement on when I begin to care for what is mine," Colin said, drawing his sword.

"You'll have him when I say you'll have him," Sir Etienne spat.

Jason tugged on Ali's arm. "No need to watch," he said. "The garrison will be full of the tale later. And you'll have the amusement of counting how many days Sir Etienne spends in the healer's house, unable to rise from his bed."

"Think you?" she wheezed.

Jason looked at her sideways. "Can you doubt it? Surely even France is afire with tales of Colin's prowess."

"Well . . ."

"Listen for yourself tomorrow and see why few dare to challenge him." He nodded toward the hall. "You need something to help ease your pain. Let us see to it immediately."

Perhaps he had it aright and she had no need to watch Colin doing what he did best. Besides, the very sight of it might be enough to send her fleeing in terror from the lists and she wasn't sure she could flee anywhere at present. So she nodded to Jason, then limped along next to him back to the hall, grateful for the slowness of his pace and his lack of comment on her smell, which even she could tell was horrendous beyond the norm.

"A bath," Jason announced, "then something proper to eat. And I'll see that you can eat it in peace."

A bath? Nay, she couldn't have a bath. When, by the blessed saints, was the last time she'd been forced to do the like? At her christening?

Sybil had bathed occasionally, but that was to remove encrusted food from her person. Then again, the lady Isabeau had bathed quite often and never suffered any ill effects afterward. Well, that was fine for Isabeau, but Ali doubted it would go as well for her.

Especially in her current straits.

But before she could escape, she found herself in the kitchens, staring down at a tub placed in one of the darkest corners of the chamber.

It was then that she began to look about her for an exit.

Jason caught her by the back of her tunic. "A good scrubbing will serve you."

"But—"

"We'll find other clothes for you."

Ali wasn't sure how she was going to escape this tangle, but she knew she had no choice but to try. She could not allow anyone to see her naked.

She watched as the tub was filled, standing still until Jason's grip loosened before she made an attempt to bolt. Apparently, though, Jason was not as big a fool as she'd hoped, for even though she managed to jerk herself away from him, he had her back well in hand before she'd taken two steps.

"Shy, are you?" Jason asked, turning her to face him. Then he looked down at her face and stopped still. "By the saints—"

Ali made it a point to never be so close to anyone, lest the sight of her beardless face give her away. She pulled away from Jason and tried a bit of bluster.

"I've no need of aid," she said gruffly.

But Jason continued to stare at her as if he had found an entirely new species of some kind of vermin and 'twas his knightly duty to discover everything about it he could. Ali could see the thoughts running amok in his handsome head and wondered desperately how she could make them stop.

"I have scars," she blurted out suddenly. "They shame me."

"Scars?" he echoed.

"Powerfully foul ones," she said, nodding vigorously.

"Do you indeed?" he asked. His look of disbelief was complete. "I daresay scars aren't what you have at all."

"Would you cause me such embarrassment as all that?" she demanded, trying to sound manly. "Ruin my pride? Grieve me beyond measure by making me show things that shame me?"

He pursed his lips. "Very well. A screen, then. We all have things to hide, I suppose," he added in a mutter.

If you only knew, she thought, suppressing the urge to roll her eyes.

Then he looked at her suddenly, pleased, as if he'd just hit upon a foolproof scheme. "Can you get out of your clothes, or will you require . . . *aid?*"

By the blessed saints, would this fool never concede the battle? "I can do it myself," she said archly.

"You're very stiff. How can you deny yourself help when you need it?"

"Very easily. Begone."

He looked at her closely for another moment or two, then turned away thoughtfully and began to ask kitchen lads for the things she would require for her bath. Ali turned back to the tub and wondered what she was going to do next. She could scarce lift her arms, and bending and breathing were completely beyond her. How would she ever manage to get out of her clothes, or her mail? Besides, she had no intentions of Jason knowing about the coins she carried inside her under-tunic. Those were her means to freedom and she would tell no one of them, no matter how trustworthy the person might seem.

It was quite some time before Jason returned and by then servants had filled the tub half full of steaming water. Jason carried clothing in his arms and a servant followed behind with a screen. The screen was set in the appropriate place and Jason laid the clothes on a small bench. Then he turned to face her.

"You know," he said carefully, "you won't be able to get your mail off by yourself."

"I need no aid," she said, crossing her arms over herself and gasping at the pain of movement.

He drew his knife. Ali backed away, wondering if he intended to stab her to get her to cooperate.

"I'll cut your surcoat from you," he said patiently, "then I *will* help you with your mail. Then you can see to the rest if you insist, though I could close my eyes, if you like."

"And why would I need you to do that?" she snapped.

He looked at her with one eyebrow raised. "You would know better than I."

"You think too much."

"And you are powerfully cheeky for a mere knight."

"I could be a lord's son," she bluffed. "Your equal."

"I suppose so," he said slowly. "But," he added with a wink, "I would still close my eyes to help you undress, did you but ask it of me."

Ali merely glared at him, then held open her arms and

didn't flinch as he cut away her surcoat. He gently pulled off her mail, then removed the cross garters from her legs.

"Thank you," she muttered, knowing she sounded ungracious, but unable to put any other tone in her voice.

"My pleasure," he said, with a low bow. "I will await my young . . . lord's pleasure beyond the screen. Screech if you need aid."

She could only hope that aid would come in the form of a serving wench, but then again, perhaps that would go ill for her as well. She would just have to hasten from the bath, dress herself in new clothing and hope that she managed it before anyone saw. And if they did, she would claim that the cloth around her ribs was to ease their soreness, not bind what little served for her womanly attributes. She had found, over the course of two years of trying to hide what she was, that people saw what they expected to see.

She'd been lucky enough to have had a garderobe always to hand, so relieving herself hadn't been a problem. And her flux had been something else entirely, but looking back on it now, she realized that every time she'd had it, the lady Isabeau had kept her near her, reading or doing some other such activity in the ladies' solar. It had come upon her seldom enough, the saints be praised, and she had assumed that was because of either some saint's doing or because she was most often terrified of being discovered. Each time it had arrived, though, the lady Isabeau had been there, demanding some undemanding service from her.

But then a truly awful thought occurred to her. Who would look out for her once she departed with Sybil to Colin's home? Colin himself?

She stripped, set her coins aside, then cast herself into perilous waters before she could give that ridiculous idea any more thought.

The water burned her like hellfire and she had to clamp her teeth together not to cry out from both fear and pain. But she sat just the same, because sound would have brought any number of people running to see how she fared.

She looked around her and found that a glob of soap had been left for her, as well as water for rinsing and a fine linen towel. She'd never used any cloth so fine in her own house, though she'd seen Marie use the like. She raised her eyebrows in silent speculation over that. Was her father given such luxuries, or was he left with rough cloth as well? She wouldn't have been surprised to find that was the case.

She realized then that she had lingered long enough. She washed—faintly alarmed at the skin she seemed to be rubbing off with the soap, for the skin underneath was certainly a far different color than that above—then did the same to her hair and hoped she wouldn't lose any more of it than she had already. She'd cut off her hair when she'd fled, leaving behind four feet of it in an unmarked grave in the deep woods near her home. Now, not a lock of it was more than the length of a finger, though she suspected she should have had someone besides herself sawing at it with a knife. The saints only knew how unkempt she looked.

She crawled from the tub, dried herself off as quickly as ever a body had, biting her tongue to keep from making any noise, then pulled on new hose that almost fit. They still required a bit of string around her waist to do the task for her, but at least there was little danger of them falling down. She hesitated putting back on the bandage around her chest, given how filthy it was, but she knew she had no choice. She wrapped and wrapped it until she'd done what she could, then tucked the edge under the top as was her wont.

"So, how do . . . you . . . um . . ."

Ali whipped around in surprise, winced at the pain of sudden movement, then found to her displeasure that Jason was standing there with a cup in his hand and a look of utter satisfaction on his face.

She gritted her teeth and yanked the tunic he'd brought her over her head. She snatched up her coins, shoved them under her shirt, and then carefully folded her arms over her chest and glared at him.

"What are you staring at?" she demanded.

He returned her look of challenge. "Something I suspected from the start."

" 'Tis an old war wound," she snapped.

He laughed.

She drew herself up and gave him the same look she had seen the lady Isabeau give Lord Humbert's fellows when they'd had far too much ale and had seemed to find her potential sport. "Be off with you," she said.

Jason leaned against the wall and took a long drink of his brew. "You'd best confess your secret," he said conversationally, "lest your soul be in peril."

"Never." *And let my soul be damned.* Better that than finding herself receiving Marie's tender ministrations.

He looked quite unconcerned at her refusal. "Well, now I know *what* you are; the question becomes *who* you are. And you should know that I am a master at solving mysteries of all kinds."

No doubt. The saints only knew what this one had learned at his master's knee. Did he charm his victims into submitting, or had Christopher of Blackmour taught him darker, fouler arts to gain his ends? Ali knew that if she told him her name, he would want to know more, and who knew where it would end? Would he go to Colin and tell him the tale?

He was smiling at her now. Ali pursed her lips. So, it was to be charm that he wielded like a sharp blade. That she could resist.

"Confess," he urged. "Unburden your soul. Perhaps I can aid you."

She took a deep breath. "Never."

"You should."

"I will *never*."

He smiled, taking up the challenge. "Then I will find you out."

"Not whilst I live."

He lifted his cup in salute. "So be it."

The saints preserve her, the man was in earnest.

And she'd thought the previous two years had been dangerous. She suspected the next half hour might be far more perilous than anything she'd endured in the past.

Chapter 8

C olin walked into the hall, well satisfied with his brief morning's exercise. He supposed he could have taken more time with Sir Etienne's instruction, but what was the point? The man had deserved a good thrashing, he'd gotten it, and now he would have a goodly amount of time to think over his poor choices as he lay in the healer's house for a handful of days, recovering.

Colin made his way through the kitchens, looking over the day's possible offerings on his way, and noted the screen blocking off a corner. Was his newly acquired garrison member having some kind of tryst already with a handsome serving wench? Well, a lad did what he had to to restore his dignity. And after the thrashing Henri had taken today, Colin honestly couldn't blame him for doing whatever he had to do in order to accomplish that.

"Confess."

"Never."

Colin paused and frowned. That was Jason, to be sure, and that womanly voice surely belonged to the lad, Henri. But what could Jason possibly be intending to find out? And what could Henri have to confess?

He rounded the screen and took in the scene before him. Jason was leaning against the wall, looking quite unconcerned—a sure sign the lad was set to use whatever methods necessary to discover whatever he'd set his mind to. Henri stood in the corner, his dark, shorn hair dripping down into his very pale face. His chin, however, had a very stubborn set to it.

Well, obviously the lads were fighting over some serving wench. Mayhap Henri had wooed someone Jason had taken a fancy to and Jason sought to find out how it had been done.

Though Jason wasn't the sort of man to tumble serving wenches, and Henri didn't look man enough to woo anything.

Colin shook his head and sighed. If he weren't careful, he'd be trying to beat the tale from the both of them. He was just certain the details couldn't possibly be worth the effort. He crossed the floor and slapped Jason heartily on the back.

"Leave the lad alone."

Jason stumbled forward, trying to save the last of his ale from spilling from his cup. Colin turned to the lad.

"You seem little worse for thé wear," he remarked.

The lad only quivered—in fear, no doubt.

"Henri, isn't it?" Colin asked.

"Sir Henri," Jason said, straightening with a groan.

Colin looked at the boy. "However did you earn your spurs?" he asked, in frank astonishment. "You fight like a woman."

"Valor," Jason put in. "The lad was knighted for valor. I daresay his training has been less than adequate, though."

Colin grunted. That was being kind, but Artane's get was nothing if not kind. He himself, however, was never troubled overmuch by that sentiment when it came to matters of war.

"Your training is nonexistent," he said bluntly. "I'll not have a man in my house who cannot fight." He considered whom he might foist the lad off upon, then had another look at the terror-stricken child before him. Nay, this was one who would require a master with peerless skill. Colin sighed. "I suppose I'll have to see to you myself."

Jason burst out laughing.

Colin glared at him, then turned back to Henri, who looked even paler than before. Well, the boy was certainly not showing the amount of joy he should have at such a declaration. After all, how many men had the opportunity to even cross swords with him and come away unvanquished? That he should even take the time to consider a helpless lad's training should have left the helpless lad in question weak with delight.

Perhaps Henri was so intimidated, he couldn't muster up the appropriate responses. Aye, that was obviously the case.

Jason, however, seemed to have no trouble expressing himself. He was leaning against the wall, gasping quite helpless with mirth. Colin glared at him.

"Be silent, you," Colin commanded.

Jason raised his cup in salute, then buried his giggles within that cup. Colin looked at Henri. There was no time like the present to be about discovering just how far his lack of skill extended.

"Have you spent no time in the lists?" Colin asked sternly.

"N-not m-much," the lad answered.

"Then what, pray, have you been doing with yourself?" Colin demanded. "Playing the lute for your mistress in her solar?"

"Um—"

"Answer enough. But why?" Colin demanded. "None other willing to do it?"

"Ah—"

Colin shook his head in disgust with thoughts he simply could not voice. The lad was in dire straits and that only added to his own personal burden. An untrained knight, a bride who would not emerge from a bolted solar, and a journey to see his father.

A lesser man would have been simply borne down to the dust under like circumstances.

But, fortunately for all involved, he was not a lesser man, and even such heavy tasks as those that lay ahead of him were not enough to discourage him. He tossed Henri's sheathed blade at him.

"Here's your sword. You left it behind in the lists."

The lad, predictably, jumped out of the way, allowing the blade to land quite forcefully on the floor.

Colin sighed. This was going to take longer than he'd thought.

"Leave your mail here," he said briskly. "We'll have a squire see to it and bring it to you later. Let us seek out a meal and you will tell me of yourself. Once I've determined just how little you know about swordplay—"

Jason cleared his throat. "If you'd care to have me train Sir Henri, I would be pleased to do it. I think I would be particularly suited to seeing to our Henri's . . . um . . . particular needs."

Colin snorted. Jason was better suited to ridding women of their clothing. Besides, why should Jason care what happened to Henri? He shook his head. "Don't need you," he said. "I'm perfectly capable of seeing to Henri's training myself."

"Um," said Henri, sounding faint. "You needn't trouble yourself—"

Colin fixed Henri with a steely look. "I have decided to train you. Many would kill to be in your place."

"Ah," Henri said, looking as if he might just fall down in a dead faint.

"The lad is obviously overcome with gratitude," Jason said dryly.

Henri did indeed look quite overcome. Still not an appropriate amount of enthusiasm, to Colin's mind, but perhaps the lad couldn't be blamed for that. Perhaps he was weak with quiet pleasure. After all, that he himself should deign to share his own vast knowledge and enormous skill with one such as this was truly a remarkable and noteworthy event.

He paused and frowned. Passing odd, that he should feel such a compulsion to aid the lad.

Ah, well, what was the use of his skill, if he didn't use it to some charitable purpose now and then? He turned back to Jason.

"Begone," he said shortly.

Jason only bowed politely. "My lord Christopher has no need of me today. I am at your service."

Wouldn't want your service was almost out of his mouth before Colin thought better of it. If he was to concentrate on Henri's training, he might need a bit of aid with less important matters. He nodded to Jason. "Well then, if you've nothing better to do with your time, go see if you can lure my bride from her hiding place. I should likely have speech at least once with her before we wed. And," he added reluctantly, "we should likely leave for my brother's monastery soon. Perhaps even within the fortnight."

"Will you have me come with you?" Jason asked. "To help you contain your, um, entourage?"

And keep your bride from escaping? Jason hadn't said the words, but Colin had heard them well enough. He gave Jason a look he hoped spoke well enough his irritation with the sudden tendency Jason's mouth had acquired of quivering, as if he could barely contain a smile.

"I doubt they'd let *you* into a monastery," Colin said curtly. "Your reputation is nearly as foul as Christopher's, and well deserved, I might add."

Jason inclined his head. "Perhaps, but you know the truth of it."

Colin snorted. "What I know is where you spend your leisure time. One cannot consort with witches and remain unsullied."

Sir Henri began to sway a little. Colin reached out and clamped a hand on the lad's shoulder.

"Aye, lad," Colin said heavily, "witches. Three of them, and viler practitioners of the art you'll never meet."

"Here?" Henri whispered.

"If you want to know where not to go, all you must do is follow Jason. He knows the way to their chamber well enough."

"And you don't?" Jason asked with a laugh.

Colin drew himself up. "They seek *me* out."

"Aye, to sprinkle you with all manner of things to improve your aspect," Jason agreed. He reached out and tugged Henri away from Colin. "Come with me and I'll introduce you to those healers Colin so callously refers to as sorceresses. No doubt they'll have something that might even improve *your* swordplay."

Henri looked even less than enthusiastic about that than he had about Colin's most generous offer, and Colin honestly couldn't blame the lad. He tugged on Henri's other arm.

"What will improve the lad's swordplay is time in the lists with me," he said, looking at Jason pointedly.

Jason tugged Henri back his way. "I'll take him with me."

Colin took a firmer hold and fair lifted the lad off the

ground as he pulled him his way. "And *I'll* keep him with
me."

Henri squeaked.

"We're going to pull the lad apart, do you continue to tug
on him thusly," Jason said. "Let him go."

"He's mine now," Colin said, "and I'll worry about him."

"I doubt you've the time," Jason said. "Needing to see to
your bride and all."

"You go see to her," Colin said, glaring at the youngest
lad from Artane. "Release you my lad here. You're going to
break him before I have the pleasure."

Henri truly began to teeter then, and damn him if he didn't
slip right from Colin's hold and sway right toward Jason.

Obviously Colin had work to do to teach the lad some
taste.

Jason held the lad up with an arm around his shoulders.
"I'll watch over him whilst you're about your business of
wooing your bride. After all, surely she is your highest pri-
ority." He smiled pleasantly. "And it would be a great honor
for me if you would allow me to accompany you on your
journey. I could certainly be prevailed upon to give young
Henri the closest scrutiny possible."

Henri pushed away from Jason, looking perfectly horrified
at that thought. And rightly so. Colin felt somewhat cheered
to know that Henri was not completely confused when it
came to matters of character.

Colin dismissed Jason without further comment, then took
Henri by the scruff of the neck. "Let us see to a meal," he
said. "You can watch me as I think on your training."

Henri whimpered.

Colin assumed it was from pain and loosened his grip on
the lad. Obviously, the training would have to wait a few
hours until Henri had recovered some of his strength.

He pulled Henri with him through the kitchen, sniffing
appreciatively. Things smelled good and he was hard-pressed
not to filch bits from platters as he passed. But he was, of
course, nothing if not disciplined, so he forbore.

But the saints pity Gillian of Blackmour if she stood in
his way of a decent repast.

He came to a dead halt at the entrance to the great hall. Diners were already seated at various tables, and who should be gracing the lord's table but Sybil of Maignelay-sur-mer herself. Awake. Lucid. And helping herself to a substantial amount of everything in front of her.

"By the saints," Jason said, sounding as stunned as Colin himself felt, "she's out."

"And conscious," Colin agreed.

"A miracle," Henri muttered.

Colin considered his options. He could, of course, remain in the shadows and allow the girl to gain some sense of peace. But then again, why should she be afeared of her own betrothed?

Decision made, he strode out into the great hall. The souls who made Blackmour their home took no notice of him. The wenches who stood behind Sybil took one look at him and, as one, screeched in fear.

Colin quickened his pace until he stood directly before his bride.

"My lady," he began.

She stood, her eyes rolled back in her head, and then she fell over backward, over the arm of the chair and onto the floor in a flurry of skirts and legs.

Colin sighed. Would the nightmare never end?

He leaned over the table and peered down at her. She was quite senseless, with her feet sticking straight up in the air. Fortunately for her, her skirts were covering all they should, leaving only her ankles and feet open to the view of anyone who cared to look. Her wimple covered her face, and her voluminous veil seemed to have pillowed her head well enough. He then watched as something rolled out from beneath her coiffure.

An egg.

Apparently Cook was boiling them into rocks today.

Colin was unsurprised, either by their condition or by the fact that Sybil had been hiding them in her hair.

Her maids fluttered around her like frantic butterflies, trying to pat her back into sense. Colin could have told them it was a useless exercise, but he suspected they wouldn't take kindly to his instructing them in their duty. He looked about him for someone useful. With a sigh, he settled for Jason.

"Carry her up," he said.

"Of course," Jason said promptly. "And I will happily take Sir Henri with me. I'm certain you wish him to be watched over quite closely."

"I am fine on my own," Henri protested.

Colin looked at the lad. Well, the first thing he would be teaching the lad was how to sound less like a woman and more like a man. "Henri, you should likely go with him," Colin agreed. "You've a way with the wench. See if you can't calm these squawking harpies surrounding her."

Jason moved promptly to do his bidding, slinging his arm around Henri and dragging the lad with him around the table to collect Sybil. Colin watched Henri put up quite a good fight at being thusly wrenched about. He certainly couldn't blame the lad. Jason's good cheer could be quite annoying at times.

Though why Jason was so interested in Henri was beyond Colin to fathom. The lad was much more likely to latch on to a handsome wench than nursemaid a fledgling knight.

Colin scratched his head over it for a moment or two as he watched the little party disappear up the stairs, then shrugged. Perhaps Jason had witnessed more of Henri's beating than he'd been able to stomach. Well, at least Henri could count himself well avenged.

Colin leaned on the table, wondering what he was supposed to do with his bride now, when he was distracted by the delicious smell of sauce wafting his way. He looked over the table to find Gillian looking at him purposefully.

"Don't want to hear it," he said crossly, stuffing a hefty hunk of meat into his mouth and chewing industriously.

"Questing is a noble venture," she offered mildly.

"I've no interest in questing," he said, making a purposeful grab for as much sauce-covered meat as he could fit in his fist. He knew exactly of what quest she spoke—and he had no desire to speak further of any attempts to find the missing and no doubt very dead Aliénore of Solonge.

"The prize might be worth it," she said.

"The prize is rotting in a shallow grave, no doubt," Colin said, reaching for Sybil's trencher and beginning to liberate it from its coverings.

Gillian looked unconvinced. "I'll say no more."

"A body could only hope," he muttered, then lifted the trencher and moved it to one of the lower tables. At least there he would eat in peace. The men said nothing as he sat with them. He accepted their silent sympathy without comment.

Well, at least Sybil had ventured forth from her hiding place. If she did it once, she could do it again. He should have removed the bolt from the solar whilst he'd had the chance. It would have saved him the future aggravation of trying to get her to open the door. He sighed as he bypassed the cup and reached for a jug of wine. Apparently he would be doing more waiting than he'd like for her to come to her senses. Or perhaps he could merely post Jason at her door and wait for the lad to charm her from her lair.

Aye, that might be wise. Jason could do what he did best, and Colin could concentrate on his strengths—such as focusing his efforts on Henri's training.

Turning that womanly lad into a warrior would be task enough for the present, one fully worthy of his considerable skill and attentions.

How could Henri not be eternally grateful for that?

Chapter 9

Ali knelt in the alcove next to the lady Gillian's solar, looked about her once more to make certain she was alone, and then quickly stuffed her coins into a crevice in the rock. She pushed dirt in after them, then placed the small stones she'd removed earlier back over the hole. She sat back on her heels and studied her work. Well, it looked unremarkable enough. At least there would be no danger of her future being discovered if she had the sorry misfortune of being forced to bathe again. 'Twas far safer to have her coins in a place that was, for the moment, far from her own person.

That task finished, she rose and stood, uncertain of what to do now. All she knew was that she couldn't remain out in the passageway. If she were going to avoid all the souls in the keep who seemed to want something from her, or seemed bent on discovering who she was, she would have to find a better place to hide than directly before Sybil's door.

It wasn't as if she hadn't already been about searching for a place that morning. She'd braved the kitchens first thing. Cook hadn't seemed to want her lingering there, no doubt because of her inability to judge a stew properly. The stable master thought she was about some kind of mischief. 'Twas rumored that Sir Etienne still languished in the healer's house, even after three days of recovering from Sir Colin's gentle ministrations, which included a broken nose and much bruising, so there was no hope of hiding there. Even the chapel and the resident priest had been unresponsive to her pleas, the latter having found her appearance to be too suspicious for his taste. How the man could determine that when she was surrounded by warlocks, witches, and warriors of fiendish and dubious character, she couldn't have said.

Inside Sybil's solar was no place for her, either. She'd managed to get herself inside the night before with Sybil and her ladies yet shove Jason out the door before he could give her any more knowing looks. And since she'd been in a goodly amount of pain, the solar had seemed a perfect retreat, a safe harbor for her to rest in and be shielded from the stormy seas without.

Until the seas began to heave within.

Sybil had confined herself to sniffles for the evening—once she'd regained her senses and had a bit more sustenance. The sniffles had been followed hard on the heels by quiet weeping, then weeping that grew in volume and intensity until Ali had known that if she didn't escape, she would go mad. That she was willing to abandon the security of the solar for the perils of the keep spoke eloquently of her misery.

But the saints only knew what she would do now.

Especially given that Colin of Berkhamshire had taken such an interest in her. Her, a knight in sore need of training.

By him.

Personally.

Ali would have put her face in her hands and laughed herself ill over the complete improbability of it all, but she found that laughing was simply beyond her. If Colin had his way, he would soon discover that she was not exactly *what* she seemed to be, and then he would eventually discover just *who* she was.

And then he would make good on his vow and remove her head from atop her shoulders, thanks to his blade across her throat.

"You look like you could use a good cup of courage."

Ali blinked and realized that Gillian of Blackmour was standing before her. Damnation, but how did the woman move so quietly? Ali revised her opinion of Gillian's state of betwitchedness. And that forced her to reconsider the likely truth she'd being trying her best to ignore:

The whole place was under a spell.

"Sir Henri?"

Ali smiled weakly. At least Gillian was holding true to her word about not giving away any secrets.

"Forgive me, my lady," she said, with a little bow. "My mind seems to be elsewhere."

" 'Tis perfectly understandable," Gillian said. "I was thinking about you and suspected you might wish for a peaceful place to rest for a bit. Would you care to come with me?"

Ali knew that she must have looked pathetically grateful, because Gillian only laughed and took her arm. She went along without hesitation. After all, the woman had offered her peace. Who was she to refuse?

They walked up and down stairs and through passageways until Ali was quite thoroughly lost. Either that or she was falling further and further under Blackmour's spell. Whatever the case, by the time Gillian paused in front of a door and knocked, Ali had no idea where she was or how she'd gotten there.

The door opened and an old woman stood there, appearing as harmless as an old woman should.

"Ah, Gillian, love," said the woman, reaching out for Gillian's hands. "A pleasure, as always. And who do you have here?"

"Someone who requires aid," Gillian said. "Of your particular sort, of course." She looked at Ali. "This is Berengaria."

Berengaria's smile seemed to invite all it reached to come, sit, and be at ease. "I am Lord Blackmour's . . . healer," she said.

Ali frowned. "I thought the healer was a man in the inner bailey."

"Ah, well, he does what he can. When souls have difficulties beyond his art, they come to me."

Well, there was surely more to that than those simple words, but before Ali could venture any more questions, Berengaria had reached for her and was pulling her into the chamber. Ali paused, feeling herself on the verge of something quite tremendous. To step over that threshold . . .

She found herself, quite suddenly, standing in the middle of the chamber and wondering how she had gotten there. She whirled around to look behind her only to find Gillian giving her a friendly wave and retreating back out into the passageway.

The door closed.

Ali took a deep breath. Gillian would not have led her to a place of danger. Perhaps this Berengaria was just what she said: Christopher of Blackmour's personal healer.

But just exactly what that meant, Ali didn't know.

She took the chance to look about the chamber. The place looked as if a healer dwelt there. Shelves lined the walls, wooden shelves filled to overflowing with pots of various sizes, though most of them were smallish, as if they held precious things. There was a window in an alcove with two benches flanking it, made for comfortable sitting with sunlight to aid in any kind of handwork.

Unfortunately, on one of those benches sat none other than Jason of Artane, whom she most earnestly wanted to avoid.

"Um," Ali said, backing up.

Berengaria put her arm around Ali's waist and drew her across the chamber.

"You know my lord from Artane," Berengaria said easily. "Nothing to fear there."

Ali tried to disagree most heartily, then realized that no one, including Jason, was paying her any heed.

"And I say that it cannot be made," Jason said, folding his arms across his chest, "without the petals of a new rose."

"Ha," said the woman facing him. She was of Berengaria's age, and she shook her finger at Jason as if he'd been but a lad of eight or nine. Ali recognized her immediately from the skirmish she'd been privy to days earlier. What was she doing here? "And what would you know of it, my lord? Wet behind the ears are you still, and there's no doubt of that."

"Now, Nemain," said a wispy-haired woman, who stood nearby, nervously fingering a long wooden spoon, "he's a fine student. He knows where all the pots are and his charms seem to work well enough—"

"Be silent, Magda," said Nemain with a glare. She turned that look on Jason, but it softened to mere skepticism. "At least you haven't burned anything yet."

"I can cook," he agreed. "And I've an excellent memory.

And, my lady Nemain, 'twas you yourself who told me that the proper way to woo a woman was with a potion made from the petals of a new rose."

"A pink rose," Magda offered.

"Red, I'd say," said Nemain, scowling. "Brings the blood to a lass's cheeks, does that."

Ali found Jason looking at her quite suddenly. He stood. "Good day to you," he said with a little bow.

Nemain threw a glance her way, then scowled at Jason. "Why're you standing for a knight?" she demanded. "Sit down, whelp, and let's finish your lesson for the day. I've important work to do after I'm finished with you."

Berengaria pulled her over closer to the alcove. "Nemain," she said calmly, "I hear Sir Colin has a victim still in the healer's house. He's being offered nightshade to soothe him—"

Nemain threw up her hands. "Hopeless! Helpless! Is there no rest for an old woman?" She rose and pulled Magda along behind her. "Carry my pots and let us be away to save the man from the ministrations of that fool in the bailey. By the fires of Hell, is there no one but me who can brew a proper healing draught?"

Ali watched as Magda was loaded down with a basket full of pots, then dragged from the chamber. The door shut with a bang. She looked first at Jason.

"Potions? Charms?"

Jason shrugged with a rueful smile. "I dabble."

And then it occurred to her where she was and with whom she was keeping company. She stared at Berengaria in horror. Why, this was a witch! A witch, one of the three Colin had spoken of, likely ready and exceedingly willing to ply her trade on a hapless soul brought to her lair for that express purpose! Ali backed away.

"I know what you are," she said, holding out her hands to ward off any stray charms. "I know what you do."

"I know what you are as well," Berengaria said. "And why you hide."

Ali didn't doubt it in the slightest. She looked quickly to her left to judge the distance from her own self to the doorway. Could she gain the doorway before she was put under a foul spell, or would she perish right there in the middle of the chamber, writhing in horrible agony as she died a frightful death from witchly curses?

"Now, my dear, there is nothing to fear here," Berengaria said gently. "Come. Let me aid you."

"How?" Ali said, easing her way out of the alcove. "By spelling me to death?"

"Oh, by the saints," Jason said, rising and taking Ali by the arm. He pulled her bodily back into the alcove and pushed her down onto one of the stone benches. "She's not going to hurt you. I've known her for years and she has yet to do anything unseemly to anyone that I've seen."

"You're hardly one to judge, apparently being one of them yourself," Ali accused, wrapping her arms around herself.

"Do I look like I cast spells?"

"How can I tell? The entire place is bewitched!" Ali exclaimed. "You likely *all* cast spells!"

Jason sighed and looked at Berengaria. "Perhaps a soothing brew of harmless herbs would aid her. Then she'll see we mean her no harm."

Ali considered trying to escape again, but she'd already tried to escape from Jason before without success. So she remained on the bench where he'd placed her and watched closely as Berengaria went to her worktable. The woman poured wine, then sprinkled it liberally with several different kinds of herbs. In truth, Ali couldn't have told the difference between dried rose petals and a pinch of hemlock—which gave her little comfort. When Berengaria returned, Ali gestured toward Jason.

"Let him taste it," she challenged. "If he breathes still, then I'll try it."

Jason sighed heavily, but sipped the wine. Then he handed her the cup with a smile. "See? Still alive, still breathing, still just as charming as always."

Well, he *could* have been a warlock himself, and immune to Berengaria's spells. She gave that thought as she swirled the wine about in the cup and studied Jason for telltale signs of bewitchment. All he showed, however, was a lethal charm that couldn't have come from a sack of herbs.

She sniffed the wine, wished briefly for Sybil's ability to judge brews from a whiff alone, then tasted hesitantly. It didn't taste poisoned, or as if it had been laced with spells. It tasted like sweet wine with a few herbs sprinkled on top. She leaned back against the wall and finished the cup.

And the longer she sat there, the more ridiculous her suspicions seemed.

Jason was no warlock; he was merely a man who looked at her kindly, if not a bit assessingly. Berengaria was no witch; indeed, she looked more like someone's *grand-mère* than she did one who brewed potions and cast spells in the depths of night.

"You must be tired of hiding."

Ali looked at Berengaria and blinked. "What?"

"Hiding for so long," Berengaria said. "You must be tired of it."

Ali wondered if she was gaping or if her mouth had simply decided it couldn't be bothered to stay closed any longer.

"She has the sight," Jason offered, draining his cup. " 'Tis impossible to keep secrets from her."

Ali looked at Berengaria. The sight, whilst a bit unnerving, was nothing to fear. "If you have it truly," she countered, "then tell me what you've seen."

Berengaria looked at her with a smile she likely used on all those who disbelieved in her skill, but she answered readily enough. "I've seen your stepmother hunting you; she hunts you still. I've seen your sire so deep in his grief that he can scarce think of you without weeping. He would give much to have you found."

Ali pursed her lips. Those were things that anyone who knew she had a sire could have divined.

"And," Berengaria added slowly, "I've seen that you should be very careful when you return to Solonge."

Jason's cup fell from his fingers and landed on the wooden floor with a dull thud. Fortunately for them all, the cup had been empty.

"Solonge?" he managed in a strangled voice.

Ali felt just as strangled. *When* she returned to Solonge? Why, she had no intention of ever setting foot inside that accursed bailey again!

Jason continued to wheeze.

Ali looked at him crossly. "You're having trouble breathing. Did you finally find something foul in your cup?" He looked as if he were torn between laughing and weeping. After a moment of his mouth working silently, he sat back and blew out a heavy breath. "Aliénore of Solonge," he said, shaking his head with a small laugh. "Who would have thought it?"

"Who, indeed?" she muttered. She buried her nose in her empty cup, wondering if there might be a place to hide permanently that didn't entail her own poor self in a crypt under the floor of a chapel. She looked at Berengaria, who she had to concede might indeed be able to see further than she herself could. "Thank you for the wine. It was pleasant," she said.

"Wine with a sprinkling of courage atop," Berengaria said.

"Courage?"

Berengaria looked at her and Ali felt as if every secret she called her own was suddenly laid open before the woman's gaze. Perhaps the old woman had the sight in truth. But, despite herself, she wasn't afraid. Never mind that there were now three people in this keep—Jason, Gillian, and this woman here—who could betray her to her death.

"Courage," Berengaria repeated, "though you've more of it in you than you realize."

"If I had been courageous, I would have followed the path my father laid out for me," Ali said with a sigh.

"I very much suspect," Berengaria said thoughtfully, "that had you done so, you never would have set foot on the shore of England. Marie wouldn't have allowed it. There are many places in the sea where a body might sink to his death and no one but the murderer be the wiser."

"Think you?" Ali asked in surprise. She could believe many things of Marie, but murder?

Berengaria rubbed her gnarled hands together. "I daresay she's not above that. I wouldn't be surprised to learn she'd done it before."

Ali knew that Marie was feared and hated by many, but to suspect such a thing of her was, well, almost more than she could stomach. Though she certainly could have seen herself coming to a bad end at the woman's hands.

Berengaria rose. "We'll keep you safe whilst we can. But for now, I'll leave you to my lord Jason's care whilst I go to forage for herbs." She smiled. "One can never have too many, you know."

Ali watched her pull the alcove's curtain across and supposed that Berengaria had no need to listen to her sorry tale. Like as not, she knew it all already. But that left Jason to hear it; and there he sat, looking at her as if he'd never seen a woman before.

"What?" she grumbled.

He only smiled faintly. "You're famous here, you know. There was quite a stir when you disappeared."

"No doubt," she said wearily.

"I am intensely curious about how you came to find yourself with spurs on your heels instead of keys on your belt. Will you not tell me of it?"

She hesitated.

"I am a vault," he added. "A veritable repository of secrets that must be kept upon pain of death."

And if any secret fit that description, it was hers.

"Come, Aliénore, and unburden yourself."

The sound of her name caught at her so suddenly and so tightly that she could do nothing but clutch the stone bench with her hands and struggle to breathe normally. And then, of course, she had to weep. Jason shoved a bit of cloth in her hands, patted her head a time or two, then sat back and waited for the deluge to subside. Ali found, eventually, that she had run the well dry for the moment. She leaned back against the wall and dragged her sleeve across her eyes.

"Womanly weakness," she said, with another sniff.

He laughed. "Aye, to be sure. Now, give me the tale of your spurs. I daresay you didn't kill anyone for them."

"I might have, for all you know of it."

"How?" he asked. "By breaking a sewing basket over some poor fool's head?"

She glared at him. "You are a rude boy."

"I am not a boy, and my mother tells me I am quite polite, but we aren't discussing my flaws. I daresay *you* are more skilled at filching than killing. Am I right?"

"I stole spurs from my brother François," she admitted reluctantly. "And he deserved to lose them, the drunkard."

"His sword too?"

"He tormented my dolls when I was little."

"His mail?"

"He was senseless. It seemed a just recompense."

"The poor lad. What then?"

There was little point in boring him with the events of the past two years. Indeed, they were memories better left forgotten. So she shrugged, as if neither the time nor the danger had meant anything to her.

"I fled Solonge," she said, "found myself at Maignelay-sur-mer as Sybil's keeper, and now I am here."

"Here being the last place you would have chosen," he said with a dry smile. "Poor girl. But you've told me so little. How did you manage the pleasure of being Sybil's keeper? Were you the most patient of Maignelay's garrison?"

She shook her head. "Sybil's mother, the lady Isabeau, gave me the task. I daresay she knew from the start what I was, else she never would have sheltered me thusly." She paused. "I owe her much for her protection."

"She will be blessed for it. You needn't fear here, either. We will protect you now, Berengaria and I. I would imagine if Gillian brought you here, she knows as well."

"Aye, she does." She stared down at her cup in her hands. "Though I daresay there is nothing any of you could do."

"I can protect you from Sir Etienne."

"I wouldn't refuse that aid, but he isn't whom I fear the most."

"Colin?" he asked in surprise. "Think you that you need protection from him?"

"He vowed to kill me did he but ever find me."

He shrugged. "Idle words, spoken in anger. I doubt he meant them. Besides, your contract with him no longer stands if he's to wed with Sybil."

"He would likely kill me just the same to remain true to his word. And who knows," she continued, "if he'll actually succeed in forcing her to the altar? If the wench had any spine, she'd flee for a convent, for I daresay she would prefer that. Especially if she could have the calling of cellarer."

"Not something I would choose," he said with a shudder.

"I've considered it."

"You? A nun?" He looked at her, slack-jawed. "Is that what you intend?"

"I've no idea what I intend," she said. "I have no skills, nothing of value to offer anyone. I am a lord's daughter, born to be a wife, mother, and chatelaine, but I have no talent for any of those things either."

"Oh, Aliénore," he said, shaking his head with a sad smile, "surely you undervalue yourself."

"You aren't familiar with my lack of skills—especially my stitching. I am as inept at that as I am at swordplay."

"Think you that is all a man wants?" he asked. "A woman who can sew a straight seam?"

Ali sighed. "I don't know what a man wants, and it hardly matters anyway as I now have no man to want me. I have coin, at least some, but no idea what to do with it."

He stroked the rim of his cup for several moments in silence, staring down at it, then he raised his head and looked at her. "You know," he said carefully, "I would trust Colin of Berkhamshire with my life."

"You didn't flee a betrothal from him."

"True enough." He looked at her and laughed suddenly. "But now look at you. First his bride, now his liege-man. I daresay, Aliénore, that you have traded downward in your choice of obligations to our lord from Berkhamshire."

"I'll judge that later."

"I can judge it now. You've never seen Sir Colin in full flush in the lists. I don't envy you the pleasure."

She scowled at him as he rose. "Have you anything else cheery to add, my lord, or will that suffice you for the day?"

"Give me time," he said, holding out his hand and pulling her to her feet. "Let us find some way to amuse ourselves today. I've no doubt Colin will have you at your labors at first light tomorrow." He pulled back the curtain, then paused. "Did you hear the door close just now?"

"Nay, I did not."

He hesitated, then shrugged and looked down at her with a smile. "I was mistaken. Let us be about your final day of leisure. You'll think back on it fondly when Colin has left you in the dirt continually for a fortnight or two before he announces that you may someday learn which end of the sword points away from yourself."

"Do you intend by that to buoy me up, or convince me that the life of a nun is the one for me?"

He put his arm around her shoulders and led her to the door. "Learning a bit of swordplay is always a very useful thing, even for a nun. Besides, it will give us ample time to discover what it is you would truly care to do with your life. A pity, though, that Colin can't know you. He would admire your courage."

"What there is of it."

He paused at the door and looked down at her seriously. "I know of few men who would have the courage, the determination, or the wit to hide for as long as you have. Can you see Colin in skirts for that long?"

"Subterfuge can hardly be a life's work," she said.

He smiled down at her. "You would be surprised. I should tell you of my father's grandfather, a spy for the French king. Do you know that he hid for several decades in the guise of a nun? With his lady wife as his abbess? Indeed, there would be many in my family who would be offended did you tell them that subterfuge is a small thing."

She swallowed with difficulty. "I don't think I could spend the rest of my life spying."

" 'Tis but one thing to consider, and it is something you're quite good at, apparently. We'll put it at the top of our list. Whilst Colin has at you in the lists, I'll give your life's work a bit more thought. Perhaps at the end of each day, we'll review the possibilities and see if any suit you. You'll be wanting to lie down on the floor and rest anyway, and no doubt listening will be all you're capable of."

He was taller than she, but not so tall that he couldn't be

flicked on the ear, which she saw to without hesitation. She received nothing but a grin and wink in return, and somehow that cheered her. Ah, that she might have had a brother such as this. Perhaps if she'd had, she would have found herself wed to a man who would have cared for her.

Not facing the prospect of being the garrison knight of someone who would surely hate her did he but know who she was.

"Come, my friend," Jason said, pulling her out of the chamber. "To the battlements. 'Twill likely be the last day you'll have the strength to get yourself up to them."

"You, my lord, have a passing unpleasant sense of the jest."

"I wasn't jesting."

Which was exactly what she feared. But as she walked with Jason of Artane up to the roof, she found that her heart was, for the first time in months, almost light. So she would find herself facing Colin of Berkhamshire in the lists quite soon. It could have been worse. She could have been facing him in front of a priest. She could have been facing Marie over a sharp blade. She could have been facing Sir Etienne over his fists.

"Alewife," Jason muttered to himself. "Midwife. Pig-herder's wife."

Pig-herder's wife?

Being Colin's garrison knight was beginning to sound almost appealing.

She studiously avoided thinking about the truth of it. She was going to soon be facing over blades the most feared man in England, and likely France, and to take that lightly was sheer folly. She would have to be careful, watch every step, consider every word.

And pray that she could survive the encounters.

Chapter 10

S ir Etienne pulled the healer's door carefully to, then drew himself back into an alcove. He stood silently in the shadows and watched as a man and a woman left said healer's quarters and made their way to other amusements. He would have stroked his chin thoughtfully, but his entire face hurt like a company of demons had been using it to dance upon for a fortnight. And he knew just whom to blame for that.

Sir Henri.

Or, as he might be more commonly known, the lady Aliénore of Solonge.

Smiling hurt his face as well, so Sir Etienne settled for a snort of pleasure. To think all this had come about thanks to the ministrations of the Butcher of Berkhamshire. Sir Etienne enjoyed the irony of that for a moment, then relived the delicious moments that had led up to his standing where he was at present.

He'd gone to seek Blackmour's private healer on the advice of a more disreputable-looking member of the garrison, though he'd been warned in very strong terms that the woman was more than she seemed. Healer, witch, he hadn't cared what she was. She would have herbs to dull his pain and his wits.

He'd been prepared to use whatever tactics were necessary to persuade her to give him what was necessary. To his surprise, he'd been making his way down the chamber only to see her leaving ahead of him. How fortunate for him that he would be able to paw through her stores without her in attendance.

He'd slipped inside the chamber only to hear weeping coming from the curtained alcove. He'd suspected some silly wench was about some sorry tale, and that had concerned him not in the least—especially since such weeping would cover any unplanned noises he might make himself.

After finding enough willow bark to send himself into oblivion for a se'nnight, he'd listened to the weeping in the alcove cease and more conversings begin.

And it was then that he realized he would leave the chamber with more than just herbs.

He'd listened in open-mouthed astonishment as the lady Aliénore of Solonge had laid out her life before that over-indulged, pampered brat from Artane. He'd been hard-pressed not to shout with laughter. Two years of hiding, two years of pretending to be a knight wasted, and all because at the moment of crisis, she couldn't keep her mouth closed.

So like a woman.

Well, at least he now understood why she was such a pitiful excuse for a knight.

He leaned back against the wall and wondered how he might use his newfound knowledge. For gain, surely, but what kind of gain and for how long? She'd said she had coin. Was she wearing it, or had she hidden it? He would have done the latter, but there was no telling what a foolish wench might do. He would just have to follow her closely and watch. No doubt she would either count it on her person or return to its hiding place to make certain it was still there.

Should he demand her coin and leave her helpless? Or should he just exact other, more personal gifts from her?

The mind reeled at the possibilities.

He would bide his time, watch how things progressed, and see what else he could discover, what he could use ruthlessly for his own ends.

It was almost enough to make up for the condition of his nose.

Chapter 11

Colin tested the ground beneath his feet for sturdiness, scanned the surrounding terrain for things that might hamper his morning's enjoyment, then turned back to the task at hand—namely training the pitiful whelp who stood before him, quaking in his boots and looking as if he prepared to enter Hell itself to be tortured by the most inventive demons there.

Colin nodded to himself in satisfaction. Now that the boy had the proper attitude, 'twas time to begin what promised to be a wonderful day of work. Such was certainly preferable to anything else he might have been doing—especially if that anything included trying to have speech with his bride, who slipped into senselessness every time he came within ten paces of her.

And given that she'd only clapped eyes on him twice, he was beginning to wonder if she was pretending the malady merely to avoid him.

Ah, but never mind that now. He had Henri standing before him looking terrified, and time on his hands to use that terror to his advantage. Really, could any man wish for more?

"We will begin," Colin announced, folding his arms over his chest, "with the manner in which you hold your blade."

Henri looked as if he would rather have been grasping a fistful of asps.

Colin felt no impatience. He was determined to teach this lad swordplay, no matter the effort nor the time involved. That such training might happily prevent him from taking his journey south any time soon was something he steadfastly refused to acknowledge, not being one to shrink from the unpleasant, of course.

The same apparently couldn't be said for Henri, unfortunately. Colin had been forced to hunt Henri down that morning, then remove him with encouraging words from his hiding place amongst Cook's barrels of ale. No doubt the lad feared to disappoint him in the lists. Colin could understand Henri's apprehension, given his own tremendously intimidating self, but how could the lad disappoint when he had absolutely no skills and there was nothing for him to do but improve?

And no time better to improve than as quickly as possible. He fixed Henri with a purposeful glance.

"Draw your blade," he instructed, "and let us see how it sits in your hand."

The boy was nervous, any fool could see that, but Colin did nothing to startle him. He merely watched as Henri struggled to pull forth his blade from its sheath. It was then that Colin realized that much of the lad's problem came from the fact that the blade was too heavy for him.

That led him to wonder how Henri had come by it. Surely no lord would have been foolish enough to give a boy a man's sword such as this. Then again, perhaps his lord had been poor and this the best he'd been able to offer.

Colin made his decision. There was no use in causing the boy shame over the gear he had. There was also no use in trying to train him with what he possessed at present. Besides, Colin could not only see the bruises on his face, but noted the way he flinched as he tried to do as Colin bid him. 'Twas a certainty that he still suffered after-effects from the thrashing Sir Etienne had given him. Another day or two of rest would likely do him good before the true work of becoming a knight began.

But first the matter of the blade.

"How attached," Colin asked abruptly, "are you to that?"

Henri's sword point made abrupt contact with the ground. "I beg your pardon?"

"That sword. Has it especial meaning for you?" Colin asked. "Would it grieve you to lose it?"

The boy looked as if he simply couldn't comprehend what Colin was saying. That gave Colin pause. He couldn't train the lad if he had so few wits that he couldn't understand the simplest question. Then again, perhaps terror had rendered him speechless. Hoping that was the case, Colin pointed to the sword.

"Put it up," he commanded, "and follow me."

Henri managed to resheath his sword after several tries, then cast a gaze heavenward before he trailed after Colin obediently, muttering various prayers to sundry saints. Not being opposed to prayers, and having heard more than his share over the course of his long career as a swordsman, Colin merely continued on his way and left the lad to follow along behind him.

Colin made straight for the smithy. Blackmour's blacksmith was a skilled sword maker whom Colin had used often himself in the past to fashion implements of death. Colin had no doubt that the man could make something quite adequate for the boy behind him.

Colin stopped at the opening to the very well-stocked hut.

"Master Stephen?" he called.

"Aye, my lord," said the man, looking up from his pounding.

Colin noted the arms bulging with strength and the sweat pouring down the man's face. He beamed his approval on such displays of smithlike prowess, then gestured to Henri next to him—who was actually behind him and needed to be dragged forward.

"A blade for this one," Colin announced. "How quickly can it be done?"

Master Stephen put away his work, then came across the floor to examine Henri more closely.

"Good day to you, sir knight," he said, with a little bow. "If I might see what you have?"

Henri had the same difficulty drawing his sword this time as he'd had the last. Colin waited for Master Stephen's verdict.

"Too heavy," Master Stephen announced.

"Aye, my thought too. How quickly might a new one be fashioned?"

"A pair of days. But I'll need the lad now and then to have him test the balance."

Colin doubted Henri would know a goodly fashioned sword from a poor one, but there was no use in saying as much. He would obviously have to accompany him on these visits.

"He will be at your disposal," Colin agreed. "Can you begin today?"

The smith considered. "This afternoonts, if that suits."

"It suits." Colin gestured for Henri to hand the sword to the smith. "Melt this down or keep it for some other goodly purpose. It doesn't serve the lad here. I'll see to the expense of a new blade."

"Of course, my lord."

That task seen to, Colin left the smithy and paused to reassess his day. Sir Etienne was vanquished, so there was no further labor there. No sense in inviting the man back into the lists before he was fully healed. His morning of training had vanished like the morning fog. He supposed he could have run through Blackmour's garrison to distract himself, but that would have felt too much like he was avoiding his fate.

He sighed and dragged his hand through his hair. Perhaps Fate itself was speaking to him, telling him to get on with getting himself wed. There was aught to be said for that. The sooner the sorry business was begun, the sooner he could concentrate all his energies on planning Henri's training. And then he could be about the happy task of grinding the lad into dust and rebuilding him.

But first the details of their journey. Colin supposed the first thing he would need to do was get the lady Sybil out from behind the door where he actually might wed her. He sighed deeply and started across the inner bailey.

"Come, Henri, and let us have speech together about your mistress."

"My lord?" came the squeak from behind him.

"By the saints, man," Colin said, stopping to turn and scowl at the boy, "you squeak too much."

"Um . . ."

"And you sound barely past your tenth summer. You've certainly no beard to show for your years, however many those might be." He looked closely at the lad and wondered just how it was he avoided hair on his face. "You may as well give me your tale as well whilst we're working on our ale," he said with a grumble. "I'm just certain 'twill be as difficult to believe as whatever you can tell me about your mistress."

The lad looked quite pale all of a sudden. Colin assumed it was over the prospect of having to discuss Sybil of Maignelay for the afternoon. He clapped a hand on Henri's shoulder, waited until he'd righted himself again, then led the way to the great hall. Surely there would be something to eat laid out somewhere. If not, Colin knew the way to the kitchens and had come to an agreement with Cook in which Cook gave him what he wanted, and in return he didn't slit Cook's throat.

"Sometimes, my lad," Colin said, "you just have to know how to inspire others."

Henri emitted another squeak.

Colin frowned thoughtfully. Perhaps he would spend some time that afternoon teaching the boy how to curse like a man. 'Twas no wonder Sir Etienne had used him so ill—though Colin couldn't countenance that kind of beating of a boy. Still, those squeals of terror were annoying. Aye, teaching the boy proper manly expressions of anger, frustration, and, the saints pity him, terror, would be first on the afternoon's list of tasks.

The hall was empty and there was absolutely nothing on any table that resembled food. Colin looked at Henri.

"No food," he announced. "We say 'bloody hell' at this point."

Henri looked at him as if he'd lost all his wits.

"Bloody hell!" Colin shouted.

Henri, predictably, ducked.

Colin rolled his eyes, then grasped the boy by the shoulders. Damned bony shoulders, if anyone had been interested, and bony enough that Colin began to wonder if the lad were starved. That or much younger than he claimed.

Had he lied about his spurs?

Colin put that thought in the back of his head where he could examine it later at length. He shook Henri.

"I'm not shouting at you. I'm showing you how to express your displeasure. You squeal like a girl."

"Oh," the boy whispered.

"Aren't you hungry?"

The lad blinked. "Hungry?"

By the saints, was he going to have to explain every nuance of every bit of life that came the boy's way?

"I'm teaching you manly expressions so you sound less like a girl," Colin explained. "We came in the hall to eat and we see that there is no food. We must voice our displeasure and not by means of a squeak!" He knew he was shouting, but sometimes a man could do nothing less.

"Bloody hell," Henri squeaked.

Colin looked at him, then grunted. This was going to take much longer than he'd anticipated.

Mayhap it would take several months.

Colin considered the possibilities there. After all, he couldn't in good conscience leave his bride with this kind of guardsman, could he? Surely 'twas his duty as a knight and future husband to train this lad to protect the lady Sybil—and not to wed her until he'd done the like.

Wasn't it?

He decided quite abruptly that it just might be.

With that happy thought to warm his insides, Colin headed back toward the kitchens. Obviously his focus would now be on Henri's training, that he might better prepare the lad to guard the lady Sybil. He could do nothing less, and surely he shouldn't move on to other things until that was at least well underway.

Henri was walking behind him, muttering under his breath. Colin came to a sudden halt and spun around to look at the lad.

"What?" he demanded.

Henri looked up at him. "Bloody hell," he said, with something that at some far distant point in the future might resemble Colin's mildest show of annoyance on his most good-humored of days.

Well, it was a start.

"Well done," he said, clapping Henri on the shoulder. He frowned down at the lad who now lay sprawled on the rushes. With a sigh, he reached down, pulled the boy to his feet, then continued on his way.

Cook was, as usual, less than pleased to see him, but didn't offer any resistance when food was demanded. A wooden trencher was provided, topped liberally with enough food for half a dozen starving men. A jug of ale was shoved into Henri's arms along with two cups. Colin nodded his thanks, then returned to the great hall. He set down his burden, sat himself down and set to without further ado. He looked up midway through his first whole fowl to find Henri still hovering near his chair.

"Sit," Colin said, indicating the chair next to him with a half-gnawed leg. "Eat. You're too skinny."

Henri sat. Colin took the jug from him, unstopped it, and took a long, hearty drink. He set it down with a bang and turned back to his meal.

Unfortunately, he didn't have as long to enjoy it in peace as he might have, for who should have followed his nose to the high table but Jason of Artane. Colin had managed to avoid having that one underfoot that morn by having Christopher find something for him to do. But there he was, turning up again like a foul waft of cesspit stench. Colin scowled at the young man, a scowl that should have sent him scampering back the way he'd come. But somehow, somewhere along the way, Colin had lost his hold on the lad. He wasn't as intimidated as he had been in his youth.

"Go," Colin said bluntly.

Jason sat down on the far side of Henri. "Now, my lord Berkhamshire," he said in that smooth voice he'd inherited from his equally charming sire, "how can you refuse a body sustenance?"

"Easily. Go get your own."

"I've come to inquire about our Henri's training."

"He's not *our* Henri. He's *my* Henri and I haven't begun

with him. I have, however, finished with you. Get you gone."

Jason only smiled, an innocent smile that Colin often wished he himself had been able to manage, damn the boy. "I might be able to aid you," he said in tones as lilting as any trained minstrel's.

"Hrumph," Colin said. "Aid me in what?"

"In whatever endeavor you're undertaking at present," Jason said pleasantly.

Colin frowned. He was never one to shun aid, but to have it from that one he would have to endure Jason's smirking *and* his uncanny ability to leave all maids in the vicinity swooning. Nay, that would be just too much for him to bear. Better that he make do on his own.

"One day, young de Piaget," Colin grumbled, "your reputation will catch you up and then you won't have such an easy time of things."

"Spoken by one who knows," Jason said dryly.

"I'm merely fierce. I don't brew potions."

"Healing draughts," Jason corrected.

And then, miracle of miracles, Henri made a noise. Colin looked at him in astonishment.

"Did you snort?"

Henri looked as if his fondest wish were to hide beneath the table. He ducked his head and stuffed whatever was in his hand into his mouth.

"Well done," Colin said, slapping him on the back.

Unfortunately, Henri spewed out that food across the table.

"That looked good," Colin said in dismay.

"Oh, by the saints," Jason laughed, handing Henri a cup of ale. "I'll fetch you more, my lord, when you've a need of it. Perhaps you should leave off with your expressions of approval toward poor Henri. He'll never have a decent meal otherwise."

Colin gave thought to Jason's offer. If he was going to do the fetching of more food, there was no sense in not finishing quickly what was on the table already. For some reason, Cook always seemed to give Jason the finest things from the kitchen. Like as not, the lad had spelled him into doing so, and he likely spelled Cook quite well, given the skill of his teachers. Colin shook his head, remembering his own brushes with those three women who called themselves healers but routinely ground up thumb-bones of whatever wizards they could find.

Healing draughts? Ha!

Colin shoved the trencher at Jason just the same. "Fetch me more."

Jason inclined his head, then rose. "Leave the interesting bits until I return."

Colin glared at him, then turned to look at Henri.

Then he paused, dumbstruck.

Perhaps it was the light from the fires, or the faint light from torches in sconces, or perhaps 'twas because he'd just had the beginnings of a fine meal and had more to look forward to, or perhaps he had just lost what few pitiful wits remained him.

Whatever the case, he was hard-pressed not to believe he was looking at a girl.

And a lovely one at that.

He clapped a hand to his forehead, hoping to restore some of his good sense. He looked again, then nodded to himself. He'd had but a moment of weakness. By the saints, this was no girl. 'Twas a boy, surely, but a young one, and one who if he had his spurs, had got them from some lord with no wisdom.

Obviously facing the prospect of marriage was wreaking havoc on his own poor self that he hadn't anticipated it could.

But what was Henri's tale in truth? He frowned at the lad. "How old are you? How did you earn your spurs so early?"

The boy looked to be struggling with his answer.

"I won't beat you for telling me the truth, but the truth you must tell. I can't abide lies."

The boy ceased with all movement, which more than any-thing told Colin that he was regretting mightily all the lies he'd already told.

"You didn't win your spurs fairly," Colin stated.

The boy looked away, but the misery was plain in the set of his shoulders.

"Did you steal them?" Colin pressed.

The boy was long in answering. "Aye."

"Did you kill for them?"

The boy whipped his head around to look at him with wide, startled eyes. "By the saints, nay."

Well, there was something.

"Why'd you do it?" Colin asked, reaching absently for a hunk of bread. "To escape?"

The boy nodded.

"A cruel master?"

There was a pause, then the boy smiled a half smile with no humor at all. "A cruel mistress," he said quietly.

"I see." Colin supposed he could understand the desire to make a better life for oneself. But there was no sense in letting the boy think he approved of his methods. "Stealing is not an appropriate knightly activity," he announced. "Never do it again."

"Nay, my lord."

"Nor is lying. If I catch you in a lie, you'll be sorry for it."

"Aye, my lord."

Colin chewed thoughtfully, then belched. Having satisfactorily made room for more food, he looked with great interest at what Jason was setting down before him.

"I don't suppose," he said, reaching for the quantity of meat he could surely never garner on his own, "that you'll tell me how old you are."

"A score, my lord."

Colin grunted. With that unmanly face? 'Twas almost more than he could stomach. Well, at least Henri's age was accounted for. Now, to pry further details from the lad.

"Whence hail you?" Colin asked. "If you'll tell me."

Henri looked as if he couldn't believe Colin didn't intend to beat the tale from him. "I have that choice?" he asked, sounding incredulous.

Colin shrugged. "Can't make a man do what he won't." He looked at Henri sideways. "Will you tell me?"

Henri sat up the slightest bit straighter. "Nay, my lord. I would have to lie."

Colin grunted. Feebly voiced the lad might have been,

he was certainly showing flashes of being quite quick on the uptake. "Fair enough," Colin said, washing down his meat with more ale. "So let us begin with your time at Maignelay. I daresay I don't want to hear how you got there."

"I daresay," the boy agreed.

Colin looked at him sharply and the boy lowered his eyes. "Better," Colin said. No sense in giving the lad too free a rein yet. "So you arrived and Maignelay put you to work. As what?"

"The lady Sybil's keeper."

"And needed she a keeper?"

"Her father thought so."

Colin grunted. Perfect. Mayhap he would have to train up this lad in truth if his betrothed was of that ilk.

"Spent you no time in the lists?"

"None," Henri admitted. "I attended the lady Sybil."

Colin grunted and speared a hunk of cheese with his knife. He chewed on it for several moments, resigning himself to the task of beginning Henri's training from the very beginning. He'd thought he might have to, of course, but knowing the truth of things was a bit disheartening.

But he was nothing if not determined, and he never turned away from something he'd set his mind to. Henri would be trained, at his expense, and by his own hand.

Colin sighed. "So you were forced to attend Sybil from the start. Tell me truly, is she so weak-constitutioned as all this? Hiding in her chamber? Indulging in that unmanly business of fainting at the slightest provocation?"

Henri looked very uncomfortable. "I daresay . . . my lord . . . that, um, your . . . reputation—"

Colin waved away the words. "Say no more, lad, for 'tis the usual reason my brides bolt. They've heard the tales and haven't the courage to face me."

"You *are* rather intimidating," Henri offered.

"Aye, well, true enough," Colin agreed.

"And your reputation is widespread."

Colin would have puffed out his chest in pleasure, but he'd heard the like too many times before. 'Twas his lot in life to be well-known and well-feared. A heavy burden, to be sure, but one he bore stoically and without complaint.

"No doubt the tales are greatly exaggerated," Jason said dryly.

Colin threw him a glare that should have felled him where he sat. But Artane's get had a strong stomach and only smiled politely in return. Colin turned back to Henri with a grumble.

"And at her home, was she so helpless?"

"She is the youngest," Henri said, "and perhaps a little overindulged because of it."

"Must you wed with her?" Jason asked, blinking a time or two. "What of your other would-be brides? Surely you could trade Sybil for one of those."

Colin shook his head. "They're all wed now, and no doubt quite happy to be rid of me."

"What of the last one?" Jason persisted. "The daughter from Solonge?"

Aliénore was on the tip of Colin's tongue, but he bit the name back. Why did everyone persist in speaking of her? She hadn't wanted him, the bloody wench, and he certainly wouldn't have her now.

Colin scowled at Jason. "She's gone missing and is likely dead."

"Wouldn't you rather have her, if she could be found?" Jason prodded.

Colin stood, pushing his chair back. "She can't be and I wouldn't. Come, Henri, and let us be about our business. No doubt the smith has need of you."

Henri followed him. Jason squawked suddenly and Colin looked over his shoulder. Jason had shoved his chair back from the table and was brushing frantically at his tunic and the sodden mess that had once been clean hose. Henri was wiping his hand surreptitiously on his own tunic, but Colin saw the movement and deduced that Henri had somehow dumped the contents of a pitcher of drink onto Artane's youngest. With the way Jason was swearing at the boy, Colin knew he had things aright.

Colin watched Henri scamper toward him in a most unmanly fashion. The poor lad looked a damned goodly bit like a girl, the saints pity him.

Well, there was obviously a *great* deal of heavy labor here to turn this one into something useful. And who was he to shy away from heavy labors?

Nay, he would take the burden upon himself.

'Twas a much more appealing project than marriage to a witless girl who fainted at the very sight of him.

Chapter 12

A *li* stood in the lists with the sun beating down on her head and thought back with fondness to the time when she'd imagined that being Colin of Berkhamshire's bride would be what killed her. Now she knew that having him train her in the gentle arts of war would be what did her in.

"We'll do that stroke again."

Ali wanted nothing more than to leave her sword where it was—point down in the dirt—and crawl off to somewhere cool and have herself a long rest, preferably without any mail, swords, or other trappings of war. Unfortunately, that wasn't a possibility at present, not with the Butcher of Berkhamshire at the helm of her ship, as it were. They'd been at this training business for only three days, but Ali suspected that Colin very much begrudged the sun its going down, for it robbed him of time to grind her further under his heel.

And he didn't even have her death on his mind. She pitied those who weren't as fortunate as she.

Not that she actually considered herself all that fortunate, and not that she'd lost any of her fear of him. He was, after all, who he was, and every moment in his presence reminded her of why she'd fled in the first place and what she had to lose if he discovered her.

Colin reached out and tapped her blade with his. "Again, Henri."

Ali swallowed back her fear, cast a final desperate prayer heavenward, and lifted her blade. Her arms shook as she did so, even though her newly fashioned sword was much lighter than her brother's had been. It was a beautiful sword; even she had to admit that. And it flashed quite nicely in the sunlight. She finished her stroke, then looked at the blade with admiration.

That she should have a newly fashioned sword was possibly the most noteworthy thing that had ever happened to her. She'd never owned anything so expensive. She'd watched the smith during his various labors and realized quite fully all that had gone into its construction. She'd also watched Colin hand over substantially more coin than she'd ever seen, and surely far more than she herself had tucked into one of Blackmour's passageway walls, and hand it over as if it meant nothing to him. When he'd given her the blade with but a " 'tis yours now, may it serve you well," she'd been tempted to weep.

Her very own sword.

It had been almost enough to give her the desire to learn how to use it properly.

Of course, that enthusiasm had faded with every subsequent day that passed—especially given that those days had begun at dawn the very morning after her sword had been finished, and lasted without fail far into the afternoon.

On the first day, she'd passed half the day learning to draw her sword, then put it away again. After a hearty meal, Colin had taken her back out to the lists where she'd learned to hold her blade properly. The only reason she'd known he had been satisfied with her work was because he'd then moved on to a proper fighting stance. That had been followed the next day by an examination of the previous day's work, then an immediate commencement of the first few swipes with her blade.

And, as Jason continually reminded her each chance he had, the true business of training had scarcely begun.

She had wondered often during the past few days if dousing him with that pitcher of ale had been wise. He'd certainly missed no opportunity since to describe in the most glorious of detail all that she would face whilst Colin did his best to make her over in his image.

She'd asked him archly the night before if all lads from Artane had such a finely honed sense of vengeance. He'd only grinned and reminded her that he would hardly be the one meting out any portion of justice over the next period of indeterminate length. That hadn't seemed to stop him from thoroughly enjoying his seat on the bench in the shade of the wall, watching her go through whatever torments Colin saw fit to inflict on her.

And damn that Artane lad if he hadn't come up with anything useful for her to be. His suggestion the night before of a fierce mercenary had almost earned him his supper in his lap.

"Henri!" Colin bellowed.

Ali snapped to attention and grasped her blade with both hands. "My lord," she said as bravely as she could. She dragged her full concentration away from thoughts of Jason's demise, the sheen of her blade, and her future, to the matter at hand. Whatever might come after, for now learning swordplay was a goodly work and one she didn't intend to fail at.

A pity Marie couldn't have seen her, or been the recipient of Ali's finished lessons.

"Are you finished thinking?"

Ali raised her blade. "My apologies, lord. Your reputation intimidates me."

Colin nodded as if such a thing were merely his due. "No doubt it does. But I am your master now, and I've no mind to separate your head from your shoulders. Unless," he added, "you continue to lose yourself in foolish dreaming."

Ali forced herself to ignore the complete ridiculousness of actually having the cheek to train with the man facing her. Apparently he thought nothing of it, so perhaps she shouldn't either.

She struggled to ignore the pain in her arms that progressed to pains in her back and then in her legs from such unaccustomed labor. Colin, though, seemed to find nothing painful about the day. He continued to deliver his instructions with calmness and a surprising amount of patience. His expression, however, gave new meaning to *inscrutable*. He neither smiled nor frowned at anything she did, no matter how many times he made her do her strokes over again.

Then again, perhaps there was nothing to be excited over yet in her quest for mastery of her blade, though Jason had told her earlier that morning that she was a good student.

Despite herself, she felt as if she were actually succeeding at something.

How ironic it was that the something was swordplay—and learned at Colin of Berkhamshire's tender hands, no less.

"Henri, I vow you've the concentration of a witless serving wench!" Colin bellowed. "Your head will never remain atop your neck if you cannot do better than this!"

Ali shook herself and gave up thinking. The remainder of the afternoon passed with her standing next to him, trying to copy the precise movement of his blade with her own. And, for the first time, the simple discipline of it gave her an odd kind of peace.

Of course that peace began to fade a bit as Colin kept her at her task the whole of the afternoon. By the time the shadows grew long and she had been released from torment, she was dripping with sweat and trembling with weariness.

Colin, still looking as fresh as if he'd just woken from a fine night's sleep, put his blade up and looked around him.

"Are they all gone?" he asked, sounding very disappointed. "No one left for a little swordplay?"

Jason rose from where he'd been lounging on the bench. "All save me, my lord, but I'm weary from just watching you train our poor Henri. 'Tis enough to make a lad consider something else as his life's calling. Smithy work? Masonry? Cobbling? What do you think, Sir Henri?"

What she thought wasn't at all what a young lady of her station could utter. Obviously she'd passed too much time in hose. She contented herself with glaring at Jason, then she turned back to see what Colin would require of her further.

She found him staring at her in a most unsettlingly probing manner.

"Henri seems to be holding up well enough," Colin conceded. "Or," he said slowly, looking at Jason, "does he seem a bit weak to you? Not as strong as a lad his age should be? These girlish tendencies he shows—"

"Not everyone can have your strength, my lord," Jason said, jumping to his feet and coming across the lists.

"Aye," Ali agreed quickly. "I crave your patience with my feeble nature, my lord."

"But 'tis a most womanly nature," Colin insisted, looking at her from under his eyebrows.

"Ah, leave off tormenting the boy," Jason said, slinging his arm around her shoulders. "Perhaps he comes from poor stock. Will you shame him beyond measure by reminding him of it?"

Ali could only nod uneasily.

"Hmmm," Colin said, stroking his chin thoughtfully. "I suppose so. Very well, Henri, I will torment you no longer. A meal, then some rest for you. Perhaps you'll overcome your weak stature at some point."

"No doubt," Jason said heartily, pulling Ali toward the great hall. "Come, Henri, and let us seek out sustenance. I'm weary from all your hard labors today."

Ali watched as Colin strode past them, making quick work of reaching the great hall before them.

She looked up at Jason. "My thanks."

"I could do nothing less."

"Think you he suspects?"

"Who you are? Never. What you are? Aye, perhaps. Unfortunately, the man is far less dense than you might think. Then again, he is so wrapped up in swordplay, he wouldn't notice you were a girl if you stood there naked—as long as you had a sword in your hand and were pointing it at him."

"I suppose," she said doubtfully.

"Don't worry. We'll put him off the scent."

"You've saved yourself another drenching, my lord."

"Oh, I've that still to repay you for," he said with a laugh, "but I'll bide my time."

"No doubt," she muttered, but went with him willingly back to the hall. It meant supper, and she found that she longed for meals like she never had before. Could the rigors of a convent life possibly be this difficult? Or the smells of pigs? Or the labors of brewing ale?

She followed Jason into the hall, but found herself sitting alone at one of the lower tables. It didn't trouble her overmuch. She had eaten more than one meal without Jason at her elbow and survived well enough. What could possibly happen to her before Jason finished his obligations to Lord Christopher?

She reached for her cup of ale, then froze as Sir Etienne appeared from the shadows of the hall and sat down across from her. She looked at him briefly, noticed the rearranging of his nose—no doubt thanks to Colin's fists—then lowered her eyes and refused to look at him again, though she could feel him willing her to do the like.

Ali turned her attentions to the high table, merely to have something else to watch. And as she looked at the faces of those sitting there, she wondered how it was that after little more than a se'nnight she could have lost so much of her discomfort at being near these people.

The Dragon she avoided just on principle, even though she'd begun to doubt that he was as full of evil as was rumored. She had given much thought to all that the lady Gillian had told her. Ali could well see where Lord Christopher's warriorly form alone could lead those around him to back up a pace and reconsider any jests at his expense. His visage, its unworldly handsomeness aside, was stern, but in nothing more than a manly way.

Ali watched him with his lady wife and saw that whilst he frowned at others around him, his look infallibly gentled when turned toward her. And to be sure, he treated her with deference enough. Gillian herself seemed to have no fear of him. Perhaps he was in truth just a man, but a man whom the gossips had cloaked with a foul enough reputation to keep everyone in fear of him.

And if that held true for him, how did it hold for Colin? Christopher of Blackmour had the very blackest, the very vilest fame reaching as far as her home, yet he appeared to be a mere man—a man with a gentle woman by his side and two very small sons who seemed to fear him not at all.

Christopher's lads didn't seem to have any fear of Colin. Ali watched as the younger one made an appearance at the table and immediately crawled over bodies and chairs until he had ensconced himself in Colin's lap. Ali watched in surprise as Colin not only allowed the familiarity, but put an arm around the lad to keep him from falling backward.

And then the true entertainment began.

The boy soon tired of Colin's food and turned to the man himself. Colin's shoulders were used as a place to perch, his hair was tugged enthusiastically, and his ears were used as reins. And all the while, Colin merely continued his conversation with Blackmour, seemingly undisturbed by the young lad's ministrations. Small fingers investigated eyes, nose, and mouth, but Colin's only response was to pat the lad on the back and settle him more firmly on his shoulders.

Ali began to wonder, unwillingly, if she might have taken rumor as fact when it should have been counted as mere fancy.

Had she made a mistake?

That was, however, a thought she simply could not entertain. She had set her foot to her accursed path and there was surely no turning back now. She purposefully turned her attentions back to her meal only to find Sir Etienne staring at her with an expression she couldn't quite identify. She glared at him briefly, then concentrated on her food.

"Beware, *boy*," he said in a low voice, leaning forward so she couldn't help but hear him. "I'll not stand for such cheek from you. You aren't his yet."

Ali felt an unwelcome rush of fear sweep through her. She remembered all too well what it felt like to be at Sir Etienne's mercy. It was the last place she would again find herself willingly. She gave serious thought to how she might escape to a place where Sir Etienne wouldn't be able to follow. Mayhap she would offer to take something up to Sybil and thereby hide herself in the solar. The foolish twit hadn't come down for the meal—again. Ali found herself quickly losing sympathy for the girl. After all, if Colin allowed a lad to crawl all over him thusly, surely he couldn't be all that bad.

His smell aside, of course. Even she, who shunned bathing as a dangerous and foolhardy practice, could see the wisdom of it in his case. Then again, too many more days out in the lists and she would be seeking out a tub of her own free will. There was something about roasting in chain mail in the heat of the day that brought out a body's most pungent odors.

The hall door opened and shut with a resounding bang, making her jump. She watched as the man who had entered the hall strode across the rushes, made straight for the high table, and bowed before Colin.

"Lord Berkhamshire," he said in a loud voice, "I bring a message from your father."

The change that swept over Colin was truly startling in its swiftness. Colin very carefully handed Blackmour's son to him, then stood to face the man standing before the table.

"Aye?" he said, and there was no welcome or warmth in his tone.

"He bids you depart for Harrowden. 'Within the hour,' said he. He is anxious to have the lady Sybil delivered."

The entire company held its breath. Ali stole a look at Sir Etienne and found that even he had stopped watching her long enough to look at the high table. For herself, once she looked back at Colin, she could not look away from him. Gone was the expression that gave nothing away. Gone, seemingly, was the endless patience he'd shown her. In its place was a cold fury that was plain to the eye. She was suddenly thoroughly grateful that she was not the focus of his ire.

The thought came to her that she surely would be, did he but know who she was.

Colin looked at the messenger with an expression of such malice that the man backed up several paces. "I'll leave when it pleases me," Colin said, each word clipped.

The messenger cleared his throat. "Your sire bid you—"

"My sire can rot in Hell!" Colin shouted. "Return and tell him I'll leave when I'm ready!" He sat down and bellowed for more wine, which a page hastened to give to him.

The messenger was no fool. He bowed, then immediately turned and made for the door, not even asking for supper.

There was silence in the hall for a goodly while after that. Conversations returned, but they were at first whispered ones.

Ali concentrated on breathing and keeping her dinner down. What a fool she had been, to think she could so easily have dealings with the Butcher of Berkhamshire! To think on him as a man who, though gruff and warriorly, was not dangerous.

Sir Etienne leaned over the table toward her. "Imagine how he will treat his wife. I shouldn't want to taste his wrath," Sir Etienne said, with an unpleasant smile. "As a woman. A defenseless, helpless woman."

"But you've already had a taste of that, haven't you?" said the man next to him, clapping him on the back with a laugh. "How did it sit with you, Sir Etienne?"

A brawl ensued and Ali wasted no opportunity to bolt from the hall. She knew she couldn't stay inside any longer, not after what she'd just witnessed. Whatever comfort she'd felt in Colin of Berkhamshire's presence was completely gone. She'd seen the side of him that grown men feared—and feared with good reason. Her only surprise had been that he hadn't reached over and pulled the messenger's innards out through his skin with his bare hands.

Perhaps with a woman he might have shown a slight bit of restraint whilst beating her or screaming at her. Perhaps. But with a man, one of his guardsmen, he would show none. He'd surely shown none to Sir Etienne.

What would he show to her when she, as Sir Henri, displeased him?

She fled down the steps and made it to the side of the chapel, her breath coming in gasps. Then she dropped to her knees and wept. What she wanted were great, noisy, wrenching sobs that would rid her of all her fear. Instead, she wept with her hand over her mouth to stifle the sounds.

He would kill her. Did he but know who she was, he would kill her, likely in the most painful of ways. But what could she do to avoid it? Flee? How, when he watched her all the time? How, when she was soon to be his as part of Sybil's dowry?

She dragged her sleeve across her eyes, her breath coming in gasps. Maybe if she banged loudly enough and wept convincingly enough, Sybil would allow her inside the solar where she might at least hide until she could decide on a plan. And if not Sybil, perhaps Gillian would aid her. . . .

She shook her head, dismissing the thought immediately. Gillian was wed to Christopher, who was Colin's dearest friend. She would be asking Gillian to turn against her husband, and that she couldn't do.

She struggled to her feet. If she could just hide for the remainder of the night, perhaps she could flee out the gates at first light. Though she would have to go back inside the keep for her coin. Leaving it behind had been a foolish decision after all. Obviously, she would have to fetch it. Putting her shoulders back, she started toward the hall.

Then she froze.

Sir Etienne stood leaning against the stone of the hall, watching her. He pushed away and started across the dirt path.

The hall door opened at the same time. Light spilled down the steps. None other than Colin of Berkhamshire stood there, looking even fiercer than her foul imaginings had made him.

"Henri," he called, "come in. I've a task for you."

Ali threw a look at Sir Etienne, but he had slipped back into the shadows.

Now, here was something to decide. Torture from Colin or torture from Sir Etienne. How could a body possibly choose between the two?

She wondered if she could make the stables before either of them could reach her. Was the portcullis down already? The drawbridge up? Would she survive if she jumped off the wall into the sea, or would she merely dash herself to pieces against the rocks below?

The chapel door opened behind her and Ali spun around, certain she was in the midst of a miracle. The priest stood there like a rescuing angel.

Ali didn't hesitate. "I want sanctuary," she said, throwing herself to her knees before him.

He frowned down at her. "Nay."

She gasped in surprise. "Why not?"

"I'll not have a sniveling knight cluttering up my chapel."

"But you must give me sanctuary when I ask it of you," she cried. "You must!"

"I must do nothing," the priest said stubbornly.

What kind of fiendish place was this, where demons ran amok and priests shirked their duties? Ali felt tears coursing down her cheeks and she could do nothing to stop them. She was doomed. Her best chance for salvation had just been denied her. She would die a horrible death at Colin's hands—

She was hauled to her feet by the back of her tunic. She squeaked in surprise.

"Damned useless priest," came the grumble from above her head. "Be off with you, Father, to where you do your best business."

The priest drew himself up stiffly. "My duties for the day—"

"No doubt continue at the ale spigot," came the reply.

The priest strode off in a fine temper. Ali wished she possessed such cheek. Unfortunately, 'twas all she could do to remain where she was, up on her feet thanks to Colin of Berkhamshire's fist in her tunic, and not weep out loud. He turned her around to face him.

"I saw Sir Etienne leave the hall," he said, looking down at her with glittering eyes. "He seems recovered enough. Was he troubling you again?"

What could she possibly say? Should the more dangerous man protect her from the less dangerous one? Or were they equally lethal where she was concerned?

Colin grunted. "You'll attend me from now on. Sybil can fetch her own food."

She blinked in surprise. "What?"

Colin looked to his left, into the shadows where Sir Etienne was no doubt still lurking, then back down at her. "A foot behind me at all times is where you will remain. Do you understand that simple instruction?"

The saints pity her, she certainly did. "Aye," she managed.

Colin looked at her with pursed lips, then shook his head and turned back to the hall. "Come. We'll seek our rest. I'm sure you're as eager as I to put an end to this foul evening."

An end? Ali had to put her hand over her mouth to keep herself from laughing in a most daft fashion. The madness wasn't ending, it was just beginning! Forever as a shadow to the Butcher of Berkhamshire? The very thing she had been trying to avoid and was now doomed to endure?

By the saints, not even her nightmares had been this diabolical!

"Henri, come," Colin said, taking her by the arm and tugging on her.

She would have dug in her heels, but the saints only knew what kind of retribution that would have brought down upon her. So as she walked up the steps to the great hall with him, she comforted herself with the small hope that he wouldn't want to damage her until he'd trained her.

She wondered, absently, what her father would have to say about her current straits. Would he have ever agreed to the betrothal if he'd known where it would lead?

She had to find another path, some other way to live her life. If she had to endure many more days of this, she was certain she would drop dead from fright.

Mayhap the convent was her only choice in truth. She might have enough coin to buy her way inside with what Isabeau had given her and if she sold the sword Colin had given her.

She shied away from the thought immediately. She touched the hilt and found the cold steel to be surprisingly comforting. Nay, she could not sell this. Whatever else she chose to do, she couldn't give up a gift that had been so freely given, given with the expectation that she could make good use of it.

Colin paused just inside the hall and his hand came to rest on her shoulder. "Stay by me," he commanded.

"Aye, my lord," she whispered.

"I'll see you're kept safe," he grumbled. "Poor whelp."

Ali gulped. A foot away from the Butcher of Berkhamshire at all times.

By the saints, could her life become any more dangerous?

Chapter 13

W*as* there truly ever a time when a man was at peace? By all the bloody saints, a body couldn't even think in the lists anymore without some foolishness or other troubling him. Colin swore in disgust. He'd been fuming for the whole of the evening before and well into the morning now. There he'd been, understandably doing his damnedest to forget about his upcoming nuptials, and he couldn't even have a decent meal without his sire pestering him. As if Colin couldn't manage to get his bride and his own sorry arse to Harrowden on his own! Nay, he apparently required a messenger to be sent after him, calling him to heel like a disobedient hound. Just the irritation of it had put him off his food and ruined his pleasure in swordplay.

Well, there was nothing to be done about it but come to heel as his father wished and have the whole sorry affair over with. Perhaps *then* he could concentrate on more important matters.

Colin looked at Henri, who stood in front of him, quaking as was his custom. The lad's sword was still hovering in the air before him and belatedly Colin realized that he'd ceased with his instruction in midswing.

He resheathed his sword and considered the boy before him. Now, here was a problem. After noticing Henri bolting from the hall the night before, then watching Sir Etienne leave off beating on one of his fellows to leave the hall as well, he'd decided that the little lad simply was not safe on his own. And when he'd arrived and found Henri quaking in the courtyard, looking quite like a rabbit preparing to be eaten, he'd known that Sir Etienne had to be nearby.

Henri's cries for sanctuary had actually touched his heart.

By the saints, when was the last time he'd watched a man be reduced to woman's weeping?

Well, the last time he'd stepped onto a battlefield actually, but that was another tale entirely.

Colin paused and stroked his chin. It had been rather womanly weeping, hadn't it?

He took three paces forward and peered down at Henri. Damned unmanly features that boy had, if his own humble opinion were being asked. Unmanly enough that they certainly could be viewed as unmanly in the extreme.

Ah, the poor lad. What torment he must have endured, with features like that. Perhaps he deserved credit for even attempting to hoist a sword, given that he likely would have been more suited to the undemanding and womanly calling of a player. Colin had no doubts that any traveling company of jongleurs he'd ever seen would have been happy to have claimed this one as one of their own. He could have filled all the women's roles with ease.

Well, there was nothing to be done about Henri's face except make certain that whoever deigned to tease him for it would pay the price with the lad's fine swordplay. And again, who better than he himself to improve that swordplay?

Unfortunately, with his father clamoring for him to come to Harrowden, Henri's swordplay might have to wait whilst Colin saw to his preparations. Unless there was someone else who might be prevailed upon to take up Henri's training for a bit.

Colin looked to his left to see Jason of Artane loitering in a most annoyingly useless fashion upon a stone bench. By the saints, hadn't that lad more to do than keep a critical eye on Henri? As if he had some interest in how the lad was trained! Well, like it or not, Jason had a goodly bit of skill and he could certainly keep Henri safe from Sir Etienne for the morning. With a heavy sigh, Colin beckoned to him.

"See to Henri's sword skills for the rest of the morning," he said reluctantly.

Jason rose gracefully from the bench and lifted one eyebrow in a perfect imitation of his father's most irritating look of feigned surprise. "You trust me?"

"I don't, but I've things to see to this morn. Teach him strokes of defense and only from the right. Do not proceed until he's mastered each one completely. You should manage at least one before supper."

"Your faith in him leaves me breathless."

"I'm not speaking of his ability to learn," Colin said pointedly, "I'm speaking of your ability to teach. When *I'm* finished with him, he'll be a match for you despite his small stature. Now, see if you can avoid undoing all my fine work, else you leave me no choice but to find someone else who can."

Jason made him a low bow. "It shall be as my lord wishes."

"You have," Colin said, pursing his lips, "many of your father's most annoying mannerisms. I vow I don't know how you came by them, given that Christopher should have pruned them from you years ago."

"I daresay 'tis in the blood," Jason replied cheerfully. "I don't know why it troubles you so. Perhaps 'tis that you have no love for my sire."

"Robin doesn't care for me."

"He respects your skill, though," Jason said. "Personal feelings for your family aside."

Well, that was something. Not that Robin, who had plundered more virginal beds—including Colin's aunt's—than he ought to have in his misspent youth, would ever have admitted the like.

Colin looked at Henri. "You'll stay no farther than a pace away from Jason until I return. Understood?"

Henri nodded with wide eyes.

Colin turned to Jason. "Keep Sir Etienne away from him. If anything happens to him, you'll answer to me."

"Such tender care you take for the lad," Jason said with a grin.

Colin momentarily considered repaying Jason for that, but decided it could wait until his other plans were seen to. He gave Artane's lad a look of promise, then patted Henri on the shoulder with a touch light enough only to send him staggering about a bit. He strode from the lists, his mind already on what he needed to prepare.

Horses, gear, men, and enough food to keep his bride alive until they reached Harrowden: The list was endless. And given what he'd seen being carried up the stairs to her lair, the last would require a large cart. Perhaps two. Not that Colin begrudged her a meal. The trouble was, she ate as much as he did, but he was the one sweating it all out in the lists. The saints only knew what sorts of things she did hiding up in that solar. Mayhap she used much energy praying that a miracle would occur and she would find that her husband was someone other than he.

It was enough to make a man consider a small trip to that chamber of horrors that masqueraded as Christopher's personal healers' quarters to see to an herb or two to make himself more desirable.

Not that Colin believed in magic. He most certainly didn't. And he wasn't at all certain he believed that any of their potions could work. Oh, they could brew a fine numbing draught. He'd imbibed a rather hefty one the night he'd learned Aliénore of Solonge had disappeared. And they could certainly brew up any number of things to ease a man's aches and pains, unplug his nose, or relieve the infection of a wound.

But potions to improve a visage?

Ha!

He found himself, however, making a most unwanted journey toward their chamber, as if his feet were no longer part of him and had decided on their own to trot their merry way toward complete folly. Colin allowed it, only because he was a bit stiff in the neck and perhaps the old wenches might have something on the fire that would serve him.

Black smoke was coming from under the door; never a good sign. Colin lifted his hand to knock, but the door was flung open before he could and he was jerked inside by women who had more strength than they should. He was shoved into a chair and commanded to sit there.

Magda was fanning the smoke with frantic motions toward the large window the chamber boasted.

They needed the damned window, what with all that that one burned.

Nemain was, as usual, cursing Magda thoroughly from head to foot. Berengaria merely sat in a chair by the small cooking fire and smiled through the clearing smoke at Colin.

"Taking up your journey, my lord?" she asked.

"Deciding upon the company," he said unwillingly. "Will likely need a healer along, I suppose."

And just from which crack and crevice of Hell had that come?

Colin listened to himself and wondered why it was he could no longer call back words that he surely hadn't meant to say, nor stop them in the first place! He gaped at Berengaria, then gaped at her two helpers who were already beginning to throw things into satchels for travel.

"We would be honored to come," Berengaria said.

"But," Colin began.

"Beauty," Nemain said, slapping Magda's hands away from her selection of pots on the wall. "He'll need all of it he can have."

"Courage, too," Magda insisted.

"Why?" Nemain asked with a mighty snort. "He has plenty of it, and to spare!"

Colin had to agree. His opinion of Nemain went up sharply.

"For his bride," Magda said.

"I know of whom you speak," Nemain snapped.

Colin suspected that the lady Sybil needed more than courage, but given that he'd only seen her a handful of times, and only one of those times was she coherent enough to sit at table, he was certainly not one to be advising anyone on what she did or did not require. He sighed heavily and looked at Berengaria.

"I suppose you can come," he said, trying to sound as ungracious as possible on the off chance she would take offense and decide to remain at home.

"Not that you need me," Berengaria agreed, "unless it was to staunch some life-threatening wound."

"Of course."

"But there may be those in your party who might have a use for us."

"No doubt," he said grimly. "Perhaps you could spell Sir Etienne into better humors."

"He is an unpleasant man."

Dangerous, too, Colin wanted to add, but he didn't. He had no use for the man and honestly couldn't understand why he insisted on tormenting Henri. Unless he was of the kind who simply couldn't stop themselves from harrying those weaker than they. Where was the sport in vanquishing a body that couldn't possibly defend himself against you? Colin did what was required on the battlefield against those less skilled than he, but he took no joy in it.

Now, did he find himself coming against an opponent who could make him sweat, aye, there was some pleasure. And besting a man of that ilk was certainly something to be proud of.

Besting young lads who looked like girls did not qualify as that.

Well, Colin would be rid of Sir Etienne soon enough, he supposed. No doubt his sire had sent word to Sybil's parents about the location of the nuptials. When they arrived, Colin would see that Sir Etienne was immediately returned to them with thanks for all his great usefulness. Then Colin would drop Sybil off in his keep with the best-stocked larder, then be on his way.

To where? was the question, but it was one he couldn't answer at present. He could always come back to Blackmour. Christopher had uses for him, if for nothing else than to put fear into the hearts of those who dared trouble him.

Besides, these folk were his family. He wasn't above admitting that he had fond feelings for Christopher, Gillian, and their little ones. And if he weren't here, whom would William find to torment at supper? The lad would have no place but his own nose for his fingers and that would likely be a lifelong sorrow for the lad. 'Twas Colin's duty to return as often as possible and spare the little lad such misery.

And if he were to be completely frank with himself, Black-mour was the one place he felt at home. His father had sent him to foster at seven, but that had been but the beginning of years of being sent from place to place. He'd never had the chance to even make himself comfortable before his father had irritated whatever foster-father he'd foisted Colin off upon, and Colin had found himself summarily being ushered out the gates and sent elsewhere.

His last master had given him a horse and his spurs and invited him to depart without delay. He'd been grateful for the gifts and left without looking back. His meandering path had led him to Artane. When Robin had learned who he was, he hadn't exactly welcomed him with open arms, but he had given him bed and board. Colin had met Christopher the next day, they had become unlikely brothers, and he had, at the tender age of ten-and-nine, found not only a purpose, but a home of sorts. Where Christopher went, Colin followed.

Of course, that had led to Christopher wedding Colin's second younger sister, and that had led to her death and Christopher's wounding, but that was a tale better left for another day.

What mattered was that his home was here, not at his father's table, and here was where he would no doubt return when his duty was discharged.

And he prayed it could be discharged painlessly.

Colin rose with a sigh, nodded at Berengaria, avoided being trodden underfoot by her helpers, and made his way from the chamber. Perhaps he had no choice now but to seek out his bride and inform her of their imminent departure.

It was with a heavy heart, and heavier footsteps, that he made his way to Gillian's solar. The door was, unsurprisingly, bolted, but no guard stood outside. Colin lifted a single finger and, in the most womanly way possible, scratched at the door. How anyone could hear such a thing was beyond him. He preferred a solid banging himself. If a body was going to announce his presence at a door, best do it well, to his mind.

But miracle of all miracles, the door opened and the giddy

maid who had opened it fell back with a screech.

More screeching ensued.

Colin clapped his hands over his ears and stepped inside the chamber before the door was slammed in his face. The sounds only intensified.

"Silence!" he roared.

Three maids fell into a pile, crawling over each other in their terror. They pushed themselves into the alcove and huddled there, sniveling and weeping.

"By the saints," Colin said in disgust, "I'm not going to carve you up and eat you for supper!"

More cries of terror ensued, but a fierce glare reduced that back to the level of sniveling and weeping. Colin rolled his eyes, then looked for his bride. She was sitting in a chair, a substantial hunk of cheese halted in midjourney to her mouth. Her eyes began to roll back in her head and Colin swore in disgust.

"Not again!" he exclaimed. "Lady, cease with that fainting! I've need of speech with you."

Her eyes miraculously seemed to find their proper position in her head.

"You're going to release me?" She breathed, her face alight with hope.

Damn all women to Hell, was he so poor a prospect? Never mind that he had no handsomeness. Could a wench not be pleased with a husband who could protect her? Protect her wee ones? Inspire terror and the soiling of hose in an entire army merely by stepping onto a battlefield?

Colin put his shoulders back and reminded himself of a few of his virtues, which included all those of a manly bent. Courage. Strength. Good humors. Thus fortified, he pressed on.

"Nay, my lady," he said archly, "I have not come to release you. I've come to inform you that we will leave on the morrow."

Sybil's eyes filled with tears.

But her distress didn't seem to extend to her belly, for she began to absently gnaw on her cheese.

"Pack your gear," he instructed. "We'll leave at dawn."

"To Berkham keep?" Sybil said, chewing industriously.

"To Harrowden," he said grimly.

'Twas nothing short of amazing how a woman could chew yet have her chin quiver in a way that portended buckets of tears to come. Colin turned and strode from the chamber before he had to witness the latter.

Harrowden. The very name made him grit his teeth and curse his sire. No doubt the man thought that if he had both Colin and Sybil there together with a priest nearby, he could bind them together before either had the chance to flee. It was also the place where his brother was currently preparing to become a monk. Colin suspected that he would be called upon once again to try to talk sense into the lad. The saints only knew if his sisters—the saints pity him that he had only two left, but those two were guaranteed to make his life hell each chance they had—would arrive to witness the madness of his nuptials.

He walked down the passageway and into Henri before he knew what he was doing. He grasped the lad by the shoulders to steady him, then frowned down at him.

"Where is your keeper?" he demanded. "And why aren't you with him? I left specific instructions that you were not to be left alone."

"I had, um, manly business to attend to," Henri said, blushing furiously.

"What manly business?" Colin demanded. "Wenching? You've no time for wenching now. By the saints, lad, you can scarce keep your mind on your swordplay as it is! How do you intend to do so if you're dreaming of a handsome maid?"

Henri's mouth worked silently for a moment or two, but no sound seemed destined to come out. He finally managed to point back down the passageway toward the garderobe.

"Ah," Colin said, "I see. Well, Jason shouldn't have left you to that by yourself. The very last thing I want to see on this accursed day is more of Sir Etienne's work on your sorry self. I suppose you'll have to forgo your training for the rest of the day and come with me on my bloody business."

"Of course, my lord."

"Is there food below?"

" 'Tis coming, my lord. But Lord Jason advised me to suggest a walk on the roof to you, should I see you before supper arrives. He said it would soothe you."

"He would, the wretch."

"My lord?"

"I do not like heights," Colin said unwillingly.

Henri looked at him for a moment or two in surprise. "Indeed?"

Colin scowled and pulled the boy down the passageway with him. "I'll speak no more of that. Just stay by me, Henri, and you'll be safe. Safer," he muttered, "than another young man you know."

Damn that Jason of Artane. He knew Colin could not bear heights. Colin fingered the hilt of his sword as he entered the great hall. Perhaps there would be yet a little time for sport in the lists this afternoon, before those unpleasant preparations for his journey had to be seen to.

He found Jason sitting next to Gillian, grinning like the empty-headed fool he was. Colin paused behind his chair and leaned down.

"You've had your sport of me," he whispered pleasantly. "Next, I'll have mine from you."

Jason said nothing, but Colin could have sworn he heard a gulp come from the lad.

"In the lists," Colin said. "After supper."

"I think—"

"You should have thought before. Don't make me seek you out."

"Now, Colin," Gillian chided. "He was just teasing you."

Colin made her a low bow. "You may tease me, my lady, and find yourself quite safe in doing so. This whelp knows better, or at least he should. Apparently he's forgotten and needs his memories stirred up. I happily take that task on myself."

"No doubt you do," Jason said dryly, then raised his cup in salute. "Very well, my lord Berkhamshire."

"I'll put a guard on the passage to the battlements," Colin promised, "lest you feel the need to flee there."

Jason hesitated and Gillian laughed. "He has you there, Jason."

"And you'll not save me, my lady?" Jason asked hopefully.

Gillian looked up. "Don't break anything, Colin. I daresay you'll wish Jason to go with you on your journey. 'Twould be a pity to ruin him beforehand."

"Why, by the saints, would I want him?" Colin asked incredulously. He was quite certain he'd already told Jason as much. Did the lad never cease with his endless plotting and planning to make Colin's life a misery?

"He could watch over your bride," Gillian said.

"Or Sir Henri," Jason offered.

"As you did just now?" Colin asked, glaring at him. "I found him wandering about the passageway, babbling about a journey to the garderobe."

"Surely he can see to that on his own," Jason said.

"The lad can't see his way across the hall by himself," Colin exclaimed. He reached behind him and grasped Henri by the tunic neck. "He needs to be watched at all times. I can see that no one can be trusted with that task but myself."

Jason laughed. Colin saw no humor in anything he'd just said, so he glared at the young man, then dragged Henri farther down the table where he wouldn't have to listen to the continual stream of mirth Artane's youngest couldn't seem to stem. Colin looked at Henri.

"He has bad habits," he said bluntly. "Do not learn any of them."

Henri nodded weakly. "Of course, my lord."

Colin grunted, sat, and turned his mind to his meal. But as he did, he realized that he would have to give serious thought to accepting Jason's aid. Perhaps between Jason and Henri, they could pry Sybil and her maids from the solar and get them on their horses. Jason could likely lead them out merely by smiling at the gaggle of silly twits. Colin had to concede there was wisdom in it.

But even that future torture didn't repay Jason for his sport. Colin looked down the table and gave Jason a meaningful glance. Jason raised his cup in salute and set to his meal as if it would be his last.

Which, Colin had to admit modestly to himself, it just might be.

Chapter 14

A *li* crept up the stairs and down the passageway toward the solar to prepare herself for the journey. It wasn't as if she had any gear, save a spare tunic inside the solar, but she wanted the chance to fetch her coins without anyone watching. Colin hadn't wanted to let her go, but she had invented the complaint of very sour bowels. Apparently, he had thought such a malady would be enough to keep even Sir Etienne at bay.

Would that it could be.

Even so, Colin had vowed that if she didn't return within minutes, he would be following her to see that she was safe. Jason hadn't been there to see to the task and she wondered why. Either he'd been sent off on some other errand or he'd fled to recover from the repayment he'd had that afternoon for having teased Colin.

She'd watched earlier, open-mouthed, as Colin had escorted Jason out into the lists, then left him looking almost as inept as she herself was. Jason had cried peace in the end, begged Colin's pardon for having used him ill regarding that never-taken trip to the battlements to relish the view, then come and slung his arm around Ali's neck and led her off the field in a perfectly fine humor.

Men.

Would she ever understand them?

What she did understand, however, was the fact that she was now being watched over almost constantly by her erstwhile betrothed in an effort to save her from another unsavoury thrashing at Sir Etienne's hands. She couldn't help but feel a little gratitude mingled with her fear. And 'twas her fear that made her scamper down the passageway when she might have, at another time, merely walked.

She didn't want to encounter Sir Etienne again alone.

She stopped in the little alcove next to the solar where she'd hidden her coin. She knelt down, pulled the rock aside, then reached into the crack for her little pouch.

She froze.

It wasn't there.

She shook her head and forced away her panic. It had to be there because she had hidden it well. She'd watched several people pass by her hiding place, but none of them had paused. She had just checked her coin herself but the day before and found it safely in its place.

She sat back on her heels, a sob catching in her throat. It couldn't be. No one could have noticed the loose rock, even if they'd had thievery on their minds. She rubbed her eyes with the heels of her hands and wondered just what in the bloody hell she was supposed to do now.

"Looking for this?"

She spun around and stared up at none other than Sir Etienne, holding a pouch in his hands and smiling in a most unfriendly manner.

She gaped at him. "How did you come by that?"

"You need to learn to watch your back more carefully."

She could scarce believe her eyes. Damnation, but the man was more clever than she'd given him credit for being. She leaped suddenly to her feet and grabbed for her coins, but he held the pouch far above her head.

"I don't think so," he growled.

"That isn't yours."

"What do you need it for?" he asked. "Thinking to flee?"

"Return it."

He sneered at her. "What kind of fool do you take me for? I have counted the coins and read the paper."

Ali cursed him. He slapped her so hard, she staggered. A whimper escaped her before she could stop it.

"I know who you are," he said.

"You don't," she said, praying it was true. Surely the oaf in front of her couldn't read. "You don't know anything."

"Ah, but I do. And I'm still thinking on what I want in trade for my silence."

"You can't read," Ali whispered. "Not you."

The swift anger in his face was enough to make her back up a pace. "I know who you are, Aliénore of Solonge," he whispered harshly, "and I can tell all of England any time I choose."

Ali felt her knees grow unsteady beneath her. Actually, it was worse than that. Her knees buckled and she went down. She would have gotten back up immediately, but her frame wasn't equal to the task. All she could do was kneel there, miserable and weak.

"Are you interested in what I want?"

She shook her head.

Sir Etienne squatted down, took her chin in his hand and wrenched her face up. "Mayhap Lord Colin is."

She could only stare at him in horror.

"I wonder how he would reward you for mocking him as you do," he mused. "I seem to remember him vowing to kill you did he ever manage to find you. And here you are, so close, so easily strangled, or beheaded, or hanged. Or perhaps he would merely take you out in the lists and allow his sword and his fists to speak for him. I've felt his displeasure. Perhaps 'tis time you felt it as well."

Ali looked at the ruin of Sir Etienne's nose and began to gasp. His grip on her chin tightened.

"Ask me what I want," he commanded.

She swallowed, hard, then spoke around her immobile jaw. "What do you want?" she whispered.

He flung her face away so hard that the whole of her met the wall with a mighty force. She pulled away and felt something coursing down her cheek. Blood, perhaps. Tears, definitely.

"I haven't decided yet," he said, fingering her coins. "But I will. Tell no one what we've discussed here. If you do, I'll shout your name long and loud from the battlements."

"But—"

"And keep Berkhamshire far away from me."

"How—"

"Do it," he snapped. "Do it, or I'll tell him."

She bowed her head, gasping for air. When she looked up,

he was gone. She didn't hesitate. She ran for the garderobe, bolted herself inside, and wept until she thought she might be ill. How had Sir Etienne found her out? And if he knew, who else knew? And whom would he tell?

That he might give her away to Colin was more than she could bear thinking on. She'd seen Colin in a fury. And there she was, having done nothing to prepare for her future save hoist a blade to satisfy the foolish whims of a man who would likely snap her neck in two if he discovered her true identity. By the saints, she should have been giving more serious thought to escape. At the very least she should have been asking where the nearest convent could be found. She could become a nun. That didn't take any skill besides kneeling in prayer, did it? She *shouldn't* have been loitering in the lists, endeavoring to learn skills that would never serve her.

She leaned her head against the door of the garderobe and wondered what to do at present. She couldn't just flee Blackmour. She had no idea where she was in relation to everywhere else, and no firm destination in mind.

Worse still, now she had no coin.

The truth of her predicament presented itself in its fullest glory. No priory would take her as she was, without dowry, without proof of her birth, without gold. No guild would take her without skills or gold. No fine hall would take her as a lady-in-waiting without title or gold. She would be fortunate indeed to find a way to keep herself alive that didn't entail either scraping along as a servant or limping along as a harlot.

With an effort, she pushed aside those thoughts. Perhaps her future didn't have to be decided upon that night. She had a bit more time. At least until Colin's company left Blackmour, she could more easily flee if she were outside the castle walls.

She thought back to his demands. How in the bloody hell was she supposed to keep Colin away from him? By force? By asking? He would scoff at either one, especially if Sir Etienne displeased him. That she should want Sir Etienne to be shown mercy would likely leave Colin shaking his head and drawing his sword to instruct the man in the finer points of chivalry.

Nay, she would have to see to humoring Sir Etienne until
she could devise a plan. Mayhap she could either steal her
coins back, or throw herself on the mercy of some group of
sisters of the cloth and beg for sanctuary. Surely now and
then they could be prevailed upon to take women simply for
the pity of it, couldn't they? She had a need. She could accept
pity.

'Twas a fair bit more promising a prospect than accepting
a knife between her ribs.

She took a deep breath and pushed open the door—only
to face the very man whom she least wanted to see.

He was leaning against the wall, his arms folded over his
chest. He frowned at her, then peered at her cheek. And his
expression turned thunderous.

"I fell," she blurted out. "I was clumsy and I fell."

"Do not lie to me," he warned.

As if she could tell him the truth! She put her shoulders
back and looked him full in the face. "I hit my face against
the wall," she said. There was truth enough in that. No matter
that she was flung against that wall against her will.

Colin studied her for a moment or two, then grunted. "I
don't suppose you'll tell me how your face came to meet
that wall, will you?"

"I would have to lie."

"As if I couldn't guess the identity of your abuser easily
enough."

"But—"

He reached out and put his hand on her shoulder. "He'll
be repaid."

"Nay—"

"Say no more," he said, shaking his head sharply. "He
cannot use you so ill and not pay the price."

She fought the desire to drop to her knees and begin to
pray.

"Then again," Colin said slowly, "perhaps 'twould be a
better justice if I taught you how to do it yourself."

"Aye," she said, nodding enthusiastically. "A perfectly
wonderful idea." She prayed fervently that he would decide
that such was the better course of action. In the time it would

take him to make her into such a warrior, she would have likely come across some way to make a life for herself. Either that or Sir Etienne would have died of old age.

One way or another, perhaps Colin might be thusly persuaded to leave the man alone and she would be safe.

For the moment.

She passed the rest of the evening at Colin's heels, watching him order men about and listening to him discuss the journey with Lord Christopher. The longer she sat on a stool behind him, the sleepier she became, until she was certain she would never manage to stay awake until they were ready to leave. Would these two never cease with their babbling?

"Enjoying your last few days of freedom?" Christopher asked politely.

Colin grunted. "I daresay I won't find myself at Berkham overmuch, even do I succeed in getting that silly wench to the altar. I'll have freedom enough still."

"She might surprise you."

"The only thing that would surprise me would be to see her coherent and without food in her hand for longer than the space of a hour. The girl is hopelessly terrified of me."

"Can you blame her?" Christopher asked. "The fierce and intimidating—and pungent, I might add—Colin of Berkhamshire as a husband? At least she didn't flee."

"She's of too little wit to flee."

Ali propped her head up against the wall and hugged herself to keep warm. Colin had it aright there. Sybil would never have thought to do aught but what her sire told her. But at least she would have Colin's larder to comfort her. It was likely all she would need for a happy life.

"Now," Colin continued, "if I could have just found a wench with wit and courage, not even to equal mine, of course, for I know that would be asking too much, but even just a bit of both, *then* I would have wed willingly. Someone with a stomach for strategy, a head for thinking, hands unafraid to hold a sword. Aye, that would be a woman I could abide for a wife."

"You don't need a wife," Christopher laughed, "you need a squire."

Colin grunted. "I've considered it. They're a far sight less trouble than a wench."

"Then you consider your little lad snoring back there on his stool to be less trouble than a wife?"

Ali pulled herself away from the too-tempting lure of sleep. Had she been snoring? She shook herself awake. Weariness was making her careless, that and the comforting sounds of Christopher and Colin's talk. She could call to mind many times of falling asleep in her father's solar whilst he talked to his allies. When she'd been younger, of course. Before her mother had died.

"Perhaps you should offer young Henri a place in your guard," Christopher said. "It would free him from having to attend Sybil at all hours. Surely he deserves some sort of reward for having endured it for so long."

Ali kept her eyes closed, but her heart began to race. A guardsman? To Colin of Berkhamshire?

Was there anything more unnecessary in the world than that?

"Don't need a guard," Colin grumbled.

Ali couldn't have agreed more.

"Perhaps not, but he needs a place, don't you think? It couldn't be any worse than being nursemaid to your lady Sybil."

"I suppose not," Colin agreed. "And the lad does need protecting. He's too pretty by halves and I daresay he's spent his life suffering for it. I doubt anyone would dare tease him, did they think he belonged to me."

There was that, Ali had to concede. But being his? In truth?

Hadn't she been trying to avoid this very thing?

She opened her eyes in time to see Christopher slap Colin on the back.

"There you go," he said, rising. "Wed the wench, then spend the rest of your time with the lad. It sounds as if you like him better anyway. I daresay you can find wenches enough for your needs, leaving Sybil happily alone with your stores and some peace. Then that leaves you with all your time to see to young Henri. Make him over in your image,

Colin." He snorted with amusement. "I'm sure he would be overjoyed at the prospect of it."

Colin stroked his chin thoughtfully. Ali managed to close her eyes before he looked over his shoulder.

"A goodly work," he agreed. "One worthy of my complete attentions."

"See?" Christopher said cheerfully. "I told you it would all work out for the best. Now, I'm off to bed before my lady comes to fetch me. What a fortunate lad Henri is to have you all to himself. I'm sure he'll realize that in time."

And with that, he walked away, laughing. Ali could see no humor in his words and she wondered with a goodly bit of suspicion if Christopher knew far more than he should have, even without Gillian having told him anything. He was the Dragon of Blackmour, after all. And handsome though he might have been, there were still those unsettling rumors surrounding him, ones Ali couldn't discredit. She opened one eye and watched him suddenly pause and guffaw so fiercely that he had to hold himself upright by walls near the stairs. He straightened and disappeared into the stairwell.

His laughter floated down behind him.

Colin belched, then rose, his chair scraping across the stone. "Henri, awake. 'Tis past time we were abed."

Ali made a great pretense of waking up whilst she tried to ignore what he'd just said.

Bride. Squire.

Was she doomed to be with this man for the rest of her life one way or another?

She found herself being peered at by that man, who had stooped down a bit to better accomplish his task. He looked at her, muttered a bit under his breath, then shook his head.

"Poor lad," he said, pulling her to her feet and turning her toward the stairs. "Too pretty by half. Well, you'll sleep just inside my door this night where you'll be safe."

"Of course, my lord. Thank you, my lord."

"Manly tones, Henri," Colin instructed. "Bring them up from your belly and put some meat on them."

Ali took a deep breath. "Of course, my lord," she said in her most squirely fashion.

Colin sighed. "We'll work more on that tomorrow. We have a long ride to Harrowden. You'll have ample time to practice."

Ample time? She had the bloody rest of her life! And with no coin, no useful trade, and no true calling to the convent, she would likely be spending that life trying to be something she most certainly was not.

She chewed on that thought until she was comfortably rolled up in a blanket on the floor of Colin's chamber, listening to him snore peacefully. Weaver? Nay. Minstrel? Assuredly not. Player?

Now, *that* was something she might consider, as she certainly had experience enough with pretending to be what she was not. She would give it further thought on her ride to Harrowden. For now, it was enough to be somewhere she could sleep safely. And to think she had Colin of Berkhamshire to thank for it. She greatly suspected that wasn't what Marie had had in mind when she'd fashioned the betrothal contract.

But, by the saints, forever as Colin's squire?

Oddly enough, it didn't sound as horrifying as it might have two years ago.

Obviously she hadn't been sleeping enough if that thought didn't send her over the edge into an abyss of terror.

She closed her eyes, pulled her blanket up over her head, and forced herself to ignore any more foolish and completely far-fetched notions. She would serve Colin for as long as it took for him to wed Sybil, then truly be about the business of fashioning herself a life. Perhaps by then she would have acquired enough skill to force Sir Etienne to give her back her coin—and that at the point of her sword. And once she had her coin, she could do as she pleased.

Chapter 15

Colin dragged his sleeve across his sweating brow. Perhaps it had been too long since he'd passed any time away from the shore. He'd grown soft and frail under the cool breezes that continually washed in from the sea. No such things so far inland. He was momentarily tempted to strip off his mail, but knew 'twould be just his luck to have his father lurking about the countryside, arrow cocked for just such an occasion.

He closed his eyes briefly and breathed deeply. Ah, but to have the leisure of loitering about in some orchard in merely a tunic and hose. To feel the warm summer sun beating down on his face, fresh fruit from a tree above just there for his pleasure, and the knowledge that everything around him belonged to him and was his to care for. Aye, there was something to be said for that. Mayhap his father had it aright and 'twas time for him to wed.

Not that he'd ever admit the like to his sire, of course.

And not, he decided as he looked over his shoulder to see his bride shielding her face from the sun with her voluminous veil—and no doubt hiding what she was seeking to shove into her mouth—not that this one would possibly appreciate the finer pleasures of such loitering. She would likely have rendered herself unconscious long before he'd managed to pry her from the cellars.

He stared at the road before him and scowled, his pleasure in the day ruined. After a se'nnight's travel, he could come to no other conclusion than that his father's sole design in making him come to Harrowden was to irritate him. Unfortunately, the wily old bastard's plan had succeeded all too well. His temper, which had been simmering since before he'd left Blackmour, was coming to a boil quite rapidly. He feared that the least thing would set him off in an eruption that would live on in memory long after he'd gone down into his grave.

If only he'd had some reason nearby for that temper to truly show itself, he certainly could have made himself much more comfortable. He looked about him for a likely cause—and found a half dozen of them surrounding him. Beginning with his bride.

Aye, there she was, huddled on her mount, swathed in enough cloth for three of herself, in which she had no doubt hidden various and sundry items to stave off starvation. Colin wondered if she ever lost that aroma of ripe cheese that clung to her like perfume.

Could he perform his husbandly labors with that scent to greet him in bed?

Best not to think on that overlong. He quickly turned his attentions to his three healers. They had behaved perfectly, uttered not a peep, and offered only the mildest and most traditional of brews when asked for "a little something to ease the pains of travel." Damn them anyway. He would have truly enjoyed skewering a witch or two on his blade.

He turned disappointedly away, then sought out another likely victim. His gaze fell immediately upon Jason of Artane, who rode easily, traveled easily, and was a fair companion on a long journey.

Damn him as well.

Colin had tried to bait the lad numerous times thus far, just for a bit of sport, but found him frustratingly unresponsive. It had made Colin all the more determined to rub the lad the wrong way, as it were, but perhaps that would have to wait for later when he'd had a chance to think up something truly annoying. For now, a glare would have to suffice.

But Sir Etienne, now *there* was food meet to assuage his irritation. The man stared at him boldly, as if he dared Colin to come and challenge him. Ah, the perfect chance to do the like. Colin started to, deciding that he could come up with a suitable reason afterward for why he'd beaten the man to a bloody pulp.

He suddenly found Henri in his way.

"Move," he said briskly.

"My lord," Henri said, bobbing his head deferentially, "tell me of our destination. Will your family be there?"

Colin glared at him. "My family be damned. I've a lesson in manners to teach Sir Etienne and you're in my way."

"But, look, my lord," Henri exclaimed, pointing with a trembling arm to something in front of them, "is that something there on the horizon?"

"Aye, trees and a little hill," Colin said, not sparing the view a glance. "Now, move aside. I've business here."

"My lord, nay," Henri pleaded, sounding altogether quite frantic. "Surely not. Your family will expect you in good time, aye?"

Colin paused and stared at Henri in surprise. Why, the lad was fair frothing at the mouth to prevent an altercation. But for what reason? Colin looked at the boy, noted the bruises and healing cuts on his smooth cheeks. What would possess this lad to endeavor to protect the man who had used him so ill?

Well, there was mischief afoot here, Colin could smell that from a hundred paces. He looked over Henri's head to find Sir Etienne smirking in triumph. Colin frowned, then returned his regard to Henri only to find him very enthusiastically avoiding having to meet his eyes.

He considered halting and solving the mystery right then, then decided against it. He would see to it later, after he'd gotten on with the unpleasantness that awaited him ahead. Best have that over with so his mind was distracted. He relented with a scowl, then urged his mount forward. He would just ignore Sir Etienne.

For now.

They continued on without further interruption. And he had to admit, as he rode under the late spring sun, that this part of the land was pleasant enough. His sire's keep was several miles to the north, but in just as pleasing a bit of countryside. Colin supposed it would be his keep in the end. Or mayhap his father would insist Colin take the title and the land immediately, then settle his own sorry self into some kind of monastic keeping.

And mayhap faeries would spring up from the grass and invite him to dine with them in the boughs of a willow tree.

Colin decided that perhaps he had been traveling overlong. He turned his face forward and concentrated on reaching his destination before he lost what few befouled wits he had left.

They made a brief halt at midday for a bit of supper, then continued on. Colin could see his brother's monastery in the distance, but the sight of it brought him no joy. The closer it came, the closer came his doom and he had little liking for either.

By the saints, did every man dread his nuptials thusly?

Another hour brought them to the gates. Colin found that they were expected, for they were ushered inside the gates and directed to the guest hall. Colin felt fortunate to have gotten so far. The first and only other time he'd come to visit his brother, he'd been required to remain outside the gates. Perhaps having a woman or two in his company instead of a group of grim warriors led the monks to believe he was harmless enough to let in.

He dismounted in the little yard, but no one came to look after his horse, or to offer him sustenance. It was enough to make him wonder if perhaps he'd assumed too much about his welcome. He looked about him to find that the rest of the company had dismounted. The lady Sybil, as usual, looked to be on the verge of fainting, but fortunately she had aught to fortify herself with. Colin was half tempted to ask her if he might investigate the folds of her veil for something to tide him over until dinner.

He was spared her reaction to that request by the arrival of his brother. Peter was but a novice here at Harrowden, though he stood to take his final vows within months. Perhaps their father wanted them both at the same place to spur each other on to each making some kind of commitment. Colin wasn't tempted to think of trading places with his brother. The monastic life was not for him, and it had more to do with swordplay than wenching. He could not imagine handing his sword over to whoever was in charge, surrendering the daggers in each boot and the crossbow on his saddle. Unarmed and with nothing on under that itchy-looking robe? Surely that required a kind of strength Colin did not possess. How his brother managed to muster it up was beyond his capabilities to understand.

Perhaps with Peter it was less a matter of courage and more a matter of cowardice in facing a more vigorous life. Then again, he might not be qualified to judge that. After all, it wasn't as if Colin knew Peter very well. Peter was ten years his junior, having been born following Colin and his three younger sisters. Colin had been long away from home before the lad had come along. He shuddered to think what kind of torments Peter had suffered with the girls looking after him.

'Twas little wonder the lad wanted to hide in a monastery.

Peter stopped in front of him and made him a low bow. "My lord brother," he said, straightening and giving Colin a faint smile. "Welcome to Harrowden."

Then again, perhaps Peter had peeped once too often in a polished silver platter and had no illusions about his visage, the ugliness of which dimmed his matrimonial prospects quite thoroughly. Colin stroked his chin before he could stop himself. Was he himself this ugly? Or had Peter been unfortunate enough to inherit all their father's unwholesome features and none of their mother's faint beauty?

Best not to know, especially when it might lead to speculation about his own poor face.

"Where is the whoreson?" Colin asked bluntly. "He told me to meet him here and here I am."

Peter squirmed. "I fear, brother, that our sire has not yet arrived."

Had the day suddenly sprouted tongues of fire to heat itself so suddenly? Colin dragged his sleeve once again across his sweating forehead.

"Not here?" he asked, trying to contain his annoyance. "He bid me come immediately."

"He sent word that he will arrive within the se'nnight."

Colin could not shout at his brother. It would likely cost

him any potential meals from the monks, and to be sure, it wasn't the lad's fault. Colin took a deep breath and looked about him for some kind of distraction.

It arrived in the form of his younger sister, Agnes.

Now, that one had at least inherited a bit of their mother's fairness. And she fairly bubbled over with good humor, something Colin couldn't understand in the least. He watched her come running across the courtyard, then submitted to her enthusiastic embrace.

"Colin, you're here!" she said, sounding as if his arrival had actually pleased her.

Colin never knew what to say to her. His brother he could dismiss, his father he could ignore, but Agnes he could only be baffled by. He patted her head.

"Aye," he said, then lost all inspiration for further discourse.

"And you brought your friends. How lovely!" Then Agnes's eyes widened and her one fatal flaw manifested itself in its fullest glory. "Oh," she said, her hand moving briefly to her heart before that hand stretched forth with one of her fingers pointing in a most purposeful manner, "who is *that*?"

Colin followed her pointing finger and found that, aye, nothing had changed with her. Give his youngest sister an entire garrison to choose from and she would choose the least suitable man there.

In this case, Sir Etienne of Maignelay-sur-mer.

Colin had the fleeting satisfaction of seeing horror sweep across the man's face as Agnes started toward him, her eyes fixed upon his hapless self, her finger still indicating whom she had chosen to pursue during this fortnight.

His prospects for amusement having brightened considerably, Colin cast about him yet again for some kind of servant bearing sustenance. He'd not thought but to open his mouth to demand the like from Peter when who should come striding down from the hall as if she owned the bloody place but his next youngest sister, Ermengarde.

Damn.

The only good thing Colin could find about seeing the whole cluster of his siblings in one place was that at least

Magdalina, curse her rotten soul, was safely dead and buried and could not come and torment him as well.

"You're late."

Colin scowled. "And well met to you too, sister."

Ermengarde came to a halt directly in front of him, put her hands on her hips, and gave him the kind of look he was wont to give errant guardsmen. More was the pity that she didn't have to tilt her head back all that far to meet his eye. The wench was only a few fingers shorter than he, and he considered himself quite enormous. 'Twas little wonder Ermengarde had found no man brave enough to have wed her. Even Colin, who considered himself the bravest of men, was often tempted to cower before her.

Not that he ever gave in to that temptation, of course.

"Where have you been?" she demanded. "Father sent for you almost a fortnight ago."

"I had business to see to."

"What business?" she asked, sounding as if even defending the gates of Heaven could not qualify as a proper excuse. "Decimating Blackmour's garrison? Terrorizing the countryside? Wenching yourself into senselessness?"

"All noble pursuits," he returned sternly.

"Not," she said, poking him in the chest, "when you had business here. Important business. Business particular to the carrying on of the illustrious line of Berkham!"

"If that was so important, where is that damned sire of yours?" Colin asked hotly.

"Likely following *you* to make certain you did as you were told!"

"I am not," Colin growled, "his trained cur to come to heel when he calls."

"Nay, you're of less worth than that," Ermengarde snapped, "for you cannot follow the simplest instruction, nor see to the least taxing of your responsibilities." She used her fingers and began to tick off his failings. "Neglecting your estates. Shirking your duties. Befouling our illustrious name with your foolish antics."

He suppressed the urge to hoist her above his head and heave her into the nearest cesspit. He gritted his teeth instead.

"I see to my duties when they need seeing to."

She snorted, then turned a critical eye on his company. "And who is this ragtag group of half-wits?"

Colin waved his hand expansively. "My bride, her entourage, a lordling or two, and a clutch of healers."

Ermengarde pursed her lips, then swept him with an unfriendly glance. "Your hair is overlong."

Colin stuck his chin out and remained silent. Better that than say the first of all the uncomplimentary things that were fighting to get out of his mouth.

"And can you not take a brush to those clothes now and then? I daresay I can divine your last years' worth of meals from the front of your tunic."

His hands began to flex of their own accord. Perhaps Ermengarde was still a virgin due to more than her height. Her vile tongue was enough to keep any sensible man away.

"Anything else?" he said tightly.

"Aye," she said, reaching out to poke him sharply in the belly. "You've gone to fat."

Colin threw up his hands with a curse. "That's enough!" he exclaimed. He turned around to face the company behind him. "Settle yourselves. Agnes, see to Sir Etienne. No doubt he'll enjoy your attentions. Jason, see to the healers and our gear." He strode over to where Sybil still sat astride her horse, her hand buried in her veil.

Fondling foodstuffs, no doubt.

Colin reached up and removed her saddlebag from her horse. Her look of horror told him all he needed to know about its contents. Well, at least he would have a decent meal.

"There will be food inside," he said shortly. "Seek it out, Lady Sybil. My sister Ermengarde will make you quite comfortable and direct the monks to spare no effort for you. I've no doubt," he added half under his breath, "that she's fair to booting the abbot himself from his quarters and taking over his position."

"I heard that!" Ermengarde bellowed.

Colin threw a glare her way, then stomped over and nodded curtly to Henri.

"Come with me. Training is the only sensible activity for the rest of the day."

"B-b-but . . . ," Peter spluttered, "where . . ."

Why did the lads around him have such unmanly articulations? Colin turned a formidable glare on his brother.

"They have a cloister, do they not?"

"But," Peter said, aghast, "you *cannot!*"

"The garden then."

The blood drained from Peter's face and he fell to his knees. "I beg you, brother, nay!"

"Then I'll find a bloody farmer's bloody field and pay him for the privilege of frightening his bloody crops to failure!" Colin bellowed. "Henri! Come!"

He had the satisfaction of seeing the lad immediately descend from his horse, his sword in hand. At least there was still someone in the company who was obeying him. Jason had dismounted as well, but he was laughing as he called out things to be done. Colin toyed with the idea of pausing and beating manners into that one, but decided that perhaps that was a pleasure better saved for after he'd had something to eat. For now, teaching Henri the rudiments of swordplay would have to suffice him.

He looked at Henri as they walked out the gates.

"My family," he said grimly.

Henri nodded in understanding. "I have one too."

"As bad as mine?"

Henri squirmed and seemed to cast about for something polite to say. Colin sighed heavily and waved a dismissive hand Henri's way.

"Never mind, lad. I know. There are few like them."

"Aye, my lord. I'd have to agree."

Colin took stock of his situation, looked to his future, then decided on his course of action. The list of his immediate activities was very short and took very little time to make.

Wed.

Escape.

Satisfied he'd planned out the next few months of his life to his satisfaction, he turned his mind back to the pleasures of the sword and looking for an appropriate place to enjoy them.

Chapter 16

Ali stared up at the darkened ceiling above her and listened to the sounds of breathing. She wasn't unaccustomed to that, having spent most of her life sleeping with many people surrounding her. But this was different. Firstly, she was sleeping in the guest hall of a monastery. Secondly, she was sleeping between Colin of Berkhamshire and Jason of Artane. As if she needed protection.

Which, oddly enough, she did.

Though Sir Etienne would have had to have been a fool to have assaulted her with these two as her guardsmen. He'd certainly left her in peace for the whole of that day. She hadn't seen anything of him besides a lump under his blankets that night. Perhaps she was safe.

For the moment, at least.

She sighed and continued her study of the ceiling. The monastery was, she had to admit, a very peaceful place. A priory would be just as peaceful, wouldn't it? Perhaps becoming a nun wasn't such a poor idea after all. She'd actually been considering it for most of the day. She'd hazarded the odd glance at the monastery during her afternoon's exercise with Colin in the farmer's field. She'd supposed there must be a priory close by, perhaps close enough that she might be on her way there before anyone was the wiser.

During dinner, she'd looked over a pair of monks, trying to judge their willingness and ability to provide her with an answer to that question. She'd espied Peter, Colin's brother, but had immediately dismissed him as a choice. He likely would have run straight to his brother with the tale and she would have been finished from the start.

The monk who had been in charge of seeing them fed hadn't appeared all that helpful either. He had gazed at them critically, as if he begrudged them each scrap of food that went into their mouths, and the very space on the floor they planned to use for bedding down. When she'd taken courage in hand and asked him where the nearest nunnery might be found, he'd looked at her as if she'd sprouted horns and threatened to steal his soul that very minute.

She supposed, upon further reflection, that a knight asking where the nearest convent was had to seem a bit like a fox asking directions to where the plumpest hens were kept.

Perhaps finding some kind of sanctuary would be a bit more difficult than she had supposed.

A body came inside the hall. Ali didn't bother to look to see who it might be. There had been comings and goings all night long; trips to the garderobe, no doubt. She wished desperately she'd had the courage to do the same, but leaving the safety of the guest hall meant leaving Colin's protection as well. The saints only knew how lightly Sir Etienne slept.

The footsteps stopped.

Ali looked down to find Sir Etienne standing at her feet.

He made no sound, made no motion. He just stared, his face full of evil intent, his eyes glittering in the torchlight.

Ali closed her eyes to avoid looking at him, but he stepped on her foot so hard that she gasped in surprise and pain. He kept crushing her foot beneath his, forcing her to look at him, until he seemed to be satisfied with her terror.

Then he smiled coldly, and returned to his bed.

Within moments, he was snoring loudly enough that none of them should have been able to sleep. Well, at least that way she knew where he was and what he was doing. The pain in her foot and the ache in her belly were enough to convince her that perhaps with Sir Etienne asleep, she could safely leave the hall and see to her needs.

She rose as silently as she could and limped toward the door. It opened more readily than she'd dared hope and she slipped outside before anyone could stop her. She hastened across the courtyard toward the guests' privy. She'd almost reached it when she felt a hand on her shoulder.

She whipped around, a scream in her throat, only to have Jason clap his hand over her mouth. He smiled briefly.

"I thought you might want companionship."

"A keeper, more like," she muttered.

He shrugged with a smile. "Call me what you like. You shouldn't be out here alone."

She couldn't argue with that. She nodded her thanks, then continued on her way and did what she needed to. When she opened the door, he was standing with his arms folded over his chest, staring up at the sky.

He looked at her and smiled. "My turn."

He was even quicker. The blessings of being a man, no doubt. Then he took her hand and pulled her along toward the monks' cloister.

"We shouldn't go there," she protested.

"Likely not," he agreed.

Ali dug her heels in, but he was easily as strong as he looked. She realized by the challenging glint in his eye that if she didn't give in, he would find other ways to make her come with him. Being hoisted over his shoulder was guaranteed to bring forth someone to see what all the howling was about, so she cursed him and gave in as ungraciously as possible.

He led her to the darkest part of the courtyard, then sat down on a bench there. He stared at her expectantly until she sat down next to him with a gusty sigh.

"What does Sir Etienne want?" he asked bluntly.

"What do you mean?" she asked, praying that he'd been too sleepy to notice what had just happened in the hall.

"I have two eyes and an excellent nose. The man is tormenting you and I want to know why."

"He wants nothing from me."

"You are a tremendously bad liar. They beat nuns who lie, you know."

"They do not."

"They do. They beat you for all sorts of reasons, but I'm certain lying is the most common. I'd think about that before I trotted off to a convent."

"They'll have two years' worth of things to beat me for," she said. "Another lie or two won't make any difference."

"What does he want, Aliénore?"

She bent her head and sighed deeply. "Nothing."

"Shall I ask him—"

"Don't!" she exclaimed, whipping her head up to look at him. "Don't say a word to him, if you value my life."

He looked at her with frank speculation. "I think I'm beginning to see."

"I'm certain you see nothing."

He stared off into the darkness thoughtfully. He was silent for so long, Ali half wondered if he had forgotten they were speaking. Well, he was guessing and she was denying. That hardly qualified as a conversation.

"You could solve this all," he began slowly, "by just telling Colin who you are."

She gaped at him. "Of course I can't! He would slay me on the spot."

"And I say he would aid you."

"Say what you like, but I will not tell him. He has little use for me as Henri the guardsman. He would have even less use for me as Aliénore the former bride. Nay, I must find my own way, by myself."

Jason was silent for a moment or two, then he reached for her hand. "I could wed you."

She looked at him, blinked a time or two, then laughed.

"Well, I'm so pleased the thought amuses you," he said dryly.

She shook her head with a smile. "I appreciate the offer, but I daresay your road will lead you to another who can give you what I cannot."

"A hand with no blisters from swordplay?" he asked, but there was no sting in his tone, just gentle amusement.

"Aye," she said heavily. "A soft, girlish hand with blisters only from too much stitching. No calluses from swordplay. No murderous stepmother waiting to pounce. No evil knights lurking nearby with fiendish purposes on their minds."

"How exciting it all sounds," he said.

"No doubt it does, unless you are forced to live it."

He gave her hand a squeeze. "Then we must find you another life. We've hardly begun to list all the things you might do with yourself." He rose and patted her on the back.

"Let us return before we are found out here. The saints only know what kind of ire that would bring down upon us."

"As if being in Colin's company isn't enough for these monks already," she grumbled. She walked with him for several paces, then a thought occurred to her. "Could your father use another guardsman?"

Jason laughed softly. "No doubt he could, but I feel certain this life has more to offer you than a place in Artane's garrison hall."

"I could be happy with much less than that. A small patch of ground and a bit of peace. That would suffice me."

"Then I wish you luck in the finding of it," he said quietly. "Truly I do."

So did she.

She walked with him back to the hall and slipped back inside behind him. She lay down on her straw pallet and closed her eyes to the accompaniment of Colin's snorts. Jason ruffled her hair affectionately. It made her feel safe for the first time in years.

Two years.

Ah, that such peace could be hers for longer than a single night.

She had scarce closed her eyes, when she realized what was missing. She sat up with a start and looked over to where Sir Etienne slept.

Only he slept there no longer.

Jason sat up next to her and followed the direction of her gaze.

"By the saints," she gasped, "by all the merciful saints of heaven . . ."

"He didn't hear," Jason whispered. "He couldn't have. There was no one there but us."

"It was dark," she said frantically. "How would we know who was there and who wasn't?"

Jason lay back down, pulling her down alongside him. He leaned over toward her.

"Leave it," he whispered in her ear. "The morn will bring what it will. I'll stand by you against whatever the dawn brings."

And dawn would come, of that she was certain. It would arrive with its relentless brightness and throw her entire, sorry life into full relief. Not a secret would remain unrevealed, and she would likely find herself speared on the end of Colin's sword come midday.

Dawn did arrive and Ali met it open-eyed and exhausted. If she'd slept, which she doubted she had, it had only been for moments at a time. She had startled herself awake so many times, she half wondered why she hadn't just risen and gone to pace. It would have been much less exhausting. She supposed, though, that she must have slept some, for she remembered quite vividly waking up several times and seeing Jason always awake watching the darkness. Mayhap he had slept often enough in the past that he needed no more sleep at present.

Or mayhap he was so calm because it wasn't *his* secret about to be shouted from the eaves of the monastery.

Sir Etienne was sleeping peacefully in his place when Ali finally sat up. He snored fit to wake the dead, as if he hadn't a care in the world and surely hadn't tossed and turned the night away. What of it he hadn't been out eavesdropping or combining other mischief, of course.

Ali hovered near Colin throughout the rising and preparing for the day, waiting for Sir Etienne to rise, stretch, and blurt out her secret.

Instead, he didn't spare her a look.

After breaking her fast, she passed the rest of the morning trampling another bit of a farmer's field with Colin, learning more defensive strokes. She did the best she could, partly to avoid earning any of his wrath, partly to receive those almost imperceptible nods he gave her after she'd spent hours perfecting a single movement, and mostly because she wanted to move on to offense. She certainly couldn't kill Sir Etienne if the only thing she knew was how to keep him at bay.

What she wanted to know was how to plunge her dagger into his heart.

They gathered back in the guest hall for a midday meal.

Ali watched Colin ignore his sister as she very loudly criticized him. How was it the woman dared sharpen her tongue so fully and so freely on such an intimidating brother? A pity Ermengarde couldn't see to Sir Etienne for her. Ali suspected he might step back a pace and consider conceding the battle were he but faced with that woman.

Throughout the rest of the day, Ali made certain she was one pace behind either Colin or Jason. Not only did it give her a small modicum of peace, it also allowed her to continue to convince Colin that Sir Etienne was beneath his attention. And given the way Sir Etienne seemed to open his mouth and spew forth whatever crossed his mind, that was no small task.

By sunset, she had almost forgotten why she'd been so worried. That and she was past being tired. Training took more effort than she ever would have imagined, and she could scarce wait until she could cast herself down on her pallet and surrender to peaceful oblivion.

The last danger of the day was a final trip to the privy. She looked about her for companionship, but saw no chance of it. Colin was arguing with his sister, and Jason was having himself a final nibble before bed. She couldn't bring herself to ask either of them to accompany her. Sir Etienne was laboring under Agnes's suffocating ministrations anyway, so perhaps he wouldn't trouble her. She bolted from the hall and hurried to the privy.

She saw to her needs, then opened the door and stepped back into the night air. The stars were bright and the night moonless. She wondered, briefly, how pleasant it would be to have nothing more to do than to stand there and stare up into the sky, marveling at God's creations—

She was jerked off her feet and back into the shadows. Before she could scream, she felt cold steel against her neck. She shut her mouth immediately and prayed 'twould be a quick and painless death.

"You cannot seem to control your tongue," a voice whispered pleasantly in her ear.

Ali swallowed with difficulty, trying not to slit her own throat.

"Perhaps I was unclear," Sir Etienne continued. "You are to say nothing of me. Not to Artane's brat, not to Berkhamshire, not to the monks."

Ali didn't dare move, and she certainly didn't dare speak. So she waited, knowing that whatever else he had to say to her, it couldn't be good.

"One more word to the lad and I'll kill him."

"Nay—"

"And then Berkhamshire. Or perhaps," he said slowly, "I should rather begin with the lady Sybil. First her, then her maids. Then the runt Peter. One soul slain for each word you speak. That seems fair to me."

"You wouldn't." She breathed.

"Wouldn't I? Mark who doesn't live to see the dawn—"

"Nay," she pleaded. "I'll say nothing else."

He was silent for a goodly while and Ali began to hope that perhaps he would agree. But that hope was short-lived.

"Another chance," he said. "Another chance to prove you can be trusted. But watch how I move among these souls who trust me with their lives. Watch and you'll see how easily I could slip a knife between their ribs and smile in their faces all the while."

She wanted to tell him what she thought of his disgusting self, but didn't dare. After all, even she knew it wasn't wise to insult the man who held a knife to your throat.

"As for what else I want from you," he said softly, "I'm still thinking. There are so many things."

The next thing she knew, he had spun her around in his arms, taken her face in his hand and ground his mouth down upon hers.

That was, perhaps, his first mistake.

His breath was so foul, his kiss so disgusting, that she gagged.

He stepped out of the way and flung her down to her knees. He delivered a hearty kick to her side, then strode off, muttering under his breath. Ali didn't stop to be grateful for that. She concentrated on trying to catch her breath and stop her tears.

It was a goodly while later that she returned to the hall

and lay down in her place between Jason and Colin. Colin leaned up on one elbow and looked at her with a frown.

"Do not," he said quietly, "leave this hall again without me. Understood?"

"But—"

"Understood?"

She closed her eyes briefly. "Aye."

"I don't know what he holds over you," Colin rumbled, "but it cannot be worth what you suffer."

"Nay, my lord."

He grunted and lay back. Ali stared up at the ceiling and wondered how a single day and night could be so miserable. It made her wish quite heartily that she had never left Colin's side for a single moment.

As odd a thought as that was.

She closed her eyes and allowed the tears to trickle down the side of her face unimpeded. She felt Jason's warm hand close over hers.

And then something quite unthinkable happened. Colin reached out and patted her, rather gently all things considered, on the shoulder before he rolled over and soon began to snore.

It was a very long time before she managed to surrender to sleep.

Chapter 17

Colin had passed better days in his score and twelve years upon the earth. He wondered, grimly, if he would spend the rest of his days looking back on those thirty-two years and counting them the best he'd had. If events at present were any indication, that might very well be the case.

He'd been at Harrowden less than three days and in that time had regained his healthy disgust for monks, monastery food, and his siblings. Why he had been burdened with those three things together at the same time was anyone's guess. He suspected that, again, his father had given much thought to inflicting upon him the things that would annoy him the most. Colin could only hope that his sire would arrive quickly, so that he could finish up his very unpleasant business of saddling himself with a wife and then make his escape to somewhere else. Anywhere else. Anywhere he didn't have to associate with the rest of his family.

Ermengarde was in full battle mode, commandeering her troops. That she had most of the monks cowed, and had even prevailed upon the abbot to attend their suppers, only lent credence to Colin's belief that she should have been a man. He supposed that had she been, she might have been a match even for him.

And if that thought wasn't enough to give a man pause, he didn't know what was.

Agnes had embarked on her usual journey into madness. Despite having found Sir Etienne unresponsive to her ploys, she continued to pursue him with religious zeal. Colin had to admire her tenacity, it being a virtue he considered quite important in a knight. Now, if he could only persuade her to ply that virtue on an appropriate man. Colin had begun to wonder if their sire had as difficult a time finding a husband for her as he'd had finding a bride for Colin. Then again, marrying off a daughter would mean giving a dowry, which surely answered the mystery of that well enough.

Agnes would, no doubt, remain unwed until their sire was safely in his grave.

Of course, Peter hadn't been able to keep himself out of the fray either. He had apparently taken upon himself the role of comforter to any and all maids in danger of wedding his older brother. Colin had watched—more often than he'd cared to—as his brother had sat next to Sybil, holding her hand, handing her dry cloths to wipe her eyes, and whispering words of comfort in her ear. It wasn't possible that he was regaling the silly wench with tales of Colin's prowess. Nay, knowing Peter, they would be tales of Colin's supposed flaws.

Flaws he was certain were quite overstated.

And if all that weren't enough to drive a man to the lists permanently, that morn had heralded the arrival of none other than Sybil of Maignelay's parents.

Parents who had taken an immediate and thorough dislike to him.

He supposed, if he were to be completely honest, he could have been more gracious than he had been. Perhaps after such a journey, they had deserved more than a grunt and a "she'll beggar me to feed her" thrown at them on his way out to trample more vegetables.

All of which had left him where he was now, standing in the hot noonday sun in mud up to his ankles, doing his damnedest to teach his fledgling knight the rudiments of swordplay.

It had seemed the only thing he could do to save himself and the lives of his sorry siblings.

He contemplated what he needed to do next. Today was the first day of teaching Henri the most basic and simple of offensive strokes. He suspected it was going to be a very long day.

"Nay, nay, and nay," he said, stomping over and whirling Henri around. "You thrust this way. *This* way."

He put his hands over Henri's and showed him precisely

how the movement was to be accomplished. And as he did so, he was again impressed by how slight the lad was. That led to his pursing his lips over the boy's supposed age, and *that* left him with a mouthful of very fine, wispy hair.

It was, oddly enough, very soft hair.

And it smelled not unpleasant.

Colin realized, with the appropriate amount of horror, that he was actually beginning to lust after the boy.

He leaped back, wondering if this might be just the reason to place his sword hilt-down in the mud and fall upon it. Many souls had suggested the like to him over the years, but he'd never considered it.

He considered it now.

Henri had turned around and was looking at him as if he'd lost his wits.

"My lord?"

By the saints, even the lad's *voice* was pleasing!

Colin looked about him for somewhere to run, but saw no place. Mud, cabbages, and various and sundry other vegetables stretched out far into the distance. All running would earn him was more gold in the farmer's pocket for decimating his harvest. Colin had paid dearly enough for the little plot of ground he'd now trampled into compost.

"My lord Colin?"

Colin looked hard at the boy, peering at him as closely as he'd ever scrutinized another living soul. The boy returned his gaze steadily from eyes that would have made any woman proud. And those eyelashes! What lad could possibly be proud of those things that fair curled above his infinitely delicate eyebrows? Slight of frame, fair of face, gentle of expression, completely incompetent with a sword?

Colin felt a rush of pity for the boy. It was a wonder he managed to face each day, when those were his failings.

Colin turned his mind to searching out the slightest manifestation of manliness. He scratched his cheek absently as he considered the boy before him. Henri's face was dirty enough, he supposed. Likely far too dirty for any girl to have allowed. And his clothing was patched and mended scores of times. Nay, no wench would have stood for that. And the lad was wearing mail and at least sporting a sword—never mind that he could scarce wield it to save his own neck. Surely no woman would bedeck herself with that kind of gear.

Henri's stance was also growing more manly by the day, though he certainly had Colin to thank for that. It had taken hours alone for Colin to teach the lad how to draw his blade, hold his blade and put it back up. Teaching him how to walk like a man had been a constant and ongoing process that Colin wasn't certain wouldn't last him several more months. The poor lad. Colin could only speculate as to the circumstances in his family.

"Do you have sisters?" Colin demanded suddenly.

Henri blinked. "My lord?"

"Sisters, boy," Colin said. "And are they as pretty as you, or did you come away with the prettiness and they have the beards?"

The blood drained from the lad's face and he began to sway. Colin realized in an instant that he had hit upon a very sore spot. He reached out and shook the trembles from the boy.

"Never mind, lad," he said gruffly. "We make a fine pair, for you've all the handsomeness and I have none. I didn't mean to strike at your weakness. No doubt many over the course of your life have made sport of your, um, *delicate* features."

"Aye, my lord," Henri said, looking for a moment as if he were on the verge of tears.

Colin quickly sought a diversion to save the lad's pride. "For me," he said, rubbing his own less-than-delicate features, " 'tis quite the opposite. Not a soul looks at me that they don't comment on my ugliness."

"Well," said Henri, bravely putting his shoulders back, "I've seen worse."

Colin paused. "Have you?"

"Much."

"Hmmm," Colin said thoughtfully. "Indeed."

"Besides, what does a visage have to do with swordplay?"

Henri asked. "Fair or foul, it doesn't make up for a man's skill with a blade."

"Well spoken!" Colin exclaimed. *Finally,* a lad who understood where a man's true worth lay. Colin gave Henri an approving nod, then turned them both back to the business at hand. "It is as you say, Henri, so let us see to improving your skill. In time, you might make a passable swordsman."

"Thank you, my lord," the boy said, blushing beneath his dirt.

Colin, having happily resolved his unsettling feelings, turned his mind, also very happily, away from the tangle that awaited him back at the abbey, and concentrated on the business at hand.

O_f course, the pleasures of the afternoon didn't last as far into the evening as he might have wished. He was forced to play the host to Sybil's parents, and, worse yet, try to repair whatever damage he'd already done that morning to their finer sensibilities. The mother, the lady Isabeau, was easily appeased and seemed to find his gruffness amusing. She also spent a bit of time inquiring after Henri, which led Colin to believe that she had an overly tender heart and was given to caring for the runts of any litter. An admirable trait in a woman, he supposed.

Lord Humbert, however, seemed to be well-enough acquainted with Colin's reputation that he felt the need to prove that he wasn't intimidated. Colin passed a very long, very boring evening listening to the man's exploits and trying not to yawn too obviously. It was during one such tale of eternal length that he happened to look about the chamber and saw the lady Sybil doing something besides either feeding herself or fainting.

She was, oddly enough, staring at his brother, Peter.

The would-be monk.

Indeed, she was staring at him with the same intensity that she likely used for a particularly tasty sweet she couldn't wait to ingest.

Colin frowned. This couldn't bode well, though at the

same time he couldn't help but wish he were seeing something that might be possible. By the saints, what he wouldn't
give to deposit Sybil in someone else's arms!

A pity he couldn't find himself a woman with a few of
Henri's finer characteristics—namely a willingness to hoist
a sword and tramp about in the mud without complaining
about the condition of her shoes.

He studied Peter and Sybil and supposed he had no one
but himself to blame for this turn of events. Hadn't Peter
been slobbering over the girl's hand for the past three days?
Hadn't Peter been filling her ears full of foul reports of
Colin's fierceness? Who could blame the girl for looking for
a bit of sanctuary?

Much, the thought occurred to him suddenly, as Henri had
tried to do.

By the saints, was he so fierce then that he drove anyone
with faint hearts straight into priestly arms?

Well, let Sybil have her dreams whilst she could. The time
would come soon enough when she would have to step into
the fray like a man and put away her girlish fancies. She was
betrothed to *him*, like it or not. Besides, his brother was on
the verge of becoming a priest. What use had he for a woman
to clutter up his praying?

Colin felt someone breathing down his neck quite suddenly and he looked up in annoyance to see Sir Etienne hovering over him, his knife in his hand. Colin spared a thought
for the man's foolishness even as his own hand was striking
out to encircle the other man's.

"What do you?" Colin demanded. "Putting a knife so close
to another?"

"I was reaching for cheese," Sir Etienne said, looking none
too innocent. "By your leave, my lord."

Colin flung the man's hand away from him. "There's
cheese farther down the table that's good enough for you.
Seek it out there."

"My mistake," Sir Etienne said with a little bow. "Perhaps
Henri could show me where—"

"He'll do nothing of the sort. Be off with you, fool. Sit,
Henri. We'll finish our meal."

Out of the corner of his eye, Colin watched Henri sink back down into his chair. The lad's face was unnaturally pale and he looked to be on the verge of heaving up his supper. Colin took his wine and shoved the cup into the boy's hands.

"Drink," he commanded. "Breathe. If you puke in here, we'll be sleeping in the stables."

Henri nodded weakly and sipped at his wine in a most wenchlike fashion. Colin rolled his eyes and finished his meal as quickly as possible. Perhaps the best place for him was outside where he could drive a few more manly manners into the lad before bed.

He grunted at Sybil's parents as he pushed back from the table.

"Follow me," he threw at Henri over his shoulder.

He didn't look to see if Henri would obey. He could hear the light *pat-a-pat* of the lad's footsteps as he followed obediently along. Colin thrust open the door and stepped out into the cooling evening air. Aye, there was daylight enough for him to be about a bit more training before the sun deserted its post completely.

He was just choosing an appropriate spot for a little impromptu fighting when who should appear before him in a most unsettlingly unexpected fashion but that chief practitioner of shady arts, Berengaria. Colin folded his arms over his chest.

"I've no need of you. No improvement to my visage could possibly aid me at this point."

Berengaria smiled. "Your visage suits you as it is, my lord. I merely came to see how your heart fared."

"My . . . h-heart!" Colin spluttered. "My *heart!*" he repeated. "What could that possibly matter?"

"Does being a warrior mean you can't enjoy a little happiness as well?" she asked in that wistful voice that always set his teeth on edge.

"I haven't time for that," he said, gritting his teeth to keep them from aching.

"It might make you a better swordsman," she offered slowly.

"Ha," he said derisively. "What will make me a better

warrior is a bit more time in the lists. Now, move yourself, mistress, lest you force me to aid you."

"What of the lady Aliénore?" Berengaria asked.

Colin reached out to steady Henri, who had swayed suddenly and quite violently. He gave the lad a good shake, then turned to Berengaria. "Why does everyone persist in speaking of her?" he asked in astonishment. "The wench is dead!"

"Mayhap she isn't," Berengaria insisted. "Mayhap she needs aid."

He looked at her narrowly. "You've been having speech with Gillian. You women and your foolish, romantic notions. I have a notion and that is that if that gel from Solonge isn't dead, mayhap she should find someone to see to that for her."

"Now, my lord—"

He wasn't sure there were words in common use equal to expressing his displeasure—or his discomfort—with speaking on Aliénore of Solonge and her doomed flight from her home.

"She is dead," Colin said curtly, "and if she isn't, I hope her current straits are just recompense for what she did to m—"

He clamped his lips shut. Damned errant things. This was what a man deserved for letting his tongue run free from between his bloody lips. Too much babbling and the next thing he knew, he would be spewing forth the contents of his heart.

So he folded his arms more intimidatingly across his chest and glared down at the old woman before him.

And he did so silently.

"I'll say no more," Berengaria said pleasantly.

He grunted. She'd said far too much already.

"She might," the old witch mused, "aye, she might very well be in need of your aid, however." She looked at him in silence for a moment or two. "A rescue might be in order, my lord."

Colin snorted and so forcefully that he cleared his nose of several things that had been troubling it since his last trample through the farmer's field. He dragged his sleeve across his upper lip, nodded curtly to Berengaria, then motioned with his head to Henri for the lad to follow him.

A rescue? Ha! He would sooner climb to the tallest tower in England and do a jig on the roof.

But that name. Aliénore. It rolled sweetly over his tongue and seemed to travel upward and rattle quite often around inside his head. He couldn't seem to rid himself of thoughts of her, where she was, if she were dead or alive.

If she needed aid.

He clapped his hand to his head so forcefully, he had to blink aside a great pain above his eyes.

"Henri," he barked.

"Aye, my lord," Henri squeaked.

"Never speak to women."

"My lord?"

"Bed them. Get them with child. But never converse with them. Nothing good ever comes of it."

"I'll remember that, my lord."

Colin grunted. If only he were intelligent enough to take his own advice, he would be far better off.

But what if Aliénore did need aid? Who better than he to provide that aid?

"Draw your sword," Colin said, pushing aside his momentary weakness. "Let us see what you've learned."

Which, as it turned out, was more than Colin could have hoped for, but less than he would have liked. At least Henri's failings gave him something else to think on besides a foolish wench who likely had herself in the most perilous of straits with no one there to rescue her.

Leaving him, of course, to do it for her.

Damn her anyway.

He stared at Henri and noted that the lad was hoisting his sword without trembles, for a change. A pity this one had no sister, as pretty as he was and with a bit of his courage. Colin sighed and grasped his own sword a bit more firmly. Mayhap Christopher had it aright, that he didn't need a wife, he needed a squire.

Henri would be a damned sight less trouble than Sybil, to be sure.

Chapter 18

B erengaria stood near the abbey's infirmary, as near as she could come, of course, being a woman in a man's kingdom, and watched with interest the goings-on there. Nemain apparently had no compunction about going where she pleased. And judging by the look on the abbey's infirmarian, she would continue to be allowed to trample heedlessly over whatever rules and monks she found in her way. The poor man she faced didn't look as if he'd ever come across anything like her. Berengaria eased closer to listen. The saints only knew what Nemain was choosing to torment the man about today. Likely something that would see them all merrily on their way immediately if her tongue wagged freely enough.

"Haven't seen any nightshade in your garden," Nemain said sharply. "How can you brew a proper potion without a bit of nightshade to perk it up?"

"Ah," the monk said, his hand moving nervously to his throat.

"Horehound aplenty, but what good is that if you *want* the victim to bleed to death?"

"Um . . ." Both hands were now at his throat, as if he intended to protect it from whatever Nemain was brewing.

"And all these bloody roses," she groused. "As if any of you had need of a brew to woo a woman to your beds!"

The man began to look about him—for aid, no doubt. Berengaria took a step forward, hoping to stop Nemain's complaints before they grew too horrifying for the poor monk to tolerate.

Nemain sighed with apparent disgust. "I can see your garden's of no use to me." She fixed him suddenly with an intent stare. "But what of the woods hereabouts? What's in 'em?"

"In them?" the monk asked faintly. "Good woman, I know of nothing in them save trees and grasses and the like."

Nemain snorted. "I'm not talking of flora and fauna, you silly lad. I'm inquiring about things of substance. Faeries. Bogles. The odd sorcerer with both thumb-bones still on 'im."

The monk looked at her; his eyes rolled back in his head and he fell to the ground like a small tree after the axe had taken its final, fatal swing.

Nemain turned and looked at Berengaria with a scowl. "No spine, these lads. That's the second one who's fainted on me today."

Berengaria only smiled, gave Nemain a commiserating pat on the shoulder, then left her companion staring down at the fallen man of the cloth, shaking her head in disappointment.

She could only hope the monastery would survive their visit.

The hall was full of the usual souls, namely the lady Sybil guarded by her three handmaids, with young Peter of Berkhamshire kneeling at her feet, no doubt reassuring her that all would be well.

Unless he was, of course, reassuring her that he would find a way to free her from his brother's clutches.

Berengaria shook her head at that. The lad was nigh onto taking his priestly vows, but he looked more like a lovesick suitor. Perhaps that would be a better finish to Sybil's tale, given that Colin's former betrothed was certainly hale and hearty enough to be his bride.

She made her way out of the gates and walked down the lane, enjoying the sunshine and the smells of summer. Her girlhood had been passed in country such as this, and the fragrances she hadn't enjoyed in decades brought back pleasing memories of time spent in her grandfather's care, learning his trade.

Which, she had to admit, he had never been all that skilled at. All manner of brews for hurts and discomforts, aye. But anything else?

That had been her gift alone, she supposed.

She stopped along the lane and rested her elbows on the

rickety fence there. The entertainment in a very muddy, no doubt formerly quite fruitful, portion of a field was such that she couldn't not pause and watch. She wished somehow that she might preserve the sight for generations to come. Surely some grandbabe would enjoy watching his grandfather and grandmother hacking at each other with swords.

Actually, Colin was doing the hacking. Ali looked to be just endeavoring to stay on her feet.

But even to Berengaria's eye, her progress was clear. The lass had courage, to be sure, and determination. And a goodly mind, if her cleverness in remaining hidden so long told the tale true.

Now if Colin could merely remove the scales from his own eyes and see what stood right before him, the tale might finish up as it should.

Berengaria watched until she began to feel the need to find somewhere to sit. It was, fortunately for her aching feet, at that precise moment that Colin put up his sword, clapped a friendly hand on Aliénore's shoulder, then led her from the field. Berengaria met them at the gate and received a scowl from Colin.

"Come to bludgeon me with more advice?" he demanded.

"The saints forbid," Berengaria said with a smile. "I've said my piece with you."

He grunted at her, then looked at Aliénore. "Be careful what you listen to," he advised. "And even more careful what you drink, though I daresay Mistress Berengaria's brews wouldn't hurt you. And that Magda's you can smell from fifty paces. The other one, though," he said, shaking his head slowly. "Dangerous."

"I wouldn't brew our young one here anything foul," Berengaria promised. "Only things to heal his aches, that he might train even more diligently on the morrow."

Predictably, Colin was for anything that might lengthen any stay in his makeshift lists, so he nodded in approval, then looked at Henri.

"Come with me and take your rest," he said. "We'll be at it again after lunch. I cannot bear being in that hall longer than needful."

"Of course, my lord," Aliénore said, nodding.

"Might I have at the lad for a moment or two?" Berengaria asked. "Just to see if there might be a particular ache he needs seeing to?"

Colin frowned. "I don't like leaving him alone—"

"I can keep him safe," Berengaria assured him. "We won't be far behind you. Nothing untoward could happen between here and the guest hall."

"You would be surprised," Colin grumbled. "Very well, Mistress Berengaria. I assume if Sir Etienne comes near, you can spell him into leaving Henri be?"

Berengaria only smiled pleasantly, but that was apparently enough for Colin. He looked at Henri. "Do not wander. Follow behind me quickly. Keep your sword loose in its sheath."

"Of course, my lord," Aliénore said, with a nod.

Colin looked at Berengaria. "Perhaps you can brew the lad something to make him sound more like a man. Think you?"

"That might be," Berengaria said dryly, "a bit beyond my art. But I'll try."

Colin cast a final warning look at Aliénore, then turned and strode off toward the hall. He didn't stride as quickly as he might have another time, though. Berengaria watched him for a moment, then looked at Aliénore.

"He guards you well."

"For all the good it does me," Aliénore whispered. "Things simply could not be worse. Sir Etienne stole my coin, the monks think when I ask about nearby convents that I've rapine on my mind, and Colin intends to make me over in his image."

"Poor girl," Berengaria said, putting her arm around Aliénore's shoulders and walking slowly back toward the abbey. "Is there nothing I can do for you?"

"Tell me where the nearest priory is and provide me with false proof of a dowry," Aliénore said with a sigh. "Not that Colin would approve of such lying."

"And neither would you," Berengaria said.

"At this point, my lady, I'm desperate enough to do almost anything."

Berengaria stopped and turned Aliénore toward her. "Then

why don't you try the truth?" she asked quietly. "Give Lord Colin the tale."

"You and Jason have the same poor ideas," Aliénore said grimly. "I would tell Colin who I am only to have him immediately remove my head from my shoulders."

"I daresay he wouldn't."

"He vowed he would."

"I think," Berengaria said slowly, with a smile, "that his tender feelings were bruised."

Aliénore snorted in disbelief. "Tender feelings? There is nothing at all tender about the man."

"Well, you were the only one who merely bolted," Berengaria pointed out. "The rest at least gave some sort of excuse."

Aliénore paused. "They did?"

"Oh, aye," Berengaria said. "Issuance of blood from every orifice, symptoms of plague, sudden madness that rendered them unfit to say their vows." She smiled. "Some have been quite inventive."

"I don't know why I grieved him, then," she said darkly. "Surely he's accustomed to it."

"Aye, he unfortunately is," Berengaria said. "Can you imagine how it troubles him?"

Aliénore looked down and remained silent.

"He is gruff and fiercesome, true, but I daresay underneath he has a tender heart. If a girl had the courage to look for it."

"If a girl had the chance to look for it before he cleaved her skull in twain," Aliénore returned.

Berengaria smiled. "I would trust him, no matter what he'd threatened in the past."

Aliénore pursed her lips, but said nothing as she walked beside her. Berengaria breathed deeply of the pungent air.

"A lovely day, is it not?"

Aliénore sighed. "I wish I could enjoy it. I've too many things to fear, namely Sir Etienne."

"Sir Etienne will meet his own sorry end in time," Berengaria said. "Though I daresay he will cause you much grief beforehand."

"Does your sight tell you anything else?"

"Just that you cannot forever hide behind your sword," Berengaria said gently. "You can trust the truth. Lord Colin certainly does."

"He's fierce enough to weather the consequences."

"So are you, my dear. So are you."

"If only that were true," Aliénore murmured, then bowed her head and watched her feet as they walked.

Berengaria kept her own thoughts to herself, though she surely would have loved to have given voice to them. Aliénore would have to find her own path, though, and that path to the place where she would have enough courage to reveal herself would not be an easy one. A pity, though, she couldn't have seen the end from the beginning.

Ah, well, such was her own gift, and she supposed it was both a blessing and a curse.

But, for herself, she stole a glance at the future and was well satisfied with what she saw.

Did Aliénore but survive what was to come first.

Chapter 19

The day dawned bright and fair. Ali peeked out a window in the guest hall and wondered if she might actually have another tolerable day. The condition of the sky boded well for it. The day before had been passed happily enough with a goodly amount of training with her sword—and who would have thought she would come to enjoy that—a fine meal with the comfort of the lady Isabeau's presence nearby, and no hint of Sir Etienne doing anything foul.

Of course, he'd caught her eye a time or two as he'd stood near either Sybil or one of her ladies, but she'd only nodded in understanding, then turned away. She had decided that 'twas best to go along with him at present until she could divine a way to be free of him. Having him lean over Colin at supper, however, had been something else entirely. She'd felt a panic sweep through her, though she couldn't have imagined how he would have dared such a brazen attack. The saints be praised that Colin was the warrior he was. He'd made Sir Etienne look the fool, *and* he'd managed to yet again keep her from the man's clutches.

And now that the folk from Maignelay-sur-mer were there, she had hope that the torment might end soon. They would take Sir Etienne with them when they left and hopefully the tale would be finished. He would have her coins for his trouble and perhaps that would suffice him.

That he could still reveal her to Colin was unsettling, but perhaps by then Colin would be safely wed and not care who she was.

Perhaps.

Mistress Berengaria certainly thought Colin to be harmless. Ali wasn't sure she herself had the same faith in his ability to forgive. Then again, perhaps by the time Sir

Etienne had departed and Colin was saddled with Sybil, she would have already bid everyone a fond *adieu* and been well on her way to some other occupation.

Or mayhap she would find herself forever serving as Colin's man, passing her days learning strokes of offense, and endeavoring to walk, talk, and carry herself in a very unladylike fashion. A month ago, such a thing would have been unthinkable. That it sounded less repulsive by the day said a great deal about the sorry state of her life at present.

Before she could plunge herself into fouler humors thinking on the unpleasant prospects for her poor life, the door burst open and a monk suffering a case of very undignified excitement burst into the hall.

"They're here!" he shouted.

Colin frowned. "Who?"

"Your sire! His company! They've arrived!"

Ali looked quickly at Colin to judge his reaction. His visage had lost all expression.

Indication enough, she supposed, of his distress.

She stood back and watched as Reginald of Berkhamshire swept into the great hall with the haughtiness of a king. He deposited greetings upon Sybil's parents, then looked the rest of the company over as if they'd been nothing but errant servants loitering about on benches, neglecting their duties to him. He spared only a brief glance for Colin, but 'twas a glance of complete non-interest.

Ali looked again at Colin for his reaction, but saw none. Perhaps he was accustomed to this kind of treatment from his sire.

Pity for him welled up inside her. Had the man never known love from his parents? Even after her father had wed Marie, she'd known that deep inside him, he still harbored fond feelings for her. And her mother? Ali blinked suddenly. Those ten years of great love had given her a lifetime of comfort.

Poor Colin, had he not been blessed with that same comfort?

Perhaps 'twas little wonder he was as harsh as he was.

Soon the only person present with more bluster and arrogance than Reginald himself swept into the chamber. Ali watched in fascination as Ermengarde pecked her father into a semblance of compliance. He was shepherded into a chair, given food and drink, then he submitted with a surprising lack of irritation to being berated for having left her so long with such impossibly unmanageable company to see to. Ali wondered if Ermengarde had taken her mother's place at such an early age that Reginald had succumbed to her rather forceful ways simply because she'd worn at him so long.

Ermengarde saw the important members of the company, including her father, herself, and Sybil and her parents, seated at the high table. Colin was left standing at the side of the hall, his arms folded over his chest, the very lack of expression on his face warning anyone with any intelligence whatsoever that he was not to be toyed with at present.

For herself, Ali sought cover on the opposite side of the hall, using Jason as a shield. She had no desire to be anywhere near Colin when his father finally forced him to the altar. She had no doubt he would not go quietly. Thinking on the temper his bride would face that night was enough to make her knees unsteady beneath her.

Her pity for him aside, she found herself rather relieved she wasn't going to be that bride.

Once Reginald had eaten and drunk to his satisfaction, he called the company to order with an imperiousness that any monarch would have been proud to call his own. Peter and Agnes were brought to stand before the table.

"Agnes, my only command for you is to keep your knees together," he said bluntly.

"Papa!" she gasped.

"You may go," he said, waving her away.

"But Papa—"

"I've found no mate for you yet. Go, and endeavor to keep your virtue intact."

Agnes went, her face in flames. Ali stared at Colin's father, appalled yet somehow unsurprised by his lack of compassion. 'Twas no wonder Colin found himself at Blackmour instead of his father's keep of Berkham. She would have done the same thing, in his place.

Reginald looked at Colin. "Come. Stand here by your brother."

Colin gave his sire a look that should have made the man rethink his demand. Either Reginald was too old to fear his son, or he had more courage than anyone else in the hall, for he merely snorted with impatience and beckoned again.

"Now. I'll see the both of you before me."

Colin pushed off from the wall and sauntered across the hall. He stood next to his brother then folded his arms again over his chest.

"Finish out your drama, Father," he said coldly. "I've business to attend to this day."

"Indeed you do," Reginald said, "but likely not the business you think." He stood, smoothed down his tunic, then took up his cup, as if he prepared to regale them with tales far into the night. "Now, as you all might imagine, I have spent years trying to assure myself that my illustrious line will continue after my death. Unsuccessfully, so far," he added, with a withering look thrown Colin's way.

Colin didn't reply.

"And having despaired of ever finding myself with a properly wedded heir who would provide *himself* with an heir, I took it upon myself to assure myself of the same."

Ali wondered how it was that Colin could content himself with a mere sigh. His sire was insulting in the extreme.

"And so," Reginald continued, waving his cup benevolently toward the assembled company, "we find ourselves here, enjoying Harrowden's hospitality, conveniently near the appropriate marrying authorities."

Colin's sigh was rather gustier that time.

"The marriage contract did specify that the lady Sybil of Maignelay-sur-mer was to be wed with Berkham's heir," Reginald said, "and so she shall." He paused, apparently for the drama of it, though all eyes were upon him just the same. Then he set his cup down. "Peter, step forward."

Peter blinked. "Father?"

"Come forward, you witless pup," Reginald barked. "Come forward and claim your inheritance."

"But—"

"All I own!" Reginald said triumphantly. "The lady Sybil. The keep. All my gold, all my silver, all my baubles. Yours, the whole."

"What?" Colin thundered.

Ali looked at Peter to find that he was teetering rather substantially. He continued to sway until he'd swayed right into his brother. Colin held him away with a very stiff arm.

"You've lost your wits," Colin growled. "You cannot disinherit me."

"Peter will wed with Sybil," Reginald insisted. "And he will inherit my lands and gold."

"I'm a priest," Peter said weakly.

"Not yet, and not anymore," Reginald said briskly.

That, oddly enough, seemed to bring Peter out of his swoon. He stood up on his feet, slapped his hands on the table before him and put his nose near his sire's. Not too near, but near enough.

"I'm going to be a *priest!*" he shouted.

"They don't want you here."

"They do too!"

"I've ceased all monetary gifts to the abbey. Unless you've coin hidden in your robe, you're no longer of any interest to these mercenary brothers here."

Peter began to sway again. Ali didn't have long to wonder if Colin would help him. Colin did, by pushing him out of the way with such force that he sent him sprawling onto the floor.

"I will not accept this!" Colin bellowed, leaning over the table with his nose much closer to his sire's than his brother's had been.

"It isn't yours to accept," Reginald bellowed back. "I've waited until I'm fair in my grave for you to manage to keep a bride I procured for you and I'll wait no longer!"

"You won't have to wait any longer," Colin said, stepping back and drawing his sword. "I'll send you to your grave now!"

Reginald wisely took a pace or two backward. He glared at his son. "Slay me and you'll be hanged."

"If it means you're dead, I'll go to the noose happily!"

"The gel is for Peter, not you," Reginald said, looking about him—likely for possible exits from the hall.

"I'll have her myself, or die in the attempt!" Colin shouted.

And Sybil, predictably, pitched forward into the little mound of food she'd managed to place before herself on the table, in a dead faint.

"You have a betrothed," Reginald said, backing up and finding himself with no choice but to sit down in his chair. "Aliénore of Solonge."

Ali felt herself begin to sway. She understood completely Sybil's fondness for the practice. Fortunately, she had Jason's arm to keep her on her feet. She leaned against him, gasping for breath.

Her betrothal to Colin still stood?

What, by the saints, was she supposed to do now?

"I don't want her," Colin snarled. "Too great a coward to face her fate."

Ali swallowed with difficulty. Well, he certainly had her there. Perhaps he would solve her problem for her all on his own.

"I'll have that one there," Colin continued, gesturing down the table with his sword and causing everyone sitting on the other side to fall back with a gasp.

"You can't. She's sworn to Peter," Reginald insisted. " 'Tis in the agreement both I and her parents signed. If you want a bride, go find yours."

Colin put up his sword with such a great thrust, it came close to severing its sheath. "And then?" he demanded.

"Find the lady Aliénore," Reginald said, "and then we'll discuss the other."

Colin looked ready to tear out his hair with fury. He slapped both his hands on the table before him. "Does she," he said through gritted teeth, "have to be alive?"

Ali's knees buckled. Jason hauled her up with his hands under her arms.

"Steady," he whispered quickly into her ear. "Call attention to yourself now and the tale is finished."

Ali drove herself back against the wall with her knees straight and stiff, praying she could keep herself from pitching forward into senselessness in Sybil's accustomed fashion.

Had she ever considered taking others' advice to reveal herself to Colin, then bravely face the consequences? She'd been daft to listen to them! Telling him who she was was the very *last* thing she could ever do! He'd vowed to slay her two years earlier, and apparently, given what she'd just heard, he hadn't changed his mind about it.

Reginald cleared his throat and tugged on the neck of his tunic. "I would prefer you bring her back alive, of course—"

"But?" Colin asked.

Only a fool would have dared push him, Ali decided.

Only a fool would have dared deceive him.

And, lastly, only a fool would have wed with him.

His sire gulped. "Bring her as you find her. If you can find her."

"I intend to," Colin said curtly. "And when I bring her back, this foolishness will be over. Wed the lady Sybil to Peter and ruin both their lives. But you'll not take my birthright from me."

"Bring Aliénore back and we'll see," Reginald said.

Colin leaned over the table. "You'll not take my birthright from me," he repeated coldly. "You'll regret it if you do."

Reginald made blustering noises, but Ali didn't have the luxury of staying to hear them. Colin whirled around and looked about him. Ali wanted nothing more than to disappear behind Jason. Unfortunately, Colin's gaze fell upon her first.

"Henri," he barked, "you'll come with me. I'll need the diversion of training. And I daren't leave you in this nest of asps here."

Ali couldn't even manage a weak nod. Come with him? To look for herself?

Could things worsen for her?

"Jason, you'll come to guard my back."

Jason nodded, no trace of a smile on his face.

"Lest my sire think to send someone to slay me," Colin added. "That would be foolishly done."

Reginald huffed even more loudly at that, but Colin had seemingly finished speaking to his sire. Ali was ready to march out the door with him—if nothing more than to be more at liberty to flee—when she realized he wasn't finished choosing his companions.

"I'll need a guide," he said, looking about the hall. "That I might concentrate on other things—"

Sir Etienne threw himself forward. "My lord, I offer my aid."

Ali gasped. Nay, not him. He was the very *last* person she wanted to see any more of.

"You?" Colin asked doubtfully. "What know you of anything useful?"

"I know much of many things," Sir Etienne responded without hesitation. "And I can lead you quickly and safely to wherever you want to go in France."

Colin muttered something under his breath, then sighed heavily.

"Very well," he said. "You'll come along too." He swept his new company with a look. "To France, then."

"France?" Ali squeaked. "In truth?"

"We'll begin at the beginning," Colin said heavily.

"The beginning?" she wheezed.

"Solonge," he replied.

The saints preserve her, he was going to take her home.

"Aye," Sir Etienne boasted, "I can definitely lead you there. I've been there several times myself."

Ali stared at him in surprise. Had he ever been at her home? She searched frantically back through her memories, but emerged with nothing for her trouble. If she'd seen him before arriving at Maignelay-sur-mer, she didn't remember it.

But did that matter? Colin was going to her home and dragging her along with him.

And bringing Sir Etienne to be their guide.

It was a disaster.

"But, Sir Etienne," she began.

"Knows much of France, no doubt," Colin said briskly, "and often manages to hoist his blade in an almost intimidating fashion. Surely my lord of Maignelay-sur-mer won't mind loaning him to me for a pair of fortnights."

His lord of Maignelay-sur-mer was hiding behind his cup and didn't offer an opinion on it.

Ali didn't dare look at anyone who knew her secret to judge their reactions. She found herself with no choice but to pack her gear and follow Colin from the hall.

They were mounted and on their way sooner than she would have supposed possible. Either Colin was anxious to find her—which she doubted was the case—or he was in a fiery temper—which she decided was more likely—and had to do something to give vent to it. And flinging them forward on an adventure certainly seemed reasonable enough.

She looked back at the hall just before they turned for the gates. The witches were there, and Berengaria was smiling encouragingly at her. Sybil was there, clinging to Peter, damn her anyway. The lady Isabeau was there as well. She looked at Ali with tears in her eyes.

I'll pray for you, she mouthed.

Ali suspected it would take more than a single woman's prayers to aid her in this.

Then they were out the gates and on their way before she could count up in her head just how many prayers it might take for her to survive the journey without Colin killing her, Sir Etienne killing Colin, or her killing herself to avoid having to watch either of the other murders.

"Do you think," Sir Etienne asked suddenly, as if he truly were concerned, "that the lady Aliénore might still be alive?"

Colin only shrugged.

"And if you find her," Sir Etienne pressed on doggedly, "will you kill her in truth?"

Colin paused and looked at him. "Absolutely."

"I'm not opposed to bringing back a corpse," Sir Etienne offered cheerfully.

"Good, for you likely will be," Colin said shortly.

Ali closed her eyes and wished there were some clear path across the country, for she would have taken it and thrown herself on the mercy of the first band of ruffians she'd come across. The possibilities for her future were limited to just one.

Flight.

But how? When? With Colin watching her every move, with Sir Etienne dogging her steps, with Jason mother-henning her until she couldn't move that he didn't know it?

Her chance of finding a convent was gone. Her chance of being free of Sir Etienne was gone. Her chance of seeing Colin safely wed to someone else and thereby fully and finally releasing her from her contract was gone as well.

And if those weren't foul enough tidings for the day, she had another sea voyage to look forward to!

"Henri? Are you unwell?"

Ali looked at Colin and wasn't sure even how to form words that wouldn't immediately and fully alert him to her distress. Fortunately for her, there were souls about her who knew her secret and didn't mind offering her aid.

"Mayhap the lad has been to Solonge and offended the lord there," Sir Etienne offered. "He doesn't seem over-anxious to return, does he?"

Ali swallowed with difficulty and looked at Colin. "The boat, my lord. I fear the boat."

"Don't think on it, lad," Colin said with a grimace. "I know I won't until I have to. It won't last long, then we'll be about our business and back home before we have time to truly wallow in our misery. Of course, my misery will be a far sight less than yours, given my manly constitution, but there's nothing to be done about that." He reached over and patted her companionably on the back. "You'll survive the journey, Henri. I'll see to it myself."

Sir Etienne coughed quite suddenly and with sounds that greatly resembled chuckles.

Ali didn't dare look at him. She didn't dare look at Jason to see his reaction.

And she didn't dare look at Colin.

Or her betrothed, as he might be more commonly known.

The saints pity her, she was in just as dire straits as she had been before!

Perhaps if she returned to Solonge and threw herself at her

father's feet, he might be so relieved he would rescue her.

"Stay by me, Henri," Colin said quietly. "Always in my sight. I will keep you safe."

Ah, but who would keep her safe from him?

Chapter 20

Colin stood with his backside against the ship's railing and wondered how it was that a piece of wood so thick and well-constructed could feel as if it had all the firmness of silk. It seemed to buck and sway with every gust of breeze, with every swell and dip of the sea. Indeed, the whole of the ocean about him seemed to be nothing but a billowing surge.

Yet the captain seemed to be highly pleased with such a pleasant and uneventful crossing.

Colin turned and quite casually heaved up his guts over the railing. Then he resumed his nonchalant pose against the side of the deck, dragged his sleeve surreptitiously across his mouth, and looked about him to see if anyone had noticed his moment of weakness.

Nay, no one, not even the puking fool beside him who couldn't seem to do aught but clutch the railing and spill his insides into the aforementioned billowing surge.

Colin would have clapped a hand companionably on the lad's shoulder, but he knew his own strength. It would be just Henri's luck that Colin's gesture of camaraderie would be what flipped the boy over the side—though Colin suspected that at the moment, Henri would have considered that kind of death a sweet release from the torment he currently passed through.

He watched in sympathy and a goodly bit of amazement, both that the poor lad was so ill and that a lad could be ill for so long.

"No sea legs," observed a deckhand as he sauntered by in a most annoyingly comfortable fashion.

Colin would have sworn at him, but he wasn't sure he wouldn't be spewing forth more than words, so he contented himself with a fierce scowl thrown at the man's back. How was it these sea lads managed to acquire those legs they spoke of? He suspected that there had been a time when that man had been just as green as Colin and Henri were.

Or perhaps he knew that the voyage was soon to be over. Colin was certain they had been at sea for the better part of a day. He squinted into the setting sun and frowned. Surely it couldn't take more than a single day to travel from the upper coast of England to a convenient port in France. He vaguely remembered the journey not being so long the last time, but he'd also traveled from Dover then, and his haste had been greater. He suspected that his lack of enthusiasm for this particular quest was contributing greatly to the length of the journey.

He looked to his left to find that Henri's retching had subsided and he himself had subsided into a heap on the deck. Colin squatted down next to him and leaned over, just to make certain the lad still breathed. Aye, there was moaning aplenty, soft though it might have been. Colin heartily agreed with the sentiment, though not with the voicing of it. He was fast coming to the realization that he should view heights and the sea with the same amount of aversion. Should he manage to find the lady Aliénore, he would drag her back to England and never again set foot on a ship. If the wench had a desire to see her family, she could go on her own.

The thought of Aliénore sent another wave of nausea through him that had nothing to do with the ocean. By the saints, was he doomed to wander the earth forever, searching for errant brides until he was too old to enjoy his inheritance? He couldn't be so fortunate as to have found her dead and buried.

The only thing good to come of the past se'nnight was that he was now free of Sybil. That one would have never survived marriage to him anyway. Let Peter have her and see to her endless demands for sustenance.

A particularly nasty wave sent the ship heaving and Colin sprawling onto his backside. By the saints, how did these lads bear this? And how did Jason and Etienne bear it belowdecks?

He'd only managed to poke his head down the hatch

once—with the subsequent inevitable and disastrous results—
long enough to ascertain that Jason was sleeping the sleep
of the unrighteous and uncaring, and that Sir Etienne had
drunken himself into a stupor. And given that at that moment,
they'd only been at sea for a pair of hours, that was saying
something.

"W-where . . . are . . . we . . ."

Colin realized that the lump of rags next to him was speaking. He considered giving the lad the truth, then discarded
the idea immediately. No sense in making his misery worse
than it already was.

"Near France," Colin said. That was partially true. The
ship was near France. So was Scotland, on the right sort of
map. No sense in quibbling over details that would only
grieve the lad.

"The saints . . . be . . . oh, nay—"

The sentiment was cut off by Henri crawling up the railing
and heaving again. Unfortunately for the lad, there was apparently nothing left to rid himself of. He merely retched
miserably and quite futilely. Colin clapped his hand over his
mouth in reply and forced himself to breathe normally until
his gorge had subsided back down where it belonged, in his
manly nether regions. And when Henri was doing nothing
more than clinging to the rail and weeping miserably, Colin
pulled him back down by his tunic. Henri curled up and wept
a bit more.

Colin couldn't blame the lad, though he did raise his eyebrows—carefully, of course, lest he upset the delicate balance his humors seemed to have acquired just recently—at
the unmanliness of the sobbing. In fact, it sounded a goodly
bit like the kind of blubbering a woman would indulge in
when she was nearing the end of her tether.

Colin paused.

Indeed, it sounded a damned bit too much like womanly
weeping.

The lad stirred him himself from his rags long enough to
lay his head on Colin's leg and weep some more. Colin could
do nothing but stare down in horror at the boy, who seemed
to find him a perfect substitute for his mother. He was torn

between wanting to pat the boy on the head and itching to give him a healthy shove back into common sense.

But as he considered his alternatives, he realized that Henri's weeping was beginning to abate. Colin looked at his hand and watched as the traitorous appendage reached out and, with a gentleness Colin surely didn't know he possessed, patted the lad on the head.

The boy sniffled heartily a time or two, then seemed to fall quite suddenly and without hesitation into a deep and apparently blissful sleep.

The ship heaved again, but the only thing it did was to shift Henri so that his face was pointing skyward. Colin stared down at the creature using him so guilelessly as a pillow and wondered how it was that such a womanly lad had managed to get himself through so much of life with such unmanly features and unmanly attributes. He was surprised that someone hadn't beaten the delicate ways out of the boy long before now. It might have aided him in the lists.

Odder still that Henri had never really been in the lists.

Colin had never known a boy who hadn't been desperate to hold a sword in his hands, fling himself into his training, and thereby become a man, a warrior to be reckoned with. The only souls he'd known who weren't interested in such noble pursuits had been women—and even then he'd known a pair of them who weren't above either hoisting a sword or learning a few lethal moves with a knife. Henri was completely beyond the confines of his previous experience. A lad who didn't long for manly things?

Unless . . . the lad wasn't a lad at all.

Colin shook aside the thought before it began. The boy was merely overindulged and protected. Perhaps his mother had mothered him overmuch and left him with a permanent weakness. Perhaps his sire had wished for a daughter and poor Henri had been forced to fill that role.

Walk in her shoes, as it were.

A shaft of setting sunlight fell onto Henri's upturned face and illuminated features that no lad would have been proud to have called his own.

Many a woman would have, however.

Before Colin could stop himself, he had reached out and carefully poked at the lad's cheek.

Soft.

Too soft.

Taking his courage in hand, Colin dragged his finger with utmost care down the lad's cheek, checking for any hope of a beard, any sign however slight that there was a manly bit of adornment just waiting to burst forth and make its presence known.

There was . . . nothing.

Just a smooth face that rivaled young William of Blackmour's for softness.

Colin felt the truth descend with certainty, and with that certainty a heaviness that at once reassured him and terrified him. Sir Henri was definitely not what he seemed. He possessed innumerable feminine traits, not to his shame, but to his credit.

By the saints, the boy was a girl.

Colin spared a brief moment for a sigh of relief that his instincts had not failed him. He'd been lusting after a girl after all. The saints be praised he could still spot one, even when she was sporting mail and hoisting a sword.

But that sense of reprieve left him almost immediately. The boy with his head on Colin's leg was exactly what he seemed to be: a girl dressing up as a lad.

But if that was the case, who was she?

And why was she hiding in a mail shirt?

Worse yet, why was Etienne tormenting her?

The moment the last thought crossed his mind, Colin felt a rage sweep through him that left him shaking. He remembered vividly just how horrendous Henri had looked after his, nay, her beating at Etienne's hands.

Colin wished he'd killed the whoreson instead of merely roughing him up a bit.

That made him wonder further why Henri—and he would really have to come up with a better name for the girl—was so anxious to protect Etienne now. Did the man hold something over her?

Her identity, perhaps?

But why should that matter? The girl was very likely nothing more than a servant escaping a miserable life. At least Colin supposed that a servant could conceive such a plan, but this girl would then be like no peasant he'd ever encountered. Their worlds extended no farther than the boundaries of their fields. Most never went beyond their villages during the whole of their lives.

That this girl should not only have decided to flee, but also have stolen a knight's gear and had the cheek to try to pass herself off as a knight for the saints only knew how long, was something indeed. Colin looked down at her with the stirrings of admiration in his breast. Aye, here was a wench to be reckoned with, never mind that she couldn't save her life with her blade if her life depended on that skill.

Though, now knowing what she was, he supposed he could excuse a few of her failings. After all, few women knew which end of a sword pointed away from them. That Henri had actually learned that, and not only that but a few strokes of offense, said much for her skill.

But who *was* she?

Colin found himself brushing the hair back from her face with a gentleness that surprised him. Then again, the girl likely deserved whatever gentleness might come her way. What a life she'd had. How had she managed it?

He wondered how long she had been at Maignelay-sur-mer. Long enough to have become Sybil's keeper, obviously. Long enough to have been discovered if she hadn't been very careful—and very clever. That she hadn't only spoke more fully of her wit and courage. Why, it might even be a kind of courage and wit that he possessed himself. In lesser quantities, of course—for she was a woman, after all—but of that same ilk.

A pity he couldn't have found such a bride as this.

He pursed his lips and pushed aside that thought. His bride was likely buried in a shallow grave, or rotting under a pile of leaves in the forest, or, worse yet, alive and merely awaiting a rescue. It was she that Colin had to think on, she who held his birthright in her weak, cowardly hands. And it was she whom he would be saddled with for the rest of his days, did he but manage to find her alive and drag her back to England.

A pity, though, about the wench on his leg. *There* was the kind of woman he might have found himself bound to and not regretting it.

Would she consent to being a member of his guard for the rest of her days?

Though that would mean that he couldn't reveal what he knew of her. And what kind of life would that be for her? Forever in hiding, forever trying to be something she wasn't, forever likely wanting more than she had?

Well, however her wants and desires went, he could at least keep her secret for her. Aye, that was the thing to do. He could pretend that he didn't know what she was. Indeed, he could continue her training and see that she at least had some skill to go along with her ruse.

And he could watch Etienne more closely and see if he couldn't divine what it was the man held over her. Her being a girl instead of a boy was likely the answer to that, though Colin found himself quite curious to find out if there was more to it. Whatever the case, he would at least see if he couldn't keep Etienne from the girl and spare her any further thrashings.

Though now knowing what she was, he wondered if he could possibly stand aside.

He greatly suspected that Etienne would find *himself* in a shallow grave did he but raise a hand against the girl again.

How would the wench take to a bit of fighting that perhaps wasn't as noble and knightly as what Colin had been teaching her so far? He remembered vaguely promising Jason that one day the wench would be his equal, despite her slightness of frame. Indeed, he could make her that, but it would require time, and perhaps time was what he didn't have to give her. Nay, unchivalrous combat would be what he would have to teach her. He could put his finer sensibilities to the side for that long.

Her life might depend on it.

Then again, who was to say he wouldn't always be there to protect her?

He leaned his head back against the railing, rested his hand on the girl's shoulder, and closed his eyes.

A girl. But a truly marvelous one, to be sure. One he couldn't have, obviously.

What with the way his life was proceeding at present, he shouldn't have been surprised.

Chapter 21

A *li* came back to herself very unwillingly. She remained where she was, still, until she realized that the deck beneath her was no longer moving. She opened a very bleary eye and looked around her, wondering if she should be grateful she was alive or continuing to wish she weren't.

They were on a dock. The weathered wood was very steady beneath her form, gathered as she was in a heap by a goodly bit of baggage. Legs stood in front of her and she recognized the finely made boots on those legs as belonging to Jason of Artane. He bounced up and down on his heels every now and then, as if he were actually anxious to be off and doing. The motion made her nauseated, so she quickly closed her eyes and gave herself up to the luxury of being stood guard over.

The peace seemed to last for but a moment or two before she found herself being gently urged to awaken. She squinted and tried to make out the visage above her.

" 'Tis only me," Jason said cheerfully. "We're ready to be on our way. Do you think you can stand?"

"It would be a miracle."

He laughed, took her under her arms, and hauled her to her feet. Then he continued to hold her as the world around her spun violently. Ali was very tempted to continue her shipboard activity, but she couldn't bring herself to spew anything on the front of Jason's cloak. So she clamped her lips together, willed her stomach to settle, and tried to concentrate on determining just what kind of pattern that was on the brooch that held Jason's cloak at his throat.

"What is that?" she whispered.

"A dragon and his wee kit," Jason supplied. "You can no doubt divine who gave it to me."

"Your sire must quake at the sight."

"Aye, he does. But Christopher was once his squire as well, and a very beloved one. My sire begrudges him little."

"Well, the Dragon seems to have made you into something of a man," she conceded.

"As Colin will you," Jason said, with a twinkle in his eye. "Now, what sort of jewels shall we make up for you? A butcher's knife with a small dagger dangling next to it?"

She found it in her to glare at him.

He only grinned and turned her toward her waiting horse. "Mount up if you're able. I'll see to the gear."

It took her several tries, and in the end it was Colin who came by and casually tossed her up into the saddle without comment, but she was finally astride her horse.

And wishing greatly she were back on solid ground.

Unfortunately, there was nothing to be done about it. So she clung to the saddle and reins both to give herself something solid to hold on to, realized early on that closing her eyes only made the motion worse, and wondered if it would be unappreciative of her to pray yet again for a quick and painless death.

The morning dragged on with infinite slowness. They rode for what seemed several eternities laid end to end. It was a moment-to-moment struggle for her to simply keep herself in her saddle and not heave into the undergrowth beside the road.

At least the remainder of her seasickness took up most of her energy, leaving very little to use in thinking about the state of her affairs. Indeed, the longer she rode, the more certain she was that another descent into senselessness was not only inevitable, it was imminent. At least there, loitering in the blackness, she wouldn't have to give any thought to her future.

When she was certain she could stave off the darkness no longer, she wrapped her hands tightly in the reins, settled herself as firmly into her saddle as possible, and leaned her head against her horse's neck.

And she hoped that when she fell, Colin would get to her

before Sir Etienne could trample her under his horse's hooves.

S he woke only to realize that she was indeed no longer on top of her horse, nor had she been left behind. She listened to the voices around her, tramping down a brief flash of panic that those voices might belong to ruffians bent on robbing and otherwise harming a hapless, very ill girl in knight's gear. Nay, they were souls she had no trouble identifying.

That was Sir Etienne going on and on in his most boastful voice. Colin was snorting from time to time and Jason was idly plucking the strings of a lute. She kept her eyes closed, content to be wrapped up and resting near a fire.

Unfortunately, that enjoyment lasted precisely the space of three heartbeats, for 'twas almost immediately that she began to actually hear the words that Sir Etienne was spouting.

"I already told you I've been to Solonge many times," he was saying. "I can lead you there, as well as introduce you to the lady of the house, Marie."

"The lady Aliénore's mother?" Colin rumbled.

"Nay, her stepmother. But a fine woman, surely. After all, how many would take on a keep of that size, as well as six children that she did not bear herself, yet retain such fine humors?"

Who indeed? Ali felt a chill run down her spine. Just how was it Sir Etienne knew so much? Then again, she supposed Marie's identity wasn't much of a secret. The situation Marie had married into couldn't have been either. But had Sir Etienne actually been to Solonge to learn those things for himself, or was he merely a skilled eavesdropper in the local tavern?

She had no idea, for she couldn't have said if Sir Etienne had truly been to Solonge. She'd been forever in the solar, working at some task Marie had set her to, whenever there had been company below. Indeed, since Marie had come to the keep, Ali could count easily the number of times she'd been allowed to descend for supper. She'd usually had it brought to her in the solar, cold of course, by a servant who had filched a goodly bit of it on his way up the stairs. Complaining had earned her nothing but punishment, so she'd learned not to complain.

Odd, that her life now seemed actually much easier than her life had been then. Odder still that she had Colin to thank for that.

She had meals when she needed them. She had rest enough and ample chance to be outside in the goodly air. The work of war had even begun to please her as well. Finally, something she was actually good at. Indeed, there was something quite satisfying about having mastered something well enough that Colin would actually give her a single, brief nod of approval.

It was far preferable to the endless criticisms and the constant danger of living with Marie of Solonge. The few times Ali had tried to protest her treatment at her stepmother's hands, her father had brought Marie into his solar and asked her if Ali spoke the truth.

That had always resulted in another of those afternoons alone with Marie in a remote tower chamber—those afternoons Ali didn't miss.

"How long will it take us to get to Solonge?" Colin asked, interrupting her musings. "Jason, by the bloody saints, that's foul. Can you not pick out some tune my ears can recognize?"

"Songs to accompany brawls are not my forte, my lord," came the innocent reply. "I've confined my repertoire to ballads and other such tales of courtly love."

"It all sounds of screeching to me," Colin grumbled. "Now, Sir Etienne, your thoughts on the length of the journey?"

"With fair weather and no trouble, a se'nnight," Sir Etienne said. "No more. Unless the lad continues this disturbing weakness he's showing and we're forced to wait for him."

Ali wondered if it might be time to rise and stretch, just to prove that she wouldn't delay them, then she realized how foolish that was. Wasn't delay what she wanted? The longer it took them to travel to Solonge, the more time she would have to find a way out of her current plight.

Though what that way might be she couldn't have for the life of her said.

Why don't you try the truth? You can trust the truth. Lord Colin certainly does.

Berengaria's counsel came back to her as clearly as if she'd heard the words spoken in her ear.

Tell him the truth and weather the consequences?

She was beginning to wonder if she had any other choice.

She was quite familiar with another bit of truth, though, and that was that she could not return to Solonge, not even to beg for her father's mercy. He would never understand how dangerous Marie was until Ali was lying in her grave.

Victim of a very unfortunate accident, no doubt.

"So," Sir Etienne said, "what are your plans? Tell me of them and let me see if I can improve upon them."

More snorting ensued, then Colin spoke. "We'll go to Solonge and have speech with the lord there. And then I'll try to discover Aliénore's trail."

"A waste, if all you plan to do is kill her in the end anyway."

"I will search. Perhaps the lass is merely in need of aid."

"I doubt that," Sir Etienne said with his own snort. "She's likely flat on her back with any number of soldiers, whoring her way across France."

Ali did open her eyes then, for Colin had leaped to his feet and his sword rang out as he drew it.

"That is my bride you speak of," he said, glaring down at Sir Etienne.

Ali wondered what Sir Etienne would do, but she didn't have to wonder long. He was staring at her pointedly, then a small smile came over his face.

"Well," he drawled, looking up at Colin with no fear on his visage, "I never would have said it had Henri not said it to me first. 'Twas his opinion of the good lady, you know."

Ali sat up with a start, sure that Colin would run her through for the insult. But he didn't look at her. Instead, he thrust home his blade and resumed his seat. He looked at Sir Etienne coldly.

"If he said the like, which I very much doubt he did, he

can be forgiven the insult. He is young and inexperienced. You, as a man of goodly years, should know better."

"Will you demand satisfaction from me?" Sir Etienne asked, putting his hand over his heart and blinking in feigned surprise.

Ali couldn't breathe. The moment Colin drew his sword again she would be finished. Sir Etienne would blurt out her sorry tale as he parried—of that she was certain.

Colin pursed his lips. "Not this time. But watch your words, sir knight, lest you not find me so lenient again."

Sir Etienne looked as if he had just stuffed himself full at a banquet table. The expression of satisfaction was almost more than Ali could bear. Would that Colin would teach her enough that she might slay this fool and spare them all the misery of any more of his company.

"A decision well made," Sir Etienne said. "Especially since 'tis Henri who should suffer for the insult."

Colin pointedly ignored him. "Draw you here in the dirt a map I can follow."

Ali lay back down uneasily. Colin obviously hadn't believed Sir Etienne's lies, which meant he was better at spotting a liar than she was. The saints only knew why he hadn't seen through her subterfuge sooner. Perhaps 'twas as Jason said: As long as she held a sword in her hands, he wouldn't look closer than that.

She vowed to hold her sword in her hands as often as possible from then on. If nothing else, it would keep Colin's attentions focused elsewhere. To be sure, it would improve her skill and she very much suspected that such skill would be her only means of obtaining her freedom. At the very least, she could protect herself against Sir Etienne and that was nothing to dismiss.

Because until she managed that, she would be protecting *him* against Colin.

She closed her eyes and let talk of roads and inns and places to avoid wash over her. She had best take what rest she could have, when she could have it. The road before her had taken on a decidedly sinister turn—and that more than just the fact that if they continued south, they would eventually have to head east.

To Solonge.

Back to Marie's lair.

So Colin could begin his search for his errant bride.

Ali struggled to peer into the future, just to see how the sorry tale might possibly play out. A pity she had none of Berengaria's sight. It would have aided her immensely to know if she should just pull forth her blade right now and fall upon it, or if she should wait for Marie or Sir Etienne to end her life for her.

She entertained such black thoughts until dawn was breaking against the shadows of the little glade where they'd made their camp. And during that long night, she decided nothing useful, except to accept the fact that she very well might lose her life at Marie's hands some time in the next fortnight. Perhaps it would behoove her to make peace with God.

Or perhaps she should just awaken Colin and tell him who she was. He could kill her right then and it would be done with. Then she could return as a ghost and haunt Sir Etienne for the rest of his days.

And the possibility of that was enough to bring her up to her elbow, the truth on her lips. She reached over to shake Colin's foot, then froze.

Sir Etienne stood above him with his sword at Colin's throat.

Ali didn't have to hear him speak to know exactly what he was thinking.

See how easy it would be?

But before she could either nod or weep, there was a ring of steel and Colin was quite magically on his feet with his own sword at Sir Etienne's throat.

Sir Etienne's blade was, amazingly enough, no longer in his hand.

"You should be more careful where you allow your blade to linger," Colin said coldly.

Sir Etienne bowed deeply. "My apologies, lord. I am perhaps overtired and careless."

Ali couldn't swallow. She certainly couldn't speak. All she

could do was stare into Sir Etienne's angry eyes and wonder if this might be the time in which he actually made good on his threat and blurted out her name.

She was saved from that by Colin putting up his sword.

"Finish your watch," he said briskly. "We'll rest until you return, then be on our way."

Sir Etienne bowed again, an ingratiating bow that spoke more of mockery than deference, then melted back into the shadows.

Ali watched as Colin sat down and threw a handful of twigs onto the fire to bring it back to life. She felt as if she should say something, but she couldn't. She half feared that if she said anything at all, it would turn into a confession and then where would she be?

Dead.

After all, Colin wasn't above carrying a corpse back to Harrowden. He'd said so himself.

"How do you fare?" he asked suddenly, looking at her from under his eyebrows. "Feeling better?"

She blinked in surprise at the concern. "Well, aye," she said, feeling rather unbalanced. There she'd been imagining how easily he would kill her, yet he was asking if she was well? Would she ever understand the man? "Thank you," she added.

"We'll stop early so we can train for a bit this afternoon."

"As you wish, my lord."

He nodded, then poked at the fire in silence. Ali watched him and realized, with a start, that while he could never be called handsome, he had a certain look about him that wasn't overly unpleasant. And the man certainly could defend himself, even when half asleep. Sybil certainly could have done worse.

Such as being wed to a would-be priest who likely couldn't tell one end of a sword from the other.

Ali rubbed her hand over her eyes and tried to clear them of the sight of Colin leaning over the fire, his face set in grimly serious lines, his sword by his side. Was it possible that she was actually finding him less than terrifying? Or had too much sea travel finally rid her of what few wits she possessed?

Or was she actually valuing the fact that her betrothed was the fiercest man she had ever seen? And not completely unpleasant to look at? And, on occasion, showed what a more foolish maid might have called kindness?

A movement startled her and she looked over Colin's head to see Sir Etienne lurking at the edge of the trees.

And she read the message in his eyes clearly enough.

Tell him and you'll both die.

She looked back at Colin. He had turned his head just the slightest bit toward Sir Etienne, so she was fairly certain he knew who lurked at the edge of the firelight. But he showed no sign of distress or nervousness. That reassured her somewhat, but not completely. The man couldn't stay awake and alert continually. There would come a time when Sir Etienne could have Colin at his mercy. And that she couldn't allow.

She wondered what Colin would say if she told him that what she did was partly to protect him.

Likely give her that look she'd seen before, the one that said he couldn't quite believe that anyone could be so ridiculously foolish. Him, the powerful and invincible Colin of Berkhamshire, in need of aid? Ha!

Yet aid he would need and it fell to her to give it to him, even if he never knew she did. She suddenly found herself cursing the hours that remained between dawn and the time Colin would teach her more swordplay. The more she learned, the more quickly she learned it, the easier it would be to see to Sir Etienne herself, and then he would have nothing more to hold over any of them.

Not Colin's life. Not hers. But perhaps his own.

Aye, Sir Etienne would not like what Colin made her into.

If she only could obtain enough time to let Colin manage it. Colin rose suddenly and she felt a wave of unease sweep over her. By the saints, would the man never cease to startle her? She concentrated on breathing in a normal fashion, as if it were an everyday occurrence to have a man standing over her quite suddenly, looking for all the world like an avenging god.

Why, the man could slay her merely by stepping on her!

But what fell on her was not his heavy boot, but rather a heavy blanket.

"Thought you might be chilled," Colin said gruffly, then turned and returned immediately to his place, taking his sword and beginning to sharpen it with great diligence.

Ali fought the urge to gape at him in amazement. Had he just given her a blanket, had he just stretched his black soul to do something nice for her, or was she caught in some inescapable web of foul imaginings?

So many conflicting thoughts swirled about in her head, she began to feel as queasy as she had on the ship. Colin and his sudden kindness, Sir Etienne and his wickedness, Marie and her sharp knife, she herself and her confusion about what she should do. It was enough to make her want to pull Colin's very warm blanket up over her ears and sleep until everything sorted itself out.

She was sure of nothing except that, despite her better judgment, she was beginning to trust the Butcher of Berkhamshire.

The saints only knew where that would lead.

Chapter 22

There were foul deeds afoot. Colin had a keen nose for trouble, and the stench of this rivaled, well, himself on his worst day. And most of the stench seemed to be coming from Sir Etienne's direction.

Never mind that the man had almost slit his throat—and quite intentionally, to Colin's mind. And never mind that he was tormenting young Henri for reasons Colin had yet to determine. What annoyed him no end was the fact that the man couldn't find east if his life had depended on it. Colin was presently regretting mightily his decision to allow the man to come along. Never mind that the man was a true Frenchman. Where was the advantage to that when his manners were atrocious, his personality intolerable, and, again, his sense of direction nonexistent?

It had taken them more than a se'nnight to come this far southeast, and that only because Colin had known where they were going. Had he been relying on Sir Etienne to lead in these matters, they likely would have been in Spain by now and scratching their heads over how they'd gotten there.

The only good to come of the past seven days was the opportunity to train Henri. Mayhap 'twas for that reason that their progress had been so poor, but Colin couldn't complain about it. He'd wanted the time to teach the girl something useful and he'd taken it without hesitation. She was making decent progress and that pleased him.

Of course, that goodly mood had lasted for him only until the rains had begun—and continued without abatement for the past two days. He'd finally decided that he had no choice but to seek shelter. And that had led him to the place where he stood at present, staring at the inn before him and wondering if he dared enter.

The Swinging Bucket. Colin had swung the bucket before—actually, he'd swung *from* The Bucket's sign over the
door in a very fine and noteworthy escape from French soldiers—and found himself quite unwelcome to come back for
another dip.

But rain was coming down in, aye, buckets, and there
seemed to be little they could do besides either seek shelter
here or catch their deaths from the ague outside. Colin pulled
his hood up around his face and looked at his companions.

"Do not announce yourselves or your business," he said
sternly. "We're carrying a message to Solonge. Nothing
more."

"Four of us?" Sir Etienne asked politely. "It must be a
very important message."

Colin knew that the only reason he hadn't loathed Sir
Etienne fully on sight was that he'd been distracted by other
things. But now he'd had nigh onto a month to let that feeling
swell within his breast. The man needed to be taught a lesson.
And Colin would happily do the teaching, after they'd arrived safely at Solonge. That should take them but a handful
of days more. Less, if they rode hard. He would then make
the man think twice about venturing forth from his bed, then
employ some other guide and have no more need of Sir
Etienne.

That day couldn't come soon enough, to his mind.

But those pair of days might also give him time enough
to discover what it was that Sir Etienne held over Henri's
head and that would be time well spent. How long had that
been going on? And how in the bloody hell had he been so
distracted that he hadn't noticed it sooner?

Well, having his life fall apart around him was one reason.

Discovering that his new guardsman was a woman was
another.

Perhaps he could be forgiven his lack of concentration,
given the circumstances. But no more. He was determined to
discover Sir Etienne's foul secrets and rid himself of the man
as quickly as possible, especially after that feeble attempt on
his life. He'd been awake long before Sir Etienne had come
to stand over him with his blade bared, so he certainly hadn't

been caught unawares. But that the man should dare such a thing was what troubled him.

What was the fool about, anyway?

Well, there would be time enough for those answers. He certainly wouldn't have them if he were dead from exposure. Colin took a deep breath and ducked beneath the doorframe.

Apparently they weren't the only ones seeking shelter that night. The common chamber was full to overflowing with wet, steaming bodies. Colin espied a table in the far corner and made his way as unobtrusively as possible to it.

The innkeeper's gel arrived soon enough and Colin felt fortunate that she wasn't one he recognized.

A meal was provided without delay and Colin set to with his usual manly gusto. Out of the corner of his eye he watched Henri eat and wondered why it was he'd been blind for so long. Why, even the way the girl fed herself left no doubt of what she was. She ate heartily, true, but without the grunts and snarls of most men when they were fair to perishing from hunger. Even Jason, who Colin had to grudgingly admit possessed all those manners that Gillian seemed to find so important, had a certain thoroughness and single-mindedness when it came to filling his belly. Even if he didn't use the table's cloth to wipe his mouth afterward.

Colin looked for a tablecloth, but finding none, used his sleeve. That's what the damned things were for, anyway. What else was he supposed to use? His neighbor's sleeve?

"What're you scowling about?" Jason asked, taking an elegant sip of his ale. "The fare not suit you?"

" 'Tis adequate," Colin replied. "I'm just thinking on those ridiculous rules Gillian has for a man at table and wondering how it is you manage to follow all of them while not looking remotely like a woman."

" 'Tis my gift," Jason said modestly.

" 'Tis damned annoying," Colin grumbled. He looked at Henri. "Don't you agree, lad?"

Henri mumbled something unintelligible.

"We're men," Colin pressed. "Our duty is to fill our bellies with as little delay as possible. Who needs a spoon when you've two good fists and you know how to use them, eh?"

Henri delicately dabbed her lips with some kind of cloth she'd produced from the saints only knew where. "Of course, my lord," she said, nodding. "Bloody hell!"

Colin choked and had to pour himself several cups of ale before the choking subsided. Why, the girl wasn't a servant. No servant would have those manners that Gillian was so damned particular about. This wench could be nothing less than a highborn lady in disguise. But what in the world could be so terrible that it would send a highborn wench fleeing into hose and mail?

Colin watched Henri—or whatever her name truly was—finish her meal. Gillian, he thought with a scowl, would have been fully satisfied with her comportment. He found himself less impressed by that than by the depths of her green eyes and the fairness of her face. He could hardly imagine anyone, especially a parent, lifting a hand to one such as she. Even with her shorn hair falling about her face, and that face liberally smudged with the saints only knew what, she was exceedingly lovely. Did he but have a daughter such as she, no task would have been too much, no luxury too expensive, no whim too ridiculous for him to have seen to.

And had his own girl been stolen . . . well, the saints pity the fool who dared the like.

But perhaps this girl didn't have the benefit of a sire such as he would have been to her. Mayhap her sire was cruel. Or mayhap he possessed a cruel wife. Colin could readily see how a woman might have been jealous of such a one as this. But what a woman that had to be, to have given birth to this creature, then fostered a hatred in that same breast that had given the girl life. Colin, who had seen many terrible things over the course of his life, simply couldn't fathom that.

But did the mother hate the girl thusly, or the sire for that matter, 'twas entirely possible that she could have betrothed her to the most loathsome man she could find. And 'twas also quite possible that this girl had found flight to be the only acceptable course of action for herself. But who could be so loathsome that a girl would choose a life as a boy to escape him?

No one came to mind.

He looked around purposefully and the jug was summarily deposited before him. He finished it without further ado. Fortunately for him, he could drink numerous divisions of the French army under the table and still walk away with a clear head, so the drink did nothing but restore his wits to him. Unfortunately, it didn't ease his heart.

"We should seek our beds whilst there are beds to be had," he announced. "And tomorrow, Henri, we will train. Perhaps spending another day or two here waiting out the weather will do us all good."

"And your identity?" Sir Etienne asked innocently. "Was there a reason we were to be silent about it?"

"A little scuffle," Colin said, waving his hand negligently. "But one I wouldn't want to repeat. Neither would you. You might bruise something and then where would we be?"

He watched as Sir Etienne threw Henri a glare and a look that contained something else. A warning? Colin sat back and wondered what Henri would choose to do. Protect Sir Etienne, no doubt.

Which she did, by trying to distract Colin to other things.

Colin listened to Henri babble something about baggage and horses and the like, then turned back to Sir Etienne. "I didn't have your answer. How would you fare in a brawl of that size? Poorly?"

"My lord," Henri said, leaping to her feet and upsetting her ale. " 'Tis late and I'm feeling quite ill all of the sudden. Our beds, aye?"

Colin looked at Sir Etienne and saw the satisfaction cross the man's features. And he vowed again to discover the depths of whatever it was the man held over Henri.

And then repay him for it.

"You're right, Henri," Colin said, rising and stretching. "You've need of rest after our journey. Let us be about the business of bedding down for the night. Come with me and we'll see to the horses." He looked at Jason and Sir Etienne. "See to yourselves and keep your mouths shut. I'd like decent bed and board for a day or two here."

Without waiting for their responses, he left the common

chamber and walked out into the wet. Rain didn't trouble
him. They surely had enough of it at Blackmour, and he was
well accustomed to training in it all through the year. But
Henri, well, who knew where the girl was truly from? Perhaps she didn't have much rain where she had been raised.

"Pull up your hood," he instructed. "Keep your head dry."

"Aye, my lord."

In the dark, where he could scarce see her face, much less
her shape, he had no trouble divining that she was a girl.
Why hadn't he noticed either by the full light of the sun? By
the saints, he'd been blind!

He'd been distracted by the thought of wedding Sybil of
Maignelay—that was it. And there was his intense irritation
with his sire to consider as well. Surely he could be forgiven
his blindness, in light of those things.

He saw that their mounts had indeed been housed as promised, stole a look or two at Henri by the light of the stable
master's candle, and couldn't help a small bit of marveling
over her intense beauty.

The saints preserve him.

"To bed," he announced suddenly before he did something
foolish, such as continue to gape at her.

"But, my lord, I've . . . um . . . I need to—"

He frowned. Letting her out of his sight was something he
had little liking for, but it wasn't as if he could shadow her
every moment. Especially when she had things to see to.
Womanly matters and such. She opened her mouth to elab-
orate, but he held up his hand quickly.

"Say no more," he said. "You've needs to attend to and
want privacy. I'll wait for you outside the gathering chamber.
Have you your knife at the ready?"

She gulped and nodded.

Much as he might like to, he could do no more for her
than that. Surely she could manage a trip to a bush without
getting into mischief. He walked away, wondering how she'd
managed to see to her body's needs for so long without
having been detected. He couldn't imagine himself doing the
like. A day, perhaps, no more, then he would have been

scurrying for the first handy tree and damning whoever cared to watch.

One thing he could complain of: She took her bloody time about the whole business. Colin waited until he decided that perhaps she had either fallen into a hole or been overtaken by foul forest creatures. He walked silently back to the stables, peered about the building, and then saw what he'd actually suspected deep in his heart.

Henri and Sir Etienne in deep conversation.

Never one to announce his presence when a goodly bit of eavesdropping might yield more information, he crept around the stables until he could hear clearly what was being whispered.

"I told you, you foolish twit," Sir Etienne whispered harshly, "to keep him from me!"

"I've tried!"

"You'll try harder, or you'll pay the price."

"Why don't you stop provoking him—"

A slap echoed in the stillness of the night.

Colin was halfway around the building before the thought to move crossed his mind. He stopped just in time, took a deep, silent breath, and then eased back into the shadows, sliding his sword back into its sheath. He was surprised by the ferocity of the rage that swept through him. How dare the wretch lift a hand against the girl! Colin stood in the shadows, shaking, and fought to gain control of himself.

He could rush forward and defend Henri, aye, but to what end at this moment? Much as he might want to, he couldn't kill Sir Etienne for a mere slap.

But he could kill him for something more serious. He could kill him did Sir Etienne find the courage to challenge him for some slight. He could also bide his time, learn what Sir Etienne held over Henri's head, and then slay him in good conscience for that no doubt unsavoury blackmail.

He let his breath out slowly and forced his hands to unclench. Aye, he would wait. And he would allow Henri a normal amount of freedom. He could easily keep the girl within arm's reach at all times, but that would make Sir Etienne suspicious and ruin any chance Colin might have of catching him about some goodly bit of mischief.

Of course, that didn't mean that he wouldn't be three paces away from Henri at all times, lest the girl need aid.

Aid he would happily deliver.

"You listen, woman," Sir Etienne said calmly, as if he hadn't struck her but a moment before, "and listen very carefully. If he touches me, you're finished. I'll see to that myself."

Henri's answer was a whimper.

"And as for our other business, when I've decided what it is I'll have from you, you'll know."

And with that, the man turned on his heel and strode away.

Colin stared after him, then looked at the girl he'd left behind, the girl who was now quietly weeping, and found that he had absolutely nothing to say. Other business? What other business? And what a woman Sir Etienne was, to force a girl to protect him! Colin's disgust for the man, which had run deep enough before, reached new lows.

And poor Henri! Not only the burden of pretending to be what she wasn't, but the added weight of having to guard Sir Etienne.

He watched as she shook herself, straightened, and put her shoulders back. Then she turned and started back toward the inn.

Colin swiftly made his way back there and was waiting by the front stoop as she crossed the courtyard. He pushed off from the wall with a negligent move, then folded his arms and looked down at her.

"Finished?" he asked pleasantly.

Her tears were gone and she wore a decidedly determined expression on her face. "Aye," she said firmly.

What a wench. Colin was hard-pressed not to either clap her heartily on the shoulder or haul her into his arms and give her a squeeze that might break a few things. He could scarce believe that she wasn't blubbering, but nay, her eyes were dry.

Her cheek, however, bore the print of a hand.

Colin realized how terrible his expression must be when he saw Henri's eyes widen with unease.

"I was," he announced, "thinking on past battles and a few very unpleasant foes. Nothing to do with you."

"Oh," she said, looking vastly relieved. "I hurried as quickly as I could."

"Of course you did." He paused. "I think," he said slowly, "that we should be at our training at first light. What think you?"

"Absolutely, my lord."

By the saints, the woman had the courage of a man. "Stay by me, Henri," he said. "I have found that there are many dangers here in France. You'll likely want to meet them with me guarding your back, think you?"

She looked so damned grateful that it almost made his eyes sting. But it was gratitude mixed with determination, and he found that he was almost as overcome by that as he had been by anything before in his life.

By the saints, the woman was exceptional.

He paused and considered. He couldn't be fortunate enough to find Aliénore of Solonge already wed, could he? Then again, if she'd eluded him this long, couldn't she be persuaded to elude him a bit longer? Perhaps he could pay for putting her in a convent himself, then wed where he chose.

He pushed aside those thoughts. He would face them when he arrived at Solonge and took stock of the situation. For now, he would admire the wench standing before him and not begrudge himself pleasure of it.

"Come, Henri," he said. "We'll make an early start of it tomorrow, aye?"

She nodded and he could have sworn he saw a faint smile cross her face.

He slung his arm around her shoulders—her very slight, very brave shoulders—and led her into the inn.

Chapter 23

The morning was wet, dark, and gloomy—perfect weather for learning the true business of death. Ali faced her sword master and found herself for the first time doing more than just mirroring his strokes, or standing next to him and trying to copy them. She was actually crossing swords with him.

And her head was still atop her shoulders.

Each clash of her blade against his rattled her very bones, but she found, after a bit, that it didn't trouble her. Nor was she troubled anymore by sore muscles. Indeed, lifting her sword came easily to her now, and all those hours she'd spent practicing each stroke provided her with a goodly repertoire of things to use against Colin as they parried.

She found herself smiling in spite of the rain.

"I will," Colin said suddenly, "now come at you as if I intended to slay you. Slowly, of course, and you can trust that it is with no malice. 'Tis but for practice."

Ali braced herself for the worst, but it was only as he said. His strokes were slow and sure, and she was easily able to identify what he intended to do before he did it. Still, she could see why men quailed at the thought of facing him. He was enormous, his sword was enormous, and just the sight of him coming at her—albeit slowly and with no malice— was enough to make her want to drop to her knees and plead for mercy.

Or it might have been, had she not been able to keep him at bay.

It was tempting to permit herself the same look of arrogance that Colin usually wore when feeling quite pleased with himself.

She looked at him to find that he was regarding her with

supreme satisfaction, as if he were actually pleased with what she was doing.

And that, to her surprise, was almost enough to bring tears to her eyes.

Quite suddenly, she found his warm, callused hand surrounding hers that held her blade, and his face not but a pair of hand's breadths from her own. She had to tilt her head back to look at him, of course—he was huge, after all. But as she looked into his dark eyes, she realized how easy it would be to drown in those pools.

And, for the first time ever, she felt absolutely no fear of him.

"You have," he said quietly, "done well."

He was holding on to her sword hand, so she was forced to fan herself with the other hand. She tried to do it as unobtrusively as possible.

"Think you?" she squeaked.

His eyes crinkled the slightest bit, as if a smile might have considered coming forth had it not been Colin of Berkhamshire's visage to wear it, and then he nodded just the slightest bit.

"Aye. Now, you must think on what you can do with this skill. You can always protect yourself, from any enemy. The more skill you have, the safer you will feel. And then, when the time comes that you have an enemy you must slay—and that time will come, believe me—you will have the skill to do so."

She looked up into eyes that were still a mossy shade of green with brownish mud near the center and couldn't help but wonder who it was that he had killed over the course of his years, who drove him to the lists every day, why he had trained himself to be the kind of warrior he was.

"Who is your enemy, my lord?" she asked.

He shrugged. "I've had many."

"Who drove you when you first began your training?"

"Can you not guess?"

It wasn't hard. "Your sire."

"Aye. I daresay you can understand why."

She smiled. "Aye, I can."

He looked down at her for a moment or two, then abruptly released her hand and stepped back a pace. "You have your enemy as well. Think on him should you need inspiration to fight well."

She didn't think she needed any more inspiration than the mere thought of Sir Etienne and his callous slap the night before, but she would take Colin at his word. And when he stepped back and raised his sword, she no longer thought of him and his reputation. She thought of herself and whom she might face in the future.

And how desperately she wished she could humiliate him.

"Now, let us be about this business with a bit more seriousness and see if you can bear it."

Ali gulped as he came at her with quite a bit more seriousness. His first few strokes rattled her bones and shook the teeth in her head. Her hands stung. Her arms ached from the force of the blows.

But she didn't quit.

Neither did Colin.

He merely continued to swing his sword at her, slicing, cutting, thrusting. And she found, to her continued surprise, that she was able to fend off his attack.

Perhaps she had found something she could master after all.

That it was swordplay shouldn't have surprised her in the least.

When her arms began to tremble from weariness, Colin pulled his sword back and resheathed it.

"Enough," he said. "Now we will move on to other things."

Ali managed to get her sword home before she looked at him in surprise. "Other things?"

"Knife work."

The saints preserve her. "Knife work?" she echoed.

"A sword doesn't always serve you. There will be times in the night, in the dark, in close places where all that stands between you and death is a beautifully sharp dagger."

She shut her mouth and tried to swallow. She could see the wisdom in it, and she could only hope she was equal to the task of learning what she needed to protect herself.

"Of course," she said weakly.

"Will you quit?" he demanded suddenly.

She didn't even have to give that any thought. She shook her head vigorously. "Nay, I will not."

He looked supremely satisfied. "I thought you wouldn't."

She blinked. "You did?"

"You've a decent amount of courage about you, um, Henri."

She could scarce believe her ears. "Think you?"

"Aye, but you surely don't expect me to blather on about it, do you? Come, let us be about our work. Courage you might have, but your skill is still lacking. I wish to remedy that as quickly as possible."

By the saints, had the man actually paid her a compliment? Given her words of praise? She could hardly believe what she'd heard, but her ears certainly weren't deceiving her.

Nor were her arms, for they were soon burdened with the task of holding Colin off with one whilst the other strove to poke at him with her knife. And when she thought she could go on no further, he changed tactics and taught her how to fend him off with just her fists—which went less well than her other lessons, but she did her best.

By the time she was allowed to stop, she was shaking from weariness and strain. But she was smiling. Perhaps she shouldn't have been, for she surely didn't have the skill to defend herself should a man come at her truly. But she had more skill than she'd had a fortnight ago and perhaps that was enough for now.

The next pair of days passed in like manner, full of as much swordplay and knife work as she could stomach—and at times much more, truth be told. But she didn't argue. Colin seemed just as driven as she felt. And she had more reason to press on than just keeping Sir Etienne far from her. Should she by some unhappy chance find herself in Marie's sights, she didn't want to be completely defenseless.

Not as she had been before.

One of the happy turns of events during those days was the absence of Sir Etienne. Ali suspected that he was either drinking or wenching himself into oblivion. At least he was gone and for that she was grateful.

After the first morning, Jason spent most of his time watching her train. He offered no opinion, but readily took the chance to hone his own skills against Colin's when Colin had finished with her for the day. It was those times that she rediscovered humility. She might have been able to hoist her sword, point it in the right direction, and swing it about with a very small bit of skill, but she was a bumbling page compared to Jason.

And nothing at all compared to Colin.

But that didn't stop her from watching him just the same, and marveling at his skill. The man was enormous, to be sure, but he moved with a grace that was riveting to watch. And once he and Jason began to truly hack at each other, Colin became nothing more than a part of his blade, an extension of the metal that flashed in the stray bits of sunlight. Jason was almost as tall as he, and would no doubt one day be as muscled, but even with his considerable skill, he could no more have bested Colin than she could have.

She was gaining, she had to admit, a great appreciation for the skill of her erstwhile betrothed.

Perhaps he wasn't as erstwhile as she might have thought. And for the first time since she'd first heard his name fall from Marie's lips, she managed to look at him occasionally without any feeling of fear at all.

If *that* was not terrifying in the extreme, she didn't know what was.

Too much training, no doubt. It was having an ill effect on her common sense.

When they finally did take up their journey again, she found that she very much disliked having Sir Etienne rejoin the company. She hadn't missed him, for more reasons than just his unpleasant personality. Colin, though, seemed to have decided that no matter what Sir Etienne said to him, he wasn't going to rise to the bait.

Ali wondered what price she would pay for that.

Their first night away from the inn, she had the first watch. It was the easiest, to be sure, for 'twas rare that Colin wasn't still sitting at the fire when she returned to her own blankets. More often than not, she would find him on his feet, watching her as she watched over them. She supposed he didn't trust her with their safekeeping. Perhaps he had reason.

But that night even he seemed to succumb to slumber readily. Sir Etienne was snoring in his usual fashion—fit to bring down any and all ruffians in the area upon them. Jason made no sound, but rested on his back with his hands folded over his breast, and his sword lying by his side.

Ali rose as quietly as possible and made her way into the trees. She looked about her, found nothing, and decided that it was a perfect opportunity to relieve herself. She chose a likely spot, saw to what she needed to, then pulled up her hose and straightened her tunic.

And then she realized that she was far from alone. She whipped around at the crack of a twig behind her and saw Sir Etienne leaning against a tree. Ah, nay, not again! Would the man never give her any peace?

"See anything interesting?" she snapped.

"Very," he said with a leer.

"What do you want?" she demanded, trying to sound as intimidating as Colin might have in the same situation.

He took a step closer to her and she drew her knife. This was a perfect time to use all those lethal maneuvers she had so diligently practiced. Sir Etienne was unimpressed, but he also took no step closer. That was enough for her.

"What do you want?" she repeated, holding her knife with the pointed end toward his belly. "Tell me and be gone."

He looked at her with a smile that made her skin crawl.

"How bold you've become, little mouse. One would think you have begun to consider yourself my equal."

"I don't," she said bluntly. "But I'll also not be ground under your heel."

"We will see about that. I'm still in need of a whore."

She merely stared at him silently. The saints only knew how she would keep herself from that, but she'd sooner blurt out her secret to any and all who might be interested than meet with this man that way.

"What do you want?" she asked calmly.

He folded his arms over his chest, seemed to consider, then smiled again. "Something only you can get me."

"I've no mind to get you anything."

"I daresay you'd decide differently did I but prod Lord Colin awake and give him my tale."

Ali pursed her lips. "Perhaps he wouldn't care."

"Will you test that?"

She glared at him, but remained silent. Nay, she wouldn't test it. Colin's good humors likely only extended so far throughout that powerful form. Best not to overtax them unnecessarily.

"I have decided," Sir Etienne began expansively, "what it is I'll have you fetch for me. And that won't be your virginity. Not yet."

The saints be praised for something, at least.

"Aren't you curious?"

"I'm tired of listening to you," she said without thinking, then bit her lip. That was a sure way to make him demand more than he'd intended.

He took a menacing step toward her and raised his fist. "I'll give you something else to listen to, then."

She raised her knife and gave him her best look of bluster. But she said nothing. No sense in goading him further.

"I'll have the treasury of Solonge," he said curtly, dropping his fist. "Get it for me."

She felt her jaw slide down. "The *what?*"

"You heard me."

Aye, she had, but she could scarce believe her ears. "I don't know what you mean—"

"Liar," he snarled. "You know very well what it is and whence to fetch it. Get it for me. Get all your sire's gold for me or everyone you know dies."

"You wouldn't—"

He grasped her wrist and had her knife pointing skyward,

useless, before she could gather her wits. He stepped in close and breathed down on her with his foul breath.

"*All* your father's private cache of gold," he repeated. "Once you have it, I'll tell you what you'll do with it."

She could only imagine. She jerked her arm away from him and stumbled backward, rubbing her wrist.

"Get me what I want or everyone you love dies," he said coldly. "From the least cur in Solonge's kitchen to your beloved sire."

She stared at him for several minutes in silence, then felt a hardness enter her heart. He boasted, to be sure, but could he really do what he said? He would be killing no one if Colin killed him first.

"I think I should just go tell Colin everything," she said.

"Tell him, and you'll regret it," he snarled.

"How will I regret it, if I'm dead?" she asked.

Unfortunately, Sir Etienne was much quicker with his fists than she was with her ability to duck. She found herself suddenly sprawled on the ground with him standing on her wrist and grinding it into the dirt. She thought to cry out, then felt the unyielding chill of steel against her throat.

"You've seen how he is when he's furious," Sir Etienne hissed, leaning down toward her. "Tell him, and I'll take your tale and add to it myself. He'll hear how you've passed the last pair of months laughing at his blindness, mocking him behind his back, calling him all manner of names he wouldn't like in the least. Kill you? Nay, I doubt he'll do that until he's avenged those insults."

Ali closed her eyes. She didn't want to believe that of Colin. She didn't.

"And," Sir Etienne continued softly, "if you tell him, you can rest comfortably in your grave, knowing that you'll soon have a goodly bit of companionship there. Berkhamshire will find himself soon lying next to you, still and cold. Then the pampered puss from Artane. Then the lady Isabeau—"

"Nay." She breathed.

"Aye. And if you think I won't do it, think again."

"But why?" she whispered. "Why would you do such horrible things—"

"Because I can," he snapped. He jerked his blade away and removed his foot from her wrist. "Because I can. And I *will*. We're only a pair of days from Solonge. I'll expect my treasure very soon after that."

"What then?" she asked dully.

"Then I'll find other uses for you. I'm sure you'll enjoy them as much as I will. Until then, think on what I've said. And be certain that should you even think to speak to Berkhamshire, someone you love will pay the price."

And with that, he kicked her heartily in the side, making her gasp, and stalked away, heedlessly crunching branches and twigs underfoot.

Ali lay there, gasping for air and willing herself not to weep. The tears came anyway and she lay there and wept silently until the pain in her wrist was a dull throb and the ache in her side subsided enough to allow her painful but possible breaths. She heaved herself to her feet, leaned against a tree, and put her face in her hands. Her father's gold? How was she ever to come by that without revealing herself? Steal the key to her father's treasury and then plunder it? By the saints, what guarantee did she have that she'd be able to manage it?

The guarantee of the lives of those she loved, she supposed.

She shook her head and returned to camp. She stood at the edge of the small fire's light and looked at both Colin and Jason. 'Twas hard to believe that both of them had become dear to her in such a short time. Well, perhaps it was an easy thing to love Jason of Artane. He was handsome and very personable.

Colin was about as personable as a sharp blade.

But even he had a certain charm that she couldn't deny. And, more than that, he possessed honor and courage. Any man would have felt himself blessed to have such a one as he guarding his back. And that he should offer to guard her back? It inspired something strong in her. Loyalty, surely.

Love?

Quite possibly.

She couldn't help but wonder what she would have decided if she'd but had a passing acquaintance with more than the man's foul reputation. Hadn't Gillian of Blackmour said the same thing? Ali shook her head. Aye, she'd made a perfect mess of things and now found herself becoming more and more entangled in the snares of the lies she'd told so far.

She wondered what Colin would say did he but know a fraction of the lies she'd spewed without remorse.

Perhaps that wasn't worth thinking on.

She knelt down on her blankets, bowed her head for a moment, and listened to the comforting sound of Sir Etienne's snores. It was nothing short of miraculous how the man could go from threats to slumber in such a short time. Mayhap that was how it went for those whose hearts were completely full of evil. They had no conscience to wrestle with.

She sighed, lifted her head, and reached out to touch Colin's leg to wake him—only to find him already awake and watching her. He rose, his face completely expressionless. The next thing she knew, he had squatted down next to her, grasped her face in his hand and lifted it up. It was gently done, but even so, the lip she realized only then was cut stung as if the wound had been made afresh.

The flash of rage on Colin's face was truly frightening to behold.

He rose in a single, fluid moment and Ali had no doubts what he intended to do. But if Colin merely beat Sir Etienne to a pulp, he would still be alive to come after not only her, but those dear to her.

She reached out and wrapped her hands around Colin's ankle. He looked down at her, his lips tight with fury. She met his eyes and shook her head. Just once. She couldn't manage more than that—especially since she wouldn't have minded in the least if he'd taken his sword, strode around the fire, and plunged that blade into Sir Etienne's black heart. He looked down at her, then took a deep breath and visibly shook off the hard set to his shoulders. He knelt down again in front of her and put his hand on her shoulder.

"My apologies," he said gruffly, in a mere whisper. "I did not intend to leave you defenseless by succumbing to sleep."

"But it wasn't your fault," she said, surprised at his apology. "It was my watch. I just didn't watch very well."

"You left me undamaged," he muttered. "I wish I could say I had done the same for you. Now, what is it that whoreson holds over you?"

She shook her head. "Nothing."

"We both know you're lying."

She looked him in the eye. "Will you beat me for it?"

He snorted. "You've become powerfully cheeky, haven't you? You know, few dare to speak to me thusly."

" 'Tis my goodly courage you ever praise that emboldens me," she said with a smile, then she winced at the pain of her lip. She put her finger to it. " 'Tis nothing, my lord, but foolishness between him and me. Nothing important."

Colin grunted at her. "I would prefer to judge that for myself, but I can see you won't give me the tale. Perhaps from now on, I should take your watch with you. Two pairs of eyes are better than one, after all."

She knew she should have told him nay, but her face hurt, her wrist throbbed, and she still couldn't breathe as well as she would have liked. So she nodded reluctantly.

"As you will," she said.

He patted her very gently on the shoulder. "Rest now, Henri. And forgive my weakness. My fine form failed me this eve, and I can make no excuses for it."

"Nay—"

"Aye," he said grimly, " 'tis true, as unpalatable a truth as it is. But rest assured, he will be repaid. If not by your hand, then by mine—and much as I wouldn't deny you the pleasure, I would rather take that pleasure for myself. He won't enjoy his recompense, believe me."

She did. No one who saw the expression on his face could have believed otherwise.

Colin looked at her very closely, then sighed and rose. Ali lay down, turned toward the fire, and pulled her blanket over her shoulder. Well, at least she would live another day, and so would her comrades. Perhaps she could ask for nothing more than that. Another day of life.

Another day to learn how to inflict death.

And as she cradled her injured wrist to her breast, she vowed to throw herself even more fully into her lessons. And the next time Sir Etienne had her alone, he would have more than her weeping as his reward.

Chapter 24

S ir Etienne finished his business with his newfound friends, then mounted his horse and rode back to camp. It had cost him the remainder of Aliénore's coin, that business, but he was certain it would be worth the expense. And what did his empty purse matter, when it would be filled within days with untold riches from Solonge's treasury?

He chortled to himself as he rode along slowly, enjoying the chill of dawn and the knowledge that he was truly about some fine venture. After all, it wasn't every day that a man found himself on the verge of possibly slaying the beguiling Jason of Artane, potentially humiliating the Butcher of Berkhamshire, and forcing the errant Aliénore of Solonge to make him richer than he'd ever dreamed he might be. He was allowed a bit of good humor when that was the case.

Of course, he had his own sweet self to thank for finding himself where he was with the knowledge he had. If he hadn't been such a temptation to Marie of Solonge that pair of years earlier, he wouldn't have known anything about Solonge's coffers. But damned if the woman didn't boast of the most amazing things whilst being tumbled in a hayloft. Apparently she'd been trying to impress Sir Etienne with more than just her delectable attributes.

He'd been more than impressed by everything she'd offered.

And when Lord Humbert of Maignelay had needed a message sent to Solonge, Sir Etienne had never found it beneath himself to volunteer to deliver it. He'd passed several very pleasant evenings in the lovely and dangerous Marie's company, taking full advantage of both her body and her arrogant, blathering mouth. One wouldn't have thought a woman so calculating could be so indiscreet, but there you had it.

Reason enough, he supposed, for why he had never wed, nor intended to do so.

Besides, nuptials meant a wife, and a wife meant children, which meant dowries and other expenses he had no intention of incurring. Nay, his wealth would be for himself and his own pleasure.

And he could scarce wait to begin indulging in his pleasures.

But all that in good time. Aliénore would provide him with what he'd requested, and then he would no doubt send her back for more from other sources. Solonge was wealthy, but he suspected that Berkhamshire was far wealthier. And the man would eventually have to return to England once his search for his missing bride had proved fruitless. And who better to rob him blind than his trusted man-at-arms, Sir Henri?

Of course, it had concerned him, that show of spine Aliénore had displayed the night before. The way to his life of comfort was made possible only by her fear of him and his ability to force her to do his bidding. That she'd even contemplated blurting out the secret of her identity to Berkhamshire had been disturbing.

It had, naturally, left him no choice but to see to the morning's entertainment, which would be catching them up in but a handful of hours—entertainment that would surely convince her that he could do what he claimed he could.

And with young Artane dead, Berkhamshire wounded or shamed, the only pause on the journey to Solonge would be a quick funeral and whatever demented rituals the Butcher would have to go through to regain his dignity. Sir Etienne supposed he could endure those.

Especially knowing that Marie would be at the end of his travels, no doubt ready and willing to take him to her bed and make him laugh yet again with tales of her husband's foolishness.

He espied the camp up ahead and put aside his thoughts and plans. All would happen as he'd planned. Just a bit longer to wait and then he'd have all he desired—and deserved.

Chapter 25

Colin rode slowly with his hood over his head to shield it from the drizzle, and cursed the French, their weather, and everything else associated with them. In his opinion, their ground was hard, their rain continual, and their ability to produce anything other than good drink nonexistent. Did they have no concept of a proper road? Winding, twisting affairs that left ample room on each side for scores of ruffians to hide and pounce upon the unwary traveler were not, to his mind, proper roads.

Fortunately, he was a very wary traveler and was ready and willing to dispatch any group of unsavouries that might come his way. That he had to be on his guard wasn't what troubled him. It was continually watching Henri and wondering when Sir Etienne would strike out at her again that was so irritating. That and knowing that to find out, he had no choice but to let events proceed on how they would. With Henri's safety hanging in the balance.

Damnation, but he wished he had a better name for her than that.

Of course, that wasn't all that was setting his teeth on edge and leaving him with the desire to decimate whatever enemy might come his way—and pray, let there be many of them that he might assuage his foul mood. What irritated him the most was reliving his own failure the night before. He should have protected Henri, yet he hadn't been equal to the task.

He gritted his teeth at the memory of watching her come back to the fire. It had taken no great gift of observation to divine that she'd been hurt. She had breathed poorly, she'd held her wrist to her belly, and her face had been smudged with tears. He'd been enraged over that. Then he'd seen the cut on her mouth and a fury had consumed him, the like of which he'd never felt before. Perhaps esteem and great admiration for a wench would do that to a man.

She'd stopped him, though, damn her, with that touch on his leg and the pleading in her eyes. It had fair done him in to humor her, but he had given in. He wondered how that might bode for the man who had the privilege of her for the rest of his life.

It wasn't the first time he'd wished he might be that man.

And that kind of thinking had led him to wish again, in the deepest part of his heart he rarely visited even on his most maudlin day, that he might somehow find Aliénore safely tucked away in a convent, already committed to her vows. That would leave him free of his obligation to her.

Free to wed where he willed.

Free to try to convince a young woman with astonishingly green eyes that he might make her a good husband.

He rubbed his hand over his face and cursed himself for even having allowed that thought to cross his mind. Like as not, Henri was betrothed to another. And even if she could break free of that, she likely wouldn't have him. After all, she was beautiful.

And he was most certainly not.

He turned his damnably fertile imagination to other things. Immediately, ideas on how he might finish Sir Etienne's sorry life surged forth in bright and delicious detail. Aye, the man would pay, and pay dearly for every bruise he'd put on Henri. Colin would see to it. Perhaps sooner than later, when Henri wasn't looking. A pity he couldn't have done it that morning. He'd woken only to find Sir Etienne gone yet again—and he wondered where the man went and what kind of wickedness he wrought.

Unfortunately he'd known that such a happy misplacing of the man couldn't last. The oaf had returned just as Colin was hopping spryly upon his horse, ready to leave him behind. Disheveled and sweating, he claimed he'd gone to pursue ruffians who had foul designs on their company.

Colin hadn't believed it for a moment.

He suspected he would feel a great deal better when they were inside castle walls. At least there, he could check a confined space for enemies instead of having to keep watch on the entire countryside.

The day passed and Colin alternated between glaring at Sir Etienne and watching the horizon. And as he scanned the countryside for rogues, he gave thought to his plans for the next few days. Mayhap they could stop at the priory and rest for a bit there. Jason would surely receive a warm welcome from the nuns, given that his family had so richly endowed the place. Colin had no qualms about availing himself of that luxury. Besides, that would give him ample time to question Sir Etienne and find out just how much the man knew about Solonge.

Then they would proceed with all caution to the keep where Colin would meet Aliénore's father, do his duty of offering to search for her, then be on his way as quickly as possible. He would, of course, find a quite plausible reason to leave Sir Etienne behind in Solonge's capable hands.

He'd just begun to contemplate that happy time, when Jason bellowed in rage.

It was as if Hell itself had unleashed an attack upon them.

Men swarmed out from the trees and bushes on the side of the road. Colin scarce had time to count their number, which was ten and five, and finish off a pair of them before he realized something quite startling about the attack.

It was all aimed, oddly enough, at Jason.

Colin fought quickly and killed without hesitation, because that was just what he did, but as he did so, he watched the pattern of the assault and wondered greatly at it. Sir Etienne engaged a pair of men and rather feebly, truth be told. Jason had eleven surrounding him, trying to hack at various parts of his form.

Henri, the saints be praised, was left completely alone.

Colin left his two expiring in the bloody dirt, then pushed ahead to lend Jason aid. He almost paused to ask the lad if he minded help, but perhaps apologies could be offered later if Jason's sensibilities had been offended. For now, there were eleven against two and those were odds enough to make Colin smile even on his most foul-humored day.

He dispatched three more with three mighty swipes of his

sword, then slid off his horse to the ground. His mount, who had seen this all before, backed away, leaving Colin ample space for a goodly morning's exercise.

It certainly didn't escape his attention that Sir Etienne seemed to be taking a bloody long time finishing off his attackers.

A quick look behind him revealed that Henri had her blade drawn, but it rested unwielded in her hand—her left hand, damn her—but what choice did she have? Sir Etienne had done her right some sort of injury. Well, she was likely safe enough for the moment. Satisfied by that at least, Colin turned his attentions to the men before him. They were ragged and filthy, but knew which way to point the business end of their swords.

Colin smiled pleasantly. "Who next?" he asked. "Or shall you all come at once?"

Ah, a brawl. He couldn't have been more pleased. Casting himself joyfully into the fray, Colin swung and cut and hacked with gleeful abandon. Men screamed out curses and prayers both. Blades didn't flash thanks to the lack of sun, but Colin supposed that was something he could live without. He was doing what he did best, and he did it thoroughly.

He finished his ten, leaving them in various states of death and incapacitation, then saw that Jason, thanks to a bolt in his right arm, was having to fight his last foe with his left. Colin leaned upon his sword and watched as Jason and his mount managed to finish off their last man.

And then Sir Etienne rode up, chest heaving, his hose covered in blood.

"Bloody thieves," he gasped.

Colin looked at him narrowly. "Aye. Interesting, don't you think, that they all made straight for young Jason?"

"The richness of his trappings, no doubt," Sir Etienne said with a sneer he didn't seem to be able to hide.

"Hmmm," Colin said thoughtfully, then looked up at Jason still astride his horse. "How do you fare, lad?"

Jason was clutching his right shoulder. "Well enough, I daresay. Lucky for us, the abbey is reachable. The nuns there are goodly healers."

"Bah," Colin said, waving a dismissive hand. " 'Tis but a scratch. Let me pull the arrow out and spare them the trouble."

"I don't think so," Jason said, stretching out his bloody hand to hold Colin off. "I'd rather have their tender ministrations than yours, thank you just the same. We're not that far. I'll last."

Colin shrugged. " 'Tis your shoulder, not mine." He looked at Henri. "And you? How do you fare, um, Henri?"

Damnation, but he was going to have to either confront her and learn her name, or stop speaking to her at all if that was the best he could do. He was, he had to concede, a very poor liar. Pretending that he still believed she was a boy was using up much energy that could have been expended somewhere else.

Her face was, unsurprisingly, white with fear and strain, but her sword was still upright and she wasn't weeping. Those, to his mind, were very good signs.

"I am well," she managed. "Well enough."

"And our good Sir Etienne seems to be unhurt, though quite filthy. Best, then, that we're off to our destination as quickly as may be. Sir Etienne, perhaps you would care to lead the way, since you seem to have such a perfect sense of direction. Who knows, you may be more successful at spotting ruffians than I was."

"Likely so," Sir Etienne said, puffing his chest out. "I surely would have spotted those sooner."

"No doubt," Colin said briskly, then swung up into his saddle. "Lead on, then. We'll follow quite happily."

Sir Etienne rode out ahead. Colin motioned for Henri to go before him, then pulled back to ride alongside Jason.

"Interesting, don't you think?" he asked quietly.

Jason looked almost as angry as Colin had felt the night before.

"Deliberate, I'd say."

Colin looked at the shaft protruding from what had been a very nice tunic but a handful of moments before. "You're going to need a few days' rest with that. I think we'll leave you with the good sisters and carry on."

"Are you daft?" Jason asked, clearly stunned. "You need me!"

Colin shrugged. "I'll manage."

"But Henri—"

"Can fend for himself."

"He most certainly cannot!"

Colin scratched absently at his chin. "He's learned a great deal. He'll manage well enough."

"Solonge is a nest of vipers," Jason insisted.

"And what should that matter to our young knight? He's a lad. No one will harm him."

Jason looked so concerned that Colin began to suspect that he might know much more than he was admitting. And then hard on the heels of *that* thought came the unpleasant realization that Jason likely knew—indeed, had likely known for some time, damn the lad—just what Henri was.

And if his charm hadn't failed him, he likely knew *who* Henri was as well.

Why he had chosen not to share either of those things with Colin sooner was annoying in the extreme.

Colin glared at him. "I hope that hurts."

Jason blinked in surprise. "Why?"

"I just do."

"Nasty of you, I'd say."

"Why are you so concerned about Henri?"

"He's young," Jason said promptly. "Inexperienced. Needful of protection."

"Hrmph." Colin pursed his lips. He would have to beat the answers from Artane's youngest, that was for sure, and repay him as well should those answers reveal a knowledge that Jason should have shared long before now. But later, after the lad had healed. There was no pleasure in taking sport of a man who had an arrow protruding from his shoulder. "You can put your mind at rest. I'll watch over Henri."

"I don't like it."

"Neither do I," Colin returned. "I won't be long at Solonge, for I've no liking to drag this out any longer than I have to. I intend to rid myself of Sir Etienne there and the sooner that's done, the happier I'll be. Then we'll be about our sorry business of a search."

"Well," Jason said, sounding quite relieved, "if he's going to be left behind, then I agree."

"Generous of you."

"I thought so."

Colin grunted at him, then turned his attentions back to the road. "Several more hours, wouldn't you say?"

"At least."

"Interesting time for an attack."

"That as well," Jason agreed.

Colin looked at him. "Far enough from the priory that you might have ample time to die en route."

"Aye, and I like not that thought."

"You wouldn't," Colin agreed, "considering you're the one paying the price for it." He looked out over the fields next to them. "I'll have to be more on guard."

"Hard to spot it, I'd think," Jason mused. "These kinds of attacks."

"That depends on how closely one shadows the instigator."

Jason nodded thoughtfully. "True enough."

Colin turned his attentions back to the countryside and gave himself over to thinking on what he'd just discovered. To be sure, he couldn't doubt that Sir Etienne had a hand in what they'd just experienced. But why? What was he trying to prove? To whom did he intend to show his cunning?

Henri, perhaps. But that again raised the question of why? Colin ground his teeth in frustration. Did he but know what the man held over her, he could see to it and dispatch the cretin. And the sooner the better, as far as their health was concerned. He would not take a chance with Henri's life, for who knew at whom the next attack would be aimed?

He fixed his full attentions on his surroundings. He would keep them safe as far as the priory, have Jason seen to, then perhaps leave at a time Sir Etienne wouldn't have expected. Even did they travel by dark of night, that would be preferable to arrows in the back during the daylight.

And then he could be rid of that bloody Sir Etienne. That day couldn't come soon enough, to his mind.

He wondered briefly if it might be safer to leave Henri behind with Jason. He dismissed that idea immediately. Jason hardly needed any more time to use his devilish charm on the girl and, despite his own two recent failures, Colin remained convinced that the safest place for Henri was right next to him.

At least he would have the pleasure of watching her whenever he so chose.

Aye, he would most certainly keep her near him.

Who could blame him for it?

Chapter 26

A*li* dreamed of her mother. She sat next to her at the priory, in front of the fire in the guest hall, and listened to the worn, soft voice of the abbess. She couldn't understand the words, but that didn't matter. Her mother held Ali's hand in hers. Every now and again, she would look at her and smile that smile full of love that made Ali feel as if she were the most precious thing in the world.

Then her mother turned back to the abbess. Soft laughter was exchanged, and more quiet words that washed over Ali and wrapped her in their warmth as if in a blanket. And all the while, her mother never let her go.

Ali was certain she'd never felt so at peace.

Her mother turned to look at her, then reached out and put her hand on Ali's shoulder. And then, quite suddenly, the hand was not so gentle and the touch on her shoulder no longer resembled a gentle caress. It was shaking that left Ali gasping in surprise.

And then she realized that the face leaning so close to hers was not her mother's, but rather Colin of Berkhamshire's. He already looked annoyed.

"Aaaack!" she exclaimed, sitting up and groping for her dagger.

"Damnation," Colin said, jumping back, " 'tis only me. You needn't poke me."

Ali drew her hand back. "Forgive me, my lord. I thought—"

"You thought I was an enemy and did as you should have. But, as you can see, I am not the enemy and you need not fear me. Aye?"

Ali rubbed her eyes with the heels of her hands and struggled to shake the sleep from herself. She looked at Colin to find him kneeling next to her, looking very concerned.

"Are you unwell?" she asked. "Sour bowels?"

He grunted at her. "I am perfectly sound. 'Tis you whom I worry about."

"You woke me in the middle of the night. How do you expect me to react?"

"I suppose," he said doubtfully.

"Why am I awake?" she asked, dragging her fingers through her hair.

"We're leaving. I think it best we travel during a time when we might not be expected."

Given the events of the day before, she could well understand that.

"We'll have time enough to rest at Solonge," he said, "though I've no desire to stay overlong there." He peered at her closely. "Do you have an opinion on it?"

"On what?" she asked with a frown.

"On how long we stay at Solonge."

I'd rather not go at all was the first thing that came to mind, but she decided against saying as much. So she smiled weakly.

"I've no desire to linger," she said finally. "Nothing there for me."

Besides death.

But there was no use in saying that either.

"I've no reason to dawdle there myself," Colin said. "Let us be on our way, be about our business quickly, and then we'll see where our path leads us. But for now, let us make haste. We'll leave Jason behind, lest he slow our progress."

She rose and packed her handful of belongings. She was ready far sooner than required and followed Colin silently out to the courtyard, where their mounts were saddled and ready. She wished, absently, that she'd had more time to spend at the priory. Her memories of it were quite faded, but definitely pleasant ones of time spent with her mother alone. No wonder she had dreamed so deeply and vividly of the woman.

She shook her head suddenly to clear it before she broke down and wept. By the saints, she was not feeling herself lately. Just the slightest thing made her give in to tears. Perhaps she had spent one too many days as a man. It was likely enough to wreak havoc on the most sensible of women. Or perhaps it was that she was on the verge of going back to the very place she had fled in terror and vowed never to return to.

Would Marie recognize her on sight? Would one of her bloody brothers blurt out her name the moment she walked through the door? She couldn't have been fortunate enough to return and find them all safely wedded and ensconced in other keeps. François, at least, would still be hanging about, doing everything but an honest day's work and passing all his hours trying to convince their sire that he should merely give François what he wanted without question.

She was not looking forward to seeing her brother.

She could only hope he wouldn't recognize his mail shirt—even altered as it had been by Blackmour's smith. At least she had no fear of her brother recognizing his filched sword. That had been melted down to fashion the saints only knew what. Cleaning tools for Blackmour's cesspit, if there was any justice at all in the world.

She mounted her horse and followed Colin from the courtyard, listening with half an ear to the vociferous complaints Sir Etienne couldn't seem to keep to himself. Colin ignored the man, and she followed his example zealously. She could feel Sir Etienne glaring at her, even in the dark, but Colin seemed determined to keep himself between the two of them, so perhaps she would make out all right in the end.

She thought back on the attack of the day before and knew it for what it was. Somehow beyond reason and beyond belief, Sir Etienne had arranged the entire thing. Hadn't the ruffians gone only for Jason? Colin had been assaulted by a token pair of men, and Sir Etienne by the same number, but Jason had been assailed by the bulk of the force. Of course, she might have had her doubts, but one thing had told her beyond doubt that it had been no accident: the pointed look Sir Etienne had given her as soon as the bushes had discharged their hidden members.

And now Jason lay in the priory, wounded. At least he

wasn't dead. She supposed he had Colin to thank for that. Watching him had been a revelation. She'd believed the rumors of his skill, of course, seen for herself his displeasure with others, even watched him parry mercilessly with Jason. But to see him actually protecting those he cared for was something else entirely.

He had chortled. He had fought with grace and ease, making those who came at him look as if they'd never held swords before. He had either slain or maimed eleven men, fighting many of them *en masse*, and he'd made it seem as if it were nothing more than an easy morning's exercise.

But as enlightening as that had been, it hadn't compared to what she'd discovered as she stole a look at Sir Etienne during that little bit of fighting. She supposed what she'd seen on his face was something he would have concealed if he'd known she'd been watching.

Envy.

Naked, hungry envy.

She considered that as she rode alongside Colin in the darkness. Sir Etienne was jealous? She could understand that well enough. But to kill Colin because of it? Or mayhap he only used that as a threat to her, to get her to do what he wanted. That he might actually accomplish the deed was something she just couldn't believe.

And that likely galled him to the depths of his soul.

Perhaps he would have his recompense after all.

She found, a goodly while later, that she had been dozing in her saddle. The sky was growing light and the forest around her was beginning to take on familiar shapes.

She realized, with a start, that she was nearing the place where she'd buried her clothes and her hair.

And she thought she just might be ill.

"Henri?"

She looked at Colin. "I am well, my lord."

He turned to Sir Etienne. "Take the lead. Through the forest path, then on to the keep."

"Aye, just as I told you," Sir Etienne said, but he didn't sound pleased. "And 'tis a road far better traveled at midday."

"So you said. I prefer to travel under cover of darkness."

Sir Etienne huffed in irritation, and spurred his mount ahead. Colin looked at Ali and motioned for her to go before him. He put his hand meaningfully on his sword hilt. Ali took a deep breath, loosened her sword in its scabbard, and moved in front of him.

And she prayed she would be able to avoid notice once she reached her home.

Soon, though, she was no longer praying but merely wishing desperately that she were anywhere else, that she had confessed to Colin weeks ago, that she was safely in her grave where she did not have to face what awaited her but a half hour ahead. She wished most of all that she didn't recognize her surroundings. Unfortunately, she could number every tree, recognize most all the bushes, and list in her mind the dips and swells of earth that would eventually spew her out before her father's gates.

She wished, absently, that she might have vomited up all her fear. A pity she couldn't seem to manage it. Perhaps she'd passed too much of the sea voyage doing the like. She would have stopped to ponder that, but worrying was her current, all-consuming passion. She found herself powerless to resist entertaining in her mind all the possibilities that might await her.

Death.

Torture.

A long, slow, painful death after a goodly bit of torture.

By the time she'd reached Solonge's gates, she was trembling with fear and merely praying that she could avoid drawing attention to herself by not falling off her horse.

Colin made no move to take the lead through the barbican gate. Ali kept her eyes down and her hood pulled close around her face. All she needed was for one of the guards— and she couldn't be fortunate enough to have it be the one she'd bribed to let her from the keep—recognize her and alert her father.

Who would, no doubt, immediately take the happy tidings to his beloved wife.

They rode into the courtyard. Ali forced herself to look at

the ground. There was no point in looking about her anyway. She knew what her home looked like. Indeed, the very smell of the place hadn't changed. She felt for a moment as if she hadn't left at all.

Only now she was on the Butcher of Berkhamshire's right hand, something she never would have imagined in her foulest nightmares.

Colin dismounted and she followed, standing close to him. She suddenly found Sir Etienne's hand on the hood of her cloak. He likely would have pulled it back had Colin's fingers not wrapped themselves around his wrist so quickly.

Sir Etienne cursed. "What do you?"

"Release Henri's cloak."

"We should uncover our heads, out of respect for the lord here."

"You great horse's arse," Colin said impatiently. "Leave the lad be. Can you not sense his unease? He may keep his head covered the length of our visit, should he wish to. See to your own head and leave his alone."

Sir Etienne spluttered, and continued to splutter as Ali suddenly found herself deposited on Colin's other side, the side comfortably far from Sir Etienne and his busy hands. Apparently Colin wasn't satisfied with that, for he gave Sir Etienne a mighty shove that placed him several feet away from them.

More spluttering ensued.

Ali wished desperately that she had remained behind, safely ensconced in the priory with Jason. But it was too late for anything like that. She bowed her head and fixed her gaze to the ground.

The door opened and a man stepped out into the overcast morning light. Ali only had to see the boots to know it was her father. The boots took a few steps down toward the courtyard, then came to an abrupt halt.

"Um," her father said, sounding very unsure.

"Colin of Berkhamshire," Colin said, sounding not the least bit unsure. "Sir Etienne of Maignelay. My man-at-arms, Sir Henri."

"Ah . . ."

"You once begged me to seek your daughter out. I refused then. I've come now to take up the task."

Ali felt her jaw begin to slide south and she hurriedly retrieved it. Her father had begged Colin for his aid? That Colin had refused didn't surprise her. His pride had likely been mightily wounded. She did, after all, have the distinction of being the only one who hadn't found a plausible excuse for not standing before a priest with him. She suspected he had been less than impressed with her tactic.

"You have?" her sire asked, sounding stunned.

"He only intends to kill her once he finds her," Sir Etienne put in.

Ali just couldn't believe Colin would do the like, even if he laid hands on the missing Aliénore of Solonge. Shout at her? Aye. Glare, complain, and make her life a misery for quite some time? Very likely. But slay her?

Ali suspected he just didn't have it in him.

Which was enough to make her think all sorts of thoughts of truth and confession that she likely shouldn't have.

Her father, however, didn't have the benefit of two months in Colin's company. She looked at him from the shadows of her hood and saw that he had gone quite gray in the face.

"Is that true?" he asked. He raised a trembling finger and pointed it at Colin. "Do you seek her merely to kill her?"

"Words spoken in anger," Colin said dismissively.

"But—" Sir Etienne protested.

"Words spoken in anger," Colin repeated, throwing Sir Etienne a glare that Ali herself felt the heat of. "Sir Etienne, as you can see, has a rather loose tongue."

"Aye," her father said absently, his eyes still fixed on Colin, "he's been here before. I know his kind."

Sir Etienne, predictably, began to splutter.

"Retire to the garrison hall," Colin ordered him. "Remain there until I send for you."

"I will *not*—"

"Garrison hall or dungeon. You choose."

Ali listened to her father throw that at Sir Etienne and was surprised by the sudden bite to his tone. She looked away, that she might not see whatever expression Sir Etienne wore and the look he would no doubt give her.

"I will go," Sir Etienne said stiffly, "only because I might have a decent meal there. But I will return."

"When we send for you," Colin said briskly.

Sir Etienne cursed as he walked away, and his words were hardly complimentary to either of the men standing near her.

"My lord Denis," Colin said quietly to her father, "I do not trust him and I would have you watch him just as if he were an enemy."

"Done," Denis said.

"And might we have speech together? Alone?"

"Of course. I'll send for my wife."

Ali thought she might faint. Indeed, she suspected that doing so was the only sensible course of action. That way, she wouldn't have to feel Marie's blade sliding between her ribs once she discovered who had come home.

She swayed. Colin grasped her shoulder and held her upright.

"I think this is a tale better left between men. Not that I don't have a great esteem for women," he added quickly, "but I think I would be more comfortable . . ."

Ali stole a look at her father and saw him nod in understanding. "Aye," he said, "I know. No sense in doing anything to upset their delicate constitutions."

Delicate constitutions? Ali barely stifled her snort before it burst forth from her. Marie's constitution was hardly delicate. Indeed, Ali suspected the woman could either bed or fight the entire French army and merely yawn when she was finished.

"Now," Denis continued, "your lad there can see to the horses—"

"Nay, he stays with me. Sir Etienne bears him ill will and I'll not have him harmed."

Denis shrugged. "As you will. Come then, and we will have refreshment in my solar."

Colin looked at her briefly, then inclined his head toward the hall. Ali followed, because the alternative was remaining outside where Sir Etienne would no doubt come to lurk the moment he thought Colin and her father were safely inside.

She walked across the great hall, shivering. If she did but survive this part of her adventure, then she would surely confess to Colin and face his wrath. It could be no worse than being back in her own home and wondering who would be the first one to see beneath the dirt and shorn hair.

She found herself soon in her father's solar, sitting on a stool in the darkest corner of the chamber, clutching a cup of wine and the plate of foodstuffs Colin had shoved into her hands. She drank and ate only because she thought it might serve her later. When she was finished, she had no memory of the meal.

But she did remember every word her father said. She leaned back against the wall and watched him as he opened his heart to Colin.

A heart full of grief.

So, it was as Berengaria had once said—that her father's grief was consuming him. Ali listened to him speak of her mother and realized how much he had loved her. Indeed, that love had been so strong, he'd hardly been himself after she'd died. Marie had been at the keep already as one of Ali's mother's ladies, so when she had wormed her way into his affections, he'd been almost powerless to deny her whatever she wanted.

Which had included, oddly enough, betrothing Ali to Colin of Berkhamshire.

Ali listened with a growing sense of amazement and distress. A pity she'd been too young then, too cowed, to have seen beyond her own misery to her sire's. But what could she have done? There was no denying that he had been so far under Marie's sway, likely nothing she could have done would have changed that.

Yet now to listen to his grief over having lost her was enough to have her continually wiping the tears from her cheeks.

"Can you not find her?" he asked Colin. "The cost means nothing to me."

"I will search for her as diligently as may be," Colin assured him. "And I am an excellent tracker."

"But," Denis said, after a goodly bit of silence, "what will you do when you find her? Surely you wouldn't slay her in truth."

Colin was silent for a very long time. Ali found herself torn between wanting to quake in fear and wanting to wallop him strongly over the head with the bottle of wine at her feet. The man had no intentions of slaying any woman. Why was he tormenting her father so?

"My lord?" Denis prompted. "What will you do with her? If you intend to slay her, then I will give you no aid."

"She is my betrothed," Colin said heavily. "When I find her, *if* I find her, then we will decide what is to be done."

"I wonder if you have any mercy in your soul," Denis said quietly.

"Many people wonder that," Colin agreed. "I often wonder the same thing."

Ali pursed her lips. She knew him better than that. He had mercy enough, he simply didn't like to show it overmuch. Might ruin his precious reputation.

"What else am I to do?" Denis asked, sounding quite pained. "I must trust you with my daughter's life whilst fearing you will end that life if you find her." He rose and looked down at Colin. "You're no doubt in need of more sustenance, and then my wife will see you settled in our finest chamber. I can only hope," he added sternly, "that when you find my girl, you will consider how you would feel in my place, were you forced to trust another with your girl's safety."

Colin nodded. "Aye, my lord. I will consider that."

Denis grunted, then led the way from the solar. Ali found herself pulled to her feet by Colin, and then she followed him from the chamber, keeping her head down.

"Stay close to me," Colin whispered over his shoulder. "I've no liking for this place. We'll leave as soon as possible."

"The saints be praised," she muttered. That moment couldn't come soon enough, to her mind.

But for the duration, she was certainly content to keep herself one pace behind Colin down the passageway. It occurred to her, as she watched him continually peek over his shoulder to make certain she was still behind him, that it was passing odd that she should be in her own home, the home she'd fled to avoid this man, and now she found herself being protected by him.

A pity Sir Etienne was still lurking about.

She might have been tempted to tell Colin the truth otherwise.

Chapter 27

S*ir* Etienne cursed as he paced in the garrison hall, a completely unsuitable, completely inadequate, fully filled, and foul-smelling place where only a lowly garrison knight should have found himself. Not him, though. Not Sir Etienne, who would find himself lord of a keep someday with men attending *him*. And women as well. He would stock himself a bloody harem when the time came if he so pleased.

But first he would have to have Solonge's gold. A pity he couldn't have the daughter of Solonge whilst he was about it. That was certainly the quickest way to find himself lord of something. No doubt her father would amply reward the man who could slay Colin of Berkhamshire, just as the butcher was preparing to slay the lady Aliénore.

Sir Etienne considered that idea, then tossed it aside. If he rescued her, he would have to wed with her and he wasn't sure that would be worth her dowry. If she'd been betrothed to Berkhamshire, perhaps her dowry wasn't as massive as he'd hoped. After all, Lord Colin had to have been desperate enough for a bride to take whatever he could get. Hadn't he accepted Sybil of Maignelay? 'Twas a certainty she had brought nothing with her.

Nay, better that he press on with his original plan.

Which he would do, if that damned Marie would respond to his message. He'd said it was urgent. Was she so witless that she couldn't sense what he was about?

He'd almost decided that perhaps he should go search for her when a page came running into the hall, asked every soul there if he happened to be Sir Etienne, then finally looked about in confusion until Sir Etienne strode over and ripped the missive from the lad's hands. He gave the boy a goodly shove as a reward, then unfolded the disturbingly small scrap of parchment.

I'm occupied now. Meet me in the stables after dark.

And that was all. Sir Etienne had a devil of a time making out those words alone, as his skills were certainly not what they likely should have been, but what did he need with reading when he would some day hire a man to do it for him?

He ground his teeth in frustration. Who did the wench think she was, sending him to the stables like a naughty kitchen lad bound for a whipping? He wanted her bed, damn her to hell, not a poor bit of straw. And did she not have more on her mind than his fine form? He had plans! He had schemes!

And he decided, in that instant, that he would say nothing of them to her. He stroked his chin thoughtfully and let that thought build in him until he was fully satisfied with it. Aye, he would keep his knowledge to himself and revel in the fact that he had a secret. And whilst he was about his business with her, he would pry tidbits from her. No doubt she'd seen the inside of Solonge's treasury and would happily list items and amounts for him.

And when he was finished with her, he would toss her aside as callously as she had done him.

Besides, he would soon have Solonge's wealth and be on his way. Marie would just have to content herself with lesser men, for he would most certainly no longer be available to her.

He bellowed for wine, but no one rushed to serve him. He sighed, cursed, and promised himself a household of servants who lived breathlessly to see to his needs.

He deserved nothing less.

Chapter 28

C olin sat in the great hall and fidgeted, nervous as a cat. The keep was crawling with intrigues of all kinds and he could scarce wait to be free of the place. He wondered, absently, how it was that Aliénore had borne it all those years. He knew that he certainly would have fled at his earliest opportunity. He felt very lucky to be a man with the freedom a sword could buy. The poor wench hadn't even had that to save her. Which made him wonder, and not for the first time, just what had happened to her.

He sighed, drank deeply of wine that was scarce drinkable, and wished her peace, wherever she was.

He stole a look over his shoulder at his other problem. She stood in the shadows behind his chair, still as stone. Her hood was still over her face and he supposed that was a boon. When they'd sat for supper and Denis had bid her remove her cloak, Colin had said that the lad's face was horribly marked by the pox and shamed him to show it. He'd barely managed to choke out the lie, but what else could he have done? No sense in letting anyone here know that the lad was really a girl. The saints only knew what would befall her then. Having met the lady of the house, Colin suspected quite fully that young Henri would have found herself revealed, mocked, and perhaps even humiliated, merely for Marie's sport.

The only thing of a goodly turn Colin had noted in the past hour was that Marie wasn't fully the lord of the manor. She certainly hadn't been able to argue with her husband about young Henri's lack of manners in keeping his head covered.

Colin, of course, had his own opinion on manners in general, but he kept that to himself.

"Would you care for more wine?"

Colin looked to his left to find the viperess in question offering to refill his cup. He looked at her and wondered how it was that Denis of Solonge couldn't see past the beauty to the exceptional coldness of her eyes. Then again, he himself wasn't sure how to comport himself with this woman. He'd trotted out his best table manners and tried to keep his thoughts to himself. Marie, however, was apparently unused to being thwarted, for she continued to pepper him with questions ranging from how he found the weather to what he would do to Aliénore when he found her.

Colin limited his responses to as few words as possible.

"Two years," Marie mused. "A long time for a girl to hide."

Colin, holding to his course, merely grunted and reached for meat.

"I've looked in the convents," she continued easily. "My concern for her was great."

Colin was hard-pressed to smother his snort of disbelief. Whatever this woman had felt for poor Aliénore, it hadn't been concern. Even Colin could tell that, and he hadn't known her an hour.

"I sent men to Spain as well," she said.

Colin was surprised at that. "Did you indeed?"

She smiled at him, and he shivered in spite of himself.

That was not a pleasant smile.

"I was concerned," she repeated with that same, cold smile. "How could I spare any expense in my search?"

"Lord Denis did not search?" Colin asked uneasily.

She dismissed her husband with a look of disdain. "He hasn't the stomach for anything so unpleasant. I took the task on myself."

No wonder Aliénore had fled.

"Not in Spain, not in France. Not even in England, or so the reports go." She looked up at him. "Perhaps she is dead."

He couldn't even manage a grunt.

"I fear your search may be in vain."

"So be it," he said.

"But, should you find her," Marie pressed, "what will you do?"

Colin opened his mouth to reply, but found that his reply was unnecessary.

"Punishment would be just, I should think," Marie said thoughtfully. "Beatings would be just. I daresay you would know how to administer one properly."

Colin found his tongue. "I do not, my lady," he said stiffly, "beat women."

"She has earned your ire."

"I do not," he repeated, "beat women."

"Then perhaps I should find her for you," Marie said pleasantly. "I'm sure I could instill a proper sense of remorse into the girl, then deliver her to you meek and tractable. What think you?"

What he thought wasn't fit for a lady's ears, so he refrained from comment. Even so, he seriously doubted that anything he could say would shock Marie of Solonge. By the saints, the woman was evil. Colin lifted his gaze above her head to find Lord Denis calmly and steadfastly plowing through his supper. Perhaps he had listened to this venom for so long that it no longer shocked him.

Colin heartily pitied the man.

He began to count on his fingers under the table the hours he must needs remain before he could depart.

The evening lasted too far into the night, as far as he was concerned. What he wanted was to seek his bed, then rise, dredge up a few polite words, and bolt back to the convent where souls were pure and motives uncomplicated. The intrigue that flowed through Solonge like a river befouled with refuse was almost enough to finish him, and he considered himself quite above being finished by almost anything.

And then a ray of hope broke through the clouds.

Marie yawned.

It wasn't the delicate yawn of a woman whose life was governed by Gillian's rules. It was the yawn of a fierce huntress who had finished her kill, but knew without a doubt that she would kill again and be satisfied.

It sent chills down his spine.

Marie looked at him. "My servant will show you your chamber." She smiled that smile that made his skin crawl. "Solonge's finest, of course. A warrior of your stature deserves nothing less."

He inclined his head, but found he could muster no polite response.

Marie rose and stretched.

Colin gulped.

She leaned over and twined her arms around her husband's neck. "Don't be long, my love. I've needs that cannot wait."

"Of course," Denis said absently.

"I must make a short visit to the stables," Marie said. "A quick nighttime assignation, you know."

"How skillfully you jest," Denis murmured.

Marie looked at Colin, winked, then sauntered from the hall.

Colin reached for his wine and downed it in a single gulp. Then he set the cup back down with shaking hands and looked over his shoulder.

"Henri," he rasped, "come and sit. Eat. There's ample left for you." He held out Marie's chair.

The girl balked.

"Come," Colin said impatiently. "Nothing here to fear. Lord Denis will not snap at you, I'll warrant."

Lord Denis continued to stare vacantly out into the midst of the great hall and offered no comment.

Yet still Henri didn't move.

Colin sighed, reached around and pulled the girl forward. He sat her down, then shoved a trencher in front of her. "Eat," he commanded. "The wine is ghastly, but it will wet your throat. Eat whilst you may, for who knows when you'll have this kind of fare again."

Hopefully only if they both were thrust down to Hell, but he didn't say as much.

He wondered if politeness required him to converse with Lord Denis, but the man seemed burdened by his own black thoughts, so Colin forbore. Instead, he found himself watching as slight, delicate fingers reached out and hesitantly brought food to a mouth that, though Colin couldn't see it, he knew was just as delicate. He was momentarily tempted to thrust those pleasing observations away, then shrugged his shoulders. He'd endured almost the entire day in this hell-hole; didn't he deserve a respite? And what better a respite than watching Henri and allowing himself the luxury of wondering about her?

He leaned his elbows on the table and scratched his cheek thoughtfully with his dagger. What *was* a beautiful girl such as this doing hiding in filthy lad's clothes, wielding a sword, and pretending to be what she was not? And what could possibly inspire such fear in a gel that she would choose this life?

She said she'd fled a cruel mistress. Immediately Marie's image came to mind, but Colin shook that aside with the appropriate shudder. Passing unpleasant woman. Or had Henri lied to him? Was she fleeing a cruel mistress, or a cruel betrothed?

A cruel betrothed, aye, that was likely the answer. But could there really be a man so fierce and terrible that any alternative besides wedding with him could seem appealing? An alternative such as dressing as a man?

Colin searched through his vast memories of men he'd encountered in the course of his life and came up with no one who seemed that intimidating to him. He supposed many might feel that Christopher of Blackmour was that ruthless. Though he merely thought his dearest friend a fierce and cunning warrior, he knew that others found the man quite terrifying. He remembered vividly going to fetch Gillian and the fear she had displayed when she'd learned to whom she was to be wed. But who could possibly have a fouler reputation that Christopher of Blackmour?

He thought on that for quite some time.

Then he stopped scratching.

And the blade fell from his hand.

Who indeed?

"My lord Berkhamshire?"

Colin blinked to find Lord Denis looking at him with concern.

"Are you unwell?" he asked.

Colin looked at Lord Denis, then about the hall at the few guardsmen still left there, then finally at Henri. He found that, for the first time in his life, he simply could not form words. The realizations piled upon him so quickly and with such force, he could do no more than struggle under their weight.

He was the kind of man brides fled from—or pretended life-threatening maladies to avoid wedding with. *His* was the reputation that sent maids and men alike scurrying for cover with prayers for deliverance on their lips. *He* was a betrothed fierce enough of reputation to leave a maid thinking she had no choice but to flee into hose for safety.

Was he the betrothed *this* girl had been fleeing?

If so, that would make her . . .

Aliénore of Solonge.

Colin looked at her, blinked, then blinked again.

Then he clapped his hand to his head and wondered where it was he'd lost all sense. This couldn't be Aliénore. It couldn't be. This wench was full of wit and courage. Aliénore was full of, well, he didn't know what she was full of, but it couldn't be those fine, manly traits. She was likely soft, mewing, and afeared of her own shadow. After all, she'd fled him, had she not? Nay, that wench possessed no redeeming qualities, no courage, no cleverness.

Not like his Henri.

Then again, Henri had certainly been terrified of him at first.

He retrieved his dagger from where it had come close to impaling him high up on the thigh—too high, he noticed with alarm—and used it to pick carefully through the remaining meat on the wooden trencher before him. He put the pieces one by one before Henri, on the pretense of feeding her, when he was in truth looking very closely to see what sort of creature she might really be. He could see little inside her hood except the shape of her nose.

A nose, he discovered upon further study, that looked a damned sight like a feminine version of Denis of Solonge's.

He cast about frantically for a plausible explanation. Noses were noses, weren't they? Many people had similar ones, and that didn't guarantee they were related to those similar noses.

Perhaps hers was merely a *French* nose. Aye, that was it. Colin nodded, feeling much more comfortable.

But that comfort was very short-lived when he actually got down to the business of examining the facts.

Henri had fled a cruel mistress. Marie, perhaps? She was certainly not a servant, which could only make her either an excessively cheeky freewoman or a highborn lady in disguise.

She had served Sybil how long? He wished he'd asked when he wouldn't have startled her with the question. He certainly couldn't lean over now and prod her for an answer. Though finding out she'd been at Maignelay-sur-mer for a pair of years certainly would have cleared up a few things for him.

He blinked, then looked and realized that Lord Denis was speaking to him.

"Eh?" he asked, dragging himself back to the present.

"I asked you if you thought you might find my girl in truth."

Colin looked at the man and wondered if he might have his clarity of vision just the same with a well-spoken query or two.

"Do you care?" he asked bluntly.

Henri's shoulder twitched.

"Care?" Denis asked hoarsely. "What kind of man are you to ask that?"

"You betrothed her to me, knowing what kind of man I am. What does that say for your care?"

"*I* didn't arrange it," the older man said stiffly. "Marie did."

"And you allowed it?" Colin asked, surprised. Perhaps Marie held greater sway here than he thought.

"I was . . . ," he paused for several moments, looking away. "I was not myself. Not thinking clearly."

"Thank you," Colin said dryly.

Lord Denis looked at him and flushed slightly. "No offense to you, of course."

Colin shrugged. "I am accustomed to brides finding a way

of avoiding coming to the altar with me. I'm not accustomed to them bolting outright."

"Aliénore is very resourceful," Denis admitted. "Smarter than all my lads put together is that one."

"She sounds a tolerable wench," Colin said, watching Henri's hands. "Likely no match for me, but I suppose that could be endured." Henri had stopped eating whilst Lord Denis was speaking. Now she clutched her fork and knife as if she'd fancy using them as weapons.

On him, perhaps?

"I heard you vowed to kill her should you ever find her," Denis continued.

"Aye," Colin said. "So I did."

Henri dropped her knife. Colin reached over casually and handed it back to her.

"Were you in earnest?"

Colin made a few noises one might associate with deep reflection, then shrugged his shoulders. "I was at the time," he said.

"And now?"

"Now . . . well, I suppose now doesn't matter, as I am unlikely to find her, am I?"

Denis pushed his chair back with a deep sigh. He looked at Colin, and the hurt plain on his face was enough to make Colin regret having toyed with Henri at Lord Denis's expense.

"I had hoped," he said quietly, "that the rumors of you were not true. You had given me hope this afternoon that I might find you a different sort of man. I'd wished it, for my Aliénore's sake."

And with that, he turned and walked toward the stairs. Colin felt remorse prick at him fiercely. He clapped Henri on the shoulder.

"Wait for me. Do not leave the hall."

Henri only nodded. Colin rose and quickly followed Lord Denis. He stopped the man halfway up the stairs.

"My lord," Colin said quietly, "I could not speak freely before my man there, but I will tell you here that should I find Aliénore, no harm will come to her by me."

The man's eyes filled with tears. Colin had to roll his to keep them from filling up likewise in sympathy.

"She is a good girl," Denis said quietly. "Beautiful and courageous. I fear she finds herself in dire straits with no hope of rescue. I had hoped, at first, that perhaps . . . you . . ."

"I will," Colin said. "I will find her. And when I do, I vow I'll protect her with my very life."

"But there is so little hope," Denis said faintly.

There is much more than you realize, Colin said silently. He merely nodded to the man and turned back to the great hall. He stood at the foot of the stairs and looked at Henri, alone and hunched over the table. Could this be she? Was there a way to know, short of asking her?

In case she didn't want him, of course.

He walked over and sat down next to her.

"Aliénore," he began slowly.

Her startled jump was telling.

"Aliénore needs us," he finished, reaching for his wine. "We will consult with her sire tomorrow, then begin our search. Will you aid me, Henri?"

The hood turned toward him slowly. "And when you find her, my lord? What will you do then?"

"What do you think I should do?" he asked. "Slay her? Beat her? Shout at her for making me fodder for jests all over England?"

"Were you that?" she asked, sounding surprised.

"Only by those with a mind for a shortened life," he replied.

She laughed.

The sound so startled him that he could only gape at her. By the saints, it was heavenly music he'd just heard. And he realized, then, that he had never once seen her smile—well, except at Jason, but that hardly counted where he was concerned—or heard her express any kind of humor or joy.

"That amuses you?" he asked, wondering if he might startle her into another such sound.

She shook her head and he could have sworn he saw the remains of a smile on her shadowed face.

"Nay," she said quietly. "Nay, my lord, it doesn't. But

surely your reputation protected you from her cowardly actions."

He couldn't correct her without spewing forth more than he dared, so he merely remained silent and waited for her to turn back to her supper. When, after several minutes, he realized she had no intentions of eating any more, he rose.

"Come, Henri, and let us see if we can find a safe place in this hall of horrors. I assume that that soul loitering by the stairs in that useless fashion is Marie's servant. Mayhap he'll be capable of showing us our beds."

Henri only nodded and rose to follow him.

Henri. Aliénore. He scarce knew what to call her.

But as he bedded down a short while later on the floor of a very small, very filthy chamber with her next to him, he found that for the first time in years, he had a reason to do something besides scowl.

The woman he loved and the woman he was betrothed to finding home in the same body.

Miracles never ceased.

Perhaps he should have worried that she wouldn't want him. Perhaps he should have worried that if he revealed what he knew, she would flee again. Perhaps he should have offered to release her from her contract.

Tomorrow, he decided. He would think on all that tomorrow. He would decide when and how to reveal what he knew to her. He would decide what was to be done with Sir Etienne—for 'twas a certainty he couldn't let the man go unpunished. He had more reason than ever to see him earn his just reward. And he would have to decide how to free Aliénore from Solonge without Marie harming her.

Which would likely be the most difficult task of all.

But for now, it was enough to enjoy the complete improbability of finding himself feeling . . . happy.

How his father would have ground his teeth at the thought!

He turned his head to look at his betrothed. "Sleep well," he said quietly.

She was silent for a moment or two, then sighed. "Thank you, my lord. You, too."

He smiled inside.

Chapter 29

A li stood up to her ankles in mud and wished for nothing more than to go back to bed where she was comfortable. She'd had such a peaceful night's rest. There was something to be said for having the Butcher of Berkhamshire sleeping but an arm's length away from you—especially when you had no fear of him.

Which was a most noteworthy and amazing thing in itself.

After such a wonderful night, she'd found herself coming quite close to a day of leisure. Colin had woken her with quite purposeful plans for the day, plans that had included having speech with her father in his solar. 'Twas just her luck that her sire had been unwell. Unfortunately, that had left Colin with nothing else to do but drag her out into the lists, where she had been for the past pair of hours. Those hours seemed more like years. It was taking all her strength merely to lift her sword and fend off Colin's very lukewarm attack.

"Bloody hell," he said, sounding thoroughly disgusted, "what are you thinking about? I could have removed your head from your shoulders a score of times this morning."

Ali forced her thoughts back to the task at hand and lifted her sword with all her concentration. Of course it didn't help that Solonge's entire garrison was gathered nearby, watching her. And it certainly didn't help that she'd seen four of her brothers at the table that morning, with promises of a fifth to stumble from his bed—and that would have been François, of course—by noon.

Did she but manage to survive the day, 'twould be nothing short of a miracle.

Too many watchers were beginning to make her very nervous. Her sword felt unfamiliar in her hands, and the complete familiarity of her surroundings only added to her unease. She dodged a particularly unpleasant thrust only to lose her balance and go down heavily on her backside in the mud. She sat there and looked up at Colin. He only sighed deeply, then put up his sword. He reached over and hauled her to her feet. Then he steadied her with his hands on her shoulders.

"We all have days," he said quietly, "when 'tis perhaps best to stop early." He peered down at her. "Is there aught that troubles you? Something you would care to tell me about?"

Ali frowned at him. What was it with the man of late? He would have rivaled a priest with his solicitousness! Was he beginning to go soft, or was Solonge working the same foulness upon him that it ever wrought on her?

"Henri?" he prompted.

"Trouble?" she asked. By the saints, she scarce knew where to begin in describing all the things that could be listed as troubles. "Ah, nay. No troubles."

"Well," he said, looking faintly disappointed, "I suppose if you have a moment, you might think of a few to share with me. And," he added, "with any luck we'll escape this accursed place before either of us encounter any more."

"Will we leave soon?"

"Are you ready to leave?"

"I was ready never to come here," she said, then bit her lip. Aye, that was wise, giving him reason to wonder why.

But he only nodded sagely. "Understandable. You'd likely heard rumors of the lady Marie, aye?"

"Aye," she said weakly.

"We'll leave after I speak with your—I mean, after I speak with . . . um . . . *our* good lord of Solonge. I've a thing or two to inquire of him, then we'll be on our way. Things about Aliénore, you know. That I might know better where to search."

Ali hardly cared where he searched as long as he managed to get them out of Solonge in the near future. She would worry about his searching once they were free of the keep.

And hopefully free of Sir Etienne.

Would that one be satisfied with whatever she could filch from her father's trunk, or would she find herself having to endure his presence further?

She looked up at Colin. "What of Sir Etienne? Will you leave him behind?"

"With any luck," he muttered. "Now, if you would forgive me, I feel the need to grind something into the dust and I daresay you would prefer that something to not be you. Perhaps the garrison here would be willing to indulge me."

She suspected they would, if only to be able to boast of having faced the man once during their lives—never mind if they walked away, or crawled away more likely, completely humiliated. Ali trudged across the field to the wall. She sat on the bench and dragged her filthy hands through her filthy hair. What she wanted was a wash and a warm fire. Perhaps Colin could be prevailed upon to end his torment of her father's garrison soon. She didn't relish the thought of sitting out in the rain, even if it allowed her to watch Colin do what he did best.

The men came, just as she'd thought they would, and with more enthusiasm than she would have suspected. Perhaps to have bested him would have been something to boast about all the way to the grave.

It didn't look like anyone would have anything to boast of any time soon, however.

Whatever beauty Colin's face lacked, his swordplay more than made up for. The man might have been huge, but he was, she had to admit, very graceful when it came to this deadly dance of his. He neither smiled nor cursed. He merely exercised his considerable skill and made no sound of boasting.

That is, until somewhere in the second score of men, when her father's largest and fiercest guardsman stepped to the fore.

Colin smiled pleasantly.

Ali had the feeling it wouldn't go well for the other man.

She searched back in her memory for the name: Osbert, from some little fief beholden to Solonge. Aye, she remembered him, now that she gave it some thought. He was the self-proclaimed fiercest of the lot, fiercest from his village, and, by his own estimation, sure to be sought after for any army with victory in mind.

All of which he recounted for Colin as he stretched various parts of himself and flexed his fingers.

Colin looked, predictably, quite bored.

And then Osbert drew his sword. And Colin drew his.

Osbert took a mighty swing. The clash of swords jarred Ali even where she sat and she wondered, briefly, if Colin might have met his match in this man. He was easily as large as Colin, seemed to be as strong, and his swordplay showed no small lack of skill. Colin merely kept to his task, parrying and thrusting, hacking and poking, using both hands when necessary.

A goodly while later, they were still at it; the only difference was that Osbert was beginning to grow quite red in the face.

"Your reputation," he said with a sneer, "overstates your skill."

"Does it?" Colin asked mildly.

"I've been but toying with you up to now," Osbert proclaimed loudly. "Now the true work of the day will begin."

"By all means," Colin said, inclining his head politely, "work away."

Osbert came at him with a whirlwind of strokes that left even Colin being forced to take a step or two backward.

Ali held her breath, suddenly quite unsure she could bear watching him be vanquished.

Indeed, Osbert seemed to find the falling back much to his liking, for he continued his relentless assault, spewing forth curses and taunts along with his merciless and very impressive attack. Even the garrison leaned forward in anticipation.

"See?" said a voice next to her ear. "I told you he was nothing."

Ali looked up in surprise to meet Sir Etienne's unpleasant visage. She quickly looked away and said nothing.

"Where is my treasure?"

"Locked up, likely."

His hand suddenly in her hair hurt very much, but she didn't allow him the satisfaction of knowing it. What she did notice was that Colin had looked her way and seen Sir Etienne's movement.

And then the unthinkable happened.

He went down in the mud.

Ali knew she had to do something, so she elbowed Sir Etienne in the groin as hard as she could, then glared at him as he knelt gasping next to the bench.

"I'll get it tonight," she said. "But trouble me again for it and you'll never have it."

"You foolish twit—"

"Trouble me again," she said, rising and putting her hand on the hilt of her sword, "and I'll tell Colin immediately everything he might wish to know and then *he'll* see to you. I daresay you wouldn't last long against him."

Sir Etienne continued to curse her, but it was interspersed with such gasps that she couldn't make much sense of it. She glared at him then and hurried farther down the wall.

Her father stood there, but perhaps he was protection enough for her purposes. She stood on his far side, putting him between herself and Sir Etienne. Then she looked back to the field and nodded to Colin. He spared her another brief glance before he rolled, just in time to miss being skewered on Osbert's sword.

"A fine warrior," Denis remarked.

"Lord Colin?" she asked, then gulped. "Lord Colin?" she repeated, making her voice as husky as possible.

Her father stilled, then looked down at her. She looked quickly away, realizing that she had left her cloak on the bench. Damn, what was she to do now? She kept her face averted, praying he wouldn't find her interesting enough to study at length.

"Aye, Lord Colin," he said slowly. "Have you served him long?"

"Many years," she lied.

"I see," her father said, sounding powerfully weak. "He wishes to speak to me. I suppose I must, then, after he's finished with this business here."

Ali stole a look at her sire and was surprised at how pale he was. Had he eaten something foul the night before? Or did the mere thought of Colin wreak havoc on the man? She watched him focus his attentions on Colin standing in the lists, and saw him shudder. She understood, of course. Colin was quite formidable. Well, at least her father was concentrating on his onetime son-in-law instead of her own soft and unmanly features.

The ring of swords drew her attention. She turned her attentions away from her father and concentrated on what was going on in front of her. Colin might have fallen and his clothing might have been mud-splattered, but apparently he was finished with humoring Osbert. He seemed to cast every bit of himself into his assault until there seemed to be no separation between him and his blade. Osbert was allowed no chance to rest and recover. Whereas he had been the aggressor, now he was fully on the defense and hard-pressed to keep that to an acceptable level.

And then Colin pulled forth strength and skill from a reservoir no merely mortal man should have possessed, and finished Osbert with half a dozen decisive, merciless strokes.

Osbert's sword went flying.

He went down on his knees.

And Colin turned to the unvanquished of the garrison.

"By twos, now," he said. "I've a mind for some true work this morning."

Osbert fell over into the mud with a groan.

Her father shook his head. "What a man. Too bad he has no kindness in him. I should have been glad to have him as a son otherwise."

Ali had to bite back a reply, then bit her tongue anyway when she realized she was near to defending Colin in glowing terms to her sire. By the saints, she was supposed to want to flee his presence at her earliest opportunity. She *wasn't* supposed to point out any good qualities he might have had. Had coming home caused her to lose all her wits?

Or had she just seen enough of Colin over the past several weeks to make her realize that he was not entirely the man his reputation made him out to be?

She drew her hand over her eyes and sighed. Her life had become a tangle she wasn't sure she would ever unravel. Then again, with all the dangerous souls about her, she might have more aid than she wished in unraveling that snarl. She wondered if any of them were nearby to offer her that help.

She looked around her father's back to see if Sir Etienne had disappeared. At least then she might retrieve her cloak and pull it on before any of her brothers decided to come to the lists to look under her shorn hair to see the kind of man Colin of Berkhamshire took on as a charitable endeavor.

Fortunately, Sir Etienne was gone.

Unfortunately, Marie had come to take his place.

Ali looked around frantically for somewhere to hide, but found nothing but an open field too wide to flee across and stone walls too high to surmount.

"Interesting display," Marie drawled, coming and slipping her arm through Denis's. "Don't you think, my love?"

"Hmmm," he agreed.

"If anyone can find that disobedient girl, he can, wouldn't you say?"

"Aye," came the answer.

"And what a man to take her in hand when he does find her. I'm certain he'll think up an appropriate punishment for her," she purred. "That kind of man thinks that way."

Ali watched as her father shook off Marie's hand. "I pray he does not. The girl has already suffered enough."

The change in Marie's expression was frightening in its swiftness. "You always did pamper that silly twit."

"She is my daughter, Marie. And I wish to heaven I'd never listened to you and allowed her to be betrothed to that man. I would have her now, safe, instead of wondering what horrible things might have happened to her."

And with that, he walked away.

Ali looked off over the field, pretending that she hadn't heard. A pity her father had listened to Marie. If he hadn't, she wouldn't have fled.

But then she wouldn't have known Colin.

And she couldn't help but feel that knowing him hadn't been completely without merit.

"Men," Marie said in disgust. "But you're one of them, aren't you?"

Ali only ducked her head and prayed fervently that Marie wouldn't come any closer.

But she did.

Marie slipped her arm through Ali's, just as she'd done with her father. "You're his man," she said softly. "What is he like? Have you seen him with any women?"

Ali shook her head.

"But he's cruel, is he not? Hard and unyielding? Surely a man like that has no gentleness in him."

Something Marie didn't sound displeased by in the least.

Ali could only nod and wonder how she might possibly extricate herself from this situation. She began to sidle to the right, but Marie was having none of that. Her fingers dug into Ali's upper arm to hold her.

"Skinny, aren't you?" she asked. "And pretty, for a knight."

Then she said no more. Ali didn't dare look at her. But suddenly she found that she had no choice. Marie's claw had grasped her by the chin and wrenched her face around. Ali tried to look away, but that was even less successful than avoiding Marie in the first place. She found herself soon with no choice but to meet her stepmother's eyes.

The triumph in those eyes was complete.

"Well," Marie breathed with a slow smile. "What do we have here?"

Ali found, quite suddenly, that she couldn't breathe. Terror? Nay, she'd never felt it before, if this paralyzing stuff that washed over her at present was what it truly felt like.

"My lady, you're frightening my little lad."

A large hand came to rest gently around Marie's wrist.

"Release him, if you will."

Ali wondered how it was that Colin had arrived to rescue her so quickly. Well, never mind that; he was there and that was all that mattered. She jerked her arm away from Marie, leaped behind Colin, and used him as a fine, large barrier to hide behind. Who would have thought he would become her deliverer? She closed her eyes and began to pray.

"Why, that is quite a womanly guardsman you have there, to my mind," Marie said smoothly.

"And it pains him, believe me," Colin said, "so I try not to speak of it overmuch. Now, might I escort you back inside? Surely this weather is too foul for a lady such as yourself to endure."

Marie tried to look around Colin's shoulder, but Colin stepped to block her view. Then he gave Marie no choice but to accept his arm and go back toward the hall. Ali kept Colin between herself and her stepmother, then snatched up her cloak and pulled it around her and over her face.

But she knew in her heart it was too late.

Marie knew.

All that remained was to see when Marie would choose to reveal her. It would be, no doubt, at the worst possible moment.

She wondered if she might manage to escape through the gates before the alarm was sounded.

She tried right then, but she suddenly found herself hauled back alongside Colin by the back of her cloak. His grip said that he wasn't about to let her go. She was thereby forced to listen to him converse with Marie. It occurred to her as they reached the great hall that he was certainly babbling about more unimportant things than she'd ever heard in her life, but perhaps victory did that to a man.

Though she'd seen Colin vanquish others before and he certainly hadn't frothed at the mouth in quite this manner.

She found herself dragged into the great hall and could do nothing but allow it. Sir Etienne was standing near the fire in the midst of the hall.

"Tonight," he snarled at her as she passed. "His solar."

She rolled her eyes as she continued her unwilling journey across the floor. First Sir Etienne, then Marie, then Sir Etienne reminding her of the thievery she must commit. Could anyone else arrive to make a demand of her?

A breathless squire began trotting alongside her.

"My lord Berkhamshire is astonishing, isn't he?" he panted.

Ali glared at him. As if she wanted to discuss any exploits of the man who refused to let go of her at present!

"Tell me of him, won't you?" said another who had suddenly appeared at his fellow's side. "It must be exciting traveling with him. Danger, intrigue, secret assignments."

Ali would have snorted, but her tunic was beginning to strangle her and she didn't have the air for it. She was finally deposited against the wall; Colin took his seat next to Marie and began regaling her with all manner of tales Ali was almost certain he was making up on the spot.

Then again, the man simply couldn't lie.

Could he have actually leaped from windows thusly? Vanquished scores of enemies with but himself and his sword? Been paid such vast sums of gold for mercenary endeavors?

The squires were panting at her side, listening with their mouths hanging open and their tongues lolling out in disbelief.

For herself, Ali could have wished for far less danger, intrigue, and secret assignments.

And when Marie threw a single smile over her shoulder at Ali, she knew she was on the verge of experiencing far too much of all three.

Chapter 30

Colin lay awake in his minuscule chamber and fought sleep. It wasn't as difficult as it might have been another time, especially given the most extraordinary events of the past many hours.

It had taken him a goodly portion of the night before—spent mostly awake, as well—to accustom himself to the thought of Henri actually being Aliénore. When the sun had risen, he'd met it wide-eyed and anxious to get on with his business. Unfortunately, finding Lord Denis indisposed had left him with no choice but to retire to the lists and endeavor to distract himself until the man recovered from whatever malady had laid him low.

Perhaps Marie had worn him down to nothing.

A frightening thought to contemplate, indeed.

He turned his mind quickly to other things. His pleasant time in the lists that morning was an appealing thing to linger over, but unfortunately not something he could permit himself at the moment. Besides, intermingled with all the memories of vanquishment were visions of Aliénore being approached by various and sundry souls who wished her no good. His concern for her had cost him a trip down into the mud, but he couldn't begrudge her that—especially after he'd seen her place her elbow with great enthusiasm in Sir Etienne's most private parts.

What a wench.

But now that wench was currently rising from her pallet with great stealth. Colin closed his eyes quickly and feigned a few snores. What was she about?

Nothing good, no doubt.

Colin had heard Sir Etienne hiss something at her earlier that evening, so perhaps she was seeing to some foul work for him. Colin waited until she had eased out the door before he rose quietly and belted his sword about him. He didn't trouble himself with his mail. Even should he encounter Sir Etienne, that man merited no more than a stiff leather jerkin to repel any of his feeble blows.

Colin left the chamber and saw Aliénore creeping down the passageway. That she was heading toward Denis's solar and not toward the great hall gave him pause. She wasn't fleeing. Then what? Did she plan to stick Marie whilst she slept? A fine plan, and one he hoped she could accomplish with all dispatch.

The sight of Marie standing next to Aliénore in the lists earlier that day would likely be a vision he would carry to his grave. Nothing short of sheer panic had propelled him across the lists so quickly that afternoon. He'd seen the knowledge in her eyes and searched desperately for something to do to distract her from contemplating it further. Not even putting forth his best imitation of a charming, boastful, talkative Artane lad at table had seemed to distract the woman from her thoughts.

But what would she do with her knowledge? That she hadn't blurted the truth out right there to him gave him significant pause. If she didn't intend to reveal Aliénore, what did she intend to do?

It couldn't be good, whatever it was.

He had decided earlier that evening that the best course of action was to go to bed. He'd done so, taking Aliénore with him, simply because the effort of talking for so long had thoroughly exhausted him. He could have spent two solid se'nnights in the lists and it wouldn't have been as taxing as passing an afternoon and evening with his mouth running as freely as a river. By the saints, how did Jason do it? Boasts, flatteries, questions he couldn't have possibly desired the answers to?

And now Aliénore, damn her, was throwing herself into danger without so much as a "by your leave."

Unless she merely planned to filch something from her father's solar, then be on her way.

Without him.

He scowled. Well, she could try, but he would find her just the same. He was an expert tracker and she a mere woman. A clever woman, to be sure, but not his equal when it came to the hunt.

He studiously avoided the thought that did he reveal his knowledge to her, she would demand to be released from her betrothal to him.

He would give that some thought later.

Later, when he'd screwed up his own considerable courage to be able to face the possible rejection.

But now his path was clear and he put his foot to it without hesitation. He melted back into the shadows when Aliénore looked behind her before entering her sire's solar. Had he entertained any further doubts about her identity, this small journey during the middle of the night would have silenced them. She knew this bloody hall far too well.

He opened the solar door, then quickly and silently slipped inside. He quickly ensconced himself in the shadows as Aliénore looked back toward the door. She cursed and came across the chamber to push the bolt home. Then she returned to the trunk under the window and went back to her task.

Of robbing her father blind, apparently.

Unfortunately, the lock was giving her trouble. Colin watched as she looked about her father's table for the key, kicked the trunk several times in frustration, then set to with her dagger. That lasted longer than he thought it would before she jabbed her knife into the top and cursed in frustration.

"If you're going to ruin the top, why not just cut the entire thing open with your sword?" he asked.

She gasped, jumped up, and whirled around so quickly, she choked. She was still hunched over, alternately choking and gasping for breath when he crossed the chamber and patted her as gently as he knew how on the back. Even so, she almost went sprawling and he had to catch her by the arm and pull her back upright.

"Theft?" he asked doubtfully. "Is this a proper knightly activity, Henri?"

"Ah . . . ah, I'm m-merely—"

He pursed his lips. "What? Stealing from Solonge's lord? Filching coin to finance an escape?"

She looked at him and he was surprised by the expression on her face. A more foolish man might have thought she looked a bit appalled at that idea.

"Nay, my lord. I was not seeking a means of escape."

Colin put that expression away in his memory to examine later. 'Twas far better a look than one that bespoke complete revulsion.

A man took what he could.

"If not escape," he asked, "then what?"

She sank down onto the trunk suddenly and put her face in her hands. She sat there silently. Colin studied her for a goodly while, then sighed.

"You aren't going to tell me, are you?" he asked.

"The truth," she began slowly, "the truth is . . . unpalatable."

"I have a strong stomach."

She looked up at him then and a ghost of a smile crossed her features. "This I fear, my lord, might sicken even you."

He wondered, with a sudden surge of alarm, if Sir Etienne had taken more from her than her peace of mind. Then he took a deep breath and shook aside the thought. The man was too greedy for rapine to be his first choice. Colin had no doubts that once Aliénore had satisfied his purse, Sir Etienne would turn to other things, but at the moment his purse was still empty.

All the more reason to stop him whilst he could.

He pulled up a stool and sat down across from Aliénore. "I have seen many things," he said, "that would finish a weaker man. I daresay nothing you could possibly say would even make me turn my nose up. So, share your burden with me. Perhaps I can aid you."

She looked at him as if she could scarce believe her ears. Colin wondered with a goodly bit of surprise if he was so truly fiercesome that such a generous offer would cause Aliénore to feel such a sense of disbelief.

He scowled. "I have a softer side, you know. Generous, even, when moved by the right circumstances."

She smiled faintly. "My lord, your reputation often does you disservice. I do not doubt that you would aid me if you could. But the tale I would give you would no doubt inspire you to other thoughts besides those of succor."

He frowned thoughtfully, trying to unravel her words. Did she not think him as fierce as he was or did she appreciate his ferocious reputation yet think him tolerable in spite of it?

How did that bode for a future with this woman?

Best not to think on that now, lest he be distracted from prying the truth from her.

"Why do you not try me," he offered, "and see?"

She looked at his hands. He held them up to show they were empty. She sighed.

"Very well. Sir Etienne wishes me to steal something for him."

Colin was unsurprised. "And if you do not?"

"He will kill you. Or perhaps Jason first. I can't remember the order at the moment."

He felt one eyebrow go up of its own accord. "Indeed."

"The sword at your throat was merely a warning," she said. "As was the attack on Jason. The next time he would succeed. I've no doubt of it."

"Well," Colin said, rubbing his hands together in anticipation, "that sounds like reason enough for me to do him in first, wouldn't you say?"

"Aye," she agreed. "Reason enough."

"At least we concur on something. Now, this cannot be the only reason you are here, bent on thievery. What else does he hold over your head?"

Aliénore bowed her head. "I cannot tell you."

"Cannot, or will not?"

She looked up at him from under her shorn hair. "Does it matter?"

He supposed it didn't. He shook his head.

"I cannot tell you," she said, "for the telling of that secret would mean my death."

"I could protect you."

She smiled again, without humor, but said nothing.

Well, he supposed she thought he would kill her if she

revealed herself to him. Given what he'd said in her presence without thinking before, he could well understand why she would. In time, perhaps he could convince her otherwise. Now, though, his task was to deal with Sir Etienne. What would Lord Denis think if he arrived in his solar to find Sir Etienne's dead body draped over his trunk?

Colin suspected he wouldn't be pleased.

He could, however, at least convince Sir Etienne that troubling Aliénore further would be a mistake. A fatal one, if the man was slow in learning his lessons.

"Al-ah, Henri," Colin said, wishing heartily that the ruse was over and he could call her by her true name. It would save him a mighty bit of aggravation. "Henri," he said, "go back to our chamber; I'll wait for Sir Etienne here."

Her mouth fell open. "You jest," she breathed.

"I do nothing of the sort. He'll come in, fumble around in the dark, and then I'll step from the shadows to greet him. 'Tis a simple plan, easily executed, and will be quite successful. I will give him reason to leave you be."

She shook her head violently. "You cannot—"

"I most certainly can, and I will." He stood, then reached out and pulled her to her feet. "Trust me. I can see to him."

"It isn't now that troubles me," she snapped, " 'tis later! What will you do when an arrow comes at you from the shadows? How can you defend against that?"

"Do you think he'll leave this chamber on his feet?" Colin asked.

She paused. "You'll slay him?"

"I'll leave him in perfect condition to pass a goodly bit of time in the dungeon. By the time he's freed, we will be well on our way back to England. I daresay he hasn't the imagination to follow us there, think you?"

She looked powerfully pale, even in the faintest of lights. "You don't know him."

"I know his kind."

"He'll never rest until he's slain us all."

"He'll invent his own ending to the tale, with him as the hero and me at his feet begging for mercy. That is a tale, I might add, that no one with any wit whatsoever will believe.

He won't bother to make another journey to England. Now, go. Be swift and silent, if you can manage it."

"But—"

"I know," he agreed, "I don't like to leave you roaming the passageways at night by yourself either, but I can see no other alternative at present. Draw your sword and go swiftly. This shouldn't take long." He took her by the arm and led her across the solar. He'd memorized where the furniture lay and had no trouble finding his way through it. He opened the door quietly, then looked out into the passageway. It was empty. He pushed Aliénore out into the passageway. "Your sword," he prompted.

She drew her sword, gave him a final look of something akin to worry—which he dismissed with a snort—and then put her shoulders back and crept back down the passageway. Colin closed the door and retreated to the darkest corner. He sat and made himself comfortable, though he supposed he wouldn't have to wait long. Sir Etienne would no doubt employ much haste to have his prize.

Colin didn't wait long. The moon had only begun to pour its light through the window before the door was eased open and a large shape came inside. The door closed and was bolted. Colin nodded to himself. Apparently, Sir Etienne had plans to have his treasure without interruption. The other man paused in the middle of the chamber, then looked about him.

"Aliénore?"

Colin nodded to himself in satisfaction. He'd suspected that this was the other part of Sir Etienne's extortion, of course. But how had the man learned who she was? And how long had he known it? Colin had no doubts that he himself had been used as a weapon to force her cooperation. No doubt Sir Etienne had promised her several choice tortures at Colin's own hands if she didn't do his bidding.

All the more reason to make it so the man wasn't capable of any more blackmail.

"She's not here," Colin said pleasantly. "But I am."

Sir Etienne whirled around with something of a gasp. "Berkhamshire," he said. "What do you want?"

"Your head adorning my gates might do for a start."

Sir Etienne huffed a bit. "You don't want me. It's that girl you want. She's your betrothed, you know."

"Aye," Colin said calmly, "I know."

That brought Sir Etienne up short. "You know?" he asked.

"Have for some time," Colin answered. That was true, he reasoned. He'd known since supper the night before, and that was some time. "So, I suppose that's nothing you can use against her anymore, is it? What else did you threaten her with? Killing me?"

Sir Etienne seemed to sway for a heartbeat or two, then regained his composure. "Let us do this," he said. "Let us cast our lot in together and go look for the gel. She has treasure enough for two, I'll warrant."

The man was inventive, Colin would give him that. And quick thinking. Apparently, though, he'd heard the tales of Colin's prowess but chosen to ignore the tales of his principles. Stealing was not an activity he engaged in.

Instruction, however, was something he felt compelled by his knightly vows to undertake as often as circumstances warranted. And this fool here needed a lesson not only in manners, but in knightly comportment. And who better to see to remedying that lack than he?

He drew his sword. That was answer enough for Sir Etienne, he supposed, for the man cursed quite furiously and drew his own blade.

Colin wondered if Lord Denis would mind if his solar were razed if the cause were a just one.

The battle was fought silently except for the ring of swords and the occasional grunt. Colin did his best to avoid cleaving any furniture in twain, but unfortunately a stool or two fell victim to his ferocity.

As did Sir Etienne in time. Colin rid the man of his sword, his dagger, and then his dignity and the already mangled shape of his nose. He supposed that perhaps breaking it a second time was unsporting, but then again, Sir Etienne had many of Aliénore's bruises and cuts to pay for. The memory of those, and of her tears, left him at his work far longer than usual. It was with sincere regret that he watched a blow he dealt Sir Etienne under the chin plunge the man into senselessness.

Being that he wasn't one to beat an unconscious man.

It wasn't chivalrous, of course.

He lit a candle from a torch down the passageway and gave himself light enough to bind Sir Etienne securely. The man would last there until morning. Colin left Lord Denis a short note regarding his wishes for Sir Etienne's care, then took Sir Etienne's weapons—given that the man would have little use for them where he was going for the next little while—and left the solar, shutting the door behind him.

It was then that he realized what had struck him as odd not a handful of moments before.

There was a lit torch in the passageway.

There hadn't been such when he'd followed Aliénore to her father's solar.

He paused, then shrugged. No doubt a guard had left it lit to make his rounds easier. Or perhaps Sir Etienne himself had brought it to make it easier to examine his gold after having received it. Whatever the case, it made little difference now. What remained was for him to sleep for the night, rise, and see if he couldn't shake Solonge's dust off his feet before midday. He had absolutely no desire to linger.

He suspected Aliénore would feel the same way.

He walked quietly back to his chamber and lifted his hand to the door.

It wasn't shut.

Colin lay Sir Etienne's weapons on the ground, drew his sword, and fetched another lit torch. A quick but thorough look inside his chamber revealed no one but a serving wench who looked as if she stood to face her death at his hands.

"Where is the lad?" he demanded.

"The lady Marie bid him come upstairs to her private solar and have refreshment with her," the girl said, her eyes wide, her chin quivering. "She bid you come as well when you arrived."

Refreshment? At this hour? The only refreshing thing he would find would be Aliénore safe and Marie trussed up thanks to her stepdaughter's skill with blade and rope.

Unfortunately, Colin hadn't taught her any knots, and he wondered if she could possibly have managed to lay a hand on her dagger before her stepmother had dragged her away to her private chamber.

Obviously, Marie hadn't been fooled by the conversings he'd tried to distract her with that afternoon. She had recognized Aliénore and come to fetch her. The only question now was, what had she done to the girl already?

Chapter 31

A *li* sat in the alcove of Marie's solar and shivered. It certainly wasn't from the cold. Sweat poured down her face, down her back, down to pool in the cloth wrapped around her chest. She'd never felt such terror in all her life, and she'd certainly passed enough time in this chamber for such to be truly a startling admission. She looked at her stepmother, who sat upon a chair, looking as serene as a summer's morn. No stray hairs escaping her wimple, no frown marring her brow, no pucker of irritation ruining the perfect symmetry of her lips.

Could evil truly look so beautiful?

Ali wondered if she might gain the door before Marie leaped from her chair and buried her knife in her back.

"I wouldn't," Marie said, as if she gently chided a child thinking to touch the thorn of a rose.

Ali realized she was halfway off the stool only because she had to sit back down. She closed her eyes against the sight of Marie's chamber and wished that she'd never left her father's solar. She could have hidden behind Colin as he did his business of death. Either that, or she should have taken a torch with her and checked to see if her own small chamber was empty.

Which it hadn't been.

She supposed that in truth she had only herself to blame. Had she never left the chamber in the first place, she never would have had Colin follow her, then shoo her away from her little bit of robbery. Then she never would have found herself standing outside her chamber with Marie's arm around her shoulders and a knife pressed against her neck. Her blade had remained in her hand, useless, until Marie had removed it and tossed it inside Ali's chamber. Refusing to accompany her stepmother up to her solar had been unthinkable. Too many years of obeying merely to avoid worse punishment had left her obeying yet again simply out of habit.

All of which left her sitting where she was, huddled in the alcove, awaiting certain death.

She'd known it would finish thusly, that she would die at Solonge. The only question that remained was who would do it. And since Marie had left a servant to direct Colin to her solar at his earliest convenience, Ali supposed she would watch the two of them fight for the privilege of slitting her throat.

Unless she could make good her escape. She did have a knife in her boot that Marie had apparently overlooked.

She slipped her hand down her leg and had almost touched the haft when the door flung inward. Who should be standing there than her betrothed, the Butcher of Berkhamshire.

Looking less than pleased.

He stared at Marie. "What," he asked curtly, "do you want?"

Marie smiled. "Not exactly an epitome of manners, are you?"

Well, the woman had an amazing display of cheek, Ali would give her that.

Colin leaned back against the doorframe and pursed his lips. "Your lord husband no doubt expects you elsewhere," he said pointedly.

Marie laughed. "Ah, that I should be so desperate for a man that I should settle for you. Nay, my lord Berkhamshire, I didn't invite you here for a tryst. I merely thought you might be interested in knowing whom you've had under your wing for these past pair of months."

Ali didn't dare look at Colin. She was far too busy contemplating the possibilities for her end.

Death at Marie's hands.

Or death at Colin of Berkhamshire's hands.

She suspected the second would hurt far worse, and it had nothing to do with the pain of a knife. She couldn't bear the thought of seeing the look on his face when he discovered the depth and breadth of the lies she'd told him. Or the expression he would wear when he realized that he was looking at the woman who hadn't even had a decent excuse for why she'd bolted on him.

Fortunately, at the moment Colin's attention was focused on Marie and not on her. She didn't dare try to divine what he was thinking. He seemed unsurprised to see her there, and Marie's announcement hadn't seemed to surprise him either. Perhaps it was just his warrior's training that left his face so expressionless.

Or anger that was so deep he didn't dare show it.

"Take off your clothes."

Ali blinked, then realized Marie was speaking to her. She looked at her stepmother in surprise. "What?"

"Take off your clothes," Marie said, with a negligent wave of her hand. "Let our fine lordling here see exactly what you are. He'll divine the who readily enough after that."

Ali swallowed past her parched throat. "Never," she rasped.

Marie paused, then cocked her ear, as if she hadn't heard aright. "Perhaps I didn't make myself clear," she said, pinning Ali with a look that spoke all too eloquently of the tortures to come if Ali disobeyed. "Take them off. All of them. And take them off now."

Ali wished desperately that she still wore her mail. Or even a leather jerkin. Her simple tunic was far too little gear to have protecting her modesty.

She darted a look at Colin, but he only continued to lean with profound indifference against the doorframe. So, she was on her own. She licked her lips with a tongue that felt as if it had spent the night outside her mouth. Could tongues in truth become so dry? A block of wood would have served her better than that useless bit of flesh.

"I," Ali began, her voice breaking, "I will . . . not."

It was nothing short of astonishing how quickly a body could move. Before Ali could do more than squeak, Marie had leaped on her, slit her tunic down the front, and shoved the sleeves down her arms. Marie tore at the cloth that hid Ali's bosom from view. Ali did fight her then, trying to dodge Marie's poking blade and save her modesty at the same time.

In the end, she was left standing there, clutching one end of the cloth over herself, her head tipped uncomfortably back as Marie held her by what little hair she had left. Marie was breathing heavily, but there was complete satisfaction in her voice when she spoke.

"Here, my lord Berkhamshire," she said triumphantly. "May I present to you the errant lady of Solonge, Aliénore."

And with that, she flung Ali down onto the floor. Ali skidded across the flat stones of the chamber and stopped just before Colin's feet. She knelt there, hunched over so she would neither have to see his face nor show him anything more than he'd just seen.

"One of your knights, I presume?" Marie asked politely.

Colin was silent.

Ali knelt there, staring at his boots, and wondered when it was he would use one of those boots to kick the life from her. Or would he use his sword? Would he hack her to bits and feed her to her father's hounds? Or would he give her to Marie, to suffer her stepmother's form of justice? Would those boots suddenly turn and leave the chamber?

"Shall you see to her for her deception," Marie asked with unnerving calm, "or shall I?"

Again, Colin was silent. Indeed, the silence grew so thick that Ali wondered if she might ever again take a normal breath. She continued to stare at Colin's boots, noting the scuffs and the mendings—rather well done, actually—and the wear that had come from miles of trudging over soil.

Looking for her.

If he did kill her, he might likely be justified for it, given the trouble she'd caused him.

The fact that he hadn't moved, or spoken, was beginning to be a bit tedious. If she'd had any courage at all, she would have sat up, looked him in the face and told him to get on with the bloody business.

But she was a coward of the vilest sort.

So she kept her head bowed and her eyes on his boots.

And then the boots moved.

She heard him cross the chamber. She heard no other foot-steps, so she assumed Marie had remained where she was. Brave woman. Then again, what had she to fear from the Butcher? *She* hadn't betrayed him, deceived him, taken advantage of his kindness.

The boots returned, carrying Colin with him, and resumed their place by the doorway. And then he spoke.

"You should get up," he said.

Never mind that over the past several weeks she had come to trust the man standing over her. That her end was so close and she so close to facing it was almost more than her poor form could handle. She crawled to her feet, shaking violently.

"You should, um, cover up," Colin said.

She did look up at him then, but he was looking away. He merely held out her torn tunic. She didn't hesitate. She re-wrapped her strip of cloth around her chest, then ripped the tunic from his hands and shoved her arms back into the sleeves. She clutched the ragged edges together.

Marie made a sound of disgust. "Perhaps you aren't as ruthless as the rumors purport. I would have thought slaying a bare-breasted woman would have been fine sport for such a one as you."

Colin didn't answer, but he did look over Ali's head at Marie. And there was nothing friendly in that gaze. Ali would have taken heart at that, but she knew it was but a matter of time before that same gaze was turned on her.

"I can see I'm to be the one to punish her," Marie said, sounding not in the least bit displeased by the thought. "I should have done it years ago. You know, her mother was weak. How she spawned so many lads is a mystery. I suppose 'twas inevitable that she should spew forth a girl, and one like this." Marie laughed, but there was no humor in the sound. " 'Twas a mercy I poisoned her dam, don't you think?"

Ali looked at her stepmother, hardly able to believe what she'd just heard. "You what?"

Marie smiled coldly. "I poisoned her. It didn't take much. It never does with those kind."

Ali felt the chamber begin to spin. And in the midst of

falling to the floor, she found herself still on her feet, with heavy hands on her shoulders, holding her up. They were, all things considered, surprisingly gentle hands.

Colin called her stepmother a very unflattering name.

"Tsk-tsk," Marie chided. "So unchivalrous. I daresay you would have done the same thing. Didn't you make a vow to slay Aliénore in the most painful of ways when you found her?"

Well, she had him there, Ali had to admit to herself.

But Colin's grip on her shoulder's didn't change. He cleared his throat.

"I don't kill for sport."

"Neither do I," Marie snapped. "I kill to rid the world of weaklings. Like Marguerite." She fixed Ali with a hate-filled gaze. "Like her daughter, Aliénore."

Ali would have likely swayed a bit more, but it was difficult to do the like when she was being held up by a man who still had his hands on her shoulders and not around her neck. Was it possible he was rethinking his vow to slay her? Promising to give that some thought later, Ali turned her attentions back to her stepmother.

"You can't poison me," she said. "I'll never again drink anything at your table." Never mind that she might not have the chance to ever drink anything else at Marie's table. It was satisfying just to say the words.

"But, my dear," Marie said with a cold smile, "you already have."

Ali swayed, but Colin hauled her back against his chest.

"She wouldn't have done it already," he said quietly. "Not until she'd tormented you first. I know her kind."

Ali looked at Marie and saw the briefest flash of displeasure cross her features. It was replaced soon enough with that annoying look of triumph, but it was enough to make Ali wonder if Colin might have it aright.

Colin patted her shoulder in his usual bone-breaking fashion. "Make her choose her weapon," he said.

Ali looked over her shoulder at him. "What did you say?"

"What did you say?" Marie echoed.

Colin shrugged. "I didn't train you for all that skill to be lost in a circle of stitchers, now did I? Avenge your dam. Kill this vexatious wench and let us be on our way."

"But . . ."

"You've the skill."

"But . . ."

"And the courage," he added. "Have her choose her weapon and her place, Aliénore, then kill her. I'll say it was provoked, that you had to defend yourself, and we'll be done with the thing."

Marie's movement was so sudden, Ali almost didn't see her coming. She turned just in time to see the blade flashing down toward her.

And Colin, damn him, did nothing but move out of the way so his tunic likely didn't get splattered with her blood.

She had little time to think on how she would curse him for that. Her mind cleared and she was left with nothing in its place but the instincts she'd had drilled into her for the past two months. She leaped out of the way of the blade, grabbed Marie's wrist, and, with a vicious twist, left her stepmother with no choice but to drop the knife.

She slammed the heel of her hand into the woman's nose and, while Marie was spewing forth both blood and curses, swept her feet out from under her and left Marie sprawled on the ground. Ali snatched up the knife and had Marie on her belly, her hand in Marie's hair, and Marie's throat bared to the blade all before Marie could damn her soul to hell.

Which Marie did all the same, of course.

"Well," Ali said, her chest heaving a bit, "I don't believe I'd fancy a visit there, especially since that'll likely be your new home. Now, do I slay you here, or leave you to my father's justice?"

"Your sire will never believe I killed your mother," Marie said, with admirable bluster given the circumstances.

"He will."

"We know you lie. He'll believe the same of Berkhamshire."

"We'll find proof."

"There were no witnesses. She was laboring with your

younger brother. I killed them both whilst the women went to heat water."

Ali tightened her hand in Marie's hair. "I should kill you," she said, tears stinging her eyes. "I would be justified."

"Do, and your father will hang you," Marie said defiantly.

A throat cleared itself from the doorway. Ali looked over to find her father standing next to Colin. His face was ashen, but he stood firmly on his feet.

Marie must have seen the same thing, for she did her best to slit her own throat on the dagger. Ali tossed the knife away, then looked about her for something to bind Marie's hands with. She found a belt dangled before her and took it, not sparing Colin a glance. She wondered if he might regret its loss later, when he was about pursuing his own revenge upon her sorry self, but she shoved that thought aside. She had enough to think on with trying to bind her stepmother's wrists behind her before the woman escaped.

It was done, not quickly, nor easily, but done. Ali jumped off Marie's still-bucking form, then stepped back and watched as her stepmother rolled over and gave her a look of such malice that she backed up another several paces.

The blood flowed freely down Marie's face. "I'll kill you for this," she vowed, spitting blood onto the floor.

"You could try," Ali said, taking a deep breath. "But I doubt you would succeed."

Marie smiled, and the sight of *that* was enough to make Ali think that facing Colin might be a blessing. Mayhap he would do her in before Marie could escape and do the deed herself. She suspected Marie's revenge would be much more painful.

"Don't fear, my girl," Denis said. "She won't touch you."

Ali looked at her father, then suddenly found herself in his arms. She closed her eyes and wrapped her arms around him tightly. There was too much to say and no time for it. She allowed herself to enjoy a moment or two of complete comfort before she pulled away.

"Well met, Father," she said, managing a bit of a smile.

He brushed his hand over her hair. "Ah, Aliénore," he said, shaking his head. "I have much to say to you, daughter."

"I long to hear it."

"Let me finish this tale," he said, "then we'll talk."

She nodded, then stepped away from him.

Unfortunately, that meant that she now had to look at Colin, which she did with a great lack of enthusiasm. His expression, damn him, was inscrutable.

"I suppose," she said heavily, "that you and I have business to finish as well."

"I daresay," he said.

Was that dryness in his tone? Humor? Or the musings of a man who contemplated just how long and thoroughly he must needs humiliate his errant betrothed before he put her in either a convent or a grave?

Though she had to admit the convent was sounding less attractive by the heartbeat. She very much suspected that a life of prayer, while it certainly might be suitable for others, was not for her.

Not enough intrigue.

Ali walked away before she could contemplate that further. She heard heavy footsteps behind her, so she knew her doom followed, but she tried not to let that trouble her. Her last few minutes of freedom should certainly be spent where she might breathe fresh air.

Mayhap Colin would put her in a dungeon of his own making where he could torment her at his pleasure. Scraps of food now and then, perhaps. Foul water. Vermin dropped on her head. Poorly sung melodies chanted at her from dusk till dawn. Truly, the possibilities were unpleasant, and vast, so perhaps it didn't serve her to think overmuch on them.

She came to herself to realize she was on the battlements, on the wall overlooking the ocean. She hadn't enjoyed the view much when she'd lived there, though she had often escaped to the roof to escape Marie.

Colin, however, had not followed her out to share the view. She could see him, though, a darker bit of shadow in the dark shadows of the doorway leading down into the stairwell that led down to the passageway. That gave her pause. She vaguely remembered his having said something about not liking heights.

Imagine. Colin of Berkhamshire having a weakness.

She sighed. "You may shout at me now, if you wish."

"For what?" came the response from safely inside the doorway. That response was accompanied by a mighty snort. "For masquerading as a knight? For leading me on a merry chase across England and France? For bringing me up to this accursed place where I will no doubt fall to my death within moments?"

She considered. He didn't sound overly annoyed. She'd certainly heard him bellow before, and there were no bellows coming from the shadows. Complaints, aye, but no shouts of fury.

"I don't think you'll fall," she offered.

Another hearty snort proceeded forth from the gloom.

Well, what to do now? She supposed the courageous thing to do would have been to bravely face whatever tortures he had in mind for her. But having so narrowly escaped death at Marie's hands, it seemed a shame to suffer that fate at Colin's. Especially when he apparently had no intentions of following her out onto the parapet.

How long could a body remain out there?

Food could be brought, true. Relieving herself would be a problem, but she'd faced like obstacles before and triumphed.

Well, if Colin expected her to simply walk off the roof and into his vile clutches where he could do her in, he would be surprised at how difficult that would be.

"I think," she announced, "that I could be quite happy here on the roof for some time."

"Daft wench," he grumbled. "You can't stay up here forever."

"I could."

"You'll catch your death. Now, show some of those fine, manly traits I've admired in you for some time and get your bloody self down to where most rational men pass their time."

"I'm not a man," she said archly.

"I knew that almost from the start."

She turned toward the doorway. "You did not."

"All right," he conceded, "I knew *what* you were on the

ship to France. I only realized *who* you were at supper last night."

She leaned her hip against the wall and folded her arms over her chest—only realizing then that her tunic was still slit down the front. She clutched the edges together and wished she weren't at such a disadvantage. It would have been easier to face her fate with dignity if she'd been fully dressed.

"Well," she said, nonplussed. "What are you going to do about it now?"

"Find my bed and sleep."

Her mouth fell open of its own accord. "That's it? That's *all?*"

"What else do you suggest?"

"I thought," she said huffily, drawing herself up, "that you'd be giving some serious thought as to how you might best put me in my grave!"

There was no answer. But after a moment or two, there was a hand, thrust out of the darkness toward her.

No comment. No invitation. Just a hand.

Ali honestly couldn't tell if she would be placing herself in a hand that would subsequently strangle her or merely help her down the stairs. Damn him, she'd been fretting over his reaction for *years* and now all he could do was hold out his bloody hand? As if there were nothing amiss with it!

But the hand was empty. No knife, no sword, no bottle of poison.

A safe hand, if you didn't think about whom it was attached to.

A hand a girl might easily put her hand into, under different circumstances.

She considered for several minutes what she might do, but in the end, when the hand began to beckon to her in a most impatient fashion, she crossed the parapet and put her hand in Colin's. So she would die. Everyone did.

But then his warm, callused fingers closed very gently around hers and pulled her through the doorway.

If she'd expected either a kiss or a knife across her throat, she received neither. Colin released her hand as quickly as he would have if she'd had the plague, then started down the stairs in front of her, giving her nothing more than a short nod of his head in the direction of down.

She followed him past Marie's solar, where horrible screeching was going on, down the stairs and to the little chamber she'd shared with him for two nights.

"You truly intend to go to bed," she said, stunned.

"What else?" he asked as he opened the door, stripped off his sword and without hesitation made himself comfortable on his pallet. Ali stood at the doorway, gaping at him.

"But—"

"Come in and close the door."

"I cannot sleep here with you!"

"Why not?" he asked. "You did last night."

"That was different."

He sat up and dragged his hands through his hair. "Aliénore," he said, sounding enormously weary, "you are as safe with me tonight as you have been for the past innumerable days. I will defend you against all enemies and protect you with my very life willingly. That is all. You can sleep in perfect peace."

"Will you kill me in the morning?"

He lay down with a groan. "If saying you aye means you'll bolt the door and go to sleep, then aye it is."

She considered for several moments. Locked inside with him, or wandering the halls with Marie potentially able to escape her bindings and Sir Etienne possibly roaming about with more stealing on his mind and her in mind to do it?

She came inside and bolted the door, then leaned back against it. "You won't slay me without a goodly bit of trouble, you know."

"I should hope not," he muttered, "as I gave you all your bloody training."

"Jason had a hand in it too."

He snorted and rolled over, pulling the blanket over his head.

She sat down on her blankets. "I don't want to die."

"Tomorrow, Aliénore," came the muffled reply. "We'll discuss it all tomorrow. You cannot fight any sort of battle on the amount of sleep we've had this night. We'll both feel much more sensible in the morning."

She lay down and stared up into the dark. "Did you kill Sir Etienne?"

"Unfortunately not."

"Did you hurt him?"

He sighed and removed the blanket from his face.

"Badly. Not as badly as I would have liked, but he'll still be many days recovering. I had much to see you avenged for."

That was something, at least. She sighed and closed her eyes. Perhaps in the morning, things would be clearer.

At least the sunlight might show her the arc of Colin's blade as it sliced across her belly.

She supposed that it would be a very long time before she managed to sleep. After all, it wasn't every day that a woman found herself revealed to her very fierce and ruthless betrothed in a such a manner.

And it wasn't every day that a girl vanquished her stepmother so thoroughly.

Of course, that didn't begin to answer all the other questions she had. Apparently Colin didn't want to kill her right away, so did that mean he could be persuaded never to do it at all? He had vowed to protect her with his very life so she might sleep in safety.

And he also snored loudly enough to wake the dead, but she supposed that was something she could accustom herself to in time.

Assuming he left her alive long enough to do it.

Well, her flight was finished. She waved a fond farewell to the convent, to the possibilities of being an alewife or the mate of a pig-herder. She was discovered, revealed, shown to be who and what she was in the most glorious and unmistakable of ways.

And what was that business of his having known?

Well. He might have his questions, but she had a few of her own. She found her sword at the foot of her pallet, dragged it up next to her, and put her hand on its hilt.

And she slept like the dead.

Chapter 32

*C*olin paced up and down the passageway in front of his chamber, feeling no less nervous than he had since he'd come to Solonge. But it had nothing to do with Marie, who was apparently safely ensconced in the dungeon with Sir Etienne, nor with Lord Denis, who had come along already that morning and asked him what his intentions were, nor with the tidings that all five of Aliénore's brothers were below waiting to see her.

He supposed that the brother she'd filched her gear from would be first in line, wanting his gear back.

He wondered why it was that her brothers had chosen now to make an appearance. He hadn't seen any of them before, not even at meals, nor in the lists. Perhaps they had been too terrified of him to show themselves. Odd, that they should choose now to reveal themselves. Perhaps they considered Aliénore's rejecting him as sport enough for their morning repast.

He pursed his lips. His unease had nothing to do with any of that, though those things certainly gave him pause. His true nervousness lay with the fact that his bride was still asleep and it was at least a few moments past dawn.

Did she intend to sleep the day away? Or was she so disgusted by the thought of finally being forced to wed with him that she didn't dare leave the chamber?

Had he not given her ample opportunity the night before to express such disgust as he stood trembling inside that doorway? Trembling from the height of it off the ground, of course, not from any fear that she might reject him outright. Hadn't he tried to put her mind at ease and give her the benefit of sleep before she made any decisions concerning him? In truth, what more could a wench have asked of him?

She, at least, had slept well. He'd slept little, if at all. He'd finally given up and risen well before sunrise, noting by the very faint starlight that illuminated the chamber that she smiled as she slept. Dreaming likely.

He could only hope it wasn't about Jason of Artane or his other quite marriageable brother, Kendrick.

He had retreated out into the passageway and tried to make himself presentable with a goodly brushing of his tunic with the edge of his knife, a straightening of his hair with his own quite useful fingers, and a goodly amount of wishing that he dared take time for a bit of whisker removal from his cheeks.

Unfortunately, that would have meant seeking out a bowl of water in the kitchen, and he couldn't leave his post.

So he had contented himself with what he could do outside Aliénore's door, then had taken to waiting.

And waiting.

Someone had brought him something with which to break his fast. He wasn't sure what it had been and he could only hope it hadn't been poisoned, though perhaps poison was a kinder wound to his heart than having Aliénore wake, look at him, and flee screaming into her father's arms and beg for a release from her contract.

Colin had, unfortunately, seen that done before.

Hark, was that rustling inside? He put his ear to the door and heard a bit of movement. Or perhaps that was his own poor blood pounding in his ears. Nay, that was definitely movement and a soft curse.

Cursing. How did that bode for him?

The door began to open and he leaped back to lean against the opposite wall. He tried to assume a casual pose as well, though he suspected the sick expression on his visage ruined the effect.

Aliénore appeared in the doorway, looking as fresh and rested as if she'd just passed an entire month lazing abed.

Colin scowled at her, just on principle.

She'd apparently donned her other tunic, for this one had no rent in the front. But she still wore hose and her scuffed boots with the dagger in the right. Her sword, however, was not belted about her waist.

"Where is your sword?" he asked, frowning.

She shrugged in a somewhat helpless manner. "It seemed . . . well, it seemed . . . foolish."

"Why?"

She sighed deeply. "Because there is no more need of ruse."

He supposed she had it aright. Now that she knew that he knew who she was, what was the purpose in pretending to be other than she was?

He wondered, absently, what she would look like in a gown.

She ran her hand over her hair, looking uncomfortable. "What now?" she asked.

She wouldn't meet his eyes. Could she truly not bear to look at him? Or was she trying to tell him that she simply could not bear the thought of wedding with him? Well, if there was something he wasn't, it was a coward. He would just put forth his questions and see what her answers were, then see where that left him. He put his shoulders back and cleared his throat.

"Perhaps—"

"Ah, there you are! I wondered when you would awake!"

Colin looked to his right and glared at the lord of Solonge, who was hurrying down the passageway. He enveloped his daughter in a large hug, rocking her, peppering her with compliments and questions alike, and generally doing all the things Colin wished he were doing at the moment.

Damn the man.

"Come," Denis said, keeping Aliénore under one arm and taking Colin in hand with the other, "let us descend and break our fast. Aliénore, your brothers are quite anxious to see you."

Colin heard a faint snort and peered around Lord Denis to find that Aliénore was wearing a look of profound skepticism. Well, that was something. Perhaps the greeting of her brothers would take less time than he feared, and then they could be about their business of being about their business.

Which he sincerely hoped included a wedding in the near future.

The morning was interminable. Colin found himself shoved to the side in the press of family, friends, and servants who miraculously appeared to shower Aliénore with attention. Colin thought she looked decidedly uncomfortable, but he didn't feel like he could suggest that she flee her relations. After all, they had two years of questions for her. Never mind that he had the same number of questions covering the same period of time. And never mind that he was her betrothed. He supposed he could wait.

But after several hours and a goodly amount of food that was substantially better than what he'd had in the previous two days, he found the waiting becoming quite intolerable. He rose, but no one paid him any heed. With a sigh, he left the hall and made his way out to the lists. There were a few guardsmen milling about and he tried to engage each one in turn, but without success. Most of them seemed to be recovering from their exercise with him the day before. Discouraged, and unaccustomedly so, he finally retired to a little stone bench and sat with his head bowed, staring at the mud between his boots.

Perhaps he was doomed to live the life of a great warrior.

Unwed.

Unchallenged by those lesser men about him.

He sighed a sigh that felt as if it had come straight from the soles of his boots. Ah, by the saints, life could be a burden at times.

He looked down and found his boots quite suddenly to be cast into shadow. He didn't bother to look up.

"If I bested you yesterday, I'll best you again today," he said wearily. "Perhaps you want to rethink your invitation."

"Actually," said a voice sounding nothing like any guardsman he'd ever heard, "I don't have much to rethink."

Colin looked up in surprise. Aliénore stood there with her hands clasped behind her back, her sword at her side. Indeed, she looked so much as she'd always looked before they began to work in the lists that he had to take a moment and convince himself that the past few settings and risings of the sun had actually happened, along with their accompanying revelations.

"You're here," he said blankly.

"I escaped," she said, with a small smile.

"You escaped?" he echoed.

"Aye. Quite a tedious bunch inside."

He stared at her and couldn't believe she had sought him out. "But your family—"

"All my brothers wanted were tales of you. I thought you'd do more justice to your escapades than I could, so I promised them your full attention later. Besides, François was beginning to look at me suspiciously, so I thought I should make my exit whilst I could."

"Very wise."

She nodded with a smile, then suddenly her smile faltered and she looked away.

"I brought my sword," she said quietly. "Just in case—"

Well, it wasn't a declaration of love, but it was something. Colin rose without hesitation.

"Of course," he said. "Let us work. You'll not want to lose your skills."

"Should I need to defend myself," she muttered.

He looked at her with one eyebrow raised, but said nothing. She obviously had something to say, but perhaps it would take a bit of swordplay to pry it from her. He was, after all, a very patient man. He could wait for her to spew out what troubled her.

He sincerely hoped it wasn't that she didn't want him.

Though why she would, perhaps, should have been a mystery to him.

She drew her sword and he followed suit. And when she did nothing else, offered no offense, he took up the cause and mounted a very gentle, very easily defended attack. She countered each stroke just as he'd taught her, with skill and precision.

And, apparently, growing irritation.

Finally, she dropped her sword and glared at him. "Well?" she demanded.

"What?" he asked in surprise.

"If you're going to do me in, will you please just be about the bloody business and be finished with it!"

He blinked. "Do you in?"

"Slay me!" She ground her teeth in frustration. "You vowed you would. I've given you ample opportunity in the past half hour. Why do you delay?"

He put his sword down in front of him and rested both hands on the hilt. "I don't want to slay you."

"You vowed you did."

He shrugged. "That was before. I spoke it in anger."

"You could have said as much," she snapped.

"To whom?" he asked. "To the lad Henri?"

"To anyone who would have listened."

"Would that have changed your mind two years ago about me?" he asked.

She pursed her lips, but apparently didn't find the question worth answering. "Well, if you don't wish to slay me, and you certainly haven't asked me to wed with you, just what is it you intend to do? I vow I've no patience for womanly hesitation in this matter."

Womanly hesitation? He mouthed the words as well, for 'twas a certainty he couldn't voice them. Then he cleared his throat and retrieved his jaw from where it had fallen to his chest.

"Womanly hesitation?" he bellowed. "I do *not* hesitate like a woman!"

She sheathed her sword with a curse, then folded her arms over her chest and glared at him. "What would you call it, then?"

He tried to wrap his mouth around several words, but none of them seemed very complimentary, or polite, so he merely gritted his teeth and scowled back at her.

"I was," he said tightly, "being patient."

"And when did your patience think it would end? After I'd worried myself sick that you truly intended to finish me?"

"Nay," he retorted. "After you decided if you wanted to wed with me or not, that's when. And not a bloody moment before!"

Her hands fell down by her sides and she looked at him in complete surprise. "I have a choice?"

"Aye, damn you," he snarled.

"But," she said slowly, "you could lose everything if I said you nay. All your lands. Your inheritance."

" 'Tis but land." There was no conceivable way this side of Heaven or Hell that his father would pass him over as his heir, but he didn't say as much. For even if he inherited all his father's wealth, it would have been an empty thing indeed without a woman at his side who wanted him.

This woman at his side.

Wanting him freely.

He stole a look at her and found that her eyes were full of tears. Damnation, what had he said this time? Was the thought of taking him as a husband so desperately unpleasant that it reduced her to tears?

"Of course, you needn't say me aye," he said heavily. "None have so far."

She was silent for so long what he wondered if she were racking her brain for a polite way to tell him that she found the thought of him as a husband completely abhorrent. He resheathed his sword with a deep sigh.

"I would understand, of course," he said, "for I am old."

"You're what?"

"Old, damn you. A score and twelve."

She scratched absently at her cheek. "Well, that is ancient," she agreed.

"And you've met my family," he said. "Detriment enough, I suppose."

"Actually—"

"And my hall. Far from the ocean. Nothing but fields. Hot in the summer. Frozen in the winter."

"Well," she said, "I loathe the sea, actually."

He blinked in surprise. She loathed the sea? Was this possible?

"Too wet," she added. "I like fields. I'd like a large garden."

Suddenly, a very small, very faint breeze blew across his soul. It smelled, oddly enough, of earth.

Orchards.

A garden in the fullness of summer.

He cleared his throat. "I have a large garden."

"Do you indeed?" she asked.

"Aye," he said. "But my foul reputation might make up for its size. And I have horrible table manners."

He looked at her from under his eyebrows, but she said nothing else. No more agreement seemed to be forthcoming. No *ah, but Colin, you needn't worry about manners when you have your own fine self to offer in the bargain.* Damn the woman, could she give him not one small concession?

"Is it possible," he asked with growing irritation, "that you might speak? I've given you my list—an *ample* list, I might add—of why you might wish to flee, and yet you remain silent. Have you nothing to say, or must I dredge up more confessions?"

She only looked at him blankly, as if she couldn't for the life of her understand what he was babbling about.

He cursed. He supposed he might have neglected a flaw or two—such as his visage, his propensity to slay those who annoyed him, and the fact that he could bear no music that didn't have the recurring themes of war, bloodshed, and victory—but who could fault him for that? By the saints, he'd laid out his very soul and all she could do was gape at him like a half-wit!

He wondered if he'd sorely overestimated her intelligence.

"I've given you all the reasons I could think of why you wouldn't want me," he growled. "Either agree with them and hie yourself off to your sire, or tell me that they don't mean anything."

He scowled at her, watched her consider his good and bad qualities, and couldn't for the life of him tell whether they mattered to her or not.

And then, quite suddenly, he found himself with a woman in his arms.

Now, *that* was certainly nothing he'd coerced from her.

He very hesitantly put his arms around her and fought the urge to squeeze her. The saints only knew what kind of damage might have resulted from that.

"Thank you for the choice," she said, her voice muffled against his surcoat.

Was that what this was about? She was grateful he was

giving her the damned choice to refuse him? He took her by the shoulders, her mail-covered shoulders, and pushed her back.

"You're very welcome for the choice, but what in the bloody hell is it? Have me or not?"

She smiled, a true smile that fair felled him where he stood. By the saints, 'twas a good thing she hadn't smiled like that when she'd been a boy. He would have discovered her straightway.

"I suppose," she said, her eyes alight with something, either humor or happiness, "that since you're not going to slay me, you'll have to wed me."

He suppressed the urge to stick his fingers in his ears to make certain they were functioning as they should. Best make certain she meant what she said. He looked at her seriously. "Is that what you want?"

"Aye," she said simply. " 'Tis what I want."

And then something extraordinary happened.

He felt as if the sun had shone for the first time on the face of the earth. Something began inside him, something very like that same sun rising slowly in the east. It grew, then grew some more until he could scarce contain whatever it was that struggled to force its way out of him.

A goodly belch?

He waited, breathless, as whatever it was erupted from him with an accompanying feeling he was certain he'd never experienced before.

"By the saints." Aliénore breathed. "You *smiled*."

Colin reached up and felt his mouth in alarm. Aye, that seemed to be the case. And this wasn't the kind of grin that came when he faced a score of men and was well on his way to sending them all speedily to the afterlife. This was a smile of, well, something he couldn't quite identify.

Joy?

"Colin," she said with a laugh, "you have a mark."

The joy immediately disappeared back the way it had come. "I do not," he said stiffly.

"You do, too. A dimple. Right there."

"I have no flaw on my visage that doesn't come from its sheer ugliness."

"I don't find you ugly."

Well, now either the wench was beginning to go blind, or too much swordplay had ruined her wits.

"Let us remove you from the sun," he said briskly. " 'Tis obvious the orb begins to blind you."

"I can think you tolerable to look on," she said. "If I want to."

Colin sighed deeply. If she wanted to continue in her madness, who was he to stop her?

"Well, how do you find me?" she asked. "My aspect, I mean."

"Breathtaking," he said promptly. "Pray our children take after you."

She grinned up at him. "Perhaps that would be best."

Well, now that that was settled, there was no sense in not seeing to getting on with things right away. Colin patted her on the back and stepped away.

"Let's go," he said.

"Where?"

"Priest," he said. "Then home. Harvest soon. Plenty of time to kick my father's sorry arse out of the keep and make ourselves comfortable."

He strode back toward the hall, then realized he didn't hear anyone striding after him. He stopped and looked behind him to see Aliénore standing much where he'd left her. He frowned and returned to see what ailed her.

"Are you unwell?"

She looked up at him in surprise. "Well, it seemed as if . . . well, we should . . . um . . . at least—"

He held out his hand. "Clasp hands on the bargain?"

She looked at him blankly for a moment or two, then smiled a smile he understood not at all and put her hand in his.

"Of course," she said. "That's what I meant."

As he took her hand, he suspected that he'd missed something important. But as he clutched her hand in his own, belatedly remembering that he could quite easily crush her

fingers were he not careful, he looked down into her beautiful—and it was very beautiful—face and felt something
else inside him shift.

More joy?

Damned if he knew.

But whatever it was, it made him feel quite pleasant in the
vicinity of his heart and he supposed it might be some sort
of affection growing in him. Not that he hadn't had vast
quantities of admiration and esteem for the wench already.
But this, this was something entirely different.

Softer.

More tender.

Definitely more terrifying.

"All right then," he said, dropping her hand and backing
away before he did something to embarrass himself. "Let us
be about this business. Where's the priest?"

"Somewhere here about, I imagine."

He caught himself before he merely trotted off across the
lists again. Grasping her hand and pulling her after him was
definitely more efficient and would save him any further de-
scents into those petrifying emotions that seemed to over-
whelm him lately.

He was obviously not sleeping enough.

"Will your father not wish to be here?" she asked as she
trotted after him breathlessly.

Colin shrugged. "Damned if I know. He can rot in Hell
for all I care."

She nodded, then fell silent. Colin stared at her, but her
well of verbosity seemed to have run dry. He frowned. What
was she about now? Was there something else he was missing?

"Aliénore?"

She looked up quickly, a brief smile on her face. "Aye?"

"Something else troubles you?"

She shifted. "Well . . ."

"Spew it forth in your most manly fashion."

"Well, don't you think we should perhaps . . ."

He hesitated. That tone . . . those words . . . It wasn't a tone
he'd ever heard used in connection with his own poor name,

but he'd heard it quite a bit when applied to the exploits and courting practices of Jason of Artane.

And that could only mean one thing.

"What?" he asked, with a goodly amount of dread.

"Well, this is a bit sudden. The wedding and such. Do you think we should perhaps, well . . ."

He steeled himself for the worst. "Aye?"

"Well . . . first . . ."

He put his hand on his sword hilt to reassure himself. He was a man unafraid, a warrior uncowed, a lord of unparalleled reputation. He was not frightened of a word that could strike fear into the hearts of lesser men, not being a lesser man himself.

"Aye?" he asked, through gritted teeth.

"Well," Aliénore said, looking unsettled, "perhaps we should . . . woo."

The saints preserve him, the word gave him all the chills he'd suspected it would.

"Woo?" he asked grimly.

"Aye."

He suspected that she didn't mean by *wooing* merely passing a few healthy hours in the lists.

"Well," he said, "I suppose so."

"Unless, of course, you don't want to," she added. "And I could understand that, of course. Given what I've put you through already."

He eyed her narrowly, but realized immediately that she wasn't wielding the sword of guilt on him. She didn't have that look about her that Ermengarde was wont to have when using her favorite tool of coercion. And he realized with equal swiftness that it would behoove him to start his marriage off on the right foot.

Who deserved wooing more than this woman? After all, she had passed countless hours in the lists with him. How could he refuse her this simple request?

But how was he to woo without some Artane lad at his elbow, giving him suggestions?

Nay, he needed no aid. After all, how hard could it possibly be? Jason seemed to do it without a second thought, dragging out that bloody lute of his and screeching out all sorts of foul things. Women seemed to fall at his feet because of it, something Colin couldn't understand in the least. Surely he, with his more astute sense of the appropriate and sensible, could invent a better style of wooing.

"Very well," he said gruffly, taking Aliénore by the hand again and starting toward the hall. "We'll woo. Just realize that it won't be any of that vacuous, empty-headed business those Artane lads engage in. This will be . . . um . . . manly wooing."

"I'm merely flattered you think me worth the effort."

He stopped suddenly, turned her to him, and put his hands on her shoulders. He looked down into her face, past the shorn hair and the dirt, into those fathomless green eyes, and marveled that she didn't just demand wooing as her right. It certainly should have been. She deserved that, and more, and he would give it to her.

In his most manly fashion, of course.

"You are worth more effort than you know," he said. "I could do nothing less for a woman who has shown your courage and wit. I might even concede that in those two qualities, you are my equal." Then he looked at her to see how she would take that.

"Thank you, my lord."

Well, she didn't look overly impressed by that concession, but perhaps he could expect no more of her at present. She was obviously quite overwhelmed by his offer to see her properly courted.

So he grunted at her, just so she would know that he was still fully in charge of his normal, warriorly mien, then took her hand again and pulled her toward the hall. It was, he had to admit, a very nice hand. And he supposed he would at some distant point in the future accustom himself to the holding of that hand.

And holding that hand led him to other quite satisfying thoughts. So he'd managed to saddle himself a wife—after he'd wooed and wed her, of course—who would enjoy his land as much as he. He could already see himself lazing beneath a fruit tree with her at his side, sleeping in the summer sun.

After having successfully and with great pleasure sent his father off to live out his remaining years in his most run-down and uncomfortable keep of course.

Colin quickened his pace. The sooner Aliénore was wooed, the sooner she would be won, and the sooner they could be home.

Hopefully whilst there was still fruit on the trees for them to pick.

Chapter 33

A *li* opened her eyes and had a brief moment of panic. She heard no snores and felt no hard floor beneath her back. Where was she? In her father's pit, in the soft earth crawling with vermin?

She patted about her frantically and was vastly relieved to find sheets and blankets covering her and a soft, goose-feather mattress beneath her back. Memory flooded back to her and she closed her eyes with a relieved sigh.

She was alive.

And, miracles never ceased, soon to be wooed.

Assuming Colin survived it, of course. He'd been rather quiet throughout the afternoon and evening of the previous day, so she'd only been able to assume that he was thinking on his strategy. She'd tried not to let the way he seemed to finger the hilt of his sword, or scratch his cheek absently with his dagger, alarm her. The man was used to planning sieges. Perhaps he thought best with a weapon in his hand.

She sincerely hoped the siege of her heart was accomplished without bloodshed.

She stared up at the canopy of the bed and wondered if she was already being courted or if he was still considering how to go about it. He'd remained by her side for the whole of that previous day, stretching himself to be polite to her father and brothers, and refraining from banging on the table when he was hungry.

He was obviously dredging up manners from previously unplumbed depths.

She rolled out of bed, pulled open the shutters and saw that it was quite late in the morning already. It was the first time in years she had slept as long as she liked and she wouldn't begrudge herself that pleasure. Besides, sleeping so long had given Colin a respite from what she was certain would be very heavy labors.

She dressed slowly, and while she did, she wondered if she might have asked too much of Colin. After all, he had waited for her for two years and then some. Was she demanding things from him she didn't deserve?

She washed her face and dragged a comb through what was left of her hair. Mayhap Colin wasn't opposed to wooing because he thought it would give her hair ample time to grow back and leave her looking less like a boy.

Though, knowing Colin, he likely didn't consider the condition of her hair. She could hardly see him setting himself to the task of brushing it for hours. He likely would rather have bid her take a knife to it anyway, lest it hamper her efforts in the lists.

That was another thing that she had to wonder about. Would he ever take her to the lists again once she was wed to him?

Did she want him to?

She slipped her dagger into her boot, then realized what she had done. She stared down at herself, garbed as she was in hose, tunic, and leather jerkin, and marveled that she could have done so without thinking. It hardly seemed unnatural anymore, but perhaps that was just as well. Colin likely wouldn't have recognized her in velvets and silks.

She looked about her father's chamber, thanked him silently for the luxury of having enjoyed it for the night, and then opened the door.

Colin was leaning against the far wall, wearing his customary frown.

Well, he didn't look overly annoyed. She smiled faintly. "Tell me you haven't been waiting for me since dawn."

He shook his head. "Ran through the sturdier lads in the garrison earlier. Tried to engage your brothers, but they were unwilling." He frowned at her. "Not even that braggart François would hoist a sword in my direction. Said the rain would rust his blade."

"Unsurprising," she said. "He's not one for overexerting himself."

Colin grunted. "It makes me wonder how it is your father got himself five such feeble lads yet sired such a fine wench as yourself in the bargain. A wench with qualities I can't help but admire: courage; stamina; willingness to draw her blade and tramp about in the mud with it."

He peered at her closely, as if he searched for some kind of reaction to that statement.

It took no great skill to realize that her wooing had begun.

So she put her hand over her heart and inclined her head. "Your compliments leave me weak, my lord."

"Feel like having a go in the lists?"

It wasn't as if she could say him nay now. So she retrieved her sword with a smile and followed him onto the very muddy field, snatching a stale piece of bread from off the high table as she passed. It was a poor meal, but she would make do. How could she do otherwise when she'd just been praised for her willingness to fight?

The rain began after only a few moments and continued without abatement until she could scarce see for the volume of it.

"A light mist," Colin shouted.

He was shouting, of course, to make himself heard over the thunderous sound of rain beating against the earth.

"To be sure," she shouted back. "Nothing more than an annoyance."

He nodded happily and continued with their light morning's exercise.

Ali began to wonder who was indulging whom.

By the time she was soaked to the skin and could see nothing for the rain coming down in sheets, Colin had seemingly resigned himself to the fact that they could no longer be about their sport in the lists. He resheathed his sword with a sigh, then beckoned to her.

"To the stables," he announced. "We'll check on our mounts."

Ali put up her sword and followed him, grateful to be out of the wet. She stood shivering beside Colin as he went to each of their horses in turn, speaking quietly to them and giving out fond rubs and pats. He looked over his shoulder at her suddenly.

"Horses like me," he said.

"I can see that."

"I treat them well."

"Of course, my lord."

He frowned. "They haven't my reputation to be afeared of, you see."

She was beginning to see quite clearly. "Colin, I am not afraid of you."

His frown deepened. "Then I must be doing something wrong."

She laughed, then reached over and stroked her gelding's soft nose. "I am, of course, still properly in awe of your immense reputation. I imagine I will spend the rest of my life treading quite carefully around you. I'll use Gillian of Blackmour as my example. She seems to live quite happily in terror of her dragon."

"Ha," Colin said with a snort. "If anyone lives in terror, 'tis poor Chris. Ever having to watch his manners, ever having to watch his tongue lest he wound her tender feelings. A hellish life for the man, no doubt."

"He does seem quite miserable," she agreed dryly.

He turned and looked at her fully, pursing his lips. "Think you that I'll find myself turning inside out trying to keep from wounding *your* tender feelings?"

She felt, quite suddenly, as if he'd just slapped her. She blinked quite rapidly. It had to be the great volumes of dust that found home in the stables. It had nothing to do with feelings the unfeeling oaf had just wounded. In truth, why could she have expected anything more? He was a warrior, after all, a man who passed his time in the business of death—

She was interrupted by the feel of a hand hesitantly brushing her hair back from her face. She looked up, wishing there weren't those damned tears standing in her eyes and feeling altogether weak and foolish for having allowed them there in the first place—

"I have no gift for this," he said with a sigh of deep resignation. "And of course I won't wound your tender feelings intentionally, damn you. Must I blurt out every feeling of my heart for you to examine at length? Can you not just look inside that maudlin, womanly bit of me and see for yourself?"

She dragged her sleeve across her eyes. "Of course you needn't expose your heart continually to me," she said, putting her shoulders back and sniffing a mighty, cleansing sniff. "I haven't the time for it either. We've important things to do, far more important than indulging in sentiment."

Now if he'd just stop looking at her that way and stop tucking the hair behind her ears as if she needed tidying up, she might be able to get on with things more vital to her future than loitering in the stables, fretting over things that didn't matter.

"Ah, Aliénore," he said very softly, "I fear you'll need more patience than courage to live with the likes of me. I'm powerfully unskilled at this business of comporting myself well with a wench."

"You needn't treat me any differently than you would one of your men," she said.

He snorted heartily. "I've obviously had you under my sway for far too long. Of course I must treat you differently. Your skill with a blade aside, I can't look at you that I don't want to treat you differently. Why, look you here at this fair skin you have. It inspires . . . well, I'm not sure what it inspires, but it isn't a brisk slap to return you to your senses."

That was something, she supposed.

He reached out to touch her cheek, then looked down at his hand. An expression of dismay crossed his features and he quickly put that hand behind his back.

"I'll admire your visage from a distance," he announced. He took her by the arm and pulled her toward the stable door. "Food," he stated. "We need food. Everything will seem much more manageable after a hearty meal. I'm feeling quite famished; what of you?"

He didn't give her a chance to answer. But as she trotted along after him, she began to consider his words and actions in a different light. Obviously, he wasn't comfortable expressing deep emotions. He was a warrior, after all, and likely didn't allow himself to feel much besides battle lust. How could he, and survive what he was called upon to do?

And then there was his hesitation at touching her to consider. He'd looked at his hand as if it had been unsatisfactory in some way. Perhaps he was afraid of her, or afraid to hurt her, or afraid to soil her with hands that were quite suited to the work of death.

Or perhaps standing out in the rain had ruined what few wits she had left.

She cursed herself thoroughly under her breath, then found herself suddenly with her nose to Colin's chest, thanks to his sudden turning about.

"What?" he demanded.

She looked up at him. "I'm just berating myself for idle thoughts."

"A dangerous business, thoughts."

"Aye," she agreed.

He looked at her for a moment or two more, as if he simply couldn't believe she was standing in front of him, then grunted and led her into the great hall.

"Food," he said, sounding vastly relieved. "We should eat."

Ali couldn't have agreed more. Perhaps something in her belly would restore the good sense in her head. She was unaccountably distressed and she couldn't for the life of her understand why. She'd slept well. She'd had a goodly bit of exercise that morning in the lists. Colin had treated her no differently than he had the past two months. And he'd certainly made it so she was free of both Sir Etienne and Marie for the moment.

What else did she want?

Evening shadows had fallen. Ali sat in her father's solar in the chair closest to the fire and looked about her. Her father was there, of course, in the chair opposite her. He was surrounded by the various and sundry persons of her brothers, who were all listening with rapt attention to the tales being told.

Tales of bloodshed, misery, and woe.

It was Colin, of course, who was regaling them with the best in his repertoire.

Ali leaned back in her chair and looked at her future husband. The firelight softened his features somehow. He would have tried to change that, no doubt, if he'd known. It would have galled him to know that at least in her eyes, he seemed not quite so fierce, not nearly so terrifying.

And that, she supposed, was the key to the man.

She'd given Gillian's few words to her much thought over the course of the afternoon as she'd watched Colin be about his wooing.

A gruff exterior, but a soft underbelly? Aye, she'd considered that well after their midday meal, when he'd fetched all her gear for her and proceeded, with great diligence, to sharpen all her implements of death.

An enormous ego that fully expected all souls in his vicinity to drop in terror when he approached? Aye, she'd seen that surely, as her brothers, one by one, had made an appearance, giving Colin a wide and respectful berth. He'd merely accepted that as his due, then set to making certain they didn't overtax her with their questions as she sat near the fire he'd commanded be built, that she might dry off and not catch the ague. And when she'd found herself stifling even the merest hint of a yawn, the lads had been summarily excused and she had been instructed to close her eyes and rest while he considered several manly matters that needed his immediate attention.

She'd suspected then that after seeing to her gear, he found himself fresh out of wooing ideas.

So she'd closed her eyes and considered Gillian's last words about Colin, that he was a man in whom the right woman could inspire great loyalty and devotion.

And she wondered if she might ever be that woman.

All of which had left her, after her apparently quite lengthy nap in front of the fire in the great hall, finding herself in her father's solar with Colin holding court. That all her brothers should have gathered together, as well as her sire, with her in attendance as well, said much about the immensity of Colin's reputation. Ali couldn't remember a time when her entire family had been together thusly. Not since her mother had died.

She turned away from that thought and concentrated on watching her betrothed. He spoke with absolutely no boastfulness, merely as if what he stated was simple fact. Her brothers, however, had to have flattered his ego. Their cries of dismay, disbelief, and admiration could be nothing but sweet music to Colin's ears.

For herself, she could only lean back in her chair and smother her smile with her hand. By the saints, the man was absolutely terrifying. What soul with any sense would possibly hoist a sword against him and think he would survive it?

The longer she watched his face, the more she realized that while it did possess no handsomeness whatsoever, it was made up of quite pleasing planes and angles. Manly ones. Ones that inspired something in her she didn't quite recognize at first.

Admiration.

Loyalty.

An intense desire to linger nearby and know that the man wearing that visage counted her as standing staunchly at his side, supporting him.

There was something to be said for earning the love of a man like that.

So he might bruise her feelings at times. He might trample heedlessly over her heart in his haste to be about some pressing business or other. She was beginning to see that none of that really mattered, in the end. Why would it, when she knew that this was a man who would, if he loved her truly, spare nothing to defend her? Hold nothing back to protect her? Keep nothing of himself when giving all of it would be what kept her from harm?

By the saints, this was the kind of man for her.

She watched him turn to look at her, then saw his words falter. He stared at her in surprise, which made her wonder at the expression she was wearing. She smiled at him, wondering if he could possibly know what she was thinking, or if she could ever tell him without sending him fleeing the other way.

He looked slightly perplexed, then turned back to his audience.

"Where was I?" he asked, scratching his head.

"Decapitating several men with one swing of the sword," her youngest brother, Pierre, said breathlessly.

"Of course," Colin said. He shot her another look of consternation, then turned back to the lads, gave himself a good shake, and plunged back into his tale. "It takes a great amount of strength, you know, to manage such a swing. And the angle must be exactly so, lest you notch your blade."

Her brothers nodded in appreciation.

Ali merely leaned back in her chair and smiled to herself. Aye, the day had been a good one, full of revelations she hadn't expected, full of realizations that would likely serve her quite well in the future.

"One more tale," Colin announced suddenly. "I've no more time this eve for this kind of thing. I've important plans to make."

"Another siege to lay?" her brother Robert asked eagerly.

Colin looked unsettled. "You might say so. But 'tis none of anyone's affair what kind of siege it is. 'Tis my own personal business and I've no need of aid."

"Of course," several of the lads murmured appreciatively.

François huffed. "Wooing my sister, more than likely, is what you're contemplating."

Colin shot him a dark look.

François shut his mouth abruptly.

Colin turned back to the rest of his audience. "Manly business is what I'm about. Now, one last tale to prove that such business is what I do best, then you can take yourselves off and ponder what I've told you. Anyone who cares for a demonstration of what I've described—" and here he gave François a pointed look—"can meet me in the lists tomorrow morning, early."

Ali closed her eyes. The man was nothing short of terrifying, and his tales were ones made to upset all but the strongest of stomachs. Fortunately for her, her stomach had seemingly been strengthened over the past pair of months, for she could listen and do nothing but look forward to the business he had to attend to the next day.

With any luck at all, that business included her.

Lists, stables, repairing her gear—it didn't matter. It would be with Colin nearby and that was enough for her.

Chapter 34

C olin sat on a very hard chair at the edge of the great hall and watched the goings-on. 'Twas a certainty he had no intention of participating in all that capering about, the swishing of skirts, and the extending of the leg in ridiculous bows. It was simply beneath his dignity.

That aside, he had no trouble watching Aliénore at it. He had to admit that she danced rather well, and it was pleasing to gaze on her and watch as she smiled and laughed with pleasure. It was less than pleasing to think she might be smiling and laughing with someone else, but Colin had his reputation to maintain. Let the other lads make themselves into cavorting arses. He would remain safely planted upon his chair.

Besides, such a firm and steady seat gave him ample time to watch his future wife and admire her skill.

He sat back, sipped his ale, and gave thought to the events of the day. It had passed rather pleasantly, all things considered. He'd begun his day with brisk exercise in the lists, finally having managed to lure several of Aliénore's brothers there. Instilling in François the proper amount of respect for his skill had taken no longer than he had anticipated. After that, he'd immediately embarked on the task he'd set himself the night before, that of repairing what damage he'd done the day before, damn his own foolish tongue.

He still cringed, very slightly and most unwillingly, every time he thought of his mindless words to Aliénore in the stable the day before. Of *course* he would have a care with her feelings. By the saints, hadn't he bent himself into unrecognizable shapes to please her ever since he'd discovered she was a girl? And even more so after he'd discovered just what girl she was? It wasn't in his nature to cause others grief—without good reason, of course.

He couldn't even say that Aliénore had caused him all that much grief. Aye, she'd wounded his feelings at first when she'd fled, but he could hardly hold that against her. He wanted to believe that if she'd truly known him, she wouldn't have run. She certainly didn't seem all that opposed to him of late. He remembered quite vividly the look on her face the night before, when he'd been recounting his more exciting escapades. Why, she'd looked at him almost fondly.

And if that weren't enough to give him hope, he didn't know what was.

All of which had left him that morning returning from the lists, determined to see her properly wooed.

Now, if he'd just had a bloody idea of how to go about it.

He'd seen her well fed. Her gear he'd taken care of the day before. He'd made sure she had another restful night in her father's chamber. Then, having done all the things he would have wanted done for himself, he'd found himself sitting next to her in the great hall, completely empty of any useful ideas.

Her father, of all people, had come to his rescue.

The man had procured minstrels from heaven only knew where, lads who seemed to have an inexhaustible supply of lays, ballads, and sundry other farces to put forth for a body's enjoyment.

It had taken all Colin's considerable powers of self-control to sit and listen with anything but a scowl on his face. Aliénore had seemed to enjoy it, though, so he'd done his best not to ruin her pleasure in the entertainment. And each time she'd looked at him, he'd produced a look that said it had been all his idea from the first and wasn't her sire clever to know what Colin had been thinking.

Unfortunately, the morning had proceeded well into the afternoon and the afternoon had produced tuneful melodies just made for dancing. Colin had drawn the line there. He would watch, aye, but he would not dance.

All of which left him where he was, sitting quite happily

on the edge of the goings-on, watching his bride.

She was wearing a gown, something he'd never expected to see her in. He supposed she had to don one eventually. It was, he had to admit, quite fetching. He watched the deep green material swirl about her as she spun. Her face was alight with laughter and he felt as if he were seeing her for the first time. He wondered, weakly, what he would have done had this been the first way he'd ever seen her presented.

He contemplated that for several moments, until he realized that Aliénore was skipping his way. She came to a skidding halt in front of him and smiled down at him happily.

"Will you dance, my lord?"

The question caught him so off guard that he could only gape at her. Of course he didn't want to dance. Hadn't he made that abundantly clear with his scowls alone?

But then he found both his hands taken by slighter, less calloused ones, and his form pulled straight off its comfortable perch by one who shouldn't have had the strength to do the like. His person was then dragged into the middle of the hall before his feet could find their wits to dig into the rushes as they most assuredly would have done at any other time.

"But—" he attempted.

"I promise you'll emerge unscathed, my lord," she said, with a winsome smile. "Put yourself into my hands and let me see to you for a change."

"Ah," he managed in a garbled tone.

"This could quite possibly constitute a full month's worth of wooing," she offered.

"Damn," he said.

She only laughed.

Well, he supposed it wasn't much different than a highly exhausting bit of swordplay. His feet, he found, weren't unequal to the task of moving about in a pattern. He was certainly adept at avoiding collisions with other dancers, given his hours of practice dodging flashing blades. And he was, he had to admit modestly, almost perfect at not treading upon his lady as they moved about through the patterns she seemed to know as if she'd been born with them burned into her flesh.

Now, if he could just dance to something besides tales of love and wooing.

"Can they play nothing else?" he complained. "Nothing of substance?"

"Should we dance to tales of bloodshed?" she asked pleasantly.

"It would be a damned sight more inspiring than this," he grumbled.

She only squeezed his hands. "My lord, you've quite a gift for this. Who would have thought it?"

"Who, indeed?" he muttered.

"You are generous to humor me thusly."

"Aye, I am," he agreed. "But we'll stop when you feel the need of it," he said, vowing that he would dance until he dropped before he would admit that 'twas a most taxing activity. "I, of course, could caper about far into the night."

She laughed at him.

He scowled at her, but only received a grin in return. And that expression of such undisguised affection was almost his undoing. He stumbled, but righted himself quickly enough.

"Bone in the rushes," he said, kicking a bit of the muck aside. "Your sire should see to it."

"I'll tell him next chance I have," she said.

"You do that." *And don't smile at me thusly again,* he pleaded silently. He was bound to fall on his face otherwise, and then where would he be?

Quite potentially rescued by the elfin creature before him whose sweet, dancing green eyes looked at him with affection.

By the saints, what had he done to deserve her?

Nothing came to mind.

What did come to mind, however, after a goodly amount of time spent humoring her, was a large cup of ale he might quaff with enthusiasm. He looked at Aliénore closely, hoping to see some sign that she might be tiring.

Damn her, where did the woman come by such stamina?

He coughed pointedly, but received only a raised eyebrow in return.

"Weary, my lord?"

"Of course not," he rasped. "Hoarse from shouting out my pleasure over this activity."

She laughed and pulled him across the hall. "Then drink you should have. I wouldn't want you feeling faint."

"Mock me if you like," he said. "And see what it earns you."

"A respite from dancing would be sufficient," she said, sitting him down and pouring him drink. She sat down in the chair next to him. "Thank you for the rescue, my lord."

He frowned at her, but accepted the cup just the same. He drank, watching her over the rim. She had seemingly lost all interest in the dance and was currently focusing all her attentions on his own poor self.

"Looking for defects?" he asked gruffly.

"Admiring your manly features," she replied.

He obviously should have ingested more of Berengaria's beauty herbs whilst he'd had the chance. It might have made Aliénore's task less onerous.

"And wondering what else could possibly equal the pleasure of dancing with you."

Well, it was likely past time when he could lure her out to the lists. More dancing? He considered, then put aside that thought. He'd succeeded at it earlier, but that might have been a happy bit of luck. But what else was there? He couldn't sing. He couldn't play the lute. He certainly had no gift for rhyme.

He looked at Aliénore and wondered if he might dredge up a compliment or two. Could that go wrong?

"You look, um, quite a bit like a girl," he said, quickly reaching for his ale and imbibing a hefty amount.

She ran her hand over her hair and looked powerfully uncomfortable.

Damnation, but this wasn't the way to please her.

"You seem a bit less adept at those steps," he nodded toward the floor, "than those other fools. There's something to be said for you. Shows you haven't wasted your entire life on frivolous prancing about."

She blinked. "Well," she began slowly, "thank you."

He cast about for something else to say, but found absolutely nothing. He'd already trotted out his most impressive tales of battle the night before, so there was no further potential there. He'd already seen to her gear. He'd already bested her sire's garrison.

And he'd already bloody taken his pride in hand and tramped about to music in the midst of her father's hall, merely to please her.

He considered a bit longer, then with a sinking heart realized there was aught yet he hadn't tried. He girded up his loins, took a deep, strengthening breath, and looked at her.

"What think you," he began, chewing a bit on his words, "of the sleeves they are showing at court this year?"

She looked at him and her jaw slid down. "Sleeves?"

"Aye. I understand they're bound to be different than they were last year."

And that was, in truth, the complete totality of what he knew of women's fashion. It was different each year, which always necessitated a new bit of stitching. That much he had learned from Gillian herself. Never mind that she found the thought ridiculous. Perhaps Aliénore was more interested in those kinds of things than Gillian was.

The saints preserve him.

"Have you lost your wits?" she asked in astonishment.

He blinked. "I beg your pardon?"

"How would I know anything of sleeve lengths? I know how long they have to be to keep me from losing my blade in them. Am I to know more than that? And when is it you think I've been to court to observe these things? Some night when you were deep into your snores?"

"I do not snore."

"You most certainly do, and that isn't the point. I've no idea what my sleeves should look like, nor do I care!"

By the saints, the wench was irritated. He looked at her, then made a decision.

"I have," he said, rising to his feet, "had enough of this."

She looked up at him. "Enough of what?"

"Enough of this business," he said. "I've danced, I've refrained from belching at the table, and I've forborne any intense harm I wanted to do to your brother François. Surely that is enough wooing for the moment." He looked about him for the appropriate marrying authority, but found no one fitting that description. "Where's the priest?"

"Are we wedding now?" she asked, rising as well.

"As quickly as might be. I'll woo you later. I'll spend the rest of my bloody life bloody wooing you. I cannot bear the strain of this another moment. Give me a pitched battle with odds that should fair guarantee my death. 'Twould be far less strain than this trying to guess how it is I'm supposed to please you!"

He realized then that he was shouting. He shut his mouth with a snap and looked down at her, fully expecting to see her recoiling in horror.

She was, to his surprise, merely looking at him serenely.

"As you will, my lord."

He took her by the hand, then turned again to see if there might not be some man of the cloth lurking about in a darkened corner, indulging himself in a bit of fortifying drink. He saw nothing but her sire, who was looking quite horrified, and her brothers, who were looking equally terrified. Colin swept them all with a formidable scowl.

"I've done my best," he grumbled. "Now, where's the bloody priest?"

Lord Denis raised a shaking arm and pointed toward the door. "Shall I fetch him?" he asked weakly. "Or do you care to go to the chapel?"

"I won't deny your daughter a proper wedding," Colin said. "We'll repair to the chapel."

"As you will," Lord Denis said. He looked less than enthusiastic about the thought.

Colin scowled at him. "I'm not going to make her life a misery."

Denis smiled faintly. "I never said you would, did I?" He reached out and put his hand on Colin's shoulder. "I wouldn't let her wed with you if I thought that."

Colin wondered how the man possibly thought he could stop the like, but he saw quite suddenly a glint of steel in those watery eyes. Aye, perhaps the man would have it in him to discourage Colin from escorting Aliénore to the altar.

Colin nodded in appreciation of Lord Denis's fierceness, then turned back to Aliénore. "My lady?"

"My lord?"

"Your last chance to bolt is before you."

She clasped his hand in both her own. They were, to his continued amazement, very soft hands considering the tortures he'd put them through. And they were willing hands, as far as he could tell.

"Colin, I'm not going to bolt."

He wondered if he should sit down briefly to digest that, then promised himself a goodly bit of marveling over it when he next had the luxury of deep thought. For now, he would wed the woman before she had second thoughts about her bold declaration.

"Are *you* going to bolt?" she asked.

He looked down at her in surprise. "What? Why would you think that?"

"Well . . ."

He scowled down at her and read the words *womanly hesitation* very clearly in her smile. He grunted, clutched her hand, and pulled her across the hall. That was the last bit of hesitation she would have from him.

Chapter 35

A *li* had a problem.
It had little to do with her wedding. The ceremony
had been brief, far briefer than the priest likely thought appropriate. Colin's hand on his sword hilt had kept the man
pressing on—and skipping over vast stretches of the text—
without hesitation.

A hasty though substantial enough wedding feast had been
provided, as well as more musical offerings by her father's
minstrels. Though Colin had begun to drum his fingers in
irritation on the table after but one verse of the first song,
he'd shown admirable restraint during the course of a rather
long evening, only heaving eight or nine sighs great enough
to untune all the lutes in the hall.

But it was this that she thought might truly bring the hall
down around their ears.

"The *what?*" Colin asked in astonishment.

"The standing up," her father said, looking baffled. He sat
at his place at the high table, wiped his mouth with a bit of
cloth, and looked at Colin in surprise. " 'Tis the custom.
Don't you know?"

"Of course I know. I just never intended it to happen to
me!"

Well, Ali thought with a smile, that sounded a little bit
like his whole marriage, truth be told.

"But . . . ," her father protested.

Colin rose from his chair and folded his arms over his
chest. " 'Tis a barbaric and undignified practice," he announced. "And it will not happen tonight."

"Perhaps 'tis best," Ali offered dryly, "lest you find yourself with a reason to flee."

The look she was favored with would have terrified her

two months before. Now she only laughed, which caused the look to darken considerably.

"Well, but of course, my lord," her father said hastily, his tone showing that Colin's scowl had at least made its intended point with someone in the hall. "I surely won't force you to do something you find distasteful. Whatever pleases you."

"What would please me," Colin said, sitting down with a grunt, "is not having to listen to any more screeching."

"Minstrels, seek your suppers!" her father called immediately.

There was, unsurprisingly, a frantic rush for one of the lower tables, where knights and other sundries were summarily pushed aside to make way for hungry musicians. Ali sat back in her chair and smiled to herself. Perhaps there was benefit after all to be wed to someone of Colin's ferocity. She looked at her father and wondered, though, if he felt differently. He was looking at her with the same kind of pity one might use for a poor, hapless soul who was about to be cast into a pit of asps.

Ali smiled at him reassuringly. After all, she'd been wooed—in Colin fashion, of course, but she wasn't going to dispute the result. She was now wed, and now that she was wed, she would engage in matrimonial activities. And to be sure, she'd heard enough about them from Sybil's sisters, who had periodically come to regale their youngest sibling with all manner of tales, told without any embarrassment, but certainly intending to shock and terrify. And on Sybil, those tales had wrought their intended work.

As for Ali herself, she had merely taken it as a fact of life. Sybil's sisters hadn't looked displeased with their lots. And did a woman but love her man somewhat, surely it couldn't be unpleasant.

But, of course, that assumed that Colin intended to see to his part in the affair. She would have asked him about his intentions, but he was industriously sniffing at various parts of his person. She tried not to stare, but she simply couldn't help herself.

A look of dismay descended on his features.

He shoved back from the table suddenly. "I will return," he said, then trotted off toward the kitchens.

Ali couldn't imagine he would bathe. Perhaps he was going to go roll himself in a bit of ale. She looked at her sire and shrugged. "I've no idea what he's about."

He reached out and grasped her hand between his own. "My sweet girl, it isn't too late. Until the marriage has been consummated, it still isn't too late. By the saints, Aliénore, I don't know if I can bear this. I can spirit you away, hide you at another keep—"

"Father," she said, amused, "I've already done that for myself, and look you now where I have wound up. Nay," she said, shaking her head, "he is a good man."

"Quite rough about the edges," her father muttered.

"But I think he's fond of me."

"But tonight—"

"Tonight will proceed as it will. Like as not, he'll prefer to pass the time sharpening his sword."

He looked at her for several moments in silence, then sighed heavily. "Perhaps you have it aright. He does look at you with great affection. I daresay he won't use you ill. At least he'd best not." He looked at her with an expression of fierceness that almost rivaled Colin's. "He'll answer to me otherwise."

"Of course, Father."

He rose. "I've something for you. Don't let him carry you off until I've returned with it."

Ali leaned back in her chair and wondered if waiting was to become her lot in life now. First for her husband—and 'twas passing strange to call Colin that—then next for her father. The saints pity her when she had a houseful of children.

But apparently her father didn't intend that she wait long. He returned with something in a small box. He sat next to her and presented it with what she could only call reverence.

"Here," he said. "My treasure."

Well, it didn't look like bags of gold. Sir Etienne would have been sorely disappointed. Ali looked at her sire. "Shouldn't Colin have this?"

" 'Tis yours by right. I only intended to give it to your spouse that he might give it to you. Open it, if you like."

Ali lifted the lid carefully and set it aside. And there, on a very worn bit of cloth, sat a small round bit of stiff cloth with a tiny portrait on it.

Of her mother.

Ali looked up at her father, tears in her eyes. He smiled, tears in his own eyes.

"Not a day has passed since that I haven't grieved for her loss. I thought you should have it, for your own comfort. And I thought your husband should see it, that he might know how much he should treasure you."

She set the box aside and put her arms around her father. And then she wept. She wept first for the mother she'd lost, then for the years she wouldn't have with her, and finally for the children of hers her mother would never see. And then she wept a bit for her father, that he'd lost something very precious to him.

And then she realized that more than just her tears were dampening her. She pulled back, but her father's weeping was confined to his face alone. Then she looked up and found that Colin was standing over her, his hair dripping down onto her and whatever else was in its path.

So he had bathed.

'Twas no wonder he looked so miserable.

"What ails you?" she asked, dragging her sleeve across her eyes.

"You regret wedding me," he said grimly. "I can see it."

"Well, of course I don't."

"Then what has wrenched these tears from your eyes?"

She handed the box to him. "Look inside, but don't drip on it."

He held it far out of harm's way, then peered closely at the portrait. Then he looked at her.

"Your dam?"

"Aye."

Colin stared at it for a moment or two longer, then looked at her father. "You loved her."

"As you should love her daughter, or you'll answer to me."

Colin seemed to take that seriously enough. He nodded, then handed the box back to Ali.

Ali took her treasure, put it away, then waited. She realized quite quickly that a growing, and very uncomfortable, silence was beginning to fill the space between the three of them. She looked up at Colin.

"Did you bathe?" she asked, surprised.

He turned a very fiery shade of red. "And what if I did?"

"Very brave."

"Very brave is the soul who follows me into that water," he said with a shiver. "And I vow the soap took off much of my skin." He looked at Denis with a scowl. "Bathing in your house is perilous, my lord."

"I'll have it seen to. Now," Denis said, taking a deep breath, "you may take my chamber, if you like. It has been prepared for your use."

"Use?" Colin squeaked.

Ali smiled to herself, then rose. "We aren't heading into a pitched battle. We're merely going to retire."

"Retire," he repeated. "Um, aye, retire. Indeed, we should likely do so."

"You can regale me with tales of danger before we sleep." She leaned over and kissed her father's cheek. "Good night, my lord. Rest well."

"You too," he managed, looking a bit green.

Colin looked green as well. By the saints, when had the men about her acquired such weak stomachs? Apparently she was doomed to take the lead in this. Ah, well, to each his own strengths, she supposed.

"Come, my lord," she said, gathering up her box, then taking Colin by the hand. "We'll retire now and recover from your day's labors. I know they were heavy ones."

Colin only grunted and followed her. Ali led the way up the steps and down the passageway, then up more steps and down another passageway to her father's bedchamber. She supposed she should have felt a bit queasy about being there with a husband, but there was almost a little satisfaction in being able to sleep in comfort whilst Marie slept in the dungeon with the vermin and slime.

Ali opened the door and entered, then let Colin pass by her. He set a candle down on a trunk, then looked about him with about as much enthusiasm as he might have at an inescapable prison.

Ali smiled to herself, lit another pair of candles, set her mother's portrait on the table, and sat down before the brazier to warm her toes. She patted a place on the wide bench next to her.

"Comfortable," she said encouragingly.

Colin shut the door, bolted it, and then leaned back against the door. "So's the door," he said.

She laughed. "You wouldn't think a man of your reputation would be nervous of anything."

"Nervous?" he said, puffing out his chest. "I am not nervous. I'm merely trying to ... um ... spare *you* any nervousness."

"Kind of you."

"Aye, I thought so."

She tilted her head and smiled at him. "Would you care to hear advice a wise man once gave me? He was referring to how one should deal with a woman."

He pursed his lips, but nodded just the same.

" 'Bed them. Get them with child. But never, ever converse with them.' "

Colin snorted. "Drivel."

"I daresay he didn't think so."

"Shouldn't listen to that kind of rot. Who said it, by the way? Artane's youngest? Nay, he wouldn't say something like that. He would speak on forever about lays and ballads and other wooing devices, if he didn't just simply talk the poor wench to death. But tell me who it was, so I can instruct the man in proper comportment next time we meet."

"It was, actually, you," she said. "In your defense, I think it was after Sybil had fainted one too many times to suit you."

He looked at her closely. "You don't seem to be on the verge of fainting."

"Nay, I'm not."

"Strong-constitutioned, apparently."

She smiled modestly. "Perhaps."

He took a pace or two forward and leaned against the foot post of the bed. "Full of goodly courage."

"Undoubtedly."

He was looking at the distance that separated him from the bench. It seemed as though he thought it to be quite large, for he looked as if he might take a step or two forward, and then he would relax and continue his leaning.

Ali wondered if he might ever come any closer.

"You could tell me how you came to know Christopher of Blackmour," she offered. "That would be a very interesting tale."

He considered. The idea seemed to be appealing enough, for he put his shoulders back, looked as if he were gathering his courage in hand, and then strode across the chasm in two great steps and sat himself down on the bench.

As far away from her as possible, of course, but at least he was sitting.

"Colin," she said with a sigh, "you needn't feel shy."

"I do *not* feel shy. I am merely . . . um . . . trying to spare you . . . er . . . any discomfort or apprehension."

"So you've said."

He scowled at her. "Lady, you are deliberately seeking to provoke me."

She sighed, then moved herself closer to him. He looked panicked, but managed to stay seated. Ali reached for his hand and held it between her own.

"We *are* wed," she pointed out.

He slipped his hand from between hers, then patted her quite thoroughly on the back. "I know. And I thank you for it." Then he folded his hands quite securely together, and pinned them between his knees. "A tale, did you say? Aye, I can humor you thusly."

Well, perhaps a tale would rid him of his nervousness and then they could see to other things. Or perhaps it would take a goodly amount of time for him to muster up his courage, as it were, and see to his business with her. She supposed she should have been grateful for a bit of time to accustom herself to being wed to arguably the fiercest warrior in England—and most of France for that matter. Indeed, many women would have been terrified by the mere thought of sitting next to the man, much less anything else.

Perhaps she had more courage than she thought she did.

"Aliénore?"

She looked at him, surprised that she was still surprised by the sound of her name coming from him.

"My lord?" she asked.

"You're not attending me."

"Forgive me, my lord."

He frowned at her. "You can't tell me that you aren't riveted by this tale."

"Of course." She was beginning to wonder, however, if perhaps she should be wearing something else. Hose, perhaps? It was possible the gown was throwing him into such a state.

"Should I put on hose?" she asked suddenly.

"What in the bloody hell does that have to do with my slicing a man's moustache from him before I sent him to his grave?"

"Nothing."

"Your powers of concentration have faded sadly," he said, looking sorely disappointed.

"I'm thinking on other things."

"Besides battle? By the saints, woman, what else is there?"

Obviously she had a goodly work ahead of her.

"Colin," she asked patiently, "wouldn't you at least like to kiss me?"

He stared at her. And he continued to stare at her. Indeed, he stared at her so long and so intensely that she began to wonder if she shouldn't have kept silent. This was the Colin of Berkhamshire she had come to know so thoroughly in the lists, a man of complete and utter focus, a man who was single-minded about whatever task he had set before himself, a man who could likely send any sensible man scampering with just a pointed look of retribution.

And now she had that look turned on her.

But she had the feeling it had nothing to do with retribution.

Then he cleared his throat.

"Did I," he began, "but begin to kiss you, Aliénore of Solonge, I daresay I wouldn't be able to stop."

Ali found that her hand was waving under her chin in a fanning motion. And given the fact that the chamber felt as if someone had thrown an entire barrel of coals on the brazier, she supposed her hand had things aright.

"Oh," she managed.

"Aye, oh," he agreed. "And know this that few have aroused such an, er, enthusiasm in me."

"In truth?"

He paused and scowled at her. "Well, I'm not a bloody virgin, if that's what you're asking. But I'm a far sight less experienced than any of those Artane lads."

"Jason doesn't seem all that preoccupied with wenching," she pointed out.

He scowled. "Must we continue this?"

"You brought it up."

He looked supremely uncomfortable and she could scarce understand it. She'd expected him to want to be about that sacred business as quickly as possible. She studied him and watched as he studied anything but her in the chamber. There were a dozen questions she could have asked, but she supposed that prying into his preoccupations was perhaps impolite. And when she'd finally decided that perhaps she should dare, he spoke.

"I know a little," he said slowly, "of bedding a wench. But I know nothing of bedding a wife."

Ah, so there was the crux of the matter. She shrugged. "I suppose, my lord, that there isn't much difference."

He looked at her then and the seriousness of his expression surprised her. "Ah, but that is where you are wrong," he said. "There is all the difference between the two."

She had nothing to say to that. She looked down at her hands clasped in her lap and had no idea what she was supposed to do now. And then she saw a large, scarred hand come into view. That hand reached over and closed over hers. It was a warm hand, and a gentle one. Ali looked up and met Colin's eyes.

"I am not afeared," he said slowly, "of trying to learn."

She only nodded, mute.

He lifted her hand and kissed it. Roughly and not very easily. Then he peered at her, as if he judged her reaction. She only smiled. The man turned swordplay into a fine, elegant dance. Perhaps that would apply to other areas of his life as well.

In time.

He lifted his arm, presumably to put it around her shoulders—

And caught her fully in the nose.

Blood began to flow.

He leaped to his feet, cursing and wringing his hands. Ali put her hand over her nose, then found herself with a rag in her hands and her head tilted back thanks to Colin's tender ministrations.

His expression was very grim.

"A disaster," he said darkly. "As I assumed it would be."

She wheezed. "I wouldn't go so far."

"By the saints, your sire will have my head for this. Is it broken, do you think?"

"I've no way to tell."

He took a deep breath, then very gently took her nose between his finger and thumb.

She found herself quite suddenly on the bed with no idea how she'd come to be there. Colin was kneeling next to her, looking very grim. She closed her eyes briefly.

"How—"

"You fainted. But not before you screamed as if the very gates of Hell had spewed forth a contingent to chase you across the whole of France. Your sire, I likely don't need to add, has already come banging on the door."

She was suddenly quite grateful she was lying down. "My nose hurts."

"I've no doubt it does."

"I think perhaps I might have had enough—"

"Of course," he said quickly. "By the saints, Aliénore, you should sleep. I'll keep watch over you. You're perfectly safe. Well, from all except me, apparently."

She reached up and touched his cheek. "It was an accident, my lord. Something amusing to tell our children."

"I fail to see the humor at the moment. Perhaps later, when you don't look quite so bruised." He heaved a great sigh. "You should sleep now. You'll feel better tomorrow."

She nodded, and that mere movement sent her world spinning fair into oblivion.

But with her last bit of awareness, she felt a hand very carefully and very gently brush the hair back from her face.

"By the saints," he whispered, "what have I ever done to deserve a one such as she? Beautiful, fearless, and with a stomach strong enough to wed with me."

Ali fought to remain still. It was difficult, especially since she was certain tears would begin to leak from her closed eyes soon.

And then came more words from her apparently rather besotted husband, words she was just certain would fill her heart to overflowing and send the tears coursing in earnest.

"Now, if I could just bed the wench properly without breaking her first . . ."

Well, some things were perhaps better left said when your spouse was asleep.

Ali fell asleep smiling just the same.

Chapter 36

Colin woke and reached immediately for his sword. It was what he did every morning when he awoke. One never knew the dangers that might be lurking just above one's head, and he was never one to meet a danger unarmed, unprepared. This morning however, when he took hold of his sword, it squeaked.

He wondered, briefly, if he had just lost his mind.

He sat up with a start, then realized he was grasping something far too soft to be his sword. It was, oddly enough, his lady wife's leg.

Memory flooded back and he looked at her in consternation.

She was still wearing her gown. And aye, she was still wearing the signs of his tender ministrations the night before.

What would her bloody family say when they saw the condition of her face?

Well, he already knew what her father would say, for he'd had a goodly dose of that the night before whilst Ali was still out of her head with pain. Colin had apologized profusely, vowed that he'd damaged the wench unintentionally, demonstrated that she was still wearing all her clothing, and sent Denis of Solonge on his way a very unhappy and scowling father.

Colin had supposed that any other start to his matrimonial life would have been quite unthinkable.

"Colin?"

He looked at Aliénore quickly, but the sight of her, even when viewed by the very faint light pushing through the shutters, rendered him quite speechless. Shorn hair and broken nose included, the woman was absolutely beautiful.

To think she was his . . .

Well, almost. He had given thought to making her his in truth several times during the night, but the sight of her had given him pause. He'd but endeavored to embrace her and look what he'd done to her. What would happen should he try to love her?

He shuddered to think.

"You're looking fierce this fine morn, my lord."

He tried to soften his expression, but found it impossible. By the saints, not only did he now have a wife, he had Aliénore of Solonge for a wife. He'd suspected from the first moment of his betrothal to her that she was not merely an ordinary woman. No woman could bear that name and not have something substantial to her.

And now he had to spare a moment or two for regret that he'd thought her so cowardly. He suspected there were few wenches who would have ever dared what she had. He *never* would have found himself dressing in skirts for any reason.

Not even to avoid himself.

"Colin, are you unwell?"

He shook his head clear of his thoughts. "Nay," he said firmly. "How do you fare this morn? Does your nose still pain you?"

She sat up with a groan. "I think I perhaps have a bit of sympathy for Sir Etienne now. And this was an accident."

"He feels worse, I can assure you. And I daresay he didn't sleep nearly as well as you last night."

She smiled. "I must admit to having truly derived a great bit of enjoyment thinking of myself in this fine bed and Sir Etienne and Marie sleeping in my father's quite disgusting pit." She looked at him. "There is justice, is there not, my lord?"

"Aye, my lady, there is."

She continued to look at him.

As if she expected him to do something.

He cast about immediately for something to say, but came up with nothing. He looked at her quickly, wondering if he should comment on her own fetching person. Surely that couldn't go astray. He looked at her hair, which was sticking out much as it had every morning he'd woken beside her. He'd not thought much of it before except to tell her that she looked like an angry hedgehog and to do something about those ratty locks. But he supposed that saying the same thing to his wife would not have the desired effect.

He frowned, at a loss.

Which left him no choice but to fall back on his usual strategy.

"I should," he announced, "go to the lists."

He looked at her quickly to judge her reaction to that idea. Her expression, damn her anyway, was inscrutable.

"Where did you learn that?" he demanded.

"From you."

"Obviously I have taught you far more than I intended," he grumbled. He looked at her sideways. "Do you want to come with me?"

"No, thank you."

No further illumination was forthcoming, apparently. Colin sighed his gustiest sigh.

"Is there aught you would rather be doing? Something that, pray, won't damage you and force your father to put my head on a pike outside his gates? Shall I read to you? Indulge you in a game of chance?" Not that he played games of chance, of course. Gambling was not a proper knightly activity.

She dragged her hands through her hair. The sight of that, something he'd been watching her do for at least two months, did something rather odd to his insides. It was all he could do not to reach over and smooth her hair down for her.

Indeed his hand was halfway to doing so.

She looked at him, then sat perfectly still.

Well, hell, there was no sense in not finishing what he started, especially since being caught doing something in a halfway manner was quite undignified.

He brushed his callused and quite work-roughened hand over her very smooth hair and hoped she didn't mind it.

Then he pulled his hand back, curled his fingers underneath themselves to hide their condition, and produced a smile.

He imagined it hadn't come out very well.

To his surprise, his hand was soon taken by his bride.

"I would like," she began, looking at him with enough seriousness that he had difficulty swallowing, "to make a little journey down the passageway."

"To see your sire?" he asked grimly.

"To visit the garderobe."

Well, that was fairly benign.

"Then I would like something to eat."

"And then?"

"And then I think we should perhaps see to a few other things. Things of a matrimonial nature." She paused and smiled. "Don't you think?"

He didn't have to think. If she was willing, he wouldn't deny her. He bounded off the bed and threw open the door. A young lad snapped to attention.

"Aye, my lord!"

"Food," Colin barked. "And a goodly amount thereof." He looked back to the bed and watched as Ali rose and opened the shutters. She walked across the chamber and stood beside him. She smiled up at him, then slipped past him.

"I'll return."

"A body could hope," he muttered.

She laughed, then continued on her way.

He leaned against the doorframe and stared at nothing. So she would return. He supposed it could have been worse. She could have been bolting down the passageway, never to return. Especially given that there was no one left to pursue her with foul intentions. Marie was safely ensconced in the dungeon with Sir Etienne, both of them recovering from various wounds. He very much suspected Marie would not like the condition of her face, did she ever have the chance to see it again.

Then again, she was due to meet with the hangman's noose quite soon, so perhaps she wouldn't have to worry about her nose for long.

Of Sir Etienne Colin had few tidings save that the man was continually raging about the injustice of his straits.

Perhaps his new life of poverty didn't sit well with him.

Ah, but no time for those happy thoughts now. Colin noticed his bride coming toward him. Best he focus all his energies on whatever other matters she intended to see to that morn.

He didn't dare speculate on what those truly might be.

"Thinking idle thoughts?"

Colin looked down at her. "Thoughts of dungeon occupants, actually."

"Is Marie really down there with Sir Etienne?"

"Aye."

"I'm certain the happy couple are enjoying a fine few days."

"Marie can count them as her last," Colin said. "I suppose your sire will release Sir Etienne eventually. Likely after we've gone."

"Are we leaving soon?"

"Soon?" he repeated absently. "Well, aye. Unless you've a mind to linger here and watch your stepmother be hanged."

"Tempting, but I think I could do without that."

"Then let's see what your sire plans to do with her before we leave."

She looked at him in surprise. "Do you intend to leave today?"

"Nay. We'll need time to have supplies from your sire." He considered her reaction to that. She seemed relieved to not be traveling quite so soon. What that meant, however, he couldn't have said. "Tomorrow?" he offered.

"That seems rather soon as well, unless you've a pressing reason to return to England. I suppose you might want to return to give your sire the happy tidings."

He grunted. "There is that."

"And Jason is no doubt waiting for us. He'll be pleased to see you."

"And you, likely." He frowned at her. "I am assuming he knew your tale at least a day or two before I did."

"Far sooner than that. He saw me covering up after my bath that first day. I told him 'twas an old war wound, but he didn't believe me. When Berengaria called me by name, I found it useless to not tell him all."

"And of course he couldn't see fit to share any of it with me," he groused.

"I daresay, my lord," she said dryly, "that he feared for my life."

Colin looked at her and rubbed his own nose in sympathy. "Well, he'll have aught to say to me when he sees your face. As will your sire. He'll wonder if I had to bloody your nose again to get you to bed." And then he realized that while he certainly had gotten her to the bed, he hadn't gotten any further than that. He sighed. "I have failed in my duties as a husband, though perhaps you are relieve—"

He would have said more, but he couldn't. His wife, and he could honestly scarce call her that without a goodly amount of disbelief that she was actually such, had put her arms around him and was looking up at him.

As if she might actually have some fond feeling for him residing within her.

He knew, at that moment, that he was completely lost. He'd suspected it might be the case, of course, but now that he actually had her willing in his arms, he knew that it would take the greater part of the French army to pry him from her. Yet still . . .

"Colin?"

"Aye," he managed.

"I daresay we could take a day or two and linger here. Don't you think?"

"Um . . ."

She pushed him back inside the bedchamber, shut the door, and put her arms around him.

"We'd best make certain our marriage is completely seen to, aye?"

"Completely seen to?" he echoed weakly.

"Consummated."

"That's what I suspected you were referring to."

She leaned up on her toes and very gently kissed him. He remained perfectly still, lest she bump her nose and begin screaming again. She sank back down and frowned at him.

"You aren't very enthusiastic about this," she said sternly.

"I fear I will harm you."

"You won't."

"But I already have—"

"Then you have that out of the way, don't you?" She patted him on the back. "Now, where is our food? I'm certain you'll need something to strengthen you for your labors."

Damn, but the woman was persuasive.

"It will also annoy my brothers to be forced to wait on us half the morning."

"Half the morning?" he asked weakly.

"Too long?" she asked with a glint in her eye. "Haven't you the fortitude?"

He managed to hoist one eyebrow. "I smell a challenge."

"Do you indeed."

He set her aside, opened the door, and looked impatiently down the passageway. To his satisfaction, he saw the page coming back down at a dead run. The lad skidded to a halt, then pointed back down the passageway where Cook himself was coming along, followed by several helpers. Colin beckoned to the cook. He allowed them to set the food down on a table, then unceremoniously ushered them back out. He bolted the door, then turned to his wife.

"Strength for my labors."

"Strengthen away, my lord."

"Aren't you hungry?"

"Aye, I'll eat enough to suit me."

He set to his breakfast with single-mindedness, in preparation for the heavy labors to follow. Who knew when he might be at liberty to eat again?

He cleaned off most of the surfaces, but stopped just short of pulling things out of Aliénore's hands. And then once he was finished, he wiped his hands on his hose, dragged his sleeve across his mouth, and turned to his bride.

"Finished."

"So I see."

His palms were, unaccountably, quite slippery. Damnation, not even an unevenly matched battle produced this kind of nervousness in him.

"Cast yourself into the fray, my lord," she encouraged.

"I'd feel more secure with a sword in my hands."

She laughed. "Well, you cannot bring one to your marriage bed. Why don't you use kisses as your weapon of choice? Remember what you said, that if you began to kiss me, you might not be able to stop—"

Aye, he remembered that well enough.

So he very carefully reached out with his battle-scarred hands and touched her face. He shifted on the bench, praying that the creaking did not herald the bloody thing's total collapse, and leaned forward.

And managed to bump her nose with his own.

Was that a whimper or a moan?

He would have pulled back, but her hand was suddenly clutching the back of his head in an inescapable grip. Damnation, where had this wench acquired that strength?

And then the sweetness of her lips commanded nothing short of his full attention. Which led to other things, of course, just as he'd known it would.

It was a burden, at times, always having things aright.

C_{olin} wasn't certain what time it was when he finally stumbled from his chamber. Noon? Dusk? Was that sunrise or sunset, coming inside through the arrow loops?

Damned if he knew—or cared for that matter.

He looked at the woman who walked by his side with her hand in his. She smiled up at him pleasantly. Well, she looked no worse for the wear, save her nose, of course. He suspected that he might be a bit pale and drawn though, thanks to the wear on his own sweet self.

The woman would have made an awful nun.

She'd told him so herself at one point during their lengthy and quite satisfactory marital interlude. He'd been appalled that she'd even considered such a thing. The lengths he had driven her to . . .

He contemplated the potential for such pleasant marital exploits over the next few days as he led Aliénore down the passageway and down the stairs to the great hall. Perhaps they would remain at Solonge a bit longer. After all, Jason would probably appreciate another few days of rest at the priory. It would be the unselfish thing. The generous thing. The very *least* he could do to ensure his wife's happiness.

That decided, he walked into the great hall anticipating a fine meal and perhaps an immediate return to bed.

Unfortunately, a calm repast was not what he found awaiting him.

The hall was full of guards, Aliénore's brothers were pacing about with their hands on their swords, and Lord Denis looked as if the entire English army had announced they were laying siege to his keep. Colin walked quickly to the high table and stopped in front of his father-in-law.

"What is it?" he asked.

Denis turned to look at him, his face ashen. "Marie has escaped along with that cretin from Maignelay. They took a dozen guardsmen with them."

Colin felt himself sway. He never swayed. That he should do so surely indicated fully the depths of his anxiety for his bride.

Of course, he felt none for himself. He had no fear of anyone, especially a vindictive woman and a boastful, arrogant buffoon. Twelve men to dispatch only gave him the almost unbearable urge to rub his hands together in anticipation.

He would have, had he not felt a goodly bit of apprehension for Aliénore. He made a decision.

"We'll leave immediately," he announced, tossing Aliénore a look. She only nodded, so he turned back to her father. "How long ago did they escape, do you think?"

"Not long," Denis replied. "At the changing of the guard, no doubt. Four hours at most."

"A guard was bribed?"

"Slain. Two of them."

"You, my lord, have traitors in your household," Colin said sternly. "Best discover them quickly. Who knows how else they might betray you?" He took a deep breath, then looked at Aliénore. "Pack our gear, lady, and don your mail shirt. I'll see to stores. We'll leave within the hour."

"I'll come as well," Denis said. "And bring guards—"

"Nay," Colin said. "We'll not travel as an army."

"But how do you intend to protect my girl?" Denis demanded. "How can you possibly—"

The man seemed to realize what he was saying and whom he was talking to, for he suddenly swallowed the rest of his words. He nodded—though a bit too reluctantly, to Colin's eye.

"Of course. But I will still come. If nothing else, I will plunge the knife into Marie's deceitful breast as I should have done days ago. The evil she's wrought has been by my inaction. I will see it righted."

"Can you wield a sword?" Colin asked doubtfully.

"Can he?" said François with disdain. "Of course he can. Likely show you a new thing or two. And if not him, I surely can."

Colin eyed him with disfavor. Hadn't he given François enough instruction in the lists earlier? Had he not left the man trembling in terror, quaking with respect, positively shivering with the knowledge of his own failings?

Obviously the lout had a very short memory.

"I'll come as well, for you'll need my skill and advice," François announced. "And we'll bring Pierre."

"I'll not have an army," Colin insisted. "We'll use stealth."

"I can be stealthy," François said, puffing up his chest. "And I'm powerfully clever."

By the saints, was he eternally doomed to be surrounded by idiots? Colin very much doubted that François had ever done anything clever in his life, but he suspected that he and his brother would likely come even if he said them nay. Well, at least he would be burdened by two and not five. Ali's other brothers looked perfectly content to stay behind and guard the larder.

Well, perhaps the best way to travel unnoticed was to take these two brothers and her sire with him. It would save them popping up at an inopportune moment and ruining all hope of secrecy, or ending their lives by mistake.

"Within the hour, then," Colin agreed heavily. "Whoever isn't ready, stays behind."

François snorted. Pierre shivered. Denis merely turned and

started very quietly issuing orders to only a pair of men. Colin turned to Aliénore.

"Perhaps I should go with you upstairs—"

She shook her head. "I can protect myself."

"You cannot hesitate," he stated. "If you must strike, you must strike a fatal blow without hesitation."

"Colin, I know. Besides, the keep is now safe."

"So we thought this morning, and see where it has led us."

She leaned up and kissed him on the cheek. "Trust me. If it comes to that, I can do what I need to."

He suppressed the urge to haul her into his arms and never allow her to escape. She had things aright. She could surely see to herself for a few minutes. He looked at her sternly. "I'll meet you here in a quarter hour. Don't be late."

"I wouldn't dare."

He looked to see if she was teasing him, but found that she was completely in earnest. He nodded, satisfied, then turned and made his way to the kitchen. Though Lord Denis's man was there as well, Colin preferred to see to his own supplies.

He, of course, received attention before anyone else, and he chose quickly and saw his kit packed with the same amount of haste. He returned to find Aliénore coming down the stairs with their small saddlebags and bedrolls. Pierre was following, reverently holding Colin's mail.

Colin accepted aid in putting it on. He looked at Pierre critically afterward and decided that perhaps this lad might make something of himself after all, especially if he managed to not follow after François in habits and comportment. He gave the lad a nod of thanks, then turned to his lady.

He took the gear from her, hefted the food as well, and then motioned toward the door. Her family could follow or not, as they would. He had no intention of giving Marie and her foolish henchmen any more time to plan an ambush than they had already. With any luck, she and Sir Etienne would be still looking for a stream to wash off the filth of the dungeon.

Colin was momentarily tempted to remain, find the traitors, and punish them appropriately for their treachery, but like as not, the traitors were the dozen who had gone with Marie. Besides, he could afford to waste no more time. After all, he couldn't defend against an arrow coming from the shadows. The sooner he left and the harder they rode, the safer they would be. He sincerely hoped that young de Piaget was ready to travel. If not, Colin fully intended to leave him behind.

He paused in the courtyard at the touch of a hand on his. He looked down at Aliénore, who was smiling up at him. He tried to smile in return, but he suspected he wasn't very successful.

"All will be well," she said.

"I'll rest easy when his head adorns my gates and she is fertilizing my garden," he said grimly.

"She would certainly deserve it," Aliénore agreed. "I daresay my mother was not her first victim. Berengaria said as much."

He shivered. "What that woman knows . . ."

"A pity we don't have her here to ask about this," Aliénore said.

"She couldn't help," Colin said. "All we need is what I can provide. I don't envy the fools when we find them."

"Neither do I," she murmured.

He patted her back, then watched as the stable master brought their horses. Only it was just one horse he brought. He looked at Colin with consternation.

"The lady Aliénore's horse is missing," he said. "Gone."

No doubt Sir Etienne or one of the lads had it. Colin sighed. "Have you another beast of the same quality? I will pay you well for it."

The stable master looked over his shoulder and nodded to one of his hands. Another horse was brought, Colin's purse was lightened, and he dismissed the stable master to quickly pack their gear.

Unfortunately, they weren't through the gates before her family was riding along behind them. Colin scowled and turned his face forward. There was no hope for secrecy now. They would just have to rely on speed to save them.

That and his sword.

He spared a brief thought for the very pleasant and productive morning he'd spent with his bride. He looked at her to find her watching him with a smile.

It was the same sort of smile she'd been wearing an hour before.

"I am less than pleased about this hasty journey," he announced.

"I daresay you are," she said dryly.

"And you aren't?"

"If you'll remember, my lord, 'twas I who suggested we might pause for a few days at Solonge and tend our marriage."

"I had been about to suggest it," he said archly.

She laughed at him.

Damn her.

He scowled, but it was without much irritation behind it. "I suppose you have it aright," he admitted unwillingly. "Rest assured, however, that I will make certain in the future that you have ample chance for adequate rests on our journey."

"You are a most solicitous husband," she said solemnly.

He grunted at her, spared her one last look, spared one last thought of regret for the comfortable bed they'd left behind at Solonge, and then turned his attentions to the task at hand.

Namely, reaching the priory with everyone intact, especially Aliénore.

Now that he'd finally managed to wed her and bed her, he certainly wasn't going to allow anyone to take her away from him.

He pitied the souls who might try.

Chapter 37

S i r Etienne stood in the clearing with a dozen grousing fools surrounding him and cursed many things.

Aliénore, that she hadn't lined his purse.

Berkhamshire, that he'd left his face a bloody mess and his form a bruised and limping wreck.

And lastly, and given his current straits, he cursed most thoroughly Marie of Solonge, for leaving him with a dozen men who were now looking at him as if he held their futures in his hands.

Or at least their hopes of a meal in the near future.

He ground his teeth in frustration. Who would have guessed that he would find himself liberated from the dungeon only to come to this pass?

It was Marie's fault. Damn the woman to hell, he hadn't even had a chance to enjoy her. Somehow the vermin in the dungeon had put her off the idea of any kind of amusement. He'd been willing, despite his own abused form. It wasn't as if she'd had the freedom to be choosy about the location for their encounter!

He supposed he had to thank her for getting him out of the pit and out the gate. They'd ridden as if demons from Hell were after them for several hours, then Marie had called a halt to see to some womanly nonsense of relieving herself in private. Sir Etienne had wondered why she'd needed her horse with her, but that was a woman for you—illogical and frivolous.

Of course, she'd been gone so long that he'd begun to wonder if something had befallen her.

And what had befallen her was a fine bit of riding that had left her nowhere to be found.

Which had left *him* with a dozen men to feed, house, and

placate before they left him dead on the side of the road.

Things would not go well for Marie, did he ever but manage to lay his hands on her again.

The lads were growing restive. Sir Etienne put his shoulders back and searched frantically through his scattered thoughts for something to calm them down. Then he struck upon it.

"Riches," he said. Such was what soothed him to sleep at night. Surely these men were interested in the same thing.

"Gold?" one asked doubtfully.

"Aye," Sir Etienne said. "Gold, silver, all manner of things that would bring a man comfort and ease."

"Where?" demanded another. "We just left our only chance of a steady meal."

"Aye," said another. "Not as if we could go back there."

"Riches are not behind us," Sir Etienne said, looking off into the forest as if he could see something the men could not. "They lie before us. On a different shore. In the keep of a man who has such wealth, even he cannot count it."

He listened to himself speak and marveled at his own cleverness. Berkhamshire was rich, that was true. And 'twas another certainty that he wouldn't be forthcoming with any of his gold here in France.

Perhaps Aliénore would yet serve him.

"A different shore?" asked one man doubtfully. "Which different shore?"

"England," Sir Etienne said enthusiastically.

He was met with blank stares, then a babble of curses that could likely be heard for leagues.

"Silence," Sir Etienne commanded. "Will you have all learn of our plans?"

"What plans?" a man said scornfully. "Sounds to me as if you haven't got a plan."

Damnation, but would these louts never stop thinking and merely follow? He longed for the time when he would have men about him who would serve him with no argument. He had little patience for peasants pretending to be knights who couldn't manage coherent thoughts if they were handed them on a fine silver dish.

"I have a plan," Sir Etienne assured them. "We will go to England, wait for the lord of Berkham, and then sell him something he wants very badly. It will cost him dearly," he continued. "Perhaps all he owns."

"Sell 'im what?" asked a man who was currently picking his teeth with his blade. "And when will we eat next? I'm hungry."

"We'll sell him back his bride," Sir Etienne said impatiently, "and that's all you need to know now. We're for England as quickly as possible."

"Dinner first," said the man with the knife in his teeth. "I can't go to England on an empty belly."

By the saints, was he going to have to do everything for these fools?

"We'll go north," he said, irritated. "We'll forage inside people's larders and take what we want. And if you're too squeamish to do that, you can leave now."

There was low rumbling, and then many shrugs and loosening of daggers in sheaths. Sir Etienne had a brief moment of panic, which he tramped down immediately and credited to no breakfast, then realized that the lads were for him and merely ready to wreak havoc in the next village they came across—not looking at him as if he might have been quite tasty roasted over a hearty fire.

"To England, then," he said, then resheathed his sword and mounted his horse. He turned it north.

Or what he hoped was north.

The lads grumbled, but tromped after him readily enough.

To England.

His fortune awaited.

Chapter 38

A*li* followed Colin into the priory's courtyard and was very grateful when she could command her horse to stop moving. The journey from Solonge had seemed endless, likely because she had feared they might be attacked at any moment.

The journey had passed, fortunately, without incident. The only thing of note was the number of times François had looked suspiciously at her gear. How he could possibly recognize his mail shirt when it was under her cloak and had been seriously altered to fit her she didn't know, but he seemed to. She could scarce wait to tell him what had happened to his sword.

She slipped to the ground and leaned her head against her horse's withers. Perhaps the beast had had enough as well, for he didn't move. Ali closed her eyes and listened to the commotion around her: Colin shouting out orders, her brother François bellowing his own orders and then cursing everyone for ignoring him, the voices of nuns who were frantically babbling about something she didn't understand.

The last finally seeped into her fogged mind and she looked up in surprise. Aye, there were nuns aplenty, and they all looked as if they'd just had a vision of the end of the world. Ali stared at them, open-mouthed, and wondered why Colin's arrival should cause such a stir.

Then she saw Jason coming across the courtyard, looking worse, if possible, than when they'd left him behind.

"What befell you?" she asked him when he'd drawn close. "And what ails the women?"

"We should speak inside. Tis safer there."

"Safer?" she echoed. "Why should you worry about safety? Were you attacked?"

"In a manner of speaking." Jason turned and looked at Colin. "My lord. I see you and our good Henri survived your journey."

"*That,*" Colin said, pushing Jason aside and putting his arm around Ali's shoulders, "is not *our* Henri. She's *my* Aliénore, and I'll thank you to take your groping hands off her."

Ali watched Jason look at him in astonishment, then turn the same look on her.

"Well," he said, a slow smile forming on his face. "I see that things have changed during my brief absence. These are tidings indeed."

" 'Tis a very long tale," she admitted. "Perhaps better left for when you're sitting down."

"I can see he didn't slay you, at least," Jason said. "You can't be displeased with that."

"I did worse than try to slay her," Colin said. "I wed the poor girl. Now, move out of my way and find a seat before you fall down. I had assumed you would be far more sturdy than this." He snorted. "Felled by a pitiful bolt. That Artane constitution is highly overrated."

Jason only smiled, took Ali by the arm, and dragged her away from Colin. "Feeling very weak all of a sudden," he threw at Colin as he leaned on Ali. He pulled her toward the guest hall. "I can scarce wait for the tale. Tell me, did he discover it on his own, or did you have to clout him over the head to bring him to his senses?"

"He discovered it himself," she said, realizing at that moment how much she'd missed Jason and his sunny smiles. "And he's been quite chivalrous about it all. You would have been impressed."

"Did he woo you, or merely drag you off to the priest?"

Ali could feel Colin's eyes boring into the back of her head and she knew he was close enough to hear every single utterance she might choose to make. Not that she would have denied him his due. He had, after all, wooed her all on his own.

"He wooed me, fiercely and in a most manly fashion," Ali said, hoping she'd put the appropriate amount of reverence into her tone.

Colin made a noise of satisfaction from behind her, so she assumed she'd managed it well enough.

"What, with hours in the lists? Tales of battle and bloodshed before the fire? A demonstration of the proper way to sharpen one's sword?"

"That and more," Ali said. She leaned closer to Jason's ear. "He danced, as well."

Jason stumbled and Ali almost went with him to the ground. He found his footing and looked at her in astonishment.

"He what?"

"He danced."

Jason shook his head. "I vow you're lying. Colin of Berkhamshire cavorting about to music? It is simply beyond my capacity to imagine such a thing."

Colin was apparently not beyond a show of displeasure. Ali watched as he slapped Jason quite enthusiastically on the back of the head and cursed him thoroughly in the bargain.

" 'Tis but the dance of death, done to foul screeching of minstrels," he said archly. "I am quite graceful, which you would know if you spent more time in the lists watching me and less time rushing about the hall, trying to lift whatever skirts aren't pinned down with nails to the floor." He looked at Ali. "His time here has obviously clouded his memory of my stealth and skill. I would remind him now—"

"I am injured," Jason said, rubbing the back of his head in irritation. "I need no instruction from you at present to further damage my poor form."

"Later, then," Colin promised. "Aliénore, if you would see this feeble child into the hall, I will see to everything else."

Ali nodded, ushered Jason into the hall, and soon found herself seated between Jason and Colin. The nuns were no less agitated, but they soon left to carry on their frantic activity somewhere besides the guest hall. Ali looked at Jason.

"What has been the trouble?"

"I'll tell you of it, but first I would hear something more of your tale. How was it exactly that this miracle of revelation came about?"

"I merely looked at her," Colin said archly. "Being quite observant, of course."

"Of course," Jason said dryly.

Colin shot Ali a quick look. "There is a bit more to it than that, I suppose, but that more is none of your affair. Ask something else."

Jason raised his cup in salute. "I'll have the full tale from Aliénore when you're off in the lists." He looked at her and smiled. "Or do you intend to keep to your current garb and occupation?"

Ali shrugged in answer. She supposed she might have looked more convincingly the part of a wife had she been wearing a gown with her hair long and pinned up under a veil, but given that she had no hair to pin up, nor a veil to cover it with, nor even a gown to don, she supposed she would just have to make do with what she'd become.

"I haven't decided yet," she said. "I suppose Colin will have something to say about it."

"Gowns drag in the mud," was his only response.

Jason smiled, then winced as he shifted his shoulder. "Well, since no more details are forthcoming from you, I'll give you my tale. The past several hours have surely been more exciting than I would have liked."

"How so?" Colin asked skeptically. "Find a nun you fancied but couldn't talk her out of her robes?"

Jason pursed his lips. "What *we* found was a nun who had been poisoned and a chapel that had been pilfered."

Ali looked at him in surprise. "How fares the nun?"

"Poorly, given that she's dead," he answered. "Hence the confusion, though I daresay that will calm itself soon enough. The stealing of the sacred relics is something that will trouble them for a goodly time to come, though."

"How did this all come about?" Colin asked sharply. "Were you robbed outright?"

"Subterfuge instead," Jason said. "We had a visitor at first light today who wanted to join the good sisters here."

"But many women seek this kind of life," Ali said.

"But not many women who go by the name of Marie."

Ali looked at Colin. "Marie? Do you suppose it is the same? Could she have passed herself off so convincingly?"

"Well," Jason said, "my constitution might be weak, but my nose works perfectly well. I can smell a liar at fifty paces—"

"Having told several colossal ones yourself, no doubt," Colin muttered.

Jason glared at him. "I do not lie."

"And all you brew is healing draughts," Colin returned.

Jason paused, then shrugged with a smile. "Very well, then, I tell what truth I can. But," he said, turning back to Ali, "this woman would have called the sky red and the grass blue without hesitation. I spotted her deception instantly."

"You're very observant," Ali said, with a faint smile. "But I knew that about you from the start."

Colin snorted. "Like as not he merely guessed. That and the wench was no doubt riding in on your horse, Aliénore."

Jason smiled ruefully. "There was that, as well."

"What did you do then?" Colin asked.

"Nothing. The good sisters here saw no reason not to take her in and I had no proof that she intended harm. But I vowed to keep watch over her."

"A bold wench, that one," Colin muttered.

"Bold enough," Jason agreed. "I mentioned to her at the morning meal that I was a very close friend of Aliénore's and had heard many tales of her life at Solonge before she was betrothed, and wasn't it odd that she, Marie, had the same name as Aliénore's stepmother? She expressed the proper amount of horror at Aliénore's troubles, then disappeared into the cloister, where I was not welcome. A pair of hours later, there was word of one of the sisters having fallen ill. Whilst we were investigating that, Marie helped herself to everything of value in the chapel and rode off quite happily."

"On my horse," Ali finished.

"Aye, on your horse," Jason agreed. "I tried to stop her, of course."

"Did she nick you?" Colin asked, peering closely at Jason's shoulder.

"She didn't mark me, but the struggle wrought a foul work on my healing wound. She fled before I could catch her and although several men from the village searched, none could find her."

"But she left Solonge with Sir Etienne and several garrison knights," Ali said. "Did you not see them?"

"She was traveling on her own from what I saw. The villagers said a goodly contingent of men rode through the fields later, and a very irritated-looking group of lads they were, so perhaps Marie was trying to leave them behind and seek safety for herself." He smiled. "I daresay she won't be happy should she encounter them again, having thusly given them the slip."

"I would put nothing past her," Lord Denis said.

Ali remembered only then that her father and two brothers were there as well. Her sire certainly seemed at peace, more so than he had in years. Perhaps ridding himself of Marie had done him some good. Would that he'd never wed her in the first place.

Then again, if he hadn't, she wouldn't be wed with Colin and she couldn't help but feel that that was worth the price.

The afternoon passed slowly, first with the chamber full of plots, strategy, and plans for reaching England alive, and then with condolences for the good sisters and their loss. Ali listened until she simply couldn't listen anymore. She leaned back in her chair and looked at Colin as he talked with her family and Jason.

And then, despite what swirled around her, she found herself thinking on how she and Colin had passed the previous morning in her father's chamber, taking care of, well, things that needed to be taken care of.

Her nose was healing nicely, truth be told.

As if her very thoughts had been divined she found her hand suddenly taken by her husband's. He rose, pulling her up after him.

"Aliénore's tired," he stated. "Where can we retire?"

Jason laughed.

"I'll see to you later," Colin promised him.

Jason only raised his cup and drained it in salute.

A nun came forward. "We have a chamber for the abbot," she offered. "You could stay there for the night, if you like."

Ali started to follow him from the guest hall when the voices behind her reached her ears.

"He bloodied her nose," Pierre whispered from behind them.

"Ah, but what did she do to him that you can't see?" Jason said with a laugh.

Pierre made noises of awe.

"I am," Colin muttered under his breath, "going to kill them both before this journey is over."

Ali kept her head down and smiled. That was perhaps the trouble with traveling with family. They felt compelled to mark and interpret every action.

The nun led them to a small chamber, then inclined her head. "For your comfort, my lord, my lady."

Colin didn't exactly shove the woman from the chamber, but he came close. Ali smiled and received a scowl in return.

"I thought you might be weary," he said.

"I daresay napping isn't why you brought me here," she said dryly.

"I thought I might seek to reassure you that I am fully capable of protecting you," he offered.

"That, my lord, is coming perilously close to a falsehood."

"Then, damn you, I am heartily sick of death and subterfuge and I thought a pleasant hour or two enjoying the fruits of my labors of finally managing to drag you to the altar might serve us both well."

"Now *that* I believe."

He said no more, but merely took her in his arms and, without further comment, proceeded to kiss her until she couldn't breathe. In truth. She finally managed to tear her mouth away from his and suck in much-needed air. He fair dropped her back to her feet.

"What?" he asked, checking her over frantically. "Did I break something?"

"Your mail," she wheezed. "My mail. It's crushing the life from me. And my nose is plugged."

"Nothing I can do about the last," he said, making quick work of removing both his mail and hers.

"You would make a fine squire," she remarked.

"I was a fine squire, but I'm a far better knight."

"So I've noticed. Now, where were we?"

"About my next objective."

"And that would be?"

He looked at her, hesitated, and then gestured for her to sit. She did, then watched as he paced in front of her for several moments in silence. Then he stopped and looked at her quite seriously.

"I have decided," he began, "that there is something yet in life that I have not mastered. I vow I will not rest until I do."

"Something you haven't mastered?" she echoed. "Is that possible? Colin of Berkhamshire, master of swordplay, terrifier of armies, man who brings souls to their very knees by the mention of his name alone? What else could there possibly be?"

"Something far more important."

She could scarce wait to hear what.

"I have decided," he announced, "that I will become as fine a lover as I am a swordsman."

The saints preserve her. She'd seen his dedication in the lists. She wondered, just as seriously, if she might ever see the outside of her bedchamber again.

"Well," she managed weakly.

He looked at her with a frown taking root between his eyebrows. "Why do you say that? Is that not a worthy goal?"

"Of course it is."

"Do you fear you lack the stamina for it?"

She wanted to sit up and put her shoulders back, but the very thought of the days and nights he would most likely want to devote to his new preoccupation was enough to keep her slumping in her chair.

"Or perhaps 'tis the thought of aiding me in this quest that doesn't sit well with you," he said grimly.

"You, my lord," she said, "think too much."

He knelt down in front of her suddenly and reached for her hands. She looked at his large paws surrounding hers, those scarred hands that had brought perhaps more justice, though likely more terror and death, than the normal pair of hands, and couldn't help a bit of marveling that they cradled hers so gently.

"Actually, I could sit no longer below," he said quietly. "I could listen no more to tales of death and destruction."

"Losing your strong stomach?" she asked gently.

"Nay, my lady. I found myself quite suddenly longing for no company but yours, even did we but sit together and speak of nothing important." He paused and an expression of deep concern descended upon his features.

"Colin?" she asked. "What ails you?"

"Think you such longings bode ill for my ruthlessness?" he asked.

She squeezed his hand. "I'll carry the secret of it to my grave."

He looked upon her with approval. "I always suspected you were a prudent wench."

"Did you now," she said, hoping that was a compliment.

"Indeed, I did," he said, beginning to warm to his topic. "If you must know, when I knew you were a girl but knew not your name, I found myself often wishing that Aliénore of Solonge had found herself a happy home in a convent."

She blinked. "Why?"

"Because I found you to be such a fine, sporting gel with a courageous heart. I found myself cursing the day that might come and saddle me with a betrothed who hadn't the spine to face me as you did."

"And when you learned who I was?"

"Well," he said, lifting her hand and kissing it in the less-than-polished way she was fast becoming accustomed to, "well, then I counted myself doubly blessed. My obligation was fulfilled to the appropriate woman, but I got the wench I wanted in the bargain as well."

That, for some reason she surely couldn't divine, was possibly the most perfect thing a man had ever said. And that it should come from the terrifying man kneeling before her looking infinitely satisfied with his life only made the words sweeter to her ears.

"I can only hope," he said slowly, "that you have no regrets. And if you do, I hope they can be overcome in time."

She leaned forward and smiled at him. "Will you know the truth?"

He looked to be steeling himself for something truly awful. "If you must," he said.

"It occurred to me, at some point in our journeys, that if I had but known *you* instead of your reputation, I wouldn't have fled."

He looked at her with his mouth open for a moment or two, then began to blink rapidly.

"Damned smoky fire," he said, waving away nonexistent clouds. "Bad wood, obviously. I'll have to have a word with these nuns before we leave."

Ali smiled to herself and rose, pulling Colin to his feet with her. " 'Tis horrible," she agreed. "Now, about that new ambition of yours . . ."

"Aye?"

"I wonder how comfortable that bed is over there."

He put his shoulders back and assumed a long-suffering expression. " 'Tis but an obstacle to be overcome by only the most courageous. I'm up to the task. You?"

"Anything for the noble cause of chivalry."

"I *knew* I was saddling myself with the right wench."

She wanted to point out that most men did not refer to their wives as "wenches," but he'd already bent his mind and energies to his task, and she found that worrying about such trivialities was simply beyond her.

As fine a lover as he was a swordsman?

The saints preserve her, she might never escape the chamber.

Chapter 39

A se'nnight later, Colin dismounted in Harrowden's courtyard, stood gratefully on ground that didn't buck and heave beneath him, and took the time to briefly contemplate several of life's more puzzling riddles.

Firstly, why was it he had spent the better part of his life on horseback, which was certainly not a ride without its own share of bucking and heaving, yet such a life had not prepared him in the slightest for the flailings and whirlings of a ship being tossed about the sea?

Secondly, how was it that Jason of Artane, still green from his wound and pale from his fever, could ride out such waves with nary a flicker of unease crossing his face and then cheerfully step off the boat with the contents of his stomach still intact?

And, lastly, how was it you could be intimate with a woman, powerfully and fully intimate with a woman, yet have that woman refuse to puke in front of you? Especially given how many times she'd done it previously on her last sea crossing in the guise of a man!

Needless to say, he had refused to leave Aliénore to her puking self, taken her cursings like the man he was, and held her head when she'd finally fallen into an exhausted slumber.

He supposed he shouldn't have been surprised when she'd woken and found that she'd been carried onto the dock senseless, yet still thanked him kindly and given him her most pleasant smile.

He'd decided then not to try to pursue the hidden meaning in anything she'd done while aboard ship. Those disturbing feminine slips aside, she had many fine, manly qualities such as courage, good cheer, and ample wit, qualities that made sense to him, and ones he would certainly choose to concentrate on instead.

Now he had reached the last pause before he arrived at his final destination of Berkham. He was pleased to be where he was, and not only because it meant he would never again have to set foot on board a ship. He had the happy occasion of his father's discomfiture to look forward to when Reginald saw Aliénore alive and well.

And apparently pleased to have wed with Reginald's son.

He took a final look about the courtyard to assure himself that no foes had followed him inside the gates, then gathered up his bride, nodded for her family and Jason to follow, and swept into the guest hall with as much bluster as his father might have managed on his best day.

Only to find his brother kissing Sybil of Maignelay-sur-mer as if robbing her of breath was the only thing that assured him of his own.

Colin came to a teetering halt and gaped at his sibling, then gaped at Sybil as well. She was wearing neither wimple nor veil. Perhaps having Peter to kiss had occupied her mouth so fully that she no longer needed to stock her larder, as it were.

The door at the other end of the hall banged shut suddenly. Peter and Sybil sprang apart as if they'd been spotted by the abbot himself.

"By the saints, at it again?"

Colin looked at his father and noted the expression of complete disgust. Apparently Peter and Sybil were not engaging in a newly discovered pastime.

"But Father," Peter protested, "we are betrothed. What else are we to do?"

"Wait for your damned bro . . . um . . ."

Colin watched as his father realized that he, Peter, and Sybil were not the only ones in the hall, then realized just who else was there. Colin had the complete satisfaction of watching his sire blanch.

Of course, that whitening of his visage didn't last long.

"Back so soon?" he asked contemptuously. "And empty-handed. I suppose I shouldn't be surprised."

Colin folded his arms over his chest. "I found what I sought."

Reginald looked the company over. "I see men, so I assume you didn't bring the silly twit back with you. Is she dead?"

"Hardly," Colin answered.

"In a convent, then."

"Hardly," Aliénore muttered from where she stood next to him.

Colin was tempted to smile, but refrained. He would enjoy that bit of humor with Aliénore later when they had some privacy. For now, he was better off scowling at his sire. "The lady is alive, hale, and hearty."

Reginald nodded in satisfaction. "You couldn't persuade her to come back with you, then. I had no doubt of it. Obviously, I made the right decision in choosing Peter—"

"To aid you in packing your gear at Berkham," Colin finished for him, "for 'tis a certainty I don't want you there any longer."

"You have no say in the matter," his father snarled, "for you have no bride."

Colin took Aliénore by the hand and led her forward. "May I present," he said calmly, "the lady Aliénore of Solonge. Or Aliénore of Berkham, as she now should be known. My lady wife."

Reginald gaped at her for a moment or two, his mouth working futilely. He seemed to be having trouble taking in air.

"Impossible," he wheezed. "This lad couldn't possibly be a woman."

"I fear she most certainly is," came another voice.

Colin looked to his right and saw that Lord Denis had stepped forward. He smiled without any warmth whatsoever.

"And this is my daughter you're near to insulting," he said. "I can vouch for her identity."

"As can I," Jason said.

Aliénore's brothers offered the same service.

Reginald looked as if his heart might be failing him right before their very eyes. He clutched at his throat and made strangling noises. Aliénore started forward, but Colin caught her by the hand.

"Ignore him," Colin said shortly. " 'Tis for show."

"But Colin," she said, aghast, "he looks unwell."

Colin pulled her along, then nodded to his sire on the way to the table set near the back of the hall. "He'll survive. See, already he turns red instead of that unattractive purple he was but a moment before. His ire will keep him from his grave long past the time when I would have rather seen him there, I assure you."

Reginald was starting to splutter, which Colin took as a sign his father was in truth not ready to be laid out and admired.

Damn him anyway.

Colin led Aliénore to the table, sat down with her, saw her family seated, and then waited for sustenance to be brought to him. What came instead was his brother crawling toward him, looking desolate.

"Does this mean," he asked, his voice quavering in a most unmanly fashion, "that my betrothal to Sybil is invalid?"

Colin studied his brother. "You want the wench?"

"Desperately." And Peter did look desperate as he clutched the edge of the table and leaned precariously over it toward Colin.

"I'm for it, then," Colin said. "Save me the expense of keeping you here, I suppose."

"My gold is not yours yet," Reginald croaked. "Not until I'm dead!"

"I can see to that for you, if you like," Colin snapped.

"You wouldn't dare."

"You would be surprised," Colin returned. He girded up his loins to launch into a full-out attack on his father, but found that he was quite suddenly distracted by the arrival of his sisters. Ermengarde came marching first into the chamber, gathered their father up, and saw him settled with food before him. Colin watched with not just a little irritation as she fussed over the old fool.

"We haven't eaten either," Colin said pointedly.

"Go fetch it yourself," Ermengarde said, sweeping the

company with a glare. "The kitchens are . . . are . . . are . . ."

Colin watched as his sister found herself rendered quite unable to finish her thought. He followed her eyes and realized she had perhaps studied his troops a moment too long. She was standing in front of the table, gaping at one of Aliénore's brothers.

François, to be exact.

And François was gaping at her in return.

Ermengarde shut her mouth with a snap. And then—and Colin knew at that moment that the world could not last but a handful of moments more if these momentous events were any indication—she reached up and tidied her hair.

Tidied her hair?

Colin could scarce believe his eyes.

"You'll need . . . food," she said breathlessly.

"You'll need aid fetching it," François said, standing up so quickly that his chair fell backward with a crash.

Ermengarde blushed.

The sight of it was, in a word, terrifying.

"She's smitten," Aliénore whispered.

"The saints preserve us," Colin whispered back.

"It had to happen sometime."

"I pity your brother."

"I pity your sister."

Colin found his father staring at Ermengarde and François as if they'd both sprouted horns and conjured up flames to lick at their backsides. Then Reginald seemed to remember that he was in the midst of being stricken with a fatal bit of grief.

"Agnes!" he cried, flailing his hands about desperately. "Come to me! Your sister has deserted me and there is no one left to see to the small comforts that an old man deserves."

"He should have been a player," Colin said with a snort. "Listen to him spout lies as if someone had written them down for him to repeat."

"Listen?" Aliénore said, with a laugh. "Rather you should look, my lord. It would seem that not even Agnes is immune to my family's charm."

It was true. Agnes had come stumbling farther into the guest hall, then come to a dead stop, her gaze fixed to none other than poor Pierre of Solonge.

Colin waited for her hand to flutter up to her throat.

It did.

He then expected the rapturous sigh, the blinking of her eyes, and the rosy blush plastering itself to her cheeks.

He wasn't disappointed.

"Who," Agnes said breathlessly, her finger pointing in its usual fashion, "is *that?*"

"Pierre of Solonge," Pierre squeaked. "Your servant, my lady."

"Nay, yours, my lord."

"Oh, by the saints," Colin said in disgust, "go help Ermengarde with the food, both of you, and see if you can get your sorry arses back here before we perish from hunger. Moon over each other all you like, but do it after I've eaten!"

Pierre and Agnes moved like souls who walked in their sleep toward the back of the hall that led to the kitchens.

"You have my brother's name," Agnes said with a reverent tone.

"And you have the face of an angel," Pierre said with another squeak.

"As if he's ever seen one," Aliénore said, sounding quite nauseated over what she'd just seen.

"Well," Colin said, "my father can count himself beggared in truth now. Dowries for his girls and the rest of his gold to me."

"I'll need something for my bride as well," Peter said. "Don't forget me."

"Forget you?" Reginald shouted. "How can I forget any of you? Ungrateful, grasping, selfish—taking an old man's last crumb of bread from his very lips? How is it possible that you sprang from my loins?"

"It is hard to believe," Colin grumbled.

Reginald leaped to his feet, swept the entire table with a heated glare, and sniffed mightily.

"I'll be lying down," he said. "Trying to regain my strength."

"Find a comfortable bed and lay claim to it," Colin advised. "I assumed you'd want to take your vows here now that I've taken mine elsewhere."

His father threw him a murderous look, then stomped from the hall. Colin sighed and went to fetch what his father hadn't eaten. He set it down in front of him, then invited Aliénore and her father, who flanked him, to help themselves.

"What of me?" Jason asked pointedly.

"Use your charm with the monks," Colin said, reaching for cheese.

"It doesn't work with men," Jason groused.

"Works with Cook at Blackmour," Colin countered.

"We have a bargain, he and I."

"What?" Colin asked. "He feeds you and you don't heap curses upon his head?"

"Nay," Jason said reluctantly. "I'm helping him woo someone."

"The saints pity the wench," Colin said, then thought better of it. "At least she'll eat well." He looked around Aliénore at Jason. "Who's the woman?"

"A certain healer we both know."

"Berengaria?" Colin asked in surprise.

"Nay, not her."

"Wise woman. Magda, then."

"She can't cook to suit him."

Colin felt himself pale. "Not Nemain."

"Impossible," Aliénore said in disbelief. "I saw them fighting over stew spices."

"I haven't yet convinced him that he'd have more success if he bit his tongue," Jason said.

Colin shivered. He could scarce believe the romantic battles that were being waged around him and he found himself quite relieved that his war was waged and won already. He looked at Aliénore.

"We've apparently begun something."

"I'd say so," she said with a smile.

By the saints, would that smile never cease to render him unfit for anything useful? He found that he could scarce grope for food and get it to his mouth with any success because all he wanted to do was cast about for something else to say that would bring her smile forth again.

"Colin?"

He blinked, then realized she was talking to him. "What?"

"Does the fare not suit you?"

"I'm having trouble concentrating on it," he admitted.

Jason, predictably, laughed.

"But," Colin added, with a glare thrown the lad's way, "I'm certainly not having trouble concentrating on whom I might destroy in the lists later."

"They don't have lists here," Jason pointed out.

"They have farmers who aren't opposed to lining their purses for my pleasure."

"I have a wound," Jason said, covering his shoulder protectively with his hand.

"You'll have more if you don't keep your mirth to yourself."

Jason only smiled, as if the thought of an afternoon in the lists facing the arguably fiercest warrior in England and France *weren't* the most terrifying thing he'd ever contemplated.

"It is merely a pleasure to see you so besotted," he said.

I'm not besotted was on the tip of his tongue, but Colin realized that he couldn't lie. So he merely clamped his lips shut and gave Jason his most formidable glare.

"And with such good reason," Jason added with a charming smile thrown Aliénore's way. "I only wonder why it took you so long to see through her ruse. Surely no lad could be so beautiful."

"My thoughts as well," Colin agreed, trying to muster up enthusiasm for the roast fowl before him.

"You know," Aliénore said, leaning toward him and speaking quietly, "you should eat."

He looked at her. "Why?"

"To keep up your strength. For whatever battle you're waging at present."

Colin was quite certain that no one would mistake the sudden flush of his face for anything but what it was.

Aye, that sudden and excessively warm breeze blowing

through the hall from the kitchens. That was it.

"You have it aright," he said, hiding behind a leg of fowl. "Shouldn't neglect my meals."

Jason had to excuse himself. Colin watched him walk off and felt his eyes narrow at the shaking of Jason's shoulders. Well, the lad could enjoy his laughter at Colin's expense now. He would certainly pay for it later.

"I think he enjoys teasing you," Aliénore remarked, picking at the monks' offerings.

"Far too much," Colin said, scowling at his supper. "He didn't use to attempt it as much in his youth. Either he's grown bold, or I've grown soft." He slid her a glance. "I think I used to be more intimidating."

She laughed, but the sound of it only made him want to do something Jason would tease him further for, such as smile in return.

"I find you still quite intimidating, my lord, so never fear that your reputation hangs about you in tatters."

"Too intimidating to have a go in the lists?" he asked. "Trample a few cabbages for the sheer sport of it?"

"Is it safe, do you think?"

"I can protect us well enough, Aliénore."

"I never thought otherwise, my lord. I just wonder about Sir Etienne and Marie. If they had the courage to follow us."

He wondered the same thing, though he'd taken every precaution he could. He'd kept careful watch during their journeyings across France and seen nothing. He'd made certain their ship was free of Sir Etienne or any of his cohorts. And he'd scrutinized every clump of grass and grouping of trees all the way from the shore to Harrowden. He was certain he hadn't missed anything.

Besides, Sir Etienne likely didn't have the stamina to follow them so far. Knowing him, he was boasting of having chased Colin and his bride from French soil.

Colin didn't care for the lie, but he wasn't about to sail the stormy seas again to put it to rights.

He sat back with a sigh. "There's no way to tell," he said. "All we can do is set our sights on home and get there without incident."

She looked more worried than he would have liked. "Will they follow us, do you think?"

"If they are fools."

Her hand closed over his and she smiled gravely. "I am very glad, my lord, that you are for me."

"And you for me," he said, with feeling.

"Home, then?"

"Aye. As soon as possible."

Which likely wouldn't be as soon as he would have liked, given the four besotted fools who could scarce carry in their burdens of foodstuffs and gaze rapturously into each other's eyes at the same time. Colin scowled at them in disgust, but they paid him no heed.

"I don't know if I can watch this," he muttered under his breath.

"Perhaps that farmer's field is the place for us," Aliénore whispered.

"It might be the only privacy we find," he agreed.

He thought to say more, to reassure her that he could protect her, but let the moment pass. She knew he could, so there was little reason to remind her of the like.

Besides, Sir Etienne had no doubt remained safely and comfortably ensconced on yonder far shore and would not trouble them again, and Marie had likely already found herself another foolish lord to mistreat.

He and Aliénore were perfectly safe trampling cabbages.

Chapter 40

S *ir* Etienne stood with his back against a tree and stared at the monastery before him. He wasn't overly fond of such places, and not just because there was so much religion going on inside. What he couldn't understand was why a man would trade wenching for prayer. And prayers all day long and through the night. Daft, it was, and he pitied the lads who were forced into it.

Being one of the lads who had escaped such forcing, of course.

Not that his sire hadn't tried. He had, with both words and fists. His mother had pleaded with tears. Being the third son of a broken-down, unskilled knight who'd been given his spurs out of some misguided sense of pity by an obscure lord in an unimportant part of France, Sir Etienne had known from the very start that any greatness he obtained, he would obtain on his own.

And the path to that greatness would never come by means of a monk's tonsure.

A pity his parents were dead, else he could have returned with Berkhamshire's gold and shown them what he'd become. His brothers wouldn't care. One was rotting in his grave thanks to an axe wound in his side and the other was rotting in a tiny monastery in that same unimportant part of France he'd never left.

Sir Etienne paused and considered. Perhaps a gift to that place wouldn't be such a poor idea. After all, even men of great stature had the occasional need of a prayer for their souls.

But first, to obtain his wealth.

Which was why he stood where he was, listening to the restive movements of the handful of lads he had left to him who waited in the trees for his instructions. Fewer lads than he would have liked, of course, but a man made do.

It had been a difficult journey.

The pillaging in France had gone well, for the most part, with only a pair of casualties in his own little army. The goods and coin had easily been enough to secure them all passage to England, but damn most of the lads if they hadn't scampered in the night, leaving him with just three. Fortunately, those three had been lads ready for adventure and dazzled with the idea of vast riches to come their way.

Not that Sir Etienne ever would have shared those riches, but he'd seen no point in telling *them* that.

The crossing had been uneventful. The true entertainment had only begun several days into the journey to Harrowden.

He'd been riding along, dreaming of what he would do with his gold, when he'd stumbled upon a small band of ruffians about their usual work of taking advantage of an apparently solitary traveler.

Who turned out to be none other than Marie of Solonge.

Sir Etienne had watched with great interest as she'd killed three of the ten men who faced her. He'd finally gotten down off his horse, wondering if he should end the skirmish—just so he could have her himself, of course; not for any other reason—when one of the men had shoved her. Sir Etienne had seen her recover from worse things, but apparently her journeyings hadn't been easy. She had tripped and fallen.

Face first into their rather large fire.

The results had been, in a word, revolting.

She'd screamed and screamed until Sir Etienne honestly couldn't bear it anymore. He'd put her out of her misery by catching her under the chin—or what was left of it—and rendering her senseless. And he'd gone so far as to kick dirt on her clothing to put out the fire. The woman was going to die anyway, what with those wounds, but there was no sense in setting the entire countryside on fire whilst she was about her business of it.

He'd turned to face the ruffians, dispatched a pair of them when they looked to him for sport, and then bargained with the other eight.

The lure of riches worked like a wonder, every time.

The additions to his little band had also provided him with reliable directions to Harrowden. He could have found the place himself, naturally, but he had other pressing items vying for his attention and had little energy to spare on trivial details. So he'd saved his strength, firmed up his plans, and ridden quite cheerfully halfway across England to where his future lay.

Or at least the means to his future.

The front gates were open, but still he waited where he was.

Then he saw motion there. He faded instantly back into the shadows and held up his hand for silence.

Who should walk out of that gate but Colin of Berkhamshire himself and his manly, though certainly very beautiful, bride, Aliénore of Solonge.

Sir Etienne could scarce believe his luck.

He waited for a guard to follow, but there was none. Could this be possible? Were they truly that foolish, that they trusted the adequate but uninspired sword skills of the Butcher?

Apparently so.

Sir Etienne smiled. This was going to be much easier than he'd dared hope.

Chapter 41

A *li* walked along the little path, holding hands with her husband and smiling in pleasure at the beauty of the day. She supposed she wouldn't think it so beautiful in an hour when she was roasting in her mail, but for now, it was lovely and the afternoon full of goodly smells. And given the fact that the only privacy she might have with her lord was out stomping about in the mud, she was willing to endure a bit of exercise to have it.

Colin squeezed her hand. "You're smiling. Thinking on the romances blossoming behind us that we're not being forced to witness at present?"

She shook her head and smiled up at him. "I'm just enjoying the day."

"And the prospect of a little swordplay?" he prodded.

One thing she could say for the man: He was consistent in his habits. "I have acquired a taste for it, you know," she said. "There is a certain peace about the discipline of practicing your skills."

He stopped her, put his free hand on her shoulder, and kissed her quite vigorously on the mouth.

"You, my lady," he said, beaming his approval on her, "are a wench without peer."

There was no higher praise from him. "My lord, your compliments leave me breathless."

"They likely should. Never given so many to anyone in my life." He slung his arm around her and continued on. "Who would have thought I would wed a woman who was handy with a blade? Not my sire, surely." Then he looked at her sideways. "But this is the question that begs an answer. Are you coming with me here because you want to, or because you're humoring me?"

"Does it matter?"

"It does."

She walked with him in silence for a bit, then smiled. "I'd say, then, that 'tis a bit of both. I also can't argue that skill with a blade might serve me. Who knows that I may be left behind to defend the hall some day."

"True enough."

"Perhaps 'tis best, then, that I don't burn these hose. Unless you would prefer me in a gown?"

He looked so startled that she laughed.

"Colin, I can't go about forever looking like a boy. What will people think?"

"Well, they'll never believe I married a lad, what with your beauty." He scratched his head. "I suppose you'll have to garb yourself like a woman eventually. A damned nuisance, those skirts. Always dragging about in things they shouldn't."

"Be grateful you aren't required to wear them."

"I am, believe me," he said, with feeling. "Ah, here we are. And look you, the industrious man has replanted."

"This will cost you," she warned.

"Well worth the expense. Come, lady, and let us see if so many hours spent pursuing our other passion has left you with no recollection of how to pursue this one."

She followed him into the field, winced at the thought of trampling such fine-looking and tender plants, then forced herself to focus her energies on the task at hand. The cabbages would grow back. Her head wouldn't, if Colin mistakenly took it off because she wasn't paying attention.

And given the way the man was swinging his blade at her, he certainly didn't seem to be holding the fact that she was his wife against her.

"You *are* in earnest about this," she said, somewhat dumbfounded.

He blinked in surprise and paused in midswing. "Of course I am. Did you think I would pass all those hours driving skill into you only to have it wasted?"

"But that was then."

"And this is now. And as you said, you may be the one

guarding the castle now and then. Best you know how to defend yourself if I'm not there to do it for you. Besides," he said thoughtfully, "you're becoming a fairly passable swordsman. With enough time, you could likely take on a less skilled knight and do him in."

"Think you?" she asked, surprised.

"Well," he said doubtfully, "perhaps a less skilled knight without mail who'd spent the night wenching and drinking himself into a stupor. But," he added quickly, "those are often the most dangerous kind of men, for they've no head for chivalry or proper knightly conduct on the battlefield."

She tipped her sword down, crossed over to him, and leaned up to kiss him softly.

"You needn't fear bruising my feelings," she said, smiling up at him. "I'll learn what I can and hopefully it will serve me, but I won't weep if I'm not your equal in swordplay."

He looked so relieved that she put her arms around him and hugged him. She rested her head against his chest and marveled. That she should embrace him so easily showed how much she had grown to trust him.

Indeed, she couldn't help but spare a wish that she'd wed him two years earlier when she'd had the chance.

She pulled back. "I don't know that I've properly apologized for bolting on you," she admitted.

"You did what you thought best. I can't fault you for it, being well acquainted with my reputation myself."

"I wasted these two years for the both of us." She looked up at him seriously. "What if our lives are cut short? We'll never have those two years back—"

"We won't have them back," he agreed, "and no one can guarantee how long life will last. But we *can* wring every drop of living from the days we do have together. Who knows, perhaps I can terrify Fate into giving us years upon years," he said pleasantly. "Otherwise, we'll just have to make do. And you know, it grows a bit warm out here. Mayhap we should seek out a bit of shade in the monk's garden and—"

Ali would have agreed with him, but she didn't have the chance.

As if the very hedge had sprouted souls and propelled them into the field, the little area where they stood was suddenly filled with men brandishing swords.

"Back to back!" Colin shouted.

Ali turned, her sword in her hand, and pressed herself up against Colin. She felt Colin swinging, hacking, thrusting, but she could do nothing more than hold her sword in front of her, point outward, and pray she didn't have to use it.

"Aliénore, *fight!*"

"Aye, Aliénore, fight," called a voice from her right. "Fight like a man."

Ali looked to see Sir Etienne holding himself out of the fray. He stood with his arms folded across his chest, smiling in a most unpleasant manner. By the saints, what did the man want? Revenge?

It was then that she noticed something quite odd.

Men were standing nearby—as near as they apparently dared when facing her sword—but they made no move to fight her.

Well, except one who only missed decapitating her because Colin had bumped her elbow and her sword went up at the appropriate time and blocked his swing.

"Not her," one of the men shouted. "Just *him.*"

"Aye," said another, "we'd be just nabbing her. But don't kill him either, else he won't be able to give us his gold!"

Ali squeaked as she found herself quite suddenly grabbed by the neck of her tunic and dragged across the field. It all happened so quickly and she was so paralyzed with fear that she could only breathe again once movement had stopped. Colin, who had practically carried her over to the hedge and backed her into it, was standing in front of her, swinging with his usual joyful abandon.

"All right, whoresons," he said, with a chortle of delight, "who's next? Only eleven of you? A pity. I'd hoped for more."

Ali spared time for a brief prayer, then put up her sword and pulled her dagger from her boot. She wasn't sure if she should continue to stare at Colin's back, or turn herself around that she might counter an attack from behind the hedge. A quick look around Colin's large form revealed that Sir Etienne stood in his same place, looking smug. His men, and she saw only three in Solonge's colors, were apparently trying to decide if they should rush Colin as a group or come at him singly.

Ali could have advised them, but decided not to, for obvious reasons.

A group of three chose to come first. A thrust, a swipe, and a two-handed cleave sent those men speedily into the next life.

The remainder of the men huddled together and consulted.

"Should I run for aid?" Ali asked breathlessly.

Colin threw her a disgusted look over his shoulder, then bounced on the balls of his feet. "Only eight left," he said dismissively. "Plus the arrogant fool there. Light exercise, beloved. Not to worry."

Five mustered themselves together. Those, however, weren't the ones who sent chills down Ali's spine. Colin could take them on easily. It was the remaining three who started for the gate in the hedge that concerned her. Were they making for her? She contemplated her sword. Perhaps with two blades she would not be such an easy mark.

Colin was obviously not oblivious to the feeble plotting going on around him. He threw himself into the fray with nothing more than a "Draw your blade, Aliénore," tossed over his shoulder. She did, but found it exceedingly difficult to do anything but watch her husband.

And be very glad she'd never come at him with his death on her mind.

He had little trouble plying his trade on the five who faced him. They fell into heaps, some missing limbs, some simply giving forth unwholesome screams of terror before they expired. And through it all, Colin's blade flashed in the sunlight in a way that seemed to stop not only her, but the remaining three lads in their tracks.

That was their mistake. Colin bounded over and engaged them before they managed to get through the gate.

Ali looked about her to see how Sir Etienne was taking the decimation of his little army.

Only to find him gone.

She whirled around and saw him clambering over the very prickly hedge directly behind her. She backed up, her blade in front of her, her dagger clutched in her hand.

"Colin, help!" she squeaked.

There was more screaming behind her, then three more quick, cut-off shouts.

And then silence.

She couldn't have cared less. Sir Etienne was standing not five feet in front of her and he had already knocked her sword from her hands.

"Haven't learned your lessons yet, have you?" he sneered.

He reached out and grabbed for her.

She buried her dagger in his forearm.

She might have been pleased with herself, but when he, howling, pulled his arm back, her dagger went with it.

But before she could commence praying, or screaming for aid, she found herself pulled around a very large form she recognized quite readily.

"We meet again," Colin said pleasantly. "Any more of your lads to see to, or is it just you left?"

Sir Etienne snarled out a curse. "You'll find me work enough, I daresay."

Ali looked behind her and saw nothing but things the farmer would most certainly not be pleased about having to clean up. Eleven bodies were scattered across the field. There were no other signs of life save Jason of Artane, who leaned on the hedge, looking faintly interested. And beside him, Blackmour's three healers, wearing various looks ranging from alarm on Magda's face to amazement on Nemain's.

"Can't believe he managed to wed her," Nemain said, with an elbow thrown in Jason's side. "Did you brew him a convincing potion to use on her?"

"He did it, if you can believe it, all on his own," Jason said dryly.

"Well, I don't believe it," Nemain said. "You've been experimenting without my permission."

"I have not."

"Aye, you have, lad, and I'll have all the details or you'll regret it."

"Aliénore," Berengaria called, "perhaps you'd care to watch from here."

Ali did care to watch from there. Colin made a shooing motion with his hand and flashed her a brief, happy smile, so she had no qualms about leaving him to his business. She joined Jason and his companions safely out of the field.

"Oh," Magda said, tapping her spoon nervously against the hedge, "I do hope he doesn't trip over any of those bodies."

"He's accustomed to that," Jason said.

"Powerful fierce, that one," Nemain agreed. She fixed Aliénore with a steely glance. "How is he at his, you know, husbandly duties? Adequate?"

Aliénore spluttered, but found nothing to say.

"I could brew him a potion, you know," Nemain offered.

"Nemain, cease," Berengaria chided. "Aliénore looks happy, Colin looks his normal self, and I daresay all is well with their marriage. You're distracting me from the swordplay."

Ali couldn't tear her gaze away from her husband. Jason had it aright. The corpses cooling behind him didn't seem to bother him. Nor did the pair of blades Sir Etienne threw at him. Colin batted them away with his sword as if they'd been annoying flies. But as interesting as that was, it wasn't nearly as riveting as what Sir Etienne was spewing as he fought.

"I'll have your gold," he boasted. "I deserve it. I deserve to be lord of a fine castle."

"Do you indeed?" Colin asked pleasantly.

"More so than you."

"And how is it you intend to buy your castle?" Colin asked. "Or do you intend to murder someone and set yourself up in his place?"

"It's been done before."

"Aye, quite successfully," Colin agreed. "And with whom by your side? The lovely and always fatal Marie?"

Sir Etienne shook his head. "She's dead."

"Is she?" Colin asked in surprise. "How's that?"

"Found her a few days ago being attacked by ruffians."

"Didn't you offer her aid?"

"She fell into the fire. I put out the flames before I left."

"Kind of you."

"She betrayed me. I didn't like that."

"No one ever does."

Ali felt a wave of relief sweep through her. If Marie was dead, then Sir Etienne was the last one who wanted her dead. Or in his thrall, as it were. Unless, of course, Colin had enemies.

But Ali couldn't imagine that.

After all, they were likely all dead as well.

"It grows hot," Jason called. "Finish him quickly, won't you?"

"I have a few things to repay him for," Colin said pleasantly. "You needn't stay to watch if you're too feeble to do so."

Jason looked at Ali. "I have a wound."

"So you've said."

He scowled at her, then turned back to the fray and shook his head. "I wouldn't want to be Sir Etienne."

"I don't think he wants to be himself," she mused.

"How so?" he asked.

"I think he'd much rather be Colin," she said, looking at him with a faint smile. "I daresay he's a little jealous."

"And who wouldn't be with you as his wife?"

"If you can't stop slobbering over my wife, Jason," Colin bellowed, "go back to the hall!"

"No hound ever created has ears like he does," Jason muttered. "The things I've regretting muttering over the years . . ."

Ali smiled, then felt her smile fade. Aye, Sir Etienne deserved his fate, but apparently Colin was deeply in earnest about exacting revenge for Sir Etienne's treatment of her.

What a lengthy and thorough revenge it was.

The sun slipped down, yet still they fought. Sir Etienne bled from dozens of wounds, but still he wouldn't concede. Concede to what, was perhaps the question to be asked. It wasn't as if Colin would let him live; of that Ali was certain.

"You will," Colin said finally, his chest heaving, "never be the swordsman I am."

Sir Etienne spat at him.

"Because there is no mercy in your soul," Colin finished.

"And there is in yours?" Sir Etienne panted.

"Aye. I know when to finish my opponents."

And, apparently, he did. Ali watched as Sir Etienne fell to the ground, twitched, and then was still. Colin stood over him for several minutes, then leaned down and closed his eyes. Then he straightened and walked across the field. He was as covered in blood as were the rest of the men lying there, but Ali suspected very little of it was his.

"A poultice or two?" Berengaria asked mildly. "For the scratches, of course."

"A bath," Nemain advised.

"A proper soothing draught," Magda promised. "I'll see to it myself."

Colin walked through the gate, stopped before Ali, and looked down at her gravely.

"I daresay, my lady, that you can now rest easy."

"Thank you, my lord."

"We could, however, still hone your skills with a sword."

"Aye," she agreed. "I did not show well today."

"There were many of them and few of us. You're allowed a bit of fear your first time in battle. You're still standing. That is enough."

Jason snorted so hard, he coughed. "What is this?" he demanded. "I've never had such kind words from the man."

Colin spared him a brief glance. "I'm not wed to you—the saints be praised. Besides, Aliénore hasn't had your training. I expect less from her."

"And you also want a place to sleep tonight that isn't with the monks," Jason groused.

"That too." Colin nodded toward the monastery. "My lady, if you will? Perhaps there is actually something on the cooking fire that we might ingest. I daresay we deserve it."

Ali took his hand despite his hesitation, and walked with him back to the guest hall. She spared a final glance over her shoulder and found herself quite glad she would never have to trample over that bloody field again.

But equal with that feeling was the gratitude that the terror was over. Marie was dead and so was Sir Etienne. She could sleep in peace, walk outside the gates with no fear, look forward to many happy years with her husband without worrying that her two foes might appear and end her life.

She squeezed Colin's hand. "Thank you."

He looked down at her and smiled briefly. "For you, lady, gladly."

"It has been a very long road to this place, hasn't it?" she asked, feeling rather wistful all of a sudden.

"Aye," he said, squeezing her hand, "but the end has certainly been worth the journey. Wouldn't you say?"

Aye, she certainly would.

And now such a happy and peaceful road before them.

She wondered what she possibly could have done to have deserved it, but she wasn't going to argue with Fate. She would take that peaceful road with her husband and walk it gratefully.

Chapter 42

C olin found himself, once again, on his horse. It wasn't that he didn't enjoy riding, or traveling a bit, for that matter. It was that instead of riding alone with his bride, looking forward to a goodly bit of peace and quiet in his own hall, he seemed to have acquired a following of immense proportions that couldn't seem to detach themselves from his pleasant company. And if that weren't enough, he was expecting guests from Blackmour when he reached Berkham!

It was enough to prompt him to ask Aliénore if she minded a fortnight or two in a tent far away from either her family or his.

Now, seeing Christopher, Gillian, and their lads was actually something to anticipate with a bit of relish. They were fine company and Colin looked forward to telling Christopher of the ease with which he'd wooed and won his bride. The lads were a joy as well and he'd missed their antics and youthful amusements. Gillian, he supposed, would have much still to say about his manners, but he supposed he could steel himself for her onslaught. She would be good company for Aliénore, and he found himself incapable of begrudging his wife whatever it was she might want at the moment.

Aliénore's father he could tolerate as well. The man had turned out to be a fine talker. And his healthy respect for Colin's reputation led him to say nothing amiss nor give any trouble.

A pity his own sire couldn't have had the same said for him.

Colin gritted his teeth as another complaint came his way with the speed and accuracy of a bolt shot from close range.

"Nay," Colin said, turning and glaring at his sire, "you

may *not* have the lord's chamber. You may gather your belongings, bid fond farewell to your favorite serving wenches, and contemplate your remaining years spent in prayer for your black soul!"

"You cannot remove me from my own keep!"

"Shall we settle this in the lists?" Colin asked pointedly.

"You," Reginald said, pointing a trembling finger at him, "are a reprehensible son!"

"You're right," Colin snapped.

"A good son would see to his father."

"As you've already said, I'm not a good son. So go live with Ermengarde. I'll see her dowered lavishly and settled in Harrowden keep."

Ermengarde made exclamations of pleasure. Reginald continued to grumble, but it was in a much lower tone.

"That way the miserable whoreson can be put in the monastery close by if he gives them any trouble," Colin muttered under his breath.

"I heard that!"

Aliénore laughed softly. Colin looked at her and noted the expression of affection on her face. Such a thing was so strange to see on any woman's face, he found that he often looked at her just to see if she wore it.

Which she did.

And quite often, truth be told.

He found that he simply could not look away from her. She was lovely, she was well-witted, and she was his.

Did miracles never cease?

She reached up and tucked her hair behind her ears. "I'll let my hair grow," she said, sounding very self-conscious. "It must trouble you as it is."

"Actually," he said, "I was just looking at you and finding myself amazed yet again that you are mine. I vow, my lady, that you've a beauty that all would wish for their own. Grow your hair if you like, or not. It doesn't matter to me."

"Doesn't it?"

"It'll get in your way training if it's too long," he said.

"I once suspected you might say something like that. You, my lord, have a most interesting way of viewing life."

He frowned, not sure if that was a compliment or not. But his lady was smiling at him as if she approved, and that was enough for him.

Now, if he could just rid himself of his various family, sundry, and guests, and apply himself fully to the task of indulging in marital bliss, he would be content.

"Oh, Colin, this is beautiful!"

He looked about him and saw his land with fresh eyes. Perhaps he'd made a mistake not coming back more often. Aliénore had it aright; it was beautiful. The hills were lush and full of goodly grasses for animals. Fields were busily producing crops that would feed him and his people for the winter. The sun shone down pleasantly and a gentle breeze cooled his brow.

Then again, he likely wouldn't have found it so pleasing without Aliénore at his side.

"Smell," she said, breathing deeply.

He did, and found himself sparing a faint wish for the tang of the sea. Though he supposed dung was a pleasing enough smell, under the right circumstances.

"You won't miss the sea, will you?" he asked.

"You know I won't." She shrugged lightly. "Though now I think I would be happy wherever I was."

"Would you? Why?"

"Because I've found a home," she said, looking at him with a gentle smile. "With you."

Colin found himself quite suddenly rubbing at his eyes. "Dirt," he said gruffly. "Damned bit of fluff flew right into my eyes. I'm fortunate I wasn't rendered sightless by the enormous quantity."

She laughed.

He couldn't even muster up enough irritation to promise her that he would see her repaid for her mirth.

"Sea, countryside," she said happily. "I don't care."

"Less dirt by the sea," he said, dragging his sleeve across his traitorous eyes a last time.

"But much sand," she said. She looked at him innocently. "Do you think you'd have the same problem there? It getting so forcefully and thoroughly in your eyes, as it were."

He pursed his lips. "Did you but know me better, you would hesitate to tease me."

"I *do* know you better," she pointed out, "and I can't resist teasing you. Would you deny me such a small pleasure?"

He opened his mouth to say that he most certainly would, then realized she was yet using him for her own sport. He scowled at her.

"You, lady, are foul."

She only smiled pleasantly and looked quite unafraid.

And that was something, he supposed.

Indeed, he supposed that her look was more than just the one a woman would wear when she was unafraid. Her look hinted at affection. Perhaps even, did he dare say it, goodly affection?

He wondered, absently, if he looked as besotted as Christopher was wont to look on occasion.

Best confine that kind of look to the bedchamber, he decided quickly. The saints only knew what would happen to his reputation otherwise.

He concentrated on the road ahead, studying the surrounding terrain as they went, looking for things that perhaps might need to be changed or improved. His father had taken marginally good care of the holding, Colin had to give him that. But there were things that could be done to make it safer, more comfortable, more pleasing to the eye.

Things he would do gladly for the sake of his lady.

They rode into the courtyard at length and Colin dismounted with relief. He helped Aliénore down, then took her by the hand and looked about him to make certain the rest of the company could see to themselves. He turned back to the hall to find his father's steward creeping down the steps. Colin had little love for the man, for he was as stingy as Reginald himself. A goodly quality in a steward, he supposed, but surely he could find another just as frugal with an aspect to him that didn't make Colin grind his teeth each time he showed that face.

"My lord—" the steward began, then looked at Aliénore. His eyes traveled down to where her hand was clasped with Colin's, and then that same gaze made its way back up to meet Colin's. The man looked near to fainting.

"My wife," Colin said shortly. "The lady Aliénore."

"Wife," the man repeated weakly. "Oh, the saints be praised 'tis a woman!"

Colin snorted. "Saints, man, have you not eyes in your head? How could anyone mistake this beautiful creature for a boy?"

"How indeed?" murmured someone behind him.

Colin knew without a doubt who it was.

"Heal yourself, de Piaget," he threw over his shoulder. "We will meet in the lists very soon. I've several things to repay you for!"

There wasn't even an audible gulp for his trouble. Colin looked down at Aliénore. "I've gone soft," he said. "He wouldn't have dared show so little response to that threat two years ago."

"Should I myself appear more terrified?" she asked, the corner of her mouth beginning to twitch in a way that looked alarmingly like something Jason would allow.

Colin favored her with a scowl. "You, lady, have learned terrible habits from that boy."

She put her arms around him. "But you tease so well, my lord. I find myself powerless to resist the temptation."

He grunted. "I would tell you to try harder, but each time you use me so ill, you seem to feel the need to soothe me, so perhaps 'tis a fair trade. And do not," he threw over his shoulder, "use that as excuse, Jason. I do not need soothing from you!"

A muffled chuckle was his answer.

Colin brushed past his father's steward, pulled Aliénore along, and entered the great hall. He paused and looked about him, trying to dredge up some pleasant memory of the place. He vaguely remembered time spent there with his mother, sitting near the fire, listening to her occasional laughter.

None of which had been directed to or shared with his father, if he remembered things aright.

"This would be a good place to start memories of our own," Aliénore said quietly, giving his hand a squeeze. "Don't you think?"

"I think," he said, looking down at her with warm feelings in his heart, "that you are a truly remarkable woman. I vow you're as sensible as any man I know."

"Such flattery," she said with a smile. "You leave me breathless."

He frowned at her. He would have rather heard that his loving left her breathless, but perhaps he hadn't polished his skills enough in that area yet. There was time enough, he supposed, for that.

He made himself at home at the high table, then passed the rest of the day watching the events of the keep unfold before him. Servants came in and out, food appeared—though after tasting it he wished it hadn't—and his family and Aliénore's made themselves comfortable. Even the witches seemed to find themselves completely at home. And when Nemain tasted supper, then made her way to the kitchens with a purposeful glint in her eye, Colin didn't bother to stop her.

He leaned back in his chair, took a deep breath, and sighed. In pleasure or relief, he couldn't tell. All he knew was that he was happy, and surprisingly so. Not that he hadn't felt waves of happiness wash over him occasionally. But this bone-deep contentment? Nay, he'd never felt that before.

He looked at Aliénore. "Thank you."

"My lord?"

"I think I am . . . happy."

She closed her hand over his. "I'm glad."

He nodded, then nodded again to himself. Aye, he was happy and glad of it. Who would have thought that a simple betrothal—for which he supposed he must needs thank his father—could have resulted in such, well, happiness.

"Father," he called.

Reginald only favored him with a glare.

"I'll see you don't lack for comforts," he offered.

Reginald's scowls ceased abruptly. "And you'll also—"

"See to nothing else. Be grateful for what you have."

Reginald subsided into soft snarls. Colin supposed it could have been worse than that. Well, his father was seen to, thankfully, so he could spare no further guilt in that direction. Nemain would no doubt see to the kitchens, leaving him to see to other things.

Was it possible his father's bed was free of fleas?

He beckoned to a servant, whispered something in the woman's ear, then smiled pleasantly at Aliénore.

"Ridding the bed of vermin."

"A fine idea."

Now, if he could just rid himself of his guests in like manner, he might be more pleased. Then again, there was no reason he had to remain below. Aliénore was beginning to look weary and there was no sense in not seeing what sort of things awaited them upstairs.

But he would let the servants see to the fleas first.

And whilst he waited, he would sit next to his lady wife and be grateful for her hand in his and her sweet smiles turned his way. Who would have thought his sire's nefarious machinations would have resulted in such a happy state of affairs? A keep of his own, a wife of his own, and the freedom to enjoy caring for both. Aye, his had become quite a good life and he supposed he might be indebted to his sire for a bit of that.

Not that the man would have planned such a thing, of course, but Colin wasn't going to quibble with the results.

And to think he had been so adamantly opposed to the blissful state of matrimony for so long. Ah, well, perhaps that had been for the best. If he'd found himself wed with the first wench his sire had tried to foist off upon him—the one who had pleaded the excuse of maggots infesting various and sundry parts of her person as reason enough not to make an appearance before a priest with him—he might have been quite unhappily wed. Or what of that empty-headed girl who'd thrown herself at her sire's feet—in front of Colin, as it happened—and pleaded a sudden onset of insanity?

He examined the score of women who'd avoided wedding with him and found not a one of them to be anywhere near Aliénore's equal. Besides, they had just used words to beg off. Aliénore had taken her fate in her hands and actually done something to avoid him.

He looked at her purposefully. "You are an admirable wench."

"Am I indeed?" she asked.

"I'd like to show you my appreciation."

"Would you?"

He rose and pulled her up with him. "Surely the fleas are gone by now."

"If not, you could frighten them off with your sword."

Why hadn't he thought of that sooner? He kept her hand in his, nodded to his guests, then promptly forgot them in anticipation of an afternoon spent showing his wife just how admirable he thought she was.

Chapter 43

A li stood in the fall sunshine and lifted her face skyward. The rains hadn't yet begun and all had been laboring diligently to bring in the harvest before they came. She had found working in the fields to be a pleasure that she couldn't deny herself.

Odd, the things a woman had time for when she wasn't passing all her time in the lists.

She stretched, her hands at her back, and closed her eyes to enjoy the fine weather. It was hard to believe she'd been at Berkham almost three months. If she'd known how happy she would be at Colin's home, she would have—well, there was no sense in trying to make sense of her decision. She'd been terrified, made the best decision she could at the time, and all had worked out for the best.

Only now she was reaping the rewards of finally having come to her senses.

She leaned down, picked up her basket, and started back toward the keep. She looked at it with fondness. Not only was it her home, it housed the one she loved.

Aye, she loved him.

And she would also love the child he'd given her.

She hadn't told him yet, but she planned to soon. He'd looked at her belly strangely a time or two, but she'd merely remarked that the fare at table had been exceptionally good and that had seemed to satisfy him. That she'd shunned the lists and been puking every morning had been something he'd obviously lumped in with his list of the womanly weaknesses she occasionally indulged in.

She smiled. How could a body not love the man?

She noticed a stooped, covered woman walking up the road, and she slowed her pace to match the woman's.

"Might I carry that for you?" she offered, gesturing to the basket.

"If you like," came the hoarse voice.

Ali took the basket and saw the scarred hand that had held it. Pity welled up in her heart for one who was less fortunate than she.

"Would you come into the keep?" Ali asked. "I'll see to a meal for you."

"Much appreciated, my lady."

Ali walked slowly alongside the woman, then turned her mind to other things. Colin would no doubt be done with his exercise in the lists and be ready for something to eat. His garrison would be ready for food and something to ease the pain.

Some things never changed.

And now that Jason had gone to Artane to visit his family, Colin's choices for a sparring partner were very limited indeed. He was continually seeking to lure fierce knights into his garrison to supplement the lads who owed him service anyway. The latter were always the ones who fulfilled their forty days and departed back to their homes with alacrity. Colin had found a few who were willing to stay as a permanent garrison, but even those he had to rotate in and out of the lists. Fighting with the man was nothing short of exhausting.

As for his other pursuit, he was not shunning those labors either. Aliénore could readily attest to that. Though she had never thought him unskilled to start with—not having anything to compare him to—she certainly had to admit that he had honed his skill with much practice and a great amount of enthusiasm.

She supposed her growing belly was proof enough of that.

As for herself, she filled her days with having her hands in the dirt, making herself known to his people, and reaccustoming herself to walking about in skirts. She had come to appreciate the odd hour in the lists merely because she could don hose and stride about comfortably.

There was, perhaps, something to be said for being a man. But being a man would have meant she had little time for offering charitable service, as she did now. She guided the woman, whom she assumed was one of Colin's villeins, up to the great hall and to one of the tables. She saw to food and would have left, but the woman seemed to hesitate. Ali felt compassion stir within her and sat next to the peasant. Perhaps she only wanted for some company.

"Have you lived here long?" Ali asked.

The woman merely bowed her head and set to her meal.

Well, perhaps talking was unnecessary when there was a belly to fill. So Ali waited patiently whilst the woman ate, then listened as that very soft voice asked for a garderobe.

"Of course," Ali said. "Follow me."

She led the woman up the stairs and down the passageway, a passageway that was certainly cleaner than when Ali had arrived. If the servants had doubted her seriousness initially, they seemed to believe she was in earnest quite readily after they'd seen her coming back from the lists with Colin, a sword at her side.

Ali wondered often what sort of reaction she might have at the English court did she but attempt the same thing.

"Here we are," Ali said, motioning to a doorway. "Now, I should likely descend—"

The next thing she knew, her hair, which had grown a bit in three months, was caught up in a grip far too strong for an old woman to have possessed. Ali might have thought it was a terrible mistake, but she felt the prick of steel in her back and heard words she never thought she would.

"Greetings, stepdaughter. What a lovely keep you have here."

Ali closed her eyes and considered screaming. Praying seemed a better choice and she hastily offered a very heartfelt one. Not for herself.

For her child.

"I thought you were dead," Ali whispered.

"Tales of my demise were, as you can see, exaggerated."

"What do you want?" Ali asked. "I daresay you'll have it, whatever it is."

"What do I want?" Marie laughed, and the sound was very unpleasant. "What I want is what you cannot give me. I want my beautiful visage returned to me. I want to walk without a limp. I want never to look at my scarred hands again. But instead, I'll take your death."

Ali flinched and the steel pricked harder.

"Not here, though," Marie said thoughtfully. "I want your husband to watch. Up on the roof, over the lists. We'll wait until he notices us. 'Tis the least I can do for him."

"He'll kill you for it."

"That would be a relief."

"Then why don't you just kill yourself?" Ali rasped. "And leave me alive to grieve your loss?"

Marie made a sound of contempt. "I know your feelings for me, Aliénore, and I think mourning me would be the last thing you would do. Besides, my death has no meaning if I don't cause yours first. Now, move, before you force me to slay you here."

Ali moved, only because the knife dug deeper. That, and she was completely unable to reach for the knife in her boot. Marie's knife had gone in only far enough to break the skin, but it would easily slide between her ribs and kill her before she could wrench away and grasp her weapon. And even if the knife slid in and left her insides mostly intact, she would likely bleed so abundantly that the babe would be harmed.

Nay, better that she do as Marie bid her. Besides, once she was up on the roof, she could easily call for help and someone would come.

Hopefully before Colin saw what was happening.

The journey there was short and silent. Well, silent except for the rasp of Marie's breathing. It was the not the sound of a healthy form and Ali wondered if perhaps she had breathed in fire and ash. 'Twas nothing short of a miracle that she hadn't died.

Ali couldn't help but wish she had.

They reached the roof far too soon for Ali's taste. She blinked against the late-afternoon sun and looked about her for guardsmen. It was difficult to see, for Marie held her head at an odd angle, leaving Ali unable to see where her feet were going. Trusting Marie that far was unsettling enough.

"Stay where you are or she dies," Marie commanded. "Go back into the guard tower and stay there."

Ali could only assume Marie was commanding Colin's guards. There was no sound of protest and Ali supposed she shouldn't have expected one. After all, it wasn't often that a man watched his lord's wife being forced to the roof with a knife in her back.

"And now," Marie announced, "we'll wait. I don't see him below, but my eyes aren't perhaps what they were before."

"He's gone visiting—"

"Liar," Marie spat. "I saw him this morning myself, giving you that disgusting kiss. Or was it disgusting? Is it a pleasure to have a man such as he is as your lover?"

" 'Tis pleasant enough," Ali managed.

That was a mistake. She cried out in spite of herself as Marie wrenched her head back farther. Ali was fairly sure she would soon fall from the walkway from having lost her balance alone. Marie surely wasn't strong enough to hold her upright, nor would she likely grieve overmuch if she failed at that task.

But Marie said no more. She merely held Ali's head back and kept the knife pressed into her ribs.

It seemed an eternity that they stood there, frozen in a deadly dance step. Ali came to the point where she thought that she might fling herself off the battlements merely to ease the pain in her body that standing thusly was giving her. She was just certain she couldn't bear any more.

"You don't want her."

Ali bit her lip to keep from making any noise. That was Colin.

On the battlements.

A more terrifying place for him there surely couldn't have been, yet there he was, come to rescue her. She wondered if he knew just how close Marie was to ending her life.

"Release her and you can have me," he said, his voice sounding very strained.

Marie laughed. "As if you would allow it!"

"Heights, they . . . um . . . distress me," he said. "You have the advantage here."

"Do I indeed," Marie said, sounding pleased. "Now, this is something I never expected."

The next thing Ali knew, she was falling to her knees and there was a blinding agony in her face. She realized, as blood dripped from her nose, that Marie had slammed her face into the rock and let her fall. Ali could scarce see for the waves of pain that washed over her. She dragged her sleeve across her eyes to clear them of her tears, then watched as Marie advanced toward Colin.

His hands, both of them, were clutching the rock before him.

Damn the man, he truly intended to allow Marie to have him in Ali's place.

She staggered to her feet, drew the dagger from her boot, and flung herself at her stepmother. It was a precarious place to be, the battlements, with the wall on her left only waist-high and a goodly drop on her right down to the roof of the great hall. Either way, a fall would be fatal.

So she drove her knife into Marie's back, then shoved her as hard as she could over the wall and down into the bailey.

Marie fell with a scream.

Ali threw herself at her husband, realizing too late that it was a very, very foolish thing to do.

He teetered.

Then he fell.

Back onto the walkway, fortunately, but it was a very un-dignified sprawl and one that came close to sending him off the roof to the right, down to grace the top of the great hall.

"By the saints," he wheezed, "do you intend to kill me as well?"

She fell to her knees and grasped him by the feet. "I didn't mean to, of course, you great oaf. Here, give me your hand and let me help you."

He shook his head vigorously. "I'll crawl, thank you just the same. Can you follow, or do you need aid?"

"Not aid from you, obviously. Go on. I'll be behind you."

And so he crawled. Ali was feeling none too steady on her own feet, so she inched along behind him as well, making herself something of a vow to never again loiter at such a height with the man she loved. Which meant that she likely shouldn't venture there overmuch herself, lest he felt the need to follow and perform another rescue.

Though given the fact that her stepmother was likely quite dead on the ground, perhaps there would never be another need for a rescue.

Colin pulled her to her feet when she reached the guard tower, then hauled her into his arms.

"She broke your nose, damn her," he said with a curse. "Did she stick you as well?"

"Not deeply," Ali said. "I'm not worried for myself. The babe, however—"

Then she realized what she'd blurted out. She looked quickly up at him to see that he had paled several shades beyond the normal paling he did when faced with such heights.

He teetered.

He swayed.

And then he fainted.

But it was gracefully done, she had to admit, as she made no attempt to stop him from swooning right onto the landing. He lay there, a large, formidable man who had been felled by the thought of the smallest, most helpless thing imaginable.

She smiled and sat down next to him to wait for him to awake.

His dagger was handy, so she cut up part of her gown and wrapped it around her middle to tighten up Marie's knife's work, then she cut up a bit more and held it gingerly to her nose. She supposed he would have to wiggle it about again, just as he had before, and that was something definitely she was not looking forward to. She supposed now her face would lose most of its beauty. Her nose would likely bear the same little crook that Colin's did. But his was attractive enough, she supposed, for a man who truly had no handsomeness.

But he had such a fine character.

And, she had to admit, that there were times she found him quite easy to look at.

Such as now, when he was lying there, stunned by tidings

she should have given him next to something softer than a stone floor.

She waited several minutes until he roused, sat up with a start, and looked at her with wide eyes.

"What happened?" he asked, looking around him frantically. "Where are the lads who attacked me? An army it must have been, surely."

"You fainted."

"I did not," he said stiffly. "I was assailed from behind."

"You were assailed by tidings of your child."

He swayed again, but she caught him by the arm.

"A babe," he said faintly.

"Aye."

He looked at her, then gently put his arms around her and bowed his head to rest it on her shoulder.

"I don't know what terrifies me more," he whispered. "That she almost killed you, or that I did nothing to save you."

"You distracted her," she said, patting his back. "Colin, you bested your greatest fear to come fight her, without weapons in your hands. Surely there is no shame in that."

He shuddered, once, then lifted his head. "Your face must pain you."

"What pains me is my vanity," she said, wincing at the clamor a smile set up on her visage.

"And I did not faint," he continued.

"You did."

"I most certainly did not."

"Colin, no one attacked you from behind."

"Worry over you then," he conceded. "My great love for you was such that I was overcome by emotion—nay, that sounds as daft as fainting." He considered for a moment, then looked at her. " 'Twas the unwholesome air up here. Being so close to the clouds cannot be good for a body. Mine is the sort of form that functions best on the ground." He frowned. "Nay, that makes me sound weak as well—"

She put her hand gently over his mouth. "I won't tell anyone that the announcement that you are to become a father was what bested you."

He kissed her palm, then moved her hand away. Then he hesitated. "You won't?"

"No one would believe it anyway."

"True," he agreed. "No sense in having anyone believe *you've* lost your wits."

"Thank you for preserving my dignity," she said dryly.

" 'Tis the very least I can do," he said, dragging himself to his feet and gently pulling her to hers. "Now, come away with me, lady, and let us see to your wounds. We should have kept those potion brewers here instead of letting them return to Blackmour. They might have served us."

"Don't you know any of their recipes?"

"Me?" he demanded, affronted. "I learned no black arts at their hands. But they did give me a batch of herbs for staunching manly wounds. I suppose that would suffice for yours as well."

"A pity Marie couldn't have waited another pair of months to come do her foul work. Your healers would have been here then. Berengaria said they would return after the harvest."

Colin stared at her in astonishment. "Why? Why would they come to torment me in my own home?"

"They're coming in their guise as midwives," she said pleasantly. "Berengaria told me when I would need her."

He started to say something, then shut his mouth with a snap and turned to descend the stairs, pulling her after him.

"I imagine they're quite skilled," she offered.

"Perhaps Nemain will stay behind," he grumbled. "I could only hope her romance with Blackmour's cook will be such that a visit here would be unthinkable."

Ali smiled as she followed him down the steps and on to their bedchamber.

She stopped smiling when he set her nose. It was every bit as painful as it had been the time before.

After she'd stopped howling, Colin turned his tender attentions to her side. She winced at the look on his face as he examined her side. The gravity there was sobering.

"Bad?" she asked.

He shook his head, then looked at her. "Could have been,

though. It isn't deep, and needs no stitching, but we'll have to watch it closely lest infection sets in. And with the . . . um . . ."

"Babe," she supplied. "Your babe."

He swallowed with difficulty. "Aye, that. I'll watch you closely for a few days." He wrapped a cloth about her side, then picked her up and carried her to the bed. "You should rest."

"Are you leaving?"

"Only to bellow for someone to go and make sure she's dead. I won't leave the chamber."

She shivered. " 'Tis foolish to fear, but—"

"Fear keeps you alive," he said simply. "A courageous man isn't one who feels no fear. A courageous man is one who acts in spite of it. As you did above."

"She was going to kill you."

He smiled briefly. "Now you know what motivates me," he said. "I pity anyone who thinks to harm you. Or the . . . um—"

"Babe, Colin. 'Tis but a babe."

He looked at her with something that greatly resembled awe. "But," he said in hushed tones, " 'tis *my* babe. Something I never thought to be blessed with."

"Congratulations, then," she said, reaching out to touch his cheek. "You'll make a fine father."

"Should I survive the birth, aye," he said weakly. "By the saints, the birth—"

"Don't think about it," she commanded, clapping her hand over his mouth. "I can't catch you now."

He reached up and gingerly touched the back of his head. "I daresay you didn't catch me on the roof, either."

"You're a large man. I did all I could."

"Which was no doubt to let me fall unimpeded." He pursed his lips at her, then rose. "Don't move. I will return to your side within moments."

Ali watched him walk unsteadily from the bedchamber, then smiled. She had to blink quite often, mostly because her eyes continued to fill with tears that had more to do with pain than anything else.

Or perhaps that wasn't as true as she would have liked. She was alive, the saints be praised. The fear of having come so close to losing her life would likely haunt her for some time to come.

But hard on those tears came ones that had nothing to do with pain. Who would have thought that she would find herself so happily wed—and to the very man she'd been certain would be the ruin of her life? But instead, there she was, wed to a man who, as Gillian had once said, had a very tender heart under all his grumbles, a tender heart that he showed her often enough to convince her it was there. And if that wasn't enough in itself, she would bear him a child come spring.

Now, if he could just survive that long without tarnishing his reputation further by these unmanly displays of emotion and weakness . . .

She smiled and closed her eyes.

Epilogue

Hearty brew shimmered and danced in the firelight as it tumbled into a waiting cup. It was swirled about, admired, sniffed by a nose well accustomed to that sort of work. Experienced hands grasped the cup and the contents were downed without hesitation.

Downed in desperation.

Downed as if the contents were all that saved the imbiber from certain destruction.

" 'Tis but a babe, my lord," Nemain said with a grumble. "No need to drink yourself into a stupor over it."

Berengaria watched as Colin ignored Nemain's advice, reached for another full cup and gulped it down in much the same manner as he had the first three.

"Those were for the mother-to-be," Nemain said sternly. "To give her strength."

"I am trying," Colin responded tightly, "to remain upright myself!"

Magda reached forward and tapped Nemain softly on the shoulder. "He looks as if he's about to faint again, Nemain. Don't be stingy."

Nemain eyed Colin narrowly, then handed him the final cup. "We'll need more, Berengaria. And why aren't you in that next chamber, seeing to the birthing of this babe?"

"Our dear Aliénore sent me to inquire about the state of her beloved husband," Berengaria said with a smile. "So, my lord, how do you? What message shall I carry to your lady, or would you prefer to carry a message yourself?"

Colin blanched, threw back another cup of brew, and rose. He was unsteady on his feet, but the man wasn't a soldier of vast renown for nothing. He put his shoulders back and fixed a grim expression to his face.

"I'm ready to go myself."

"This isn't a hopeless war, my lord," Berengaria said gently. "She is fine."

"She's been screaming."

"Screaming? Nay, my lord. Voicing a bit of discomfort, perhaps."

"My name has figured quite prominently in her cursings, lady," Colin said, looking at her skeptically. "Are you certain she wants me in truth, or is it for some foul purpose that you take me to her?"

"Berengaria!" came the shout from Aliénore's chamber.

Berengaria took Colin by the arm and bodily dragged him into the next chamber. She left him hovering by the door and arrived at the birthing stool in time to deliver his firstborn. She cleaned the baby, cut its life's tether to Aliénore, then handed the baby to her. She helped Aliénore to bed, then looked at Colin.

"Will you come see?"

He swayed, swayed a bit more, and then fell to the floor with a mighty crash.

"He'll rouse soon enough," Aliénore assured her. "Come sit by me and look. Isn't she beautiful?"

"She?" came the weak voice from the floor. "She?"

Berengaria looked to her left to see that Colin, though he was fallen, was recovering with goodly speed. He sat up and peered over the edge of the bed. He looked no less terrified than he had before, but his color was better.

"She?" he squeaked.

"Listen to your papa closely, my love," Aliénore said, stroking the babe's cheek, "for you'll not hear that sound often. Manly knights never squeak, except when they're overcome by great emotion."

"Bloody hell," Colin managed hoarsely. "A gel. A gel and I've no idea what to do with her."

Aliénore looked at Berengaria and gave her a smile full of amusement. "I daresay he'll learn, don't you think?"

Berengaria rose. "I daresay he will, love. Now, I'll leave you to introduce your daughter to her father, then I'll return and see to arranging you properly."

She walked to the door, then paused and looked back. Colin had gotten to his knees and was currently leaning over the bed.

"A girl," he said reverently.

"Are you disappointed?"

"Disappointed?" he echoed. "I should think not! There's no reason she can't hold a sword."

"Colin!" Aliénore gasped.

"But finding a mate for her, now *that* is what I will be losing sleep over. Nay, 'tis best that we just keep her by us. No man I know now could possibly be worthy of her. And since there's only one of me, I suppose she'll just have to remain unwed, forever tending my wine and sharpening her skills with me in the lists."

"Ah, Colin," Aliénore laughed, "I should expect nothing less from you."

He looked at her, wearing an expression of complete bewilderment. "What did I say?" he asked. "I'm only trying to keep her safe. Now, to think of a name. Something with a warriorly tone to it, don't you think?"

"I was actually thinking of Rose—"

"A fine effort, but not exactly what I'm looking for. What think you of—"

Berengaria closed the door with a smile, paused to listen to the raised voices inside, then shook her head and sought out the chamber for honored guests she shared with her companions. She paused before the door, saw the black smoke seeping out, and changed her mind. Perhaps she would retire to the solar for a moment or two before returning to care for Aliénore. With Magda obviously at the cooking fire, it was likely safer that way.

She sought out a comfortable chair in the solar and sat down with a contented sigh. She leaned back and let her thoughts briefly wander. They did, directly to the vision she'd once had of Colin's bride. It was proof enough that one could never judge too quickly by the outer aspect, for despite his gruff exterior, Colin of Berkhamshire had a gentle and quite tender heart. And Aliénore, though gently visaged, had the heart of a true warrior, brave and fearless. Perfectly matched, they were, and perfectly happy. And now a new little life to guide and protect.

What a fortunate little lass she was.

And how fortunate her parents were to have her and each other.

A new family, bound by love, with years of happiness to look forward to.

Berengaria smiled, content.

ROMANTIC ROOTS

MACLEOD

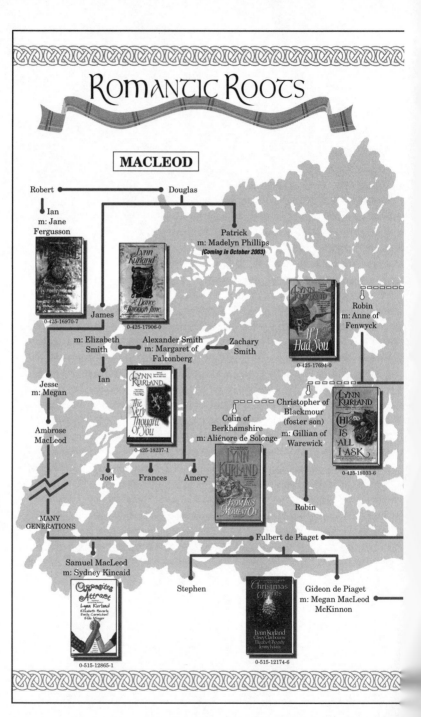

Robert ● — ● Douglas

Ian
m: Jane
Fergusson

Patrick
m: Madelyn Phillips
(Coming in October 2003)

James

0-425-16970-7

0-425-17906-0

Robin
m: Anne of
Fenwyck

m: Elizabeth
Smith

Alexander Smith
m: Margaret of
Falconberg

Zachary
Smith

If I
Had You

0-425-17694-0

Ian

Jesse
m: Megan

The Very
Thought
Of You

0-425-18237-1

Colin of
Berkhamshire
m: Aliénore de Solonge

Christopher of
Blackmour
(foster son)
m: Gillian of
Warewick

This
Is
All
I Ask

0-425-18033-6

Ambrose
MacLeod

Joel   Frances   Amery

From This
Moment On

Robin

MANY
GENERATIONS

Fulbert de Piaget ●

Samuel MacLeod
m: Sydney Kincaid

Stephen

Gideon de Piaget
m: Megan MacLeod
McKinnon

Opposites
Attract

0-515-12865-1

Christmas
Spirits

0-515-12174-6

family lineage in the books of
LYNN KURLAND

DE PIAGET

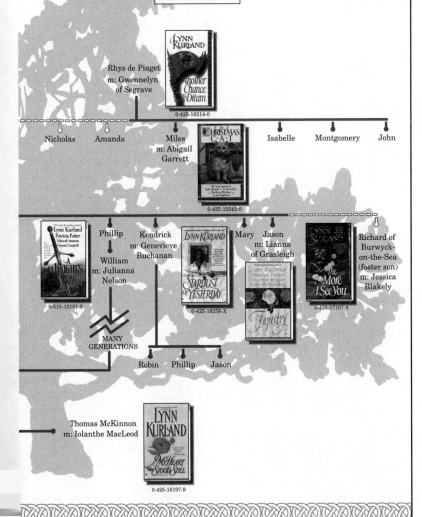

Rhys de Piaget
m: Gwennelyn
of Segrave

Another Chance to Dream
0-425-16514-0

Nicholas Amanda Miles
m: Abigail
Garrett

The Christmas Cat
0-425-15542-0

Isabelle Montgomery John

A Knight's Vow
0-515-13151-2

Phillip

William
m: Julianna
Nelson

Kendrick
m: Genevieve
Buchanan

Stardust of Yesterday
0-425-18238-X

Mary Jason
m: Lianna
of Grasleigh

Tapestry

The More I See You
0-425-17107-8

Richard of
Burwyck-
on-the-Sea
(foster son)
m: Jessica
Blakely

~~~ MANY
GENERATIONS

Robin Phillip Jason

Thomas McKinnon
m: Iolanthe MacLeod

My Heart Stood Still
0-425-18197-9